SWEET REVENGE

"Oh, Wes, don't you see? We *are* on the same wavelength." Pia sighed dreamily.

Wes drew back as scotch fumes assailed his senses. "Pia! You've been drinking again. Your mother will be furious with you, young lady!"

"I'm not that young, and we don't have to tell my mother everything, do we . . . ?"

"Your mother and I have no secrets between us, Pia. That's part of the reason I wanted to come and speak to you alone. I have something important to tell you. Something that concerns your mother and Jeanne and you and me."

"Oh, Wes!" she cried out, turning and flinging her arms so tightly around his neck that he could hardly breathe. "I've known it from the first! I knew you had to be feeling the same way about me that I feel about you. And when two people are destined for each other, age doesn't matter! Oh, my dearest, I'll make you happy, I promise I will!" Pia's lips sought his mouth.

Wes grabbed her wrists and pried himself loose.

"Pia, stop it! I came to tell you that your mother and I are going to be married!"

Mama! He wants Mama instead of me . . . ! Rage coursed through Pia's veins. Well, she silently vowed. I'll show you—all of you. Just wait and see . . .

CATCH UP ON THE BEST IN CONTEMPORARY FICTION
FROM ZEBRA BOOKS!

FORTUNE'S SISTERS

ROBIN
ST.
THOMAS

ZEBRA BOOKS
KENSINGTON PUBLISHING CORP.

ZEBRA BOOKS

are published by

Kensington Publishing Corp.
475 Park Avenue South
New York, NY 10016

First printing: April, 1989

Printed in the United States of America

For Sue

and Lillian

and to the memory of Julia

Part I

1955

Chapter One

"We'd better hurry, girls, or we'll miss the train."

Jeanne sat in a squatting position, trying to keep her body balanced while she struggled with her task. "But, Mama, I keep knotting my shoelaces—and why can't I wear Mary Janes like Pia's, anyway?"

"Because," answered Mathilde, "you've outgrown yours and we can't afford a new pair. Come here and I'll tie the laces for you."

The child edged slowly toward her mother as she smoothed the already wrinkled organdy of her pinafore. Mathilde took the child's wrist. "I wish you wouldn't use your dress as a towel, Jeanne. Your hands are all clammy—your skirt will be a fright before we even leave the house."

But Jeanne was nervous, and the more she tried to relax, the more desperate she became. Why did they have to take this stupid train ride in the first place? Did Mama actually think her daughters were pretty enough to be in the movies? Pia might be able to convince them, but she would be the biggest laughingstock of the studio—especially dressed in an organdy pinafore over a baby-pink dress that suited a six-year-old far better than a preadolescent girl of twelve. What had possessed Mama, anyway?

"Mama, do you think my hair is all right like this?" asked Pia, entering the kitchen. She had spent half an hour in front of the mirror trying to arrange her chestnut curls in a sophisticated style like those pictured in her collection of fan magazines. Her personal favorite was Elizabeth Taylor, but she was too old. Natalie Wood was second choice and, although several years Pia's senior, she was accessible. Pia had used a full-page color photograph of Natalie in the current issue of *Photoplay* as her model. She was pleased with the result but not certain of passing Mama's more critical inspection.

"Beautiful, Olympia, just beautiful," exclaimed Mathilde as her older daughter did a fashion model's full turn. How was it possible, she wondered, for two girls, barely ten months apart, to look and be so diametrically different? One dark, graceful, extroverted —a younger image of Mathilde herself—and the other, shy and awkward, pale and plain. It didn't seem fair; she wanted both her daughters to be perfect.

Mathilde walked to the hall and surveyed her own reflection in the full-length mirror. She checked the hemline of her blue-and-white polka-dotted dress, the one decent "afternoon" dress in her wardrobe. She wore blue-and-white spectator pumps with heels that showed off her shapely legs. There wasn't much that she could do with her hair in the California humidity, but the French twist served to add sophistication as well as getting the damp curls off her neck.

She leaned in closer to check her makeup. Claire, their neighbor next door, always managed to wind up with lipstick on her teeth. Mathilde grinned to check her smile. No, her teeth were fine, white as pearls. She had taken extra pains this morning with her mascara and eyebrow pencil—after all, studio makeup people were masters of their craft and would notice the slightest flaw. With a fingertip she blended in a spot of rouge she'd missed earlier. Then she stepped back and sighed. Good complexion, high cheekbones, clear, deep-set dark brown eyes; no crow's-feet at the corners yet, which wasn't bad for a woman of thirty-two raising two young daughters alone, especially in this sun-baked climate that was terrible for the skin.

Mathilde chided herself as she licked her deep pink lips. No point to all this vanity; the studio was looking for young girls, not mothers of young girls. But that didn't stop her from smoothing her bra line.

"Mama, we're ready," said Jeanne in her nasal whine.

Mathilde was certain her younger daughter would be dismissed the moment she opened her mouth.

"You must remember that you want people to be as captivated by your voice as by your physical demeanor," she said, seeking patience. She regarded Jeanne's appearance. Perhaps it was senseless, taking her along. Pia would certainly shine by comparison, but was it fair to Jeanne? It was so difficult not to play favorites, but Mathilde was determined to divide her love equally between them.

"I do wish you'd let me wear high heels today, Mama," said Pia, breaking in on her mother's thoughts. "Just for the audition. It would make people take notice. I'd be taller than the other girls—and I'd look more mature."

She was beginning to look too mature as it was, Mathilde observed. Even hidden under the dotted Swiss blouse, a bosom was forming. And the contours of her face were shedding the roundness of childhood. Her voice—never thin like Jeanne's—had assumed a richer, mellower timbre over the past few months.

Mathilde shook her head sadly. Soon she would lose

11

Pia to the world; she felt it as strongly as one might feel a sixth sense. But not just yet. "No heels," she said. "Come, girls, let's go."

She watched as her daughters walked to the street in front of her. Pia strode, confident and sure, while Jeanne, shoulders slumped as always, stepped pigeon-toed onto the grass. Mathilde didn't particularly enjoy scoldings, but, in spite of herself, she called, "Jeanne, try to stay on the sidewalk—grass will stain your shoes green." Already the whites of the saddle shoes were scuffed—and they'd been polished that morning till they shone!

The ride to the train station was a rare treat; Mathilde splurged and they were delivered in a taxi. "I like this, Mama," said Jeanne, staring out at the passing scene. "When I grow up I want to ride in taxis all the time!"

With an arm Mathilde coaxed her back to the seat and rolled up the window. Pia, sitting quietly with her hands folded in the lap of her pink-and-white gingham skirt, said, "When *I* grow up, I'm going to have a car. A big car. Driven by a chauffeur."

And somehow Mathilde knew that her daughter's statement would prove true.

The train was stuffy, but with the window open two inches at the top, a breeze managed to penetrate and circulate the stale air. The seats in the coach section were scratchy green plush, and Jeanne delighted in rubbing the backs of her legs against the fabric to soothe the previous day's mosquito bites; calamine lotion had been forbidden this morning because Mathilde feared it would soil the girls' dresses.

Olympia sat with her eyes half closed, envisioning the afternoon before them. Neither Pia nor Jeanne had ever visited a Hollywood studio, but Mathilde had appeared as an extra in several movies before the girls were born, and she had filled their heads with tales of glamorous sets and famous stars and whole towns and cities constructed on areas called lots. Not that Mathilde had ever admitted to her lowly status as an extra; in her reminiscences, she avoided the subject altogether by using one of her pet expressions: "When I was in such-and-such with so-and-so." But Olympia had rummaged through the desk in the corner of the living room and had found, stuck between two drawers, her mother's union card. It was printed with her name—her *real* name of Matilda Loran—together with the acronym SEG—Screen Extras Guild— instead of SAG, the actors' union. She had never confronted Mama with her discovery, but guarded the information jealously, hiding the truth from even her sister.

The conductor came through the car and punched their tickets.

"I'll bet you girls are in the movies, aren't you?" he asked, winking. Olympia regarded him with disdain— she hated when adults condescended to her. Jeanne's breathing rose and fell in nervous, silent gasps.

Mathilde, nonplussed, replied, "They're not yet— but they soon will be."

The conductor smiled. "Well, that's no surprise, with such pretty faces—and their mother, too, I'd imagine."

Mathilde felt the color rising in her cheeks and hoped it wouldn't be mistaken for flirting.

"Mama," said Olympia when the conductor had gone, "will there be many girls at the audition?"

"It doesn't matter, darling. My girls will stand out, even if there are hundreds."

Jeanne had broken into a cold sweat. She hated this train, hated this trip, hated the thought of lining up with hundreds of other girls and having to compete

13

with them—and for what? A part in a movie? Who would give her a part in a movie? Wasn't Mama just bringing her along so she wouldn't feel left out? And what would she and Pia be required to do? Sing? Dance? Would they have to actually *perform*—in front of an audience? She'd die first!

But the most frightening thought of all was one she didn't want to acknowledge, even to herself: What if, over hundreds, maybe thousands of girls, *what if they chose Pia?*

The noise was driving the receptionist to distraction. She tried to remain professionally cool as she checked the names of each child on the list in front of her.

There were only four girls left in the waiting room of director Neal Genesco's office. With them were four mothers. Thank God Neal didn't schedule children's auditions every day! Most of the kids were brats, but their mothers were the real problem. Neal had been auditioning girls for the role since ten that morning. These four more and it would be over.

She looked up from her typing as the door opened and a woman, sweeping in with her two charges, walked to the desk.

"Olympia and Jeanne Decameron to see Mr. Genesco."

The receptionist eyed her quickly. No spring chicken, she observed, but she sure dresses like one. Those heels—on somebody's mother? She handed a script to Mathilde and said, "Pages sixty-two through seventy. The role of Deborah."

Mathilde led them to the long leather sofa. The woman and child seated there moved over to make room for the newcomers. Motioning for the girls to sit on either side of her, Mathilde lowered herself onto the tufted cushion and opened the leatherette-covered

14

screenplay. Then she flipped through the script until she reached page sixty-two.

Jeanne glanced around the room at the other girls present. They were reading the lines aloud to their mothers. In a moment, she and Pia would be doing the same with Mathilde. Judging from the ages of the others, she knew that both she and her sister were too old for the role. It only contributed to her acute self-consciousness, emphasized by her childlike wardrobe and saddle shoes.

Pia began to read aloud. Jeanne smiled inwardly at her sister's attempt to sound like an eight-year-old. Mathilde tried coaching her by reading each line aloud, and Pia obediently repeated each phrase with the same inflection used by her mother. Jeanne thought her sister sounded more like a parrot than a person, but she had already learned that her suggestions proved futile and only fueled Pia's contempt.

Suddenly the script landed with a thud on Jeanne's lap and Mathilde declared, "It's your turn."

God, thought Pia, she really stinks!

She watched as her sister stammered and faltered her way through each line of page sixty-two, her blond bangs damp with perspiration and straggling now. It reminded Pia to check the two spit curls she had carefully plastered against her own temples. As she did so, Mathilde continued to instruct Jeanne.

"Try to read it the way I do," she said. "Just imitate my voice." But Mathilde feared that it was hopeless.

Pia leaned back against the cushion, all but dismissing her mother and sister. She was calm, confident. Her only regret was having to wear ankle socks instead of nylon stockings. Still, she knew that Mama was right. *Young* was what the studio wanted. That made her steal another glance at Jeanne, who *was* younger than she and gawky enough to appear closer to the age sought by the director. For a brief moment, anger rose within her. But it quickly subsided when she saw her sister's scarlet face look pleadingly at Mathilde and say, "Mama, I have to go to the bathroom."

Mathilde emitted a sigh. It was Jeanne's third visit to the ladies' room that afternoon. She hoped her younger daughter hadn't inherited Hank's kidneys.

"All right, then, but come right back. There's not much time, and I don't want you to miss your chance to audition."

Pia studied her sister as Jeanne made her way across the waiting room. It won't matter even if she's the *exact* age they're looking for, Pia reflected. She's skinny and pale, nervous. And shy. An actress can't be shy. Besides, no one will notice her as long as *I'm* here. It brought an upward curve to her lips.

When Jeanne returned from the bathroom, her eyes were red from fighting tears. She had tried to reduce the swelling with cold water, but it hadn't helped. For some reason, her nerves had started her thinking about Papa, and that always made her want to cry.

It wasn't that she remembered that much about Hank. It was more from the photographs in the family album. The love in his eyes as he stood beside Mama in their wedding picture. He had loved Mama so! And his daughters. Maybe he had loved Jeanne best because Pia was Mama's favorite. Oh, Mama tried to be fair, but she couldn't hide the truth. And it was okay, because Jeanne loved Papa most. She still reserved a special place in her heart for him.

He'd died a hero's death, a policeman shot in the line of duty. If he were alive today, things would be so different, thought Jeanne. She'd be able to talk to him about her books, about her dreams. She wouldn't feel so alone.

But she *was* alone. Papa wasn't coming back.

The awareness gave rise to the germ of an idea, an idea previously dormant inside her.

If a person has no one else, at least she has herself!

The sudden realization jolted her. For the very first time, she was looking inward, to herself, for help. The loneliness of her situation briefly overwhelmed her, but the reality of it—the common sense of it—gave her the strength she needed to regain her composure.

I will depend on *me*, she promised joyfully.

Her spirits flagged as she reentered the waiting room and saw the expression on her sister's face. Pia was sitting demurely with a picture-pretty innocence as she smiled blankly at Jeanne.

When Jeanne drew closer to the sofa, Pia hissed under her breath, "You'd better learn to *behave* like an eight-year-old, because you sure don't look like one now—you look like a *baby!*"

It required all the nerve she could muster, but Jeanne replied, "I'm a whole year closer to the part than *you* are!"

Mathilde had been powdering her nose. She stopped. Pia's mouth fell open. It wasn't like Jeanne to answer back.

Then the receptionist called both of their names.

While Neal Genesco outlined the audition scene to the girls, Mathilde scrutinized the director from narrowed eyes. She refused to wear glasses, and squinting clarified her vision.

Genesco was well known, and a very attractive man. His attention was focused on the two girls, making Mathilde feel left out and unnecessary. Nonetheless,

17

she smiled politely as he joked with the girls to put them at ease.

Neal Genesco would have preferred to audition each child separately, but he knew from the mistakes of other men in his position that this was unwise; girls who were under age could invent all kinds of stories about his conduct if he was alone with any of them, especially girls like these Decamerons, who were certainly more mature than the others he'd seen that day.

Still, he didn't relish having both sisters being present at each other's audition. He had suggested that one wait outside while the other read. But their mother had insisted: They'd made the trip together and would remain together. "They can learn from each other, Mr. Genesco," she'd said. Maybe it was her way of hiding partiality, he reasoned; the two girls were, after all, so unlike.

It was the end of a long day and Neal was tired. He'd forgone hiring an actor to read with the children; his own early acting career had taught him that auditions were tough enough; reading with someone who didn't care made these ordeals even tougher. He preferred to read with each of them, helping and encouraging them while assessing their abilities and natural acting instincts.

Pia read first. As she took her place on the chair at the center of the small room, Neal looked over at Jeanne. The girl sat close to her mother, almost clinging to her—or was she cringing from his glance? She wasn't a pretty child but her wan expression and the delicate features hinted at vulnerability, a depth of feeling that the child probably didn't know she possessed. Neal had to consciously force his attention back to the other sister, who was poised and ready to begin.

He stopped her midway through the first page, trying to mask his displeasure. She was no different from all the girls he'd auditioned that day. Ninety percent of them had obviously been coached and rehearsed by their mothers, burying any possibility of spontaneity.

"Olympia," he said as kindly as he could, "don't *try* to act. Let's read the scene as though we were just talking to each other."

She began again and it was better. She was already mannered and false, but the slightly rounded face, the richly dark hair with its reddish highlights, the liquid brown eyes were all employed to their best advantage. It might convey something to screen audiences—even if it couldn't be called acting.

"Thank you, Olympia," he said. Then Jeanne took her sister's place on the chair.

She stammered at first. But after the second time through, Neal saw that she was becoming more relaxed. He sensed that it stemmed not from a growing confidence but from not caring about the effect created—as if she merely wanted to have the ordeal over and done with, that if reading would bring about that objective, well then, it was worth the effort.

That made all the difference. She hardly possessed the studied charm or physical allure of her sibling, but a natural sensitivity—a sensitivity that she didn't know how to hide—more than compensated. She didn't smother the scene with "acting."

"Both of them?" Mathilde cried.

"Both," said Neal. "I'd like the producer to see screen tests. He'll have final say in the casting. They may be a little old . . . but I'm willing to risk that. Have them here Monday morning at six."

19

Chapter Two

On Sunday night Mathilde sent the girls to bed at nine o'clock. For a change she received no protests about the earliness of the hour. Pia seemed to accept as a matter of course that if one had to arise at four-thirty A.M., retiring early the previous night was a necessity. Beauty sleep, Mathilde called it. And Pia certainly wanted to look beautiful. "Besides," she told her mother, "tomorrow will just arrive sooner."

It made Mathilde smile, although at times she was awed by her older daughter's voracious appetite for competition. If she had possessed more of Pia's driving ambition, perhaps *she* would be the one scheduled for the screen test. *She* might have had a career.

But it was too late for that, she reminded herself as she poured herself a scotch, added two ice cubes, and carried the glass to her bedroom. She sat down at the vanity to set her hair for the next morning. She had helped Pia and Jeanne with their curls an hour before, although now she questioned the wisdom of having done so; anticipation of the coming day might cause a restless night, and hair curlers wouldn't help matters. Makeup could erase any signs of fatigue or strain, but as an added safeguard she'd slathered cold cream over both girls' faces—despite what it would do to their pillows.

The joints of her fingers ached tonight as she rolled the hair tightly onto each curler. She winced at the pain that shot through her arms whenever she raised them over her head. Christ, she thought, I can't be arthritic— I'm only thirty-two!

Sighing, she took a sip of her drink and glanced at the mirrored reflection of her bedroom. The cabbage roses of the wallpaper were beginning to peel. The bed sagged, and the sweet little boudoir chair she had once adored was now frayed at its arms. The house was falling into disrepair. But it was all she had. The house and the girls. Self-pity only made it worse.

She concentrated her thoughts on the forthcoming day. Everything could change for them. It depended on the girls. No, she amended. It depended on Pia.

She was genuinely amazed that Jeanne was even in the running. And although Jeanne, too, had gone to bed early without complaint, it was, Mathilde knew, more from passive acceptance than from eagerness. What can I do to help her? Mathilde wondered. She's pale, thin, withdrawn . . . so like Hank. Will she be as weak? Still, Jeanne's remark to Pia in the director's office *had* taken Mathilde aback. Perhaps she does have backbone, after all—when she isn't sinking into moodiness. But what if her brooding spells do run as deeply as Hank's did? And if so, how long before they become manifest? Oh God, please, she prayed, don't let Jeanne have her father's problems. She isn't really plain—unless she stands beside Pia. Her soulful blue eyes and her long hair are her best assets—or *would* be if she'd come to the beach and let the sun bleach her dishwater-blond hair into the gold it was in infancy.

Mathilde shook her head. Her younger daughter actually preferred sitting in her room and reading

21

her books.

Hank's books. Well, reasoned Mathilde, in all fairness, Jeanne's skin *is* too delicate for prolonged exposure to the sun. Poor child . . . why, she *likes* rainy days!

She clamped the last curler into place. I'll have to have a talk with Jeanne, she decided. Twelve isn't too young to start lightening blond hair—just a little . . .

Yes, that's an excellent idea. I'll suggest it to her first thing in the morning.

Jeanne turned her head restlessly against the pillow. A metal curler dug painfully into her scalp. Oh, why, she wondered silently, *why* did he have to pick me, too?

Her eyes were closed, but it was useless; she'd never get to sleep, and in the morning she'd have dark circles to show for it. And the curlers wouldn't work; her hair never kept a wave for more than an hour.

She opened one eye and peeked over at Pia in the bed near the window. Already asleep, her head was propped against so many pillows that she was practically sitting up! Mama had said the higher one elevated one's head, the less puffy the skin would be in the morning. Jeanne had read in a medical journal that it wasn't good for one's back, but that didn't seem to bother Pia.

Jeanne's worst fear had come to pass. She and Pia were serious contenders for the same part. It terrified her. Please, God, please, she prayed. Let Pia have the role. I'm so afraid of cameras. And there'll be all those people watching! Even if I get through tomorrow, I'll die if I get the part and have to do it every day! And Pia will hate me forever.

*   *   *

22

Pia, too, was awake. She watched as Jeanne tossed and turned in the darkness, the only light in the room coming through the slats of the venetian blinds. She pitied her sister and congratulated herself for being the kind of person who could find compassion for someone so weak-willed. It would be difficult for Mama once Pia was gone from the house and Mama was left with Jeanne. But she had her career to think of. Of course, she would have to remain at home until she was old enough to be out on her own—but by then she'd be a famous star. Maybe she'd even take Mama to live with her in a great mansion in Beverly Hills. She wouldn't leave her sister completely out in the cold; Jeanne could have this house, Papa's house with all its books and memories. *She* was about to embark upon a whole new life.

Pia finally closed her eyes and managed to drift off to sleep.

"Now stay like that until I tell you to get up," Mathilde said.

"For how *long,* Mama? I *hate* this!" Pia was being forced to lie still with two dampened teabags over her closed eyelids.

"Twenty minutes. It'll make your eyes sparkle."

"I'll go blind!"

"Olympia . . . !"

Pia grew quiet and Mathilde turned her attention to Jeanne. It was four-thirty A.M., too early for the sun to rise. Too early for any living thing to rise.

Mathilde reached over to the milk-glass table lamp at Jeanne's bedside and pressed the switch. She jumped back in horror at the sight of her younger daughter's face.

The child was covered from head to toe with bumpy

23

red splotches.

"Hives! Jeanne! Oh, dear God, how could you *do* this?"

"It isn't my fault, Mama, I swear. I'm sorry! I . . ."

"All right, all right, just let me think . . ."

How would she explain it to the studio? What could she do? Apply makeup over the rash? No; the welts were raised and would still be visible even if she were able to cover the redness. Besides, the makeup man would cleanse her face before applying Pan-Cake. What kind of first impression would Jeanne make if she appeared in this condition? And, Mathilde reasoned, even if we could disguise her skin, nerves are the culprit, and they wouldn't disappear before the camera—they'd multiply. Sooner or later, Jeanne's nerves would have to be dealt with.

Mathilde shook her head sadly as the child stared up at her with apprehension. Oh, Jeanne, thought her mother, how will you ever accomplish anything in life?

Should I insist? Force her to go—for her own sake? But Jeanne's pitiful face was too much to bear.

Shaking her head sadly, Mathilde said, "Stay home. I'll see if they're willing to reschedule your audition."

Before leaving their room, Pia took a long look in the mirror. She was more than pleased with the image reflected back at her. The chestnut hair, always shiny, now glowed beneath the Adorn that Mama had sprayed all over her head to keep the tight mass of curls in place. She couldn't see much of a difference in her eyes, but Mama insisted that the teabags had done wonders. Pia spun around to check out the rose-colored dress she wore, fully aware that Jeanne's eyes were fixed upon her. Pia tried to ignore her sister, but it was difficult. It made her long for the privacy of her

24

own room.

"Pia, aren't you nervous?" Jeanne asked.

"Silly—why?"

"Never mind."

Pia shrugged her shoulders and started into the hall. But at the threshold she stopped and glanced back at the autographed eight-by-ten glossy photograph of Natalie Wood that hung over her bed. She adopted Natalie's big smile. Then, satisfied, she went to join Mama.

They walked from the train station. Two blocks from the studio, Mathilde said, "Wait here," and went to make a call from a phone booth. Three minutes later, they stepped into a taxi.

"But, Mama, we were almost there," said Pia. "We could have walked."

"You're here for a screen test, Pia. We don't want it to seem as if you really need this job. It's always wise to look as if you have a few dollars, even if you don't. Remember that."

A few dollars was all she did have.

They were cleared by the guard at the gate and the taxi driver was directed toward Stage 22. For such a short ride the fare, including Mama's meager tip, came to less than a dollar. The cabbie made it clear that the ride had hardly been worth his time. The moment Pia and Mathilde alighted, he gunned the motor and sped off.

"Lick your lips and pinch your cheeks," Mathilde whispered as she rang the bell to the left of the soundstage door.

After three rings, it was opened by a production assistant, a prematurely balding young man in his early twenties. He referred to some papers on his clipboard

25

and then led them through the cavernous innards of the building.

"Right on time," he said. "That's good. You're lucky. You're the first to shoot today." He helped Mathilde over a rolled coil of black cable lying on the cement floor. "Sorry it's so hot, but it takes a while for the air-conditioning to get going. I'll take you to wardrobe now."

Mathilde thanked him and asked to see Mr. Genesco as soon as possible. "That's a tall order, Mrs. Decameron." Mathilde bristled at the formality; it made her feel like a matron. But she said nothing and he continued. "Neal's around somewhere, but he's pretty busy. There are three other tests besides—" He stopped and looked at Pia, then checked the names on his list. "Wait a minute. Aren't there supposed to be two of you?"

Pia was about to reply, but Mathilde grabbed her hand and said quickly, "That's what I'd like to discuss with Mr. Genesco."

"Oh, okay." He opened the door to the wardrobe room crowded from end to end with racks of costumes. "Have a seat. Edna will be here in a minute." He removed several pages from beneath the clip and handed them to Mathilde. "Here ya go, Mrs. Decam—"

"Mathilde, please . . ."

"Sure. Thanks. Okay, Matilda"—he didn't notice when she winced at the mispronunciation—"this is the script. Same stuff she read at the audition. I'll be around. If you need anything, just ask for Al."

Mathilde began leafing through the pages while Pia's eyes devoured the hundreds of costumes hanging neatly in rows. Gowns and dresses in every hue formed a glittering rainbow of color. Some were beaded or sequined and caught the bright reflections of the overhead lights. She wondered which of them would be hers.

Mathilde was concerned. There were many lines of dialogue for Pia to learn and very little time in which to do so. Mathilde worried over her daughter's ability to commit so much to memory. I should have insisted upon a script for her to study over the weekend, she thought too late.

Just then, the door opened and a dark, stern woman of fifty walked in. "Hello," she said brusquely. "I'm Edna. And you must be Olympia?" Pia nodded. "All right, honey, what size are you?"

Mathilde replied for her.

But Edna had already gone to one of the racks. The sound of wire hangers scraping against metal rods grated on Mathilde's anxious nerves as dress after dress was shoved aside, any one of which Pia would have adored. Edna glanced at Pia again and motioned for her to rise. "You're pretty tall to play a ten-year-old . . . but I'll see what I can do."

She opened the door and yelled, "Ernie! Pia Decameron's ready for you!" She turned back to them. "That's it for me. Make a right and it's two doors down. Makeup's waiting."

Before Mathilde could ask again to see Genesco, they were being ushered down the hall in search of Ernie.

Pia liked the makeup room. The enormous mirrors surrounded by frosted, round light bulbs were just as she'd imagined they would be . . . just as she'd seen in countless movies. Mathilde smiled, watching her daughter climb up onto the center chair as if she were a princess taking her rightful place upon the throne.

Ernie and his assistant Duane stared down at her from left and right of that throne.

27

"Nice curls," Duane said, almost as an aside to Mathilde. Pia saw her mother's thank-you nod, and she swelled with pride for herself and for her mother's skill. But her joyful expression was immediately transformed into a sneer when Ernie said, "They've gotta go."

"*What?*" cried Pia.

"This kid's supposed to be a waif," Duane answered. "Not a fourteen-year-old glamour puss."

"I'm twelve!" Pia lied.

"Sure," Ernie said as he brought a comb to her head. It lodged as if glued to the first Adorned curl.

Pia steeled herself for the next painful tug-of-hair. "What are you going to do with it?" She was furious with her mother for the mistake, as furious as she had been proud only moments before.

"I'm gonna *try* to straighten it. Sit tight. This may hurt."

Forty-five minutes later, Pia emerged onto the set somewhat less than the movie queen she'd envisioned in her dreams. She wore a drab, brown, shapeless shift. Her crown of curls had been replaced by a severe part at the center of her head, and her long chestnut hair had been pulled—yanked—into two braids that hung stiffly from behind each ear. Her peaches-and-cream complexion was hidden beneath the anemic pallor that Ernie and Duane had applied to every visible section of her face and neck. Pia had never resembled her sister more. She knew it. And she loathed it.

Neal Genesco approached, shook her hand, and said, "I understand that only one of you is testing this morning. I hope there's nothing the matter with your sister . . . ?"

"Oh, she's fine, Mr. Genesco," Mathilde said with

forced gaiety. "Just a mild attack of nerves. But she'll be fine tomorrow, if you're still testing—"

"I'm sorry. All the tests are being done today. The soundstage isn't free tomorrow. Still, it's a shame. I thought she might have something."

He turned to go, but Mathilde insisted. "Surely there's a way to . . . to squeeze her in . . . perhaps at the end of the day? I'm sure she'll be ready tomorrow, and—"

He cut her off. "I'm really sorry, Mrs. Decameron." And again, formality stiffened Mathilde. It silenced her as well.

Neal said to Pia, "Have you looked at the script?"

"She didn't have much time," interjected Mathilde.

He wanted to throttle this stage mother, but instead, he continued speaking to Pia. "Since we're running a little late, why don't you take the time now to go over your scene?" Indicating two canvas chairs in a corner, Neal said, "We'll call you when we're ready. And remember, there's no need to be nervous." Then he turned and began weaving his way through the mass of standing lamps and hanging cables.

Mathilde's fears had been unfounded. After studying the pages silently to herself, Pia was ready to read her part aloud. She was near-perfect by the third go-round.

Neal Genesco stood beside the camera and watched as Olympia Decameron skipped onto the set, her thick braids flapping like wings against her ears. Her mother followed close behind and stopped just short of the actual set.

The director sighed indulgently and led Mathilde to a chair that had purposely been placed five feet away from his, although still affording an unobstructed view of the shooting area.

He introduced Pia to Barry Barnes, the actor assigned to test with her. They ran lines while last-minute lighting was adjusted to Pia's skin tones and coloring. Someday, she mused, I'll have a stand-in for all this.

She already knew that Barry Barnes would spend most of the time with his back to the camera, since it was her test and her reactions would be the ones recorded.

Mathilde sat obediently, feeling helpless and worried for her daughter. There was nothing a mother could do for her now; Pia was on her own, and although Mathilde tried to catch the girl's eye to smile or nod encouragement, Pia never once looked her way.

Instead, she and Barry Barnes were chatting amicably. It's probably to put her at ease, Mathilde reflected appreciatively.

Neal positioned Barry in a chair—his back facing the camera, as Pia had expected—and instructed Pia to enter through the living-room door, cross to the sofa, and begin the scene.

"Now remember," Neal said, "you're here to admit to your father that you've stolen a dollar from the church collection plate to pay for his birthday present. You're ashamed and afraid of what he'll say."

Pia nodded and stepped behind the flat. On Neal's "Action!" she flung open the door. It banged against a wall that shook from the impact, and a framed picture fell to the floor. Pia stopped dead and looked at Neal.

He sat with a hand to his forehead. Sighing, he said, "Just keep going, Pia. I want to see what you do. We'll talk after you run it."

Smiling, she closed the door softly and sauntered to the sofa, settled comfortably, and began unwrapping a lollipop she had taken from the pocket of her ugly brown costume.

"Where did *that* come from?" Neal asked with a touch of impatience. He only echoed Mathilde's horrified thoughts.

"I brought it with me," answered Pia. "To give me 'business' to do." She'd heard the term in a movie musical about backstage life.

The prop man had already removed the "business" from her hand as Neal drew a breath and said, "Go on, Pia."

Another thirty seconds and it became apparent that instead of playing the scene, Pia was playing at being ten years old; it was much as she had done at her first reading at the audition. She came across more like Fanny Brice's Baby Snooks. But Neal let her finish the scene. Then he walked her through it, showing her where to stop, at each place previously taped on the floor. "Those are your marks," he explained.

"Oh, yes," Pia said, nodding that she understood.

Neal called a break and led her to the sofa while deciding upon the lie to tell her. "Pia . . . we've made some changes in the script. This girl is older—more your age, around twelve or thirteen. Her mother dresses her like a little girl to make her look younger." He thought for a moment. "And she didn't steal the money from the collection plate, after all . . . Her best friend did, and she's covering up for her."

"Oh!" exclaimed Pia, blushing at the sudden realization that she'd been playing the scene all wrong. But she adjusted instantly to the fact that it wasn't *her* fault; nobody had *told* her.

By the time they were halfway through the second take, everything had changed. Mathilde, seated in the background, was overwhelmed by her own daughter. Pia had allowed her well-modulated voice to emerge; all remnants of the bouncy child had disappeared.

31

They shot the scene in three takes, including one in close-up.

Pia's transformation didn't come as a surprise to Neal. He'd used these tactics in the past on far more experienced actresses. It was easier to change the actress's motivation in a scene than to teach her how to play it. And although Neal didn't think Pia was capable of genuine *acting,* he was impressed by her ability to take direction. He noted that she had hit her marks on target every time.

But there was something more. Only viewing the completed test would confirm his suspicions, but he was ready to bet money that the kid understood how to make the camera love her.

The personality test came next. It required Pia only to stand facing the camera and answer questions about herself. "Just talk directly to the lens," said Neal. "As if it's a friend."

But as the test rolled, Mathilde began to feel like a human lie detector, tallying the string of half-truths, evasions, and barefaced lies coming from her daughter's mouth.

Pia said that she was twelve; that she'd skipped two grades in school; that her hair was naturally curly— "Mama never has to set it"—and that she spent every waking hour reading and studying. It was only the start.

Her birthplace? "On a yacht, off the coast of Tahiti."

Any brothers or sisters? She almost shook her head no, then remembered that the director had met Jeanne. "Yes," she answered. "I have a sister."

Then: "What does your father do?"

Pia shot a glance—her first—off-camera to her mother, then quickly returned her eyes to the lens. "My father was a deposed prince, who lost his title in a revolution and died trying to raise his country's flag over the castle."

Mathilde buried her head in her hands, certain that it was all over.

But Neal, suppressing his grin, continued. "What country was that, Pia?"

She thought for a moment and replied, "I'm not at liberty to say."

Throughout the prevarications, Neal noticed the reactions of various members of the crew. Not one of them could take his eyes from Pia, despite hands clapped over their mouths to keep their laughter from being picked up by the sound boom.

Then came the final question: "Pia, what do you want to be when you grow up?"

Neal was hardly surprised when she answered, "A star." He hadn't expected her to say "an actress."

When the test was over, Pia marched off to the makeup room and Neal approached Mathilde, who seemed to have grown smaller from embarrassment.

"I'm so sorry, Mr. Genesco! I don't know *where* she came up with that story. She was born in—"

"Never mind. Children often invent when they fear the truth to be less . . . entertaining. The scene with Mr. Barnes was, I'm afraid, only . . . acceptable. But I think the personality test will prove to be quite successful. She's charming and quite confident. That's good."

"But the scene . . . ?"

"Well, she's very"—he hesitated, searching for a word that wouldn't go overboard—"*very* pretty, you know. That can . . . compensate for a great deal. But we'll have to wait for the producer's decision. Most of it depends upon the way she photographs, of course."

"Of course."

Neal shook Mathilde's hand and walked away as the crew began setting up for the next test. He wondered about the sister who hadn't shown up—what was her name, again?—Jeanne. How would she have acted in front of the telling eye of the camera?

Shrugging, Neal reached for his pipe and strode to his director's chair, where he would await the next little girl and the second test of the day.

Jeanne rose stiffly from the bed. She had lain in the same position all afternoon, resisting the urge to scratch the hives; calamine lotion didn't seem as effective for soothing these eruptions as it did for insect bites. The antihistamine had helped but had induced a cottony dryness in her throat. A glass of lemonade would be just the thing.

She slipped her arms into the pink terry-cloth bathrobe, although it was really too hot for any but the lightest covering. She peered briefly at her reflection in the mirror. The spots were less angry-looking than they'd been at dawn. Jeanne's thoughts wandered to her sister and her own missed screen test. Pia and Mama would be home soon, and she'd have to endure a blow-by-blow description of the whole day. Well, she reasoned, it was still better than having to undergo the humiliating experience in person.

She was looking for a cork coaster to put under the sweating glass of lemonade when the front screen door slammed. Involuntarily, her pulse quickened. She'd have to ask. Even if she didn't want to know, she'd *have* to ask.

"Well, dear, you're looking much better," said Mathilde, entering the kitchen. Pia was directly behind her, beaming with self-satisfaction.

Jeanne steeled herself; obviously, the success of Pia's screen test had exceeded her wildest expectations. Without a doubt, her sister had outshone everyone else

34

at the studio, and the front office was already brimming with plans for her brilliant career. An Oscar was imminent—probably for her very first role!

"How do you feel?" asked Pia.

"Okay, I guess. How . . . how was your screen test?"

"Just fine," answered her sister. "Sit down and I'll tell you *everything* you missed."

"Not until you've changed clothes, Olympia," said Mathilde. "Otherwise you might spill lemonade on your good clothes—lemon is a dye and it stains."

Pia's mouth curved into a sulking frown. Only hours earlier she had been the center of attention—the *star*— and now she was expected to return to a normal life! She flounced from the kitchen, to her sister's relief. A reprieve for Jeanne, although a short one; still, it postponed the pain forthcoming.

"The camera loves her," said Mathilde. "That's what the assistant told me." Then, feeling sympathy for her younger daughter who stood sweltering in Pia's hand-me-down bathrobe, her stringy hair falling over her face, Mathilde added, "I'm so sorry you weren't able to do the screen test, dear. But there'll be another time. Very soon."

"Sure, Mama." Jeanne would have agreed to anything in order to avoid the subject.

But there was no avoidance. Pia returned to the kitchen within moments, clad in navy-blue gym shorts and a matching T-shirt.

"Pia," said Mathilde, "did you hang up your dress?"

"Oh, Mama!" Pick up, put away! Why couldn't she be grown-up already so she wouldn't have to take orders from anyone? When she became a famous movie star, she'd have someone *else* pick up her clothes and put them away, that's what she'd do!

Jeanne had opened a tattered library copy of *Jane Eyre* and was pretending to read. She loved the novel, but at the moment she was in no reading mood; the book was serving as a means of escape. Escape from the gory details of Pia's day of triumph. She wondered if her sister had actually signed a contract with the studio. But she dismissed the thought. If *that* had transpired, Pia would have mentioned it first thing.

Pia, her full account rehearsed and ready, pushed the book away from Jeanne. "The movie was much better," she said.

Annoyed, Jeanne looked up. "You haven't read the book."

"Yes I have," insisted Pia.

Mathilde inhaled deeply. She admired Pia's determination and drive, but she disliked the girl's tendency to lie, especially after that morning's humiliation at the studio. "Olympia, your sister brought that home from the library on Thursday. And we don't own a copy of the book. Please don't . . . pretend . . ."

"Well, I looked at the first couple of pages and I didn't *have* to read the whole thing—the movie was much better! And when I'm a famous star, I'm going to play all the great heroines from books, just the way the authors wanted them to be played." She stopped herself before adding, "So there!"

Jeanne swallowed two almost-melted ice cubes and said, "If you don't read the books, you won't *know* how you're supposed to play the heroines, no matter *how* famous you are."

For the second time that week, Mathilde was stunned by Jeanne's response.

But Pia was angering. She didn't give a darn about Jane Eyre or anybody else. *She* wanted to talk of nothing but her screen test. Finally she found an entree to the subject.

"I think the movies can attract a whole new audience for the classics," she said. "And I plan to play a major role in that. It's why I'm so . . . *grateful"*—but she'd had to search for the word—"for today's opportunity. To *do* something important for humanity." She was pleased with the reading. Jeanne thought she might throw up.

Thereupon Jeanne was subjected to a complete reenactment of Olympia Decameron's Official Hollywood Screen Test. Mathilde listened to the retelling, amazed, as always, by her older daughter's ability to recall verbatim every word uttered, every nuance expressed. It could be one of her most valued assets—if she chose to use it creatively and not simply to impress.

Jeanne had listened intently, trying with all her inner strength not to appear too interested in the details or the outcome. Finally, in spite of herself, she asked, "Well? Did you get the part?" And her heart pounded as much at the question as at its possible answer.

"They said they'll call us," said Mathilde. "So I think we should all just be as patient as we can be." She rose from the Formica chair and stretched. "I'll make hamburgers for dinner in a little while, but first I've got to take off these clothes and put my feet up. There's leftover tuna fish in the meantime."

Pia devoured the salad while she continued to relate the day's events to Jeanne, savoring each detail and dropping names of every star she had—and hadn't—seen on the lot.

Jeanne didn't eat; suddenly she'd lost her appetite.

Mathilde yawned. She was stretched out, barefoot, on the sofa, an empty scotch bottle on the floor beside her. She hadn't meant to fall asleep in the living room—it must have been the excitement of the long day. She glanced at the alarm clock on the mantel. Eleven-thirty! Was that possible? She listened for sounds from the girls' room. Nothing. They'd probably fallen asleep hours ago.

She reached over to the scratched coffee table and opened the lid of the copper-and-chrome cigarette box. She needed something to neutralize the taste of scotch in her mouth. She withdrew a Lucky Strike and lit it, moving her head from the sofa arm to a more comfortable half-sitting position against the cushion. Her eyes moved around the room and settled on the television set in the corner. An old James Cagney movie was flickering on the round screen of the Zenith; she'd have to call someone to check the picture tube. The image seemed to have weakened recently.

The cigarette tasted bitter—or maybe it was the tobacco mingling with the scotch. My God, she thought, did I really drink that much of it tonight? Am I picking up where Hank left off? There was a fingerful of whisky remaining in the glass—a glass that had formerly held pineapple cream cheese. Mathilde was convinced that scotch whisky—even cheap scotch— would have a completely different *bouquet*—a word she'd recently learned from a magazine article on French wines—served in a crystal glass instead of an A&P giveaway special. Everything in this room, she reflected, all of it looks like giveaway specials—the dimestore plates—how could anyone call them china? —and stainless steel flatware instead of sterling silver. She could sympathize with the people at the Salvation Army; Christ, she and her girls were *living* Salvation Army! No better than the years with Hank—or those before. The Great Depression had ended, but she was still immersed in her own great depression.

Inadvertently, Mathilde's hands came to rest on her stomach. Two children, two agonizing pregnancies, but no sign of a belly. No stretch marks. Not even visible suggestions of aging—if it weren't for the fact that she'd been married and widowed so young, she could pass for a girl of twenty. Well . . . she quickly amended the estimate to twenty-five or -six.

And what did that get her? She didn't even go out with men. Oh, there were plenty around who would jump at the chance—as long as she didn't mention her two daughters—but they were locals, clerks and laborers with no future in sight other than what surrounded her now. And she was tired of sameness. Every day exactly like the one just past. Was that the way she was meant to spend the rest of her life? While jeweled matrons waddled through the fashionable streets of Beverly Hills and dined at the best restaurants? Why couldn't she have some of that—not all of it, just her fair share?

She heaved a deep sigh and stubbed out the cigarette that had turned almost completely to ashes in the glass bowl beside the empty scotch bottle. An incessant drone interrupted her reverie. The Cagney film had ended and the ugly, striped signal pattern with the TV station's logo had replaced the blinking picture.

Mathilde rose from the sofa and flicked off the set. The screen went blank. One minute here, she mused, the next minute gone. All at the flick of a switch, the press of a button, the click of a trigger. She silently cursed Hank, turned out the light, and went to bed.

Chapter Three

For the following week, with the exception of those hours in which Pia and Jeanne were at school, the star-to-be hovered around the telephone, casually leaning against a wall as she leafed through one of her movie magazines or rummaged through desk drawers for a paper she claimed to have misplaced. Whatever activity occupied her time, it never took her far from the small three-legged table and the precious instrument at its center.

And with each ring, Pia pounced upon the receiver while Mathilde's heart skipped a beat. She would press an ear closer to the wall as Pia's voice, a studied calm belying any nervous anticipation, said, "The Decameron residence. Olympia Decameron speaking."

The other two members of the Decameron residence were able to tell by Pia's deep sigh of disappointment—unmasked, no matter who the caller—that it was not Neal Genesco's office. Pia was less than thrilled that her mother had alerted the entire neighborhood; Claire called at least three times a day and always with the same question: "Any news?"

God, Pia wanted to say, if there is, how will the studio be able to get through if you're always at the other end of the line? Instead, she made certain that the conversations were kept to a minimum and was ready to cut the telephone wires altogether when Mathilde and the television repair man spent five minutes arguing over the charge for his service call.

Jeanne, meanwhile, absented herself from the house as much as possible. Her legitimate excuse took her to the local library to do research for an assigned book report on the great French actress, Sarah Bernhardt. But she admitted to herself that she didn't want to be the one to answer the phone and hear, "Miss Olympia Decameron, please. Mr. Genesco's office is calling with the offer of a starring role in a movie." She didn't care that Pia probably sensed the underlying reason for her return after six o'clock each evening—when studio switchboards were closed for the day—and knew that Pia hadn't mentioned the fact merely from gratitude. That put one less person in the vicinity of the telephone.

But the studio didn't call, and the week wore on. And on. Finally, on Friday afternoon, Mathilde could wait no longer. Pia wasn't eating properly, was unusually restless, and an air of tension in the house was bringing everyone's nerves close to snapping.

She ushered Pia from the room and picked up the receiver. There was no point in covering the mouthpiece; the shortness of her breathing betrayed to both daughters the number she gave the operator.

The studio switchboard line rang twice. Three times. Four. Mathilde glanced at the small Benrus on her wrist. Four forty-five; they couldn't have shut down for the weekend—they couldn't have!

They hadn't. At last a voice answered at the other end. Mathilde explained the reason for her call and was

41

asked to wait. Her temples pounded as she drew long, deep breaths that didn't help.

And then, after an interminable silence, came the death knell. "I'm sorry to keep you waiting, Mrs. Decameron, but Mr. Genesco's secretary says that your daughter wasn't right for the role."

"What do you mean?" The words refused to register on Mathilde's brain. *"What do you mean?"*

The switchboard operator, between clicks of her chewing gum, repeated the message, adding, "But Mr. Genesco's secretary said to tell you that she has your daughter's photograph on file and will definitely call if a role she's right for comes up."

"But there must be some mistake!" Mathilde insisted. "They said the camera *loved* her! I'd like to talk with Mr. Genesco."

"I'm sorry, but he's not available."

"Look, I'm sure he'll talk to me—*please* put me through."

"His secretary is just leaving the office. Mr. Genesco is away on location and won't be back till Monday."

"But . . . her test was wonderful—I was there!" Mathilde's bosom was heaving and the tightness across her chest was beginning to close in like a vise. "Are you sure? Absolutely *sure?"*

"Look, Mrs. Decameron, I'm telling you exactly what Mr. Genesco's secretary said. Oh, I did forget one thing. She also said they needed a girl with a name."

"A *name?* What's wrong with Decameron?" A sour taste was rising in her throat and Mathilde tried to swallow it out of her way.

The switchboard operator had dealt with hundreds of little girls' mothers whose daughters had lost roles they'd expected to win. "They needed a *star,* Mrs. Decameron," she explained sympathetically. "The part went to Natalie Wood."

"Natalie Wood. Oh, well . . ." If Pia had to lose a role to someone else, at least it had gone to someone deserving. She could live with that. And Genesco's office *had* said they'd keep Pia in mind. Beverly Hills would just take a little longer than planned . . .

Pia didn't see it that way. She had covered her ears with her hands as Natalie Wood's name burned its way into her head. She didn't wait for Mathilde to hang up the receiver. She tore into the bedroom and ripped the autographed picture of her former idol from the wall over her bed. Then, still not content, she flung it to the floor and stomped on Natalie's smile until the pent-up rage inside her was vented and no more tears would come.

Then, both mind and body spent, she sank onto her bed and fell into exhausted sleep.

Later that night when Jeanne went to bed, she lay awake, examining her feelings. The earlier envy she had felt toward Pia was gone. She had wondered for a week about the reaction she would have when the fateful news arrived. But she had anticipated the same news that Mama and Pia had expected: that Pia would get the role. None of them had been prepared for this outcome, so no appropriate feelings had been rehearsed. Jeanne experienced no triumph in her sister's disappointment. Indeed, there was a fullness in her heart, as though its capacity had deepened and, alongside that special place reserved for Papa, there was newfound room for Pia.

*   *   *

Mathilde mentioned the screen test only once, seeking to placate herself as much as her daughter. "The studio will call with something else. Something *better*. They said so and I firmly believe it. You'll be a star yet, you'll see."

"I'll be a star, Mama, but it won't be for waiting. I will never again sit by the phone waiting for *them*. They'll wait for *me*."

It wasn't said with venom, but the cold detachment and determination with which the words were spoken struck a chord of warning in Mathilde. I'd not want her for an enemy, she mused, alarmed to be applying such a thought to a child she had brought into the world.

Perhaps to help dispel the cloud that seemed to have settled over the Decameron household, Jeanne allowed herself to be persuaded into entering the annual school spelling bee championships. She didn't relish the aspect of competing with her classmates, but finally, at the urging of her favorite teacher, she gave in.

"You're the top speller in the seventh grade, Jeanne," said Mrs. Armitage. "Probably better than all the eighth-graders, too. And you're a strong contender for the district competition and the city-wide match."

She hadn't considered that the school contest was only a preliminary to the all-city finals. Otherwise she might not have agreed to enter her name.

Mathilde was thrilled that at last Jeanne was participating in school events instead of burying her nose in all those books at the library. A normal twelve-year-old needed to be more physically active and spend more time with her peers.

It temporarily lifted a burden from Pia's shoulders; everyone in the neighborhood and all the girls at school asked constantly if the studio had called with any movie offers. She regretted ever having shared the news of her screen test with anyone. In fact, she had told *everyone*. She subsequently made up her mind that in future she would keep all important matters to herself until they materialized; but for the present, the endless questions would have to be endured.

Pia was not involved in the spelling competition. Just as she knew her looks were more than sufficient for a successful movie career, she was aware that her spelling prowess was sorely lacking. Sheer laziness and indifference were responsible; she didn't care enough to study. But she did offer to help Jeanne.

"I'll say the word to you and you can spell it out," Pia suggested one evening after dinner. Jeanne was washing the dishes and Pia was toweling them dry.

Mathilde was seated at the Formica table in the kitchen and applying dark red nail polish to her ten perfectly filed ovals.

"Why, that's lovely of you, dear," she said, relieved that Pia had ceased her sulking over the lost movie role. "I'm sure you'll be a big help to your sister."

Thus began the nightly ritual. Pia would pronounce the word. Jeanne would repeat it slowly in an effort to visualize the individual letters in her mind. Then she would spell the word aloud.

Most of the words Jeanne spelled correctly. The longer, the better. The difficult words were those with "traps," as Mrs. Armitage termed them, the words with sounds and spellings peculiar to the English language. These were also the words most frequently used in championship spelling bees when the competition drew to the final rounds. They were employed for a single purpose: to trip up the good spellers and separate them from those who were truly outstanding.

45

On the third night of practice, Pia began making use of the "trap" words.

"Ukulele," she pronounced slowly.

"Ukulele," repeated Jeanne. She didn't need to take time with that one; she'd heard it spelled on the *Arthur Godfrey Show* and had never forgotten its particular trap. "U-k-u-l-e-l-e."

Pia didn't say yes or no, but went on to the next word. *"Accommodation."*

"Ac-com-mo-da-tion," said Jeanne phonetically. There was a trick to remembering its correct spelling. What was it that Mrs. Armitage had said . . . ? She closed her eyes to help her concentrate. Ah, yes . . . there it was. "Think of *two* accommodations in the room," her teacher had advised. *Two* was the memory "peg": two *c*'s followed by the two *m*'s. "A-c-c-o-m-m-o-d-a-t-i-o-n."

Pia nodded but didn't stop. *"Irresistible."*

"Okay. Ir-resist—did you say *tible* or *table?"* she asked.

Pia didn't answer.

"Would you repeat the word?"

Pia, stone-faced, said, *"Irresistible."*

"Pia, that's the same as last time. I can't spell the word right if I don't hear it right."

"I'm saying it the way everyone says it. Now spell it!"

Jeanne sighed. Most of the *ble* words took an *a,* but maybe that was why Pia had included this word on the list—because it was one of the trap words. *"Irresistible,"* said Jeanne, not slowing to phoneticize. Then, as quickly, "I-r-r-e-s-i-s-t-*i*-b-l-e."

"I guess maybe you'll win this contest," Pia said, biting her lip.

Jeanne thought she detected disappointment in her sister's reaction to the possibility. She hoped that Pia wasn't jealous. But then she almost laughed. Pia—jealous of *her?* Ridiculous!

Mathilde had closed the copy of *Coronet* magazine that she'd been reading while half listening to the girls. Now Pia rose and said, "That's enough spelling exercise for tonight. *Father Knows Best* will be on in five minutes."

The girls left the kitchen, and Mathilde, after pouring herself a cup of coffee, joined them in the living room. The old Zenith had been repaired and a relaxing TV show would do them all a world of good.

"I have an idea," Pia told Jeanne as they settled into their beds. "Those trap words could make you lose the spelling bee, couldn't they?"

"Mrs. Armitage says they're the ones that cause the best spellers to lose. Why? What's your idea?"

Pia smiled in the darkness. "I'll tell you in the morning."

Jeanne awoke to find Pia's bed empty. She glanced at the clock, at first fearful that she'd slept through the alarm and would have to rush or else miss the bus. But it was only seven-fifteen.

She stretched for a few minutes and enjoyed the luxury of the extra time. She could have gone back to sleep until the alarm buzzed at seven-thirty, but she wasn't tired. She got up, turned off the alarm button, touched her toes, and was awake for the day.

She found Pia seated at the table in the kitchen. "What're you doing?" she asked.

Her sister covered the page in the spiral notebook and shook her head. "You'll see when it's finished."

Jeanne shrugged and helped herself to a glass of orange juice.

Pia continued to write while Jeanne toasted two English muffins and poured their milk, adding some of

Mama's already percolated coffee to her glass until the liquid was the color of caramel.

"Well," Pia said at last, closing the notebook, "here. This is for you. And it'll be our secret, so don't show it to anyone."

Jeanne reached over and took the present from her sister. She opened the cover and stared at the first page. It was divided into two columns. The left side was a list of words. On the right, directly opposite each word, was its phoneticized twin. She turned to the second page, then the third, and on through twelve pages of words. All the "trap" words Pia had been able to find.

"Pia!" she exclaimed, overwhelmed by both the gift and its underlying gesture. "Oh, you're amazing!" Jeanne threw her arms around her sister and hugged her tightly.

"God, Jeanne, you'll choke me to death!" Pia stiffened and Jeanne released her grip.

"I didn't mean to . . . it's just that . . . oh, Pia, I'm so glad!"

"Well, don't start sounding like Pollyanna or you'll make me sorry I did it in the first place!"

But Jeanne felt such joy at having tangible proof of her sister's love. She could hardly wait to show it to Mrs. Armitage!

When Mathilde arose, she was surprised to find Jeanne dressed and ready to leave for school; usually she was the one who needed coaxing.

When the two girls reached the landing that separated the seventh-graders on the second floor from the eighth graders on the third, Jeanne reached out to squeeze her sister's hand. "Oh, Pia, thank you so much! I love you!"

Pia stepped back as though the words embarrassed or annoyed her; Jeanne couldn't interpret the expression in her sister's eyes. For a split-second it unnerved her and a darting pain shot through her head. But it disappeared before she could blink, and Pia, who said only, "See you," hurried up the stairs to class.

Jeanne dismissed the puzzling thought as she skipped off to room 207 to show her prized word list to Mrs. Armitage. She'd live up to her teacher's hopes: she'd *win* that spelling bee!

Mrs. Armitage stared at the opened spiral notebook and tried to interpret the intent beneath Pia's action. Pia had been a student in her seventh-grade class last year. Not a particularly good speller. That might account for it. On the other hand, the teacher recalled the older girl's disparaging remarks whenever her younger sister's name had been mentioned. But could an attack of sibling rivalry be responsible for the contents of the notebook just handed to her? And if the latter answer was the case, exactly what would she say to the unsuspecting child at her desk? That she had been sabotaged by her own sister? It saddened the teacher that a girl of thirteen might possess such capacity for premeditated cruelty. She hoped the first reason—Pia's difficulty with spelling and phonetics— explained why the twelve pages of two neatly divided columns of words and their phonetic spelling, top to bottom, listed each "trap" word *incorrectly*.

She glanced up at Jeanne. Then her eyes returned to the bottom of the final page. As though ending the list with an unconscious signature, the last word on the page was *misspelled*. Pia had written m-i-s-p-e-l-l-e-d. Mrs. Armitage checked it twice to be sure. As with all the other words, only a single letter made the difference. But the difference was everything, and it wasn't *her* mistake. One *s* definitely *was* missing.

The teacher hesitated, uncertain of the way in which

to tell her pupil. She considered borrowing the notebook overnight. She could make all the necessary corrections and return it to Jeanne in the morning, the child none the wiser.

But that was the point. *If* the misspellings—with such consistency—were truly unintentional, there was no reason to conceal the discovery. And if they had been made in a deliberate attempt to undermine Jeanne's chances of winning the competition, well, then, as painful as it would be, the child had a right to know. Needed to know. Still, the hurt would cut deeply.

She sighed. There were times when teaching required the wisdom of a Solomon. The "resourcefulness" of some children was frightening, and instinct told Mrs. Armitage that while she hoped the spelling mistakes were accidental, in all probability they were not. She liked the shy, intelligent, sensitive younger sister and had never felt a moment's fondness for the manipulative Pia. This instinct wasn't based on lessons outlined in teachers' manuals, but on thirty-five years of working with children. She could almost always spot a rotten apple.

Mrs. Armitage felt that Jeanne Decameron possessed great promise and might go far—if Pia Decameron didn't get in her way.

She shook her head and closed the notebook. "We'll talk after class, Jeanne" was all she said for the moment.

Jeanne didn't tell Pia—or Mama, for that matter—of her conversation with Mrs. Armitage. She stayed after school and together, teacher and pupil went over every word on the list until the "traps"—those visible and those disguised—had been eliminated. To anyone with the gift of perception, the change in Jeanne, however subtle, would have been noticeable. But neither Pia nor Mama possessed such abilities. Or else they never took the time and interest required. Whichever, they didn't see a thing.

Jeanne won the spelling bee. Easily. She was happy about that. Mama was there and clapped her hands the loudest of all. A picture appeared in the neighborhood newspaper and for a week Jeanne was the celebrity on the block. Claire baked her a special cake and iced it, adding a large "B" in the center.

Then came the district competition with the best spellers from each of the seventeen schools. And she won that. Jeanne accepted the compliments and good wishes with modesty and charm. Only Mrs. Armitage saw beneath the surface. But Jeanne never brought up the subject of the notebook, so the teacher followed suit. Pia was present, seated beside her mother, and dutifully hugged her sister when she was awarded the fifty-dollar prize. This time it was Jeanne who withdrew—almost imperceptibly—from her sister's embrace.

The city-wide spelling bee was held the following month. The last rounds were broadcast on the radio. Jeanne made it all the way through to the ten finalists. She came in fourth. She missed on *mellifluous*. She forgot the third *l* until she'd finished spelling the word, and the rules forbade going back.

But she was pleased, all the same. She was relieved that it was over, relieved that she had come this far. And most of all, she was relieved at having won—and lost—on her very own. She was filled with sweet sensation. *Mellifluous*. It was appropriate. The word was new to her vocabulary. It had not been among those on her list.

Chapter Four

Mathilde wasn't sure which was worse—school or vacation. During the school year, the girls had to be awakened at dawn and dressed in skirts and blouses that seemed to require endless laundering, ironing, and mending. Then there was the long day alone in the house. Not that she missed the girls themselves—she missed their physical presence. Mathilde had never enjoyed her own company that much; the girls provided distraction, even if evenings were spent coaxing Pia to study harder or worrying guiltily about Jeanne, who, after the spelling bee, had withdrawn even more into her private world of books.

At summer's approach, Mathilde had begun to wonder if she was neglecting her younger daughter's needs, but she and Jeanne never seemed to find much to say to each other; with Pia, conversation bubbled; she was simply easier to have around.

And now vacation was here. She'd have them both around until September.

Some vacation, she mused. A month had passed since Pia's screen test. Its failure had only increased her obsession with movies. She spent most of her time at Marybeth's house down the block. That part of it was a blessing for both mothers. Mrs. Michaels worked during the day and was relieved by her daughter's newly formed friendship with someone in the neighborhood; for Mathilde, the day's absence made her less demanding when Pia returned home, and she did enjoy her daughter's imaginative descriptions of the movies she and Marybeth had gone to see.

From what Mathilde could gather, the two girls spent almost every afternoon and most of Marybeth's allowance on movies—trading fan magazines or sitting through double-features at the Mercury, which changed its bill twice a week in summer. It offended Mathilde that she didn't have the extra money for Pia to pay her own way, even to treat her friend occasionally, but a policeman's pension didn't stretch far, and the thought of taking a job to augment the pension never occurred to her; what was she qualified to do besides answer a telephone? She found sufficient difficulty in balancing their meager budget—she would be incapable of calculating anyone else's—and she had never learned to type. She'd often thought of returning to extra work on films, but that insulted her sensibilities; extras were treated like cattle—with no guarantee of steady, full-time employment. Nor did the working hours coincide with mothering.

Mathilde didn't care for Marybeth's parents; nonetheless she felt compelled to extend occasional dinner invitations in reciprocation for the Michaels family's generosity toward her daughter. These evenings always cost more than the movie tickets would have, but Mathilde never thought about that until it was too late.

She also wondered if Marybeth was the right influence on Pia. Both girls lived in a dream world where Hollywood was concerned. It was well and good to plan methodically for a career in movies, but to talk and think exclusively of stardom could prove dangerous—wasn't that what had possessed Pia during her screen test? Hadn't her overripe imagination triggered all those embarrassing lies?

Jeanne, on the other hand, was no trouble these days. Aside from her reclusive behavior and her passionate devotion to her books, the long hours at the library or in her room seemed to benefit her health; her allergies were fewer, their infrequent attacks less intense, and she didn't seem to mind the heat as long as her mind was occupied by good reading.

Mathilde almost envied Jeanne's ability to lose herself vicariously in others' lives; reading had never interested her, except for her magazines. She had enjoyed *Forever Amber* when the girls were toddlers, and *Gone with the Wind* before that—but, like Pia, she preferred the movies. She had started reading *Peyton Place*, but the sexy passages made her think of Hank.

Only during the summer did Mathilde miss him; summer allowed the memory without the pain. She recalled midnight swims, moonlit picnics on the beach, and making love under the fragrant breezes wafting in the window of the room they'd shared before the girls were born.

After Hank's death, Mathilde's interest in sex had dwindled away—or she had unconsciously buried it, she couldn't say which. She didn't miss the stranger Hank had become, but the man he had been still stirred her during sleep. Especially in summer.

The long days with nothing to engage her mind, no one to confirm her own existence, began to wear her down with a now familiar fear—fear of a future yawning lazily before her. When she remembered to pray, which was not often, she prayed for *something*. Something to *happen*.

In the suffocating heat of August, something did.

The telephone rang.

"Mrs. Decameron?" a woman asked.

"Yes, speaking."

"Are you Olympia Decameron's mother?"

"Yes . . ."

"Please hold for Robert Derringer."

Who? she thought as the line clicked into silence.

It came alive moments later. A deep baritone said, "Mrs. Decameron, this is Robert Derringer at Antaen Pictures." He didn't wait for Mathilde to acknowledge his name or the studio's, but continued. "We were impressed with your daughter's screen test last month, and we'd like to offer her a small role in an upcoming feature."

"W-what . . . ?"

There was a pause and Derringer began again. "I'm calling from Antaen Pic—"

"Yes, yes. I-I'm sorry . . . I thought . . . I was told . . . that Natalie Wood . . ." But her throat closed and she couldn't speak.

"Oh, I understand. No, Miss Wood is on loan to our studio for a different movie. Anyway, as I said, it's a small role, but if your daughter is available—"

Mathilde located her voice. "Uh . . . yes. That's fine. I wasn't . . . I mean . . . er, will she have to test again . . . or audition?"

Derringer laughed warmly. "The role is hers, if you're in agreement. The director saw her test and suggested her to me."

"You mean Neal Genesco?"

"No, Mrs. Decameron, Mr. Genesco is directing the picture with Miss Wood."

Mathilde was afraid that a touch of impatience had crept into his voice. "Of course . . . I was just . . ."

"If you can arrange to pick up the script tomorrow, we can have a contract ready. You'll have to sign for her, since she's a minor."

"Certainly . . ."

"Excellent. We'd like her to begin shooting on Friday."

"F-Fri—I mean, tomorrow . . . yes . . ."

"She *is* a member of the union already, isn't she?" Derringer asked.

"Union? Uh . . . well, not yet."

"Then I suggest you go to Screen Actors Guild immediately after you sign her contract. Their office isn't far from the studio. You have the address?"

"Yes," she answered, nodding excitedly into the phone.

"Fine. Then we'll look forward to seeing you tomorrow at ten o'clock. It's the Blanchard Building on the east lot."

Long after Derringer had hung up at his end, Mathilde stood motionless, still holding the telephone receiver in her hand.

My God, she thought. They really *do* like her! She's going to have a chance! All right, it was only a small role, but they wanted her to join SAG, didn't they? That meant a *speaking* role! A start.

SAG! How much would it cost to join? Her own SEG initiation fee had been nominal, but that had been years before, and actors undoubtedly paid more to SAG than extras did to SEG. Of course, actors *earned* much more.

Mathilde hurried to her purse and withdrew her checkbook. Three hundred dollars, with a mortgage payment due. She closed her eyes and drew a deep breath. The hell with the mortgage for now—Pia's first check would pay for that—and then some!

* * *

As recently as a month ago—before the spelling bee and a growing inner confidence—Jeanne might have begged or whined or taken ill in order to stay home. Today, however, she simply entered her mother's bedroom while Pia was ensconced—for the morning, it seemed—in the bathroom. Mathilde was seated at the vanity table and spun around as her younger daughter approached and made her request.

"Mama, I'd like to stay home," she said.

"But, Jeanne . . . you're already dressed to go. Why wait until now to ask?"

Jeanne leaned against the faded wallpaper. "I can change clothes. I just thought it would save time in case you said no."

"Which you already know is my answer, dear, don't you?"

The girl paused and turned to go.

"Jeanne, please wait."

The child came to Mathilde, who gently took her daughter by the shoulders and looked into her eyes. "Jeanne, you know what an important day this is."

"I do, Mama. But you and Pia don't need me there. I'm not the one who's signing the contract or joining a union."

"Jeanne," Mathilde said quietly, "I want you there with us because Mr. Genesco seemed to take an interest in you, too. In *you,* dear. And besides, what's wrong with my wanting to show off *both* of my girls? Maybe you'll be offered a role. It's all a matter of being in the right place at the right time."

Jeanne smiled wanly as the screen image of Ruby Keeler, picked from the chorus to fill in for the star on opening night, played through her mind. This wasn't *42nd Street*, whether Mama knew it or not. Even the day of Pia's screen test, despite her own misgivings and her fleeting bout with jealousy, Jeanne had been aware

57

that the fan magazines' publicity stories were a lot of fairytale nonsense. Yes, Pia had been offered a movie role. But it wasn't a starring role, yet. Nobody became a star overnight, not even Pia. And certainly not Jeanne, simply for accompanying her mother and sister to a contract signing! That was absolutely ridiculous!

Nonetheless, she couldn't say that to Mama, whose face was radiant with happiness. And there was something more. Jeanne thought she saw relief in Mama's eyes. Mama, too, needed to maintain her dreams.

"Did you hear me, dear?" asked Mathilde. "I was saying how nice you look today."

Jeanne smiled. "Pia's awfully pretty, Mama. The kind that shows right away."

Her mother was puzzled. "What do you mean? You're pretty, too."

"Not compared to Pia, Mama," she said simply.

"You're pretty in a different way, dear. It has to be discovered, that's all. Yes. Yours is an *undiscovered* prettiness." Mathilde seemed pleased with her pronouncement—and hoped that it was true.

"Well, maybe that's the difference, Mama. I mean, Pia *knows* about hers. She isn't . . . invisible." She almost smiled to herself—there were aspects to invisibility that held their attraction. But they weren't discussing Jeanne, despite Mathilde's attempt to include her. They were discussing Pia. "She's going to be a famous movie star, Mama. It's all she's ever wanted to be."

"I suppose you're right," agreed her mother. Then, tentatively, Mathilde asked, "And . . . what do *you* want to be, dear?" She was surprised to be conversing in this manner with a twelve-year-old.

"I don't know yet, Mama," answered Jeanne. "Maybe a writer. Someone who can express herself and

58

really . . . communicate . . . her inner feelings."

Why, wondered her mother, couldn't Jeanne have simple, ordinary goals, such as making the most of her looks, perhaps doing small roles in movies, marrying well, doing something to better her life? But communicate her inner feelings? What was that all about? And where would it get her? The child was so . . . what was the word? . . . introspective.

Mathilde was overtaken by a sudden, inexplicable impulse; she drew Jeanne to her and hugged tightly. "Please, darling, come with Pia and me today. I don't want you to be left out."

Jeanne wrapped her arms around her mother and returned the embrace; it was not without sadness, as though an inner voice had told her that this was a last, rare chance for such closeness with Mama. That the closeness did not include understanding only served to deepen a profound sense of loss, although, if asked, Jeanne could not have explained it.

"All right, Mama," she answered with a sigh. "I'll come with you and Pia. Just let me brush my hair."

This time they took a taxi all the way from the train station to the studio. Later, Robert Derringer insisted on calling another to drive them from the Blanchard Building to Screen Actors Guild. It was pure extravagance, but Derringer had said to bill it to the studio— and that was what Mathilde would do.

Signing the contract wasn't half as exciting as Pia had expected. It was her mother's signature, after all, and Pia hardly stole a glance at it before the original was handed back to Derringer and the copy quickly folded and tucked into Mathilde's purse. Pia was embarrassed by the way Mama grabbed it the moment Derringer put down his pen. Was she afraid he'd change his mind? Pia wondered if Jeanne had noticed. But a peek in her sister's direction made her dismiss the thought completely.

In the taxi, Mathilde opened the script and perused Pia's two scenes. Derringer had described the character as bubbly, vivacious, energetic. He had added with a smile that she was very pretty and very rich. Everything Pia was or wanted to be. She loved the role already—even though it was too small.

Pia could hear the distant sounds of televised gunfire coming from the Zenith in the living room. Mama had insisted that Jeanne watch TV with her so that Pia could use the bedroom to study her lines. She hoped her sister wasn't terribly jealous, especially since Jeanne had been practically banned from her own room. But Jeanne spent too much time there alone as it was; Mama had said so.

Pia tried to bring her concentration back to the script lying open before her on the bed. Despite Pia's having only two scenes, Derringer had advised her to read through the entire screenplay. An hour had gone by and she hadn't passed page ten. She yawned. Her first scene wasn't until page forty. It was difficult not to skip ahead to it right away.

Pia would play Annie, best friend of the leading man's daughter. Mama had seemed impressed to learn that the father would be played by Wesley Guest. His name hadn't thrilled Pia. She knew who he was—everyone knew who he was. He was talented and handsome, sure, but if he was such a big star, why didn't she ever see stories of him in *Photoplay* or *Modern Screen*? Oh, there were pictures of him at premieres of his movies, but never any *stories*. Okay, so Mama said he had real acting ability. Still, he wasn't a

Jeff Chandler.

Once more she forced herself to stare at the script and read a whole page. She went over it twice before realizing that not a single word had penetrated. "I guess this is the worst of it," she said to the air. Then she laughed at the irony. Jeanne was the one who loved reading.

Her eyes glanced over at the nightstand. Propped against the little alarm clock was the card. Her SAG card. "Olympia Decameron" was typed on the line beside her membership number.

She reached out and picked up the card. *That* was exciting, she admitted. The *A* instead of an *E* was important.

Well, she thought, *I* am important. Or will be, anyway. Even if Mama had only been an extra. She blushed as she recalled the day of her screen test and that silly story about Papa. A prince—really!

But it was easier to remember him that way than—

Never mind. Let Papa remain a prince. She'd become the princess. And Jeanne thought *she* had been Papa's girl. Pia knew the truth, the secret. And her silence would buy the love that Papa had squandered on her sister.

Yes. A princess. Or at least a star. Papa's star.

She looked down at the script. Page eleven.

I can't stand it, she decided, flipping to page forty.

Jeanne savored the long hours alone in the house while Mathilde and Pia were at the studio. She stayed in bed until they had left for the day, although her inner clock, so accustomed to rising at seven-thirty each morning during the school year, still awakened her at the same time, as though an invisible alarm buzzer had sounded.

She spent the morning reading at the kitchen table, her coffee-flavored milk turning room temperature as the summer heat warmed the air. For lunch—if she remembered it—she made herself a peanut butter and jelly sandwich; most afternoons she forgot, so engrossed was she in her books. She waited until the end of the week and then, with pennies jingling in her pocket to pay overdue charges, she trudged off to the library, her borrowed books trailing over her shoulder in Mama's woven-string shopping bag.

The library was even quieter in summer than during the winter months. And stuffier. The air didn't seem to circulate through the musty rows and rows of bookshelves. But Jeanne felt comfortable among the worn volumes of yellowing pages. She spent twenty-five cents of one week's allowance to buy a soft kidskin bookmark, on which was hand-painted the inscription: *Books, like friends, should be well chosen.* It described her feelings; these shelves were filled with friends, friends who spoke to her, reached out to her, who lived and died and briefly welcomed her into their company.

As a result, she no longer felt lonely. When a neighbor happened occasionally to pass and offer greeting as Jeanne sat at the reading table, she behaved politely, but was relieved when, after an exchange of amenities, the intruder departed.

And one day, seated in her customary corner at the table closest to the window in hope of catching an elusive breeze, Jeanne's eyes fell upon a book that someone had unintentionally left open there. Thinking it was one of the dozen she had chosen and forgotten to replace upon its shelf, Jeanne drew it to her.

Immediately, she recognized her mistake. This wasn't a *book*. It was a *play*. She could tell by the page format. The description and stage directions were printed in italics, each character's name stood at the center of its own line, and the lines of dialogue were set apart in paragraphs and separated from the rest of the text. She glanced at the upper-left-hand corner of the page. It read *George Bernard Shaw*. In the upper-right-hand corner of the opposite page she saw *Pygmalion*. Wasn't there a movie by that name? Of course there was—Leslie Howard had played in it; Mama had mentioned that she liked him so much more as Professor Higgins than as Ashley Wilkes. She tried to recall whether she had seen it on television, but she couldn't be sure. Maybe reading a few pages would refresh her memory. She turned to page one.

She was unaware of the fly buzzing overhead and the librarian's attempt at swatting it; she didn't notice when Richie Greene took a wad of bubble gum from his mouth and pressed it to the underside of the reading table. She didn't see or hear a single distraction until she had finished reading through to the very last page of the play. When she realized that the sun was heading downward, she craned her neck toward the huge pendulum clock at the far end of the reading room. Five-fifty! She'd been there all afternoon! Had she been that engrossed in *Pygmalion*? In a *play?*

She collected the books she wanted to borrow and, placing the Shaw atop them, hurried off to the checkout counter before the library sounded its closing bell.

"Why, Jeanne," she heard from behind her in line, "what a nice surprise!"

She turned to find her beloved teacher waving a makeshift fan of accordion-pleated paper. "Mrs. Armitage! I didn't see you!" This was one person whose presence at the library was not an intrusion on Jeanne's private world.

Mrs. Armitage glanced at the title that topped the stack of books in her pupil's arms. "Ah, Shaw," she said, a smile forming. "Excellent choice. Have you read

63

any of his others?"

Jeanne stammered uncertainly. "I-I . . . n-no. It was on the desk . . . and I picked it up . . ."

"Well, I think that's the best way. That way we can discover the great writers without having them forced upon us. I've never liked spinach."

Jeanne didn't understand. "Spinach?" she repeated.

"I've never liked the taste of spinach because it was forced upon me as a child. Otherwise, I might have developed a taste for the vegetable, which is quite nutritious, you know."

Jeanne wasn't altogether sure it was proper to laugh inside a library, but she couldn't resist doing so. "Has Mr. Shaw written many plays?" she asked, stifling an errant giggle.

Mrs. Armitage nodded warmly. "Yes, dear. And I highly recommend them all. But I admit I didn't know you were interested in the theater."

"I'm not. Well, I mean I've never been to the theater, so I can't say one way or the other." Mama was always admonishing both girls about forming opinions when they had no experience with the subject in question.

"Oh, I see. Your encounter with Mr. Shaw really *is* an accident, then." But the teacher's voice bore no trace of accusation. "Well, Jeanne, you're in for unimagined delights. And perhaps when school resumes this fall, you'll enter the tryouts for the class play."

Jeanne's stammer returned. "Oh, n-no, I c-couldn't. I—"

Mrs. Armitage patted her pupil's shoulder affectionately. "Don't fear, Jeanne. I wouldn't dream of pushing you into something you didn't want to do. It's just that I do recall how well you performed in the spelling bee, all that poise under enormous pressure—"

"But that wasn't *acting*," Jeanne explained. "That was just *spelling*."

"Yes," said her teacher as the checkout line moved closer to the desk. "And acting is probably easier on the nerves than spelling."

Jeanne didn't understand how that could possibly be true, but she held Mrs. Armitage in too high regard to argue the point. Maybe acting was easier for someone like Pia, who acted in front of the mirror all the time and was simply exchanging her mirror for the lens of the movie camera.

"I wasn't referring to movie acting," said Mrs. Armitage, as if reading Jeanne's thoughts. "I meant acting onstage. It's all in the concentration. If one concentrates on one's role and listens—really *listens*—one forgets to be nervous. After all, we act offstage, don't we?"

Jeanne squinted, as if that would enable her to better understand her teacher's words. "We do?"

"Of course. The difference is that onstage, in plays, we have the opportunity of becoming so many different people. We can use our imaginations to portray all kinds of personalities in all sorts of situations. It's rather like living the lives of the characters we only read about in our books. And then, when the curtain falls, we can return to being ourselves."

Jeanne was confused. Suddenly she didn't know which was easier: to be herself or someone else, someone entirely unlike herself. She had never considered that before.

"Next!" said the librarian impatiently. "Do you want those books or not? We don't stay open all night!"

Jeanne hadn't realized it was her turn in line. She stepped forward and handed over her card.

"You can't borrow that many books at one time," said the woman behind the desk. "I've told you that before."

Jeanne's mind was only half listening.

"I said, you've taken too many. Now which ones do you want?"

"Oh . . . I . . . well . . ." And then hesitation vanished. She placed all but the Shaw play to one side of the desk. "Never mind those," she answered. "I'll just take *Pygmalion*."

The librarian muttered something about putting the rest of the books back where they'd come from, but Jeanne wasn't paying attention. She was already planning the evening ahead. Mama and Pia wouldn't be home until late, probably after nine, if the previous day's shooting was any indication. She'd make a grilled cheese sandwich for dinner and then curl up on her bed and read *Pygmalion* aloud—not just the role of Eliza Doolittle, but *all* the parts! She couldn't wait!

When she and Mrs. Armitage reached the foot of the library steps, her teacher said, "I'm driving past your street, Jeanne. Let me drop you off."

Jeanne accepted eagerly, suddenly both exhilarated and tired.

When they pulled up in front of the house, Mrs. Armitage opened the passenger door. "There's a summer stock company playing in a suburb not too far away. Perhaps your mother would let you accompany my husband and me one evening."

Jeanne's heart thrummed excitedly. "Is *Pygmalion* playing there?" she asked.

The teacher smiled and shook her head. "Nothing quite so ambitious, I'm sure. It's probably a light comedy, something the actors can learn with their eyes closed. I did stock when I was a girl. Ten shows in as many weeks. The classics were sadly avoided. But it'll give you a taste of what theater is like. I think"—this she added with full knowledge of Pia's current filming activity—"you'll find it quite different from the theater as it's generally depicted in the movies. You may be pleasantly surprised."

Jeanne looked up at Mrs. Armitage. She was already surprised. First, by learning that the white-haired woman who was older than Mama had once acted onstage—she seemed so ladylike and quiet. And then by the woman's interest in Jeanne. It didn't seem as if Mrs. Armitage was befriending her from pity. She'd ask permission to go to the summer stock performance as soon as Mama and Pia got home from the studio. She'd accept even before that, something she had never done before.

"Mrs. Armitage, I'm sure my mother will say it's all right. So I thank you so very much. I'd love to come with you to the play."

Her teacher had met Mathilde only once, after the district spelling bee. But she had understood much immediately.

"I tell you what, Jeanne, just so your mother doesn't feel we're conspiring behind her back, I'll telephone her later and ask her myself." She thought she detected momentary apprehension flash across her pupil's face.

"Thank you for the invitation," said Jeanne. "Even if Mama says no."

"I don't think she'll say no," said the teacher. "I'm sure she'll be happy to see you expanding your horizons of interest."

Jeanne nodded, but she felt as though she were indeed—what word had Mrs. Armitage used?—*conspiring*. That was new. And for some reason, she didn't mind.

Chapter Five

As the hairdresser reached for his brush, Pia quickly pulled two spit curls to lie flat against either cheek. Phillip turned to face her with a can of hair spray in his hand.

"I *told* you *no*," he said, twisting the ringlets to their former position.

"Those are my trademark."

He began spraying as he asked, "Pia, just how old *are* you?"

Her mind raced. She'd forgotten her character's age as well as the age she had earlier claimed to be.

"I'm old enough to know what becomes me," she said at last.

With his palm, Phillip shielded Pia's eyes from the spray and continued. "Then you should know that looking like a little whore *isn't* what becomes you."

Big sissy, Pia thought. But she said nothing. He applied an extra spritz of lacquer to the waves at each ear, put the can down on the dressing table, and said, "You're through." But as she started to rise, Phillip leaned in with a hand on each arm of the chair and prevented her escape. "Now let me tell you something," he said very quietly, staring directly into her eyes. "The credit line for hair on this flick bears *my* name. Those curls are all *wrong,* and if you're filmed with them, *I* get the blame, and *you* get laughed at. For the third time, *leave your hair alone.* Now go and get into costume."

Pia wriggled out of the chair and tried her best to make a grand exit.

His name was Phillip Turner. I'll remember that, she promised, and he'll never work on one of my pictures again.

She had begun a list, and his was the first name on it.

Mathilde had just poured her second cup of coffee from the tall metal urn when she noticed a woman standing at the threshold of the wardrobe room. She appeared close to Mathilde's age and wore a green smock over gray pedal pushers.

The woman seemed to be staring at something as she dragged deeply on a cigarette. Mathilde followed the direction of her gaze until she saw that the object of attention was Pia, who stood talking with one of the technicians on the set some forty feet away.

All morning, Mathilde had felt superfluous. There was no apparent reason for her presence, even though Pia was a minor. Two hours had passed since their arrival at the studio and with nothing to do, Mathilde was already bored. If she'd brought along any suggestions—which she hadn't—no one, including her daughter, would have listened or cared.

She picked up her cardboard cup, selected half a buttered roll, and walked toward the wardrobe-room door.

"Hello," she said in greeting.

The woman mumbled "hi" but her eyes were still fastened on Pia. "That's some kid," she said finally.

"Is she?" Mathilde asked.

69

"Yep. I put her in puce and she said it wasn't her color. She was right. She washed out in it."

"What did you do?"

The woman shrugged. "Asked her what color was right. 'Mauve,' she said. I had two, told her to pick one. She looks great, no?"

Mathilde admitted that she did, adding, "It was kind of you to listen to her."

"I always listen. That's why I'm good at what I do. My name's Catherine Prager. And I'll bet you're Mrs. Decameron."

Mathilde hoped she wasn't blushing. Hadn't Catherine Prager won an Oscar for best costume design last year? She managed to stammer, "Y-yes, I am. H-how did you know?"

"Everyone's busy but you. Your little girl's got schmartz. If she photographs, she's got a chance."

"Thank you," Mathilde said. "I'm glad the two of you got along."

Catherine nodded and crushed the cigarette beneath her shoe. "I think maybe it's a good idea to get along with Olympia. Otherwise, I'd watch out for her." She turned back toward the room. "Excuse me, I've got work." Then the door closed.

Mathilde remained motionless for a moment, the roll balanced delicately in her hand. A strange sensation, not unlike a chill, had run down her spine when Catherine Prager made her assessment of Pia. It had given voice to misgivings of her own.

Just then, Wesley Guest emerged from the makeup room, and Mathilde's concerns over Pia were erased by the appearance of the actor she so admired on the screen.

It was not a dramatic entrance, yet his presence was immediately felt throughout the soundstage, almost tangibly, as though accompanied by an electrical

70

current. Heads turned, conversation hushed. Mathilde observed, mesmerized, as Wesley Guest strolled casually through the maze of lamps and cables. His greeting to the crew seemed to infuse with energy even the oldest of the army of professionals. His demeanor, carriage, voice bespoke nothing studied or practiced for effect. Wesley Guest wasn't a studio fabrication. His ease came across at first glance.

Mathilde hated the word *fan,* but she had to admit that at this very moment, *fan* described her perfectly. And she suddenly understood *why,* which relieved her. Until now, she had admonished herself for reacting like a schoolgirl when watching him onscreen. Yet here he was, in the flesh, completely altering everyone's mood, charging them with enthusiasm. Talent and experience had made him a fine actor, but neither attribute was responsible for the all-but-visible energy that drew people to him like a magnet. For the very first time, Mathilde understood the meaning of the word *star.*

Since the picture had been shooting for two weeks already, introductions were made to the newcomers, Pia among them. Mathilde wasn't close enough to hear their exchange, but the expression of utter adoration on her daughter's face was definitely more than one of polite tolerance—her customary attitude toward adults.

Pia's eyes searched the shadows beyond the set until she spotted her mother and pointed to her. Wesley Guest smiled, said something to the first assistant director, and, taking Pia by the hand, began a slow saunter in Mathilde's direction.

My God, she thought, he's coming here!

"Good morning," he said in the rich voice so familiar to her. "I'm flattered that your daughter wanted me to meet you."

Mathilde *was* blushing now. She didn't believe him

71

but appreciated the gesture. His hand was extended and she accepted it. Another chill of a different kind swept through her.

He wasn't quite as tall as she'd expected him to be, although he was close to six feet. The chiseled jaw narrowed to a chin that was perhaps a bit sharp and divided by a deep cleft at its center. His dark blond hair was brushed back off a high forehead, while at each temple, softly graying waves curled over his ears.

"My daughter's manners are improving," Mathilde managed at last. The star's deep blue eyes wrinkled at the corners as his slightly crooked grin broadened to a wide smile. His teeth were perfect and Mathilde wondered if they were capped. She didn't care.

His brows knitted together in amusement.

"You look a little confused," he offered, but before she could answer, he called out, "Joey!" Instantly a young man in need of a shave came running across the cement floor to his side.

"Yes, Mr. Guest?" he answered breathlessly.

"Joey, this is Mrs. Decameron—"

"Mathilde," she put in with a smile.

"What a lovely name," he commented. "French, isn't it?"

She nodded, and he continued addressing the production assistant. "Joey, if Mathilde needs anything, or has any questions, I'm leaving it up to you to help, if I can't."

The boy turned to Mathilde and offered his hand. "Joey Crane, Mrs. D. Just let me know whatever you need."

Mathilde thanked him. Joey shrugged it off and then said to the actor, "They're ready to rehearse, Mr. Guest."

"All set, Olympia?" he asked.

"Oh yes, Mr. Guest." Pia had not lost her composure,

72

but Mathilde noticed a slight flutter in her daughter's voice.

"Call me Wes." Taking Pia's hand once again, he said to Mathilde, "Both of you."

She watched them walk back across the cavernous space and step before the cameras to emerge under the blazing illumination of the set.

Joey had set up a canvas chair from which Mathilde could watch the proceedings in comfort.

She was impressed by the set. Two walls were lined with books inside heavy wooden cabinets with glass doors. A massive mahogany desk, appointed with a brass lamp, stood left of a broad bay window. "Sunlight" from three different sources of colored gels streamed through the panes and created an early-afternoon glow in the exquisite library.

Pia sat on a wingback leather chair at the center of the set. Wesley Guest was leaning against one side of the desk that faced her; they ran lines while corners of the Oriental carpet were taped to the floor.

Pia looked beautiful. Even she thought so, Phillip's hairdo notwithstanding. The soft waves caught the light, and her budding figure had been permitted to show beneath the mauve velvet-and-lace dress.

Now Pia and Wes were on their feet and the rehearsal began. Gerry Byrne, the director, joined them as the assistant director screamed, "Quiet!"

"Okay," Gerry said, "let's try a run-through."

Pia did her best not to let her nerves show. The tension came as a surprise to her; until now, she had possessed the steely calm and clarity that she had always depended upon. But this seemed to have disappeared. Her lines were solidly memorized—she could recite them in her sleep. But all she could think of was: *What do I say next?* Everyone around her knew exactly what to do. Her primary motive suddenly became one of survival: to mask her fear of failure. The realization was dawning upon her that whatever she did or said, however or wherever she moved, *all* of it would be recorded for posterity on film by the impersonal, uncaring eye of the camera. Yes, there would be ample opportunity to do it again and again until it was right. But what if she did something terribly wrong *and* wonderfully right—during the same take? What if, during the second take, she could correct what she had done wrong—but not *repeat* what she had done right?

These thoughts raced through her mind as she paced the set, speaking her lines. She felt as if her brain were split into three sections: acting, worrying, and watching herself.

When she picked up the teacup from the desk, the cup rattled audibly in the saucer because her hands were shaking so. But Gerry said nothing, and the scene continued. And then Wesley came to her rescue. He leaned across the desk and took the shaking cup from the saucer still in Pia's hand. He lifted the cup to his lips and sipped.

"Nice!" Gerry yelled when they came to the end of the run-through. "Wes, taking that cup from her was great. Leave it in. And . . . Pia . . . if you can give me the same edge of tension when we roll, we've got a beauty of a scene." Turning from her, he announced, "Okay, everybody. We shoot the master in five minutes."

Immediately, people swarmed around Pia and Wesley. Catherine Prager adjusted Pia's hemline while the makeup man smoothed her eye shadow and powdered her down. The assistant cameraman stretched

74

a tapemeasure from her chin to the edge of the camera lens. The light man held a meter to Wesley's cheek, then to Pia's.

Amid the flurry of activity whirling about them, Wes said to her, "Olympia, I hope you weren't offended by my inventing that teacup business."

"No," she replied with honesty. "In fact, thank you . . . Wes. I was shaking so badly I couldn't do anything but hold on to it."

"Technique," he said.

"What?"

"You're new. You need to develop technique . . . and it'll come. Just keep in mind what you're supposed to be doing in the *scene."*

But then a woman in her late twenties joined them and introduced herself. "Elaine Blair." A heavy camera, suspended from a strap around her neck, hung between her breasts. "I'm continuity, Miss Decameron. Would you mind standing up, please?"

Pia obeyed, looking questioningly at Wesley. "What's this for?"

"So when you go from shot to shot, scene to scene, you always match what's been done," explained Elaine while she aimed her camera. "That is, if it's all supposed to take place on the same day. Hold it."

A blinding flash went off in Pia's eyes, and when her vision cleared, she saw Elaine pulling a rectangular packet from the side of the camera. She peeled off the dark paper. Gradually Pia saw a small photograph of herself emerging. The mauve dress was gray and her lipstick was black. There was a brownish cast over all the tones of the picture. After a minute or so, Elaine pulled a spongelike pink roll from a glass tube and rubbed it across the picture's surface. While it was drying, she took a pad and pencil from her pocket and

75

began writing, her eyes darting from Pia to the pad and back again.

"What are you doing now?" This new instant camera was amazing, but Pia was growing restless.

"One of these days they'll start making 'em for color. Till then, I've got to list everything. Otherwise you're liable to have green eyelids today and yellow tomorrow —in the same shot. See?" She scribbled a few last notes, repeated the process with Wes, and was gone.

Pia felt moderately stupid for knowing nothing about the practice of matching; still, she couldn't be expected to know everything. Not all at once.

The shooting began.

Two minutes into the scene, a loud voice yelled, "Cut!"

"What happened, Stu?" Gerry asked from his chair.

"Pia can't open the doors to the cabinet."

Oh, God, she thought. It's my fault! "I'm sorry, Gerry," she rushed to say. "I did it in the rehearsal, and I—"

"No, no," Stu interrupted. "It's not you, honey. I could see the whole off-set crew—and the camera— reflected in the glass on the doors."

"So . . . I shouldn't open the case?"

"So," he said, smiling, "you should wait until we decide to move the camera or change your cross. Relax."

"He's right, y'know," came Wesley's voice from behind her.

Pia turned. "What do you mean?"

"I mean, Olympia—"

"Pia, please . . . Wes . . ."

"Pia. I know it isn't easy, but nothing good . . . nothing creative, can be born if it's blocked."

"Blocked?" She was listening intently while basking

in the warmth of his attention.

"Nerves, dear. Up to a point, they're fine. Keep the adrenaline going. And, too, you're *supposed* to be nervous in the scene . . . Your instincts are good."

"But I thought you said nerves are bad."

"When *they* control you, they're bad. Let the nerves surface to help the scene and your character . . . not to hinder you. *You* are in control. The actor is *always* in control, no matter how harrowing the scene that's being played."

"But that's not *acting,* is it?"

He smiled and nodded. "Using whatever resources you have at hand, including your own, honest emotions . . . *that's* acting. That's truth. Anything else is just pretending."

As they went through the scene again—this time without having Pia open the bookcase—she tried putting Wesley's advice into practice. But she understood only half of it—the half that said her nerves should not control her.

"Pia," Gerry said after the first completed take, "you're letting that nice edge slip away. Get some of the earlier tension in it again."

She glanced hopefully at Wes, but Elaine was straightening the stickpin in his lapel and sharing a joke with him, while the makeup man touched up his perfect nose.

They shot the master twice more. The last take was a print. Pia had overcome her nerves completely, and realizing that Gerry *wanted* nerves in the scene, she resorted to acting *at* being nervous.

Wesley watched. He knew it was acceptable, but it wasn't good. Pia couldn't discern between a genuine performance and an imitation of emotion. Everything she did was pretense, for effect. Still, it was big—and

77

surprisingly confident, he noted, for someone so new, so young. She had sacrificed reality for melodrama, but it wasn't boring.

At least she understands that much, he mused. It had been years since he'd learned the most basic lesson of his craft: one could be bad, but one must *never* be boring.

Pia was calmer the following day, although not in a very cheerful mood. Jeanne had stayed awake late, reading a book by the light of her bedside lamp until midnight. At length Pia had lost her patience and snapped, "*You* may not have to look good tomorrow, but *I* have close-ups and I need my sleep!" She was almost disappointed when her sister silently closed the volume and turned off the light without a word.

Pia had slept restlessly. In the morning, while Mathilde clucked on and on about the magicial world of movies, Pia, yawning, yearned only to crawl back into bed. Before leaving their room, she glanced at Jeanne, curled comfortably between the sheets, and envied her sister for being free to remain at home to do as she pleased.

Nonetheless, Pia's spirits rose at the sight of the studio limousine. As she and Mathilde stood waiting for the driver to come around and open the rear passenger door, she hoped that Jeanne—or at least a few of the neighbors—were awake and watching through their windows. This was the part of movie-making that appealed to her most, although she would have liked it more had the driver been in uniform. Mama informed her that he wasn't really a chauffeur. "He's a teamster," said Mathilde.

Well, whatever a teamster was, Pia mused as she

78

settled back into the plush velvet seat, it sure beat the train—or even a taxi.

Wearing the same mauve velvet dress as she had the day before, the same makeup, and the same hated hairstyle, Pia emerged from the wardrobe shop and noticed Phillip Turner walking away from the wig room. He was headed for the exit, and Pia squinted to shield her eyes as the rising sun of daylight entered the darker soundstage area.

When the door had closed behind him, Pia approached Joey.

"Where's Phil going?" she asked.

"He's not feeling well this morning. He's going home. He's done everybody's hair already—his assistant can handle maintenance for the rest of the day."

"I hope he's all right," Pia said with more concern than she felt. "When do we start shooting?"

"Ten minutes," answered Joey, coiling a length of cable around his arm.

"Good." Quickly Pia started in the direction of her dressing room.

Wesley knelt beside Mathilde's canvas chair.

"How is Pia doing?" she asked him, partly because she wanted his opinion, partly for need of something to say. Pia was all they had in common.

"She's learning fast," Wesley answered. "She doesn't know yet to save her real performance for the close-up and use the other setups as rehearsals, but it'll come. She gave too much yesterday."

"Is that how you work?"

"It's how we all work, if we're smart. That's how

Oscars are won." Then he smiled to himself. "Well, that and studio politics."

His grin had a wry edge to it, but Mathilde said nothing. As he rose to his full height, she wondered if his last remark had slipped out unintentionally, possibly revealing more of Wesley Guest than he had planned. She knew he had been nominated twice for the Academy Award. Once for Best Supporting Actor, once for Best Actor. He hadn't won it either time. Perhaps he cared less about politics than about acting . . .

"Mr. Guest on set, please!" called a loud male voice. Wesley excused himself and headed for the "library."

Pia saw Elaine Blair coming her way, pad and pencil in hand. Hastily she turned her back and pulled the spit curls at her cheeks back into the wave Phillip had earlier created.

Thirty seconds later, Elaine said, "Okay, honey, you match yesterday." Then the woman from continuity was gone.

Pia turned around once more and laid the curls flat against her cheeks the way *she* liked them best. She didn't require a mirror; she'd practiced the arrangement in the dressing room and could do it with her eyes closed. She knew the spit curls were perfect.

She also knew that attracting undue attention to herself would provide additional opportunity for the spit curls to be noticed.

Pia willed away her nerves—not for the sake of her camera performance, but to draw as little direction from Gerry as possible; less contact with him might just cause him to miss the "continuity."

During a break, Wesley approached her. She smiled,

happy for any excuse to talk with him. Nonetheless, the smile was tentative—it might be about her hair.

It wasn't.

"Pia," he said in a fatherly tone that both pleased and annoyed her, "when we shoot your close-ups this afternoon . . . a word to the wise."

"I'm grateful for any advice from you, Wes," she answered. It was true.

"Keep it fresh. *Re-create* your performance—don't try to repeat it."

Relief was replaced with puzzlement. "What?" She had no idea as to what he meant.

"Look," he said, "let's have lunch—the three of us." He glanced over at Mathilde, who was sitting in her customary canvas chair off to one side. Then, turning back to Pia, he said, "And don't worry about your close-ups. Even though they won't need me, I'll be there."

"Won't need you? What do you mean?"

"We'll leave *that* for lunch, too."

But before the meal break, she'd find out. She hated this constant feeling that she didn't know anything about the process of moviemaking. Joey—sweet, reliable Joey—would tell her what she needed to know. She suspected that he'd developed a crush on her; that made him the most likely person to ask.

He was replacing a pink gel into a lamp, but he stopped as soon as he saw her and was eager to answer her question.

"Y'see," he said, "Wes is the star. He does his close-ups first, and if he wants to, he's free to go home. Your close-ups could be shot with a stand-in feeding you lines from off-camera."

"Thank you, Joey." She was considering asking him to join them for lunch when he spoke again.

"By the way, Pia . . . I like your spit curls."

She froze for an instant, stuttered another "thank you," and walked away quickly. Joey's presence at lunch was no longer an option. Besides, although he was very pleasant, he was, after all, only a production assistant. She doubted that stars socialized with production assistants.

In deference to her daughter—but also from the uneasiness that Wesley Guest stirred within the daughter's mother—Mathilde had tried to maintain a polite distance from the star during lunch together. But she was aware of her inability to disguise her own self-consciousness. When the jealous eyes of actresses or female studio personnel traveled from Wesley to Mathilde with quizzical expressions, it required every ounce of willpower to steady her knees and balance her fork. While she was certain that his attentions were designed to encourage Pia in her screen debut, she couldn't avoid his gaze from across the table.

Pia didn't seem to notice; her mind was on her curls.

Wesley kept his word; he gave a full, committed performance during Pia's close-ups, even though his face was never seen by the camera. Still, she anxiously wanted the day to be over.

So far, no one but Joey had noticed the change in her hairstyle; nonetheless, the constant fear of discovery kept her tense. Dodging Elaine and her instant camera was wearing her down. Only Wesley's presence enabled her to maintain control throughout her close-ups. He liked her, and the thought buoyed her flagging spirits.

The day's wrap came a full hour earlier than it had

the previous afternoon. Gerry seemed more than satisfied.

"I'll look at the rushes tonight," he said, "but I'm sure they're fine. Tomorrow we'll shoot your second scene. Get a good night's rest."

Climbing into the limousine, Pia soon shed the day's tension. In her own crinoline skirt and sleeveless blouse, her curls combed out from the stiff spray and set, she leaned back and sighed deeply. Tomorrow would be a snap, she mused as the car drove past the studio gates. Oh, sure, that annoying Phillip would probably be back and he'd impose those ugly waves on her again, but at least she had been filmed the way *she* wanted to look, if only for one day. Her second scene had less than a dozen lines. It would be an easy day.

Then Mathilde said, "It was nice of them to let you wear your hair like that."

For a change, Pia didn't gush with news when she and Mama arrived home from the set. Jeanne didn't question her sister's moodiness, but she could tell from the expression on Mathilde's face that Mama found it curious, too. Jeanne's quiet, which lately seemed less from shyness than from lack of desire to share her feelings with her sister, annoyed Pia no end, particularly this evening.

She might ask—just once—how my day went, Pia fumed silently as she slathered Noxzema on her face. She might even *learn* something! But in her heart Pia knew she wanted Jeanne to ask from jealousy, not curiosity, and it wasn't happening. Her sister didn't seem to care. *How* could someone actually not care about movies?

She didn't really want to be questioned tonight—but

she *did* want the attention. She had played her brooding to the hilt, just to have someone—all right, *Jeanne*—ask what was troubling her. Of course she'd never have *told* her sister, but the drama of forcing tears to her eyes and then turning away to walk down the long hallway to the bedroom did hold its appeal.

Or, in an alternate scenario, to quietly murmur, "It's nothing," and then to excuse herself and, with a sigh, exit to the porch "to look at the stars." Originally, the phrase "I want to be alone" had crossed her mind, but she amended the dialogue since Mama was a Garbo devotee and even Jeanne would no doubt recognize the famous line.

One fact did upset her. She studied herself in the mirror as she regarded her pained reflection—oh, why, she moaned silently, why can't a camera be recording *this* moment on film?—and realized that she was truly worried. Mama had noticed her hair. So had Joey. Perhaps others had, too, and had merely said nothing. Maybe she hadn't gotten away with it.

The driver held the umbrella up over Pia and Mathilde. The protection wouldn't cover three, so he stood soaking from head to foot as he opened the soundstage door.

Once inside, Mathilde knew immediately that something was wrong. In the first place, Gerry Byrne was already there; usually the director never showed up until an hour after the actors' call. This morning, he was standing beside the coffee urn. A cigarette bobbed up and down in his mouth while he spoke to Joey. His voice was low, but deep furrows in his brow and a tight expression warned of impending trouble.

When the huge metal door slammed shut against the rain, Gerry's eyes shot up to meet Mathilde's, then moved to Pia and stayed on her as the two figures walked toward the dressing room.

"He's here early," Pia observed as she removed the yellow rain slicker and automatically handed it to Mathilde.

"Yes," Mathilde agreed, looking around for something on which to hang the dripping rubber garment. Finally she suspended it from a metal pipe over one of the two sinks.

Pia had already kicked off her shoes and was unbuttoning her blouse. Mathilde reached for Pia's chenille robe and held it out for her to slip into.

"I'm not undressed yet!" Pia snapped.

"Pia, I'm only trying to keep you from catching cold . . ."

The girl closed her eyes in exasperation and said quietly, "I can put it on myself when I'm ready."

"Fine," answered her mother, folding the robe over the back of a chair. "I'll be outside if you need me."

Gerry Byrne had moved into the shooting area with Joey. Mathilde watched them from her position next to the coffee urn, which seemed to be the morning congregating spot. Phillip Turner was back; he stood beside the director. His face was pale under the harsh work light. Mathilde was struck by the falseness of the make-believe room without benefit of the hundreds of lamps that lit the set from above.

Just then, Elaine Blair strode across the Oriental carpet to join Phillip and Gerry. It wasn't long before their voices had grown louder, their conversation now a heated exchange. Mathilde couldn't make out what was being said, but Gerry was obviously furious, and his anger only fueled the already volatile hairdresser. Elaine's face had gone beet-red as she maintained a forced silence.

"Get Miss Decameron out here on the double!" Gerry ordered.

Mathilde spilled the coffee in her haste to head Joey off at the door to Pia's dressing room.

Too late, she watched as he knocked and entered.

Pia had heard the raised voices through the door. She had remained seated in her chair, waiting for the inevitable summons.

Now she spun around as Joey's reflection appeared in her mirror.

"Olympia, Gerry wants to see you. Pronto!"

"Is something wrong?" she asked, her throat tightening.

Joey said, "Looks that way," and left.

He was halfway across the soundstage when Pia stepped from the dressing room. Knotting the belt of her robe, she walked as slowly as she could—she needed time to think. Her pulse raced, and beads of perspiration had begun to dot her forehead.

Joey, Phillip, Elaine, and Gerry stood near the desk staring at Pia. Their faces seemed to grow larger as she drew nearer, and suddenly she was terrified. She saw her mother move in closer to the edge of the set, Mathilde's worry evident on her ashen face.

Who had told? Pia asked silently as she sidestepped a cable and moved around a camera. Was it Joey? Or her mother?

Neither, she learned from Gerry's curt answer a moment later.

"The rushes," he said.

Pia understood instantly. But perhaps her inexperience and her tender age would save her. With studied confusion, she blinked and asked, "The what?"

"The rushes!" Phillip screamed at her in a shrillness that echoed throughout the cavernous space.

"Calm down, Phil," Gerry urged, but his own eyes never left Pia's face. Then he spoke directly to her. "Pia, everything we shot yesterday—an entire day's work—has to be reshot today."

"It d-does?" she stammered.

"It does. Up to now, I was under budget, and my producer was happy. Today we go over budget, and I'm in trouble."

"But . . . why?"

"Because yesterday's footage doesn't match what we printed two days ago, Pia. You have two different hairstyles."

She knew her face had turned crimson, but she couldn't back down now. "I do?"

"Yes. And I'd like to know why. Mistakes are one thing, but we all have to answer to someone. In this business, time is money."

He cleared his throat. "Phil says your hair was perfect when he left yesterday morning. Elaine tells me you avoided her each time she tried to get a picture. Now . . . what's *your* story?"

Pia's hand went to her brow but was stayed when Joey proffered a handkerchief. She stalled, dabbing at the moisture, and finally said, "Well . . . I . . . I thought Elaine was supposed to find *me.*"

"And Phillip?" Gerry asked.

Everyone's eyes appeared to bore into her—even Mathilde's.

What can I do? she wondered, panicky with indecision. Would they fire her? It was a small role . . . less than two weeks' work. They'd already lost one day . . . would they get someone to replace her? But worse . . . far worse . . . would they—what did they call it—*blacklist* her and never let her work in movies, *ever* again?

A small voice from within her whispered: Stop it,

87

Pia! *Think!*

For all her ruminations, only seconds passed before she gave her reply: "If it's the spit curls you mean, I never touched my hair after Phillip finished with it."

Phillip Turner's eyes bulged as though he might explode, but Pia rushed on. "He said it wouldn't hurt, and that since I thought the curls were pretty, he—he'd do me a favor! B-but he was sick yesterday, and maybe"—she paused, astounded by her own performance—"maybe you didn't know what you were doing, Phillip . . . ?"

She had expected the hairdresser to shout again, but he didn't. Instead, he looked at the director, as though waiting for a cue.

After an interminable pause, Gerry said very quietly, "Pia, the only reason I'm not going to fire you is because we've already got three days' work in the can. You're lucky you didn't try a stunt like this your first day on the set." Before she could react, he announced, "All right, everybody. We start in half an hour! Reset for the top of yesterday's shoot!"

Then, turning again to Pia, he said, "Phillip will do your hair."

Pia walked toward Mathilde, took her hand, and squeezed it hard. Together they started off to the dressing room. They were intercepted at the door by Phillip Turner. His jaw was tightly set as he said to Pia, "Just remember one thing, honey. I've got your number—and you're a lying little bitch!"

Mathilde closed the door and faced her daughter, but she was unable to speak. She hadn't heard that word since before Hank's death.

"Mama," said Pia, tears welling up in her eyes, "Mama . . . I couldn't *help* it . . ."

Mathilde remained silent as she studied the stranger who was her child.

"Mama . . . *please* say something!" she pleaded as broken sobs filled the room. "Mama, I *had* to! They would have *fired* me!" Pia cried, then immediately lowered her voice, remembering that the dressing-room walls were paper-thin. "Mama . . . please don't give me the silent treatment! Yell at me! You can punish me—do anything!" She stopped abruptly, and her face assumed the expression of a startled deer. "Anything, Mama . . . except . . ."

"Except what?" Mathilde asked wearily.

"Please . . . whatever you do . . . *please* . . . don't . . . tell . . . Jeanne!"

Mathilde sighed and opened the door. Before she left the room, she said, "Stop your crying, Pia. You'll be puffy for the cameras."

Chapter Six

Jeanne was waiting in front of the house when her teacher's gray Chevrolet pulled up.

A white-haired man who could have passed for his wife's twin, rather than husband, sat behind the wheel. Mrs. Armitage waved as Jeanne approached the car. Then Mr. Armitage reached in back and opened the rear door for Jeanne. "Sorry about the lack of formality," he said in a friendly voice, "but the car's having a little problem with stiffness. Age, I suppose. And she just might not start if I don't keep her idling."

Jeanne didn't mind, but the very fact that he had apologized impressed her.

"You were wise to bring a sweater," said her teacher. "It'll grow quite cool once the sun sets."

"It was Mama's idea," explained Jeanne. Still, the pink sweater didn't go with the red sundress she was wearing. It was her best summer cotton and her only cardigan; there had been no choice. Pia had refused to lend her sister the white sweater Claire had knitted for her thirteenth birthday.

Jeanne sat back against the rough grain of the synthetic leather upholstery. She tried to stretch her legs far enough from the seat to avoid a waffle-pattern imprint on her calves. She placed the sweater across the back of the seat for the same purpose. Her own back was bare, except for the crisscrossing of the wide straps of her sundress; she was not going to arrive at the theater looking like a waffle iron!

Mr. Armitage kept up a patter of friendly talk, asking nondescript questions about school and Jeanne's interests. None of the conversation was personal, but both he and his wife made certain that their guest was never excluded. Before she realized she might be prying, Jeanne asked, "Do you have children at home, Mrs. Armitage?" It was the first time she had actually considered that her teacher might have a private life away from school.

The white-haired woman turned her head. At first, she said, "No. My pupils are my children." Then, after a moment's hesitation, she added, "Frank and I weren't able to have any of our own."

Jeanne was at a loss for words. "Oh, I'm sorry," she said.

"Don't be. At first we were, too, but now, quite truthfully, dear, I don't think I would have been a good mother."

"You don't?" Jeanne was amazed; Mrs. Armitage had so much patience, took such an interest in her pupils. A child would have been blessed with a mother like her!

But Mrs. Armitage explained. "I've come to believe that being a mother is a full-time occupation, Jeanne. As is teaching. And I don't think I could have done both without shortchanging one or the other. It would have been unfair to a child—or children—either at home or in the classroom." Then, when she saw that the girl was listening with an intensity lacking in most twelve-year-olds of her acquaintance, the teacher added, "I'm sure your mother must feel the same.

That's why she chooses to be at home with you and your sister."

Jeanne shrugged. "I don't know. She's always home, but I don't really think she likes it. She's much happier now that Pia's in a movie. Mama goes with her to the studio every day."

Frank Armitage addressed Jeanne through the rearview mirror. "Do you mean you're at home alone all day?"

Mrs. Armitage cautioned her husband with a touch to his arm. "Jeanne isn't alone, dear. She's surrounded by her books. And she spends many hours at the library—that's where we met the other day, isn't it?"

The potential for an uncomfortable moment had passed. Jeanne was thinking about the characters in *Pygmalion*. "You know," she said, "you're both like Colonel Pickering." Then she blushed. "Oh, you're not as *old* as he is! I meant he really *cares* about Eliza. He doesn't just order her around and tell her what to do. Professor Higgins treats her as if—as if she's twelve years old!"

"But that's his way of caring," said Mrs. Armitage. "People have different ways of expressing their love."

"Well, I don't think he loves anybody except himself," scoffed Jeanne. "He's only interested in his own words—not Eliza's feelings. He never treats her like a *person!*"

The passion expressed in the child's statement indicated to her teacher that the loneliness she had detected in Mathilde Decameron was misinterpreted by her daughter and perceived instead as selfishness. "Perhaps Professor Higgins has spent too much time by himself," Mrs. Armitage said gently. "Grown-ups sometimes feel that they're being neglected."

Jeanne's eyes widened. "Like children?"

"Exactly like children. We may be taller and larger—and older, to be sure. But that doesn't always make us wiser. And it certainly can make some of us sadder."

Jeanne felt a flash of tenderness for Mama. Did Mama feel neglected? It's funny, she reflected, maybe when she's busy telling Pia and me what to do, she wants someone else to tell *her* what to do. But is that *love?* Is that why Mama misses Papa? Oh, there were so many questions, questions that she knew would go unanswered, because she would never be able to ask them. Not of Mama. She wondered what Mama's life would have been like if she hadn't been able to have children, if she and Pia had never been born.

They had reached the open-air theater. A large, painted sign, carefully lettered in foot-high print, announced the "Southern California Summer Playhouse Series." Underneath, in smaller letters, it read: "Broadway hits performed by a cast of Southern California's finest professional actors." It made excitement and anticipation surge through Jeanne's chest.

The production of the week was *The Guardsman*, by Ferenc Molnar. Jeanne had never heard of the play or its author. "It's not exactly a Broadway hit," Frank said as they waited in line for their tickets. "Molnar wrote *Liliom*"—he noted Jeanne's blank expression and edited his explanation—"which was later made into the Broadway musical *Carousel*."

Mrs. Armitage smiled. "Well, then, I suppose the marquee isn't completely misleading. *The Guardsman* by way of *Liliom* and *Carousel*—*is* connected to Broadway, isn't it? As a matter of fact, the play was originally performed by the Lunts."

Jeanne had read several books about the theatrical couple and was secretly pleased at not being totally ignorant on the subject.

However, as they settled into their folding chairs within the tree-encircled theater area, it became apparent that the play was no more on a level with *Carousel* than the cast of "Southern California's finest professional actors" compared in any way with the Lunts. It was a drawing room comedy, and, as Mrs. Armitage whispered during a particularly dated scene, "It's all style and no substance. The actors don't know how to listen to one another."

There it was again—listening! It sounded so easy! That was part of what they'd talked about at the library, wasn't it? But if acting was so easy—just a matter of *listening*—why were the people onstage finding it so difficult?

Jeanne was quiet for most of the drive home. Frank Armitage and his wife spoke softly in the front seat, to avoid disturbing their guest in case she had fallen asleep.

But Jeanne wasn't asleep. The air had cooled, as Mama and Mrs. Armitage had predicted, and she was curled up on the backseat, unmindful now of any patterns stamping themselves on her legs. The pink sweater was buttoned up to her neck as she leaned her head back and closed her eyes. She had found *The Guardsman*, her first encounter with live theater, absolutely boring. And she had expected far more from the actors than the performances given. But it had not dampened her increasing interest in the art form. Instead, it had heightened her curiosity. What if the play *had* been engrossing? she wondered. And what if the actors really *had* listened, *had* communicated with each other—and thereby with their audience? They might have accomplished the same end as the characters in Jeanne's favorite novels. Or as those in Mr. Shaw's *Pygmalion*.

Could *acting* be as fulfilling as writing?

And—even in her thoughts, Jeanne lowered her

94

silent voice before daring to acknowledge the question —was it something *she* could learn to do?

Because for all the boredom endured that evening, a spark had been kindled. There was something . . . inexplicable . . . magical . . . *extraordinary* about live theater! Even amateurish, run-of-the-mill theater. It caused Jeanne's heart to pound wildly as she asked herself: Do I have what it takes? Not to become a movie star—but a genuine, real, live *actress?*

A chill passed through her, despite the warmth of her pink cardigan sweater and the coziness of the old Chevrolet.

And then she did fall asleep, right there on the backseat.

Pia had changed. She suddenly became obedient, almost subdued, on the set, keeping to herself most of the time. She was polite to the crew, especially to Elaine Blair and Catherine Prager. She avoided only Phillip Turner—unless he was dressing her hair.

The movie wrapped in the late afternoon. The party was getting under way on the set where the last scene had been shot. Within record time, the area was cleared; cables and booms and lights seemed to disappear, immediately replaced by tables laden with delicacies—beef Wellington, stuffed breast of veal, shrimp, lobster, terrines, salads, aspics, and a mountain of black caviar. Champagne and Chivas Regal were in ample supply, and Mathilde quickly downed a scotch, then accepted a glass of champagne. Even Pia was allowed to partake, although her resulting giddiness caused Mathilde to worry that she had been too permissive, even on an occasion that prompted such lessening of discipline.

"It's no matter," said a voice behind her.

Mathilde looked up to find Wesley Guest standing very close. Makeup, costume, and all traces of artifice had been removed, giving his rugged features and casual friendliness room to surface. In gabardine slacks and safari jacket, he seemed less threatening than the sophisticated, smoking-jacketed leading man filling the screen of the movie theater with his larger-than-life image.

"What's no matter?" she asked.

He nodded in the direction of Mathilde's gaze. Pia was giggling and leaning against a table for support. "That she gets drunk tonight. If she drinks enough champagne her very first time, she'll become sick. It's an excellent way to keep her from turning to alcohol later." Then he laughed as they both observed Pia's almost-stagger. "In fact, she may be sick sooner than we think!"

"It might be a good idea for me to take her home," said Mathilde. "I'd hate to see her make a fool of herself."

"Relax," Wesley advised. "It has to happen sooner or later." Then, noticing her discomfort, he added, "Look, if she gets really stinking drunk, I'll rescue both of you and no one will be the wiser." He clinked his champagne flute against Mathilde's. "Come on, you can't mother her forever."

She managed a weak smile and tried to find something clever to say. But words failed her each time she looked up into the deepest blue eyes she had ever seen. No wonder Pia fancied herself in love!

"Why haven't you been mingling?" asked Wesley. "You're hiding on the sidelines. It isn't fair—you ought to be dancing and having fun."

"Oh . . . I'm h-having fun," she stammered. "I just . . . just don't know anybody."

"Not true. You've met everyone on the set."

"No . . . I mean I don't really *know* any of them—to talk to. They all seem to be such good friends, and—"

"Don't believe it for a minute. Everybody's acting. Even wrap parties are performances."

Mathilde's eyes widened, causing Wesley Guest to laugh. "I hope you won't think this is a line from one of my movies, because it isn't. You're not only lovely, Mathilde—you're refreshing, too."

"I'm *what?*"

"Refreshing. You're not behaving like a typical stage mother."

She blushed, because she knew she'd often been guilty of exactly that in the past.

"I'd like to think that I'm the reason for that sudden flush of your cheeks, but somehow I doubt it . . ."

Mathilde was at another loss for words. She found the top button of her blue-and-white polka-dotted dress coming undone and filled the moment by securing it.

Wesley stopped her gently with his hand on hers. "Leave it open. It's much more becoming that way."

Mathilde's heart felt as though it had stopped beating. This is crazy, she told herself. He's a movie star. He's accustomed to having women fall at his feet. He's only talking with you because you're Pia's mother. Or perhaps because you haven't thrown yourself at him. Snap out of this now before you're the one who behaves like a fool, instead of Pia!

But at that moment, Pia, weaving against a potted palm that had not been removed from the set, reached out as if to grasp the air. Her eyelids fluttered, and she slid down the trunk of the tree until she was seated in a heap beside the large earthenware receptacle.

"Oh my God!" whispered Mathilde.

"It's all right," said Wesley. "Nobody's seen a thing." He hurried over to Pia as Mathilde stood watching in horror and embarrassment. But he was right; the set was jammed with so many people that Pia's "scene" had gone completely unnoticed. Wesley waved to one colleague, spoke to another, and disappeared. He returned moments later with a young studio assistant, who helped Pia to her feet and led her from the set.

Then Wesley rejoined Mathilde.

"Where did he take her?" asked an anxious Mathilde.

"To my car. We'll sneak out of here in a few minutes and I'll drive you home. She'll be fine in the morning." Then he amended the statement. "Well, if not fine, wiser."

It took longer than expected because Wesley had to stop and bid good night to so many people. Mathilde observed the ease with which he remembered to thank each person for some particular task or favor performed during the picture's shooting. And each recipient beamed in turn with genuine fondness for the actor, who seemed truly grateful to every one of them for his or her contribution to the movie. Mathilde found herself studying him during their exit. Wesley Guest wasn't "performing," as he had said of the others earlier. He certainly didn't behave like a star!

Nor did he believe in being chauffeured like a star. They finally made their way through the throng and out into the vast parking area. Wesley took Mathilde's arm and led her to his black Buick convertible. The top was up, and curled comfortably, asleep in the backseat, was Pia. When Wesley opened the passenger door for Mathilde, they could both see by the dim overhead light that Pia's face was ashen.

"Well, then," said Wesley quietly, "I'd say it was definitely sooner than later. She's probably been sick already." He helped Mathilde into the car and came around to the driver's side. "We'll leave the top as it is, but I'll open a window. The air will do her good."

It would do Mathilde good, too. She suddenly realized that she was alone, seated beside one of

Antaen Pictures' biggest stars, and he was about to drive her—with a drunken thirteen-year-old—to the small, dilapidated frame house with the weedy front yard and the secondhand furniture. Of course she wouldn't have to invite him in—but what if he had to carry Pia? She couldn't be rude. Mathilde began to feel sick—and she hadn't drunk that much.

"Do you ladies live far from here?" Wesley asked as he guided the car out of the lot, past the gate and the guard's quizzical expression, and onto the street.

"It's a long drive," said Mathilde. "But I'm sure there's a train—"

"Not at this hour," he said. "And not with what's in the backseat." He grinned to make Mathilde feel less uneasy.

"Wesley—"

"Wes, please."

"All right. Wes. This is awfully kind of you, but it isn't really necessary. I can take Pia home on the train, even if we have to wait at the station—"

"I wouldn't dream of it. Think of the scandal in the morning papers." When he saw the shocked expression on her face, he laughed. "Mathilde, relax. Nobody's going to know a thing. And if anyone at the studio does, well, frankly, my dear, they won't give a damn!" His Gable imitation finally made the corners of her mouth turn upward and a giggle did escape.

They drove in silence for a while. Mathilde leaned her head back against the back of the seat and let the breeze play against her face. A tendril of hair came free of the French twist and Wes's hand brushed it away. His touch made Mathilde jump.

"Whoa, lady, I'm not going to bite! Take it easy!" But that was physically impossible.

The Buick had entered a palm-arched road. Tall, manicured shrubbery obscured the property within; it was difficult to tell whether the residents shared the

99

area with neighbors or if one person owned it all.

"Where are we?" asked Mathilde.

"Pasadena," answered Wes. "My ex-wife has the house in Beverly Hills. I know some people are very civilized out here, with former spouses living next door, but I guess you can't shake your roots. I was born old-fashioned and I'll die that way."

"Where are you from?" And why couldn't she remember from all the fan magazines she'd read? Then she recalled. Wesley Guest never discussed his personal life in interviews.

"Ever hear of Kenosha, Wisconsin?" For the first time, Mathilde detected a trace of his midwestern accent, normally absent from his on- and off-screen speech. "My dad was with the Coast Guard there. Phyllis and I grew up together, sailed together every summer. I crewed on a boat that won the Chicago–Mackinac race. And we both studied acting at Northwestern." When Mathilde's eyes expressed no recognition, he explained, "They have a good speech department. Evanston, Illinois. Ever hear of that?"

She had, and nodded.

"Well, we came out here together. Stars in our eyes, both of us." He laughed then at a private joke.

"What's so funny?" asked Mathilde, growing more relaxed. Part of it came in learning that Wesley Guest wasn't a Hollywood snob. His beginnings weren't so different from hers. His dad, Coast Guard. Hers, the police department. Small towns, big dreams.

He was still grinning, but she sensed a wryness from the set of his jaw. "You know, most people run into marital problems because they don't have enough money. Phyllis and I were fine while we were broke. When we—when I—started making big bucks, *that* was when our troubles began. Ironic, isn't it?"

"Was it the money, or . . . or your career success?"

100

"Both. She never understood that the movie business is a crap shoot. If you take it seriously, it can ruin you. It ruined us."

He hadn't said it to evoke sympathy; nonetheless, Mathilde felt a sudden sadness. And Wes noticed it. Her uneasiness returned; it seemed that he noticed everything about her, and just now he could probably read her thoughts, which were about him. What was she supposed to do whenever they reached his house—which was obviously where they were headed? She was less concerned with what *he* might do than with what she wanted him—or didn't want him—to do. And she sensed that he knew it. How could he not know it?

Wes turned onto a gravel driveway that led through more arched palms and ended at the side of a white stucco two-story house. The style was Spanish, and while far grander than anything Mathilde had ever seen before, it did not qualify as a mansion. Still, Pia would be impressed—once she could be revived

Wes lifted Pia from the backseat and whispered to Mathilde, "Reach into my right hip pocket."

She panicked at the thought of such intimacy.

"My housekeys," he said.

She obeyed, wondering why they couldn't simply ring the bell and be admitted by a butler.

She unlocked the massive wooden door and swung it open. The foyer light revealed a splendid center staircase leading to the upper floor. The wide expanse was tiled with dark stone, and the rich wood of the beamed cathedral ceiling created an atmosphere of simultaneous warmth and coolness.

"Welcome to my parlor," Wes said, after depositing Pia on one of the two spacious sofas. "Maid's night off. I wasn't expecting company."

101

Again, Mathilde stiffened.

"Make yourself comfortable. I'll tuck Pia in for the duration. Then I'll fix us a nightcap."

He had said it nonchalantly. He expected them to sleep at his house! No question, no offer, he was taking it for granted that they'd be staying the night. And what about Jeanne? It was past one. If she telephoned at this hour, she'd frighten the poor girl to death! Well, she reasoned, during the movie's shooting, on the days they'd gone overtime and returned home really late, Jeanne hadn't waited up but had gone to bed and left a note to that effect. Tonight was probably no different.

Then why was she feeling that everything *was* different?

"Sleeping Beauty is taken care of," Wes said, reentering the living room. He noticed that Mathilde wasn't looking directly at him. "Is it something I said?"

"N-no . . ."

"Then it's something I did . . ."

She shook her head, but couldn't speak.

Wes crossed to the bar and poured two scotches. "This is your poison, too, isn't it?"

"What makes you say that?" She hadn't intended it to sound combative.

"I was watching you earlier this evening, and I noticed you had a scotch before you switched to the champagne."

"I'm not . . . accustomed to champagne," she retorted.

He placed his glass on the leather-trimmed bar and came to stand beside her. "Mathilde, what is it? Are you afraid of me?"

She closed her eyes. How could she answer that she was afraid of *herself*? That part of her wanted to move

102

away from him, and part of her didn't dare? That if she did, she might awaken and find this all to have been a dream. Dreams could be dangerous. She knew that from the past.

"Mathilde," Wes said gently, "I never thought to ask. I guess because you're always at the studio *alone* with Pia. I mean . . . is there a Mr. Decameron at home? Or . . . someone else?"

"Not anymore," she said with only a trace of bitterness. "He . . . died. A long time ago. Pia was only three."

"I'm sorry. I didn't know."

"It's not that . . . we had grown apart . . . it's just . . ." She felt the familiar tightness across her chest and sighed deeply. A tear formed in the corner of her eye and she was unable to blink it away. It trickled down her cheek and another formed. But the tears were not for Hank, no matter what interpretation Wesley Guest might give them.

Wes was standing beside her. With his index finger, he wiped the tear dry, then traced the side of her face until he reached her chin.

"Mathilde," he said softly, "I want you to believe me when I tell you that I'm not in the habit of enticing beautiful women to my house in order to seduce them. That isn't my style. I know the magazines are filled with photographs of me with glamorous starlets on my arm at this premiere or that party, but it's studio publicity, please believe me. I wouldn't do anything to hurt you, I promise."

Her heart ached at his words. She wanted desperately to believe him. She wanted Wesley Guest to take her in his arms and protect her, hold her, give her the tenderness and love so long denied. She was aware that he was removing the hairpins from her French twist. She didn't try to stop him. His strong yet gentle fingers caressed her hair as the waves cascaded to her shoulders. His hands moved to her forearms and squeezed them. Then he turned her around to face him, and when she looked into his eyes, she believed him. She didn't know whether he was worthy of her trust— she had no way of knowing—but it was his, nonetheless, for the asking. When he bent his head to press his lips to hers, Mathilde closed her eyes once more and prayed that this was truly happening, that in a moment he would sweep her off her feet and carry her up the grand staircase the way Rhett had carried Scarlett.

And when their lips parted, he did.

What in God's name am I doing? she asked herself. I must be losing my mind! With Jeanne at home alone— and Pia passed out cold somewhere in this house—Wes must be wondering what kind of mother I am. He'll think I'm no better than a . . .

Her brain refused to supply the word. Wesley had begun to unbutton her dress.

"Wes—" She lifted her head.

"Shh," he whispered, smoothing her unpinned hair against the satin pillow. Then he kissed her forehead.

"I can't stay. I've got to wake Pia and—"

"She'll be fine. You can't mother her all night."

"But I—" She tried to pull herself up, but his strong grip restrained her.

"Mathilde . . ." His fingers were brushing gently across her shoulders as he eased the fabric of her dress down to meet the lace border at the top of her slip.

"Wes, really, I—"

His eyes, glistening in the glow of the bedside table lamp, silenced her. His hands continued with their task, now sliding the straps of her rayon slip off her shoulders and down her arms.

Mathilde shivered, even though the room was warm. It grew warmer as Wesley's hand went beneath the small of her back and unfastened her bra. It fell away, and with it went any last vestige of restraint. Desire and hunger, a decade of longing, welled inside her, and as Wesley bent to kiss her breasts, Mathilde's arms went around him and pulled him to her with surprising force.

"You're lovely," he said, caressing her and exploring the contours of her body at the same time. She offered no resistance as he separated her stockings from their garters. She wasn't sure whether he removed her garter belt with or without her help. She knew only that her head was beginning to spin with a dizziness she hadn't known in years—since those long-ago summers on the beach with Hank.

Mathilde tried to banish Hank from her thoughts as Wesley's lips parted and took her left nipple into his mouth. She tried to erase Hank's image as Wesley's tongue worked back and forth. She tried to cancel all memory of the past as his hand parted her thighs and his fingers began their journey inward. She tried to pretend that this was the first time, that she was eighteen once more and everything from now on would be wonderful—as she had dreamed and wished it to be.

There was brief hesitation as Wesley rose to remove his shirt and tie. As the rest of his clothes fell to the floor, Mathilde felt a sudden surge of panic.

But then she saw him standing naked beside the bed, and her heart leapt. All she wanted was this moment, this night with Wesley Guest. She would ask no more than that. She would not demand the impossible.

When he turned out the light, she closed her eyes. And when he climbed onto the bed and entered her, only Mathilde's gasp of joy betrayed her. Wesley couldn't see her tears.

Chapter Seven

Mathilde slowly opened her eyes and took in the strangeness of the room. Sunlight filtered through the drawn rust-colored silk draperies and cut a white-gold arrow across the rust-and-brown floor tiles. The arrow extended beyond Mathilde's line of vision, and she craned her neck first to her left, where another sliver of light outlined the bottom of the bedroom door.

Gradually she became aware of the sounds of Wesley's steady, rhythmic breathing beside her. She turned her head, expecting him to be asleep, but his eyes were open, and he was smiling at her.

"You're watching me!" she exclaimed, suddenly embarrassed and pulling the top sheet high around her shoulders.

"Watching, no. Observing . . . I confess it. You're beautiful when you're awake, Mathilde, but when you're unaware that anyone is watching—observing, that is— you let down your guard." His hand brushed the side of her cheek as he added, "You let go of your inhibitions —the way you did last night."

She was certain he could see her blush, even in the semi-darkness.

"Wes . . . about last night—" She stopped. What

106

was there to say? Shouldn't she just get up, dress, collect Pia, and—

"My God!" she said at the realization that one of her daughters was asleep in this house, had been asleep while her mother and Wesley Guest were—

"What about last night?" he asked.

"I . . . I didn't mean . . . hadn't planned . . . I—"

He leaned over to stroke her hair. "Mathilde, don't start rebuilding those 'mama' barriers again."

"Those . . . wh-what?"

"Mama barriers. You're the mother of two girls—and a sensual woman, too. You mustn't allow one to suffocate the other. If you do, the neglected woman will die."

She didn't understand why his remark almost made her cry, but when he kissed her, a great sigh of longing escaped, and he whispered, "You can be both . . . you *are* both. But not at the same time."

And when he drew back the sheet and began caressing her once more, she made no attempt to resist.

Pia rolled over onto her side as light started to fill the room. She squeezed her eyelids shut as she became aware of the hammering pain in her head.

Then, carefully, she peeked once more in the direction of the window opposite the bed. Her focus was still too fuzzy to make out more than blurred silhouettes. She tried to swallow away the terrible taste in her mouth. It didn't work. She was very thirsty. Perhaps a glass of water would help. A glass of water with half a dozen aspirins in it!

The throbbing grew louder inside her head. Pia moaned—a long, low cry of agony. Maybe it was best to lie still, very still, since the slightest movement seemed to aggravate the pain.

A few minutes passed, and then she tried again. This time she was able to open her eyelids almost all the way without the urge to scream. She purposely averted her gaze away from the window and took stock of herself.

She lay in a supine position, her head propped in the middle of two fluffy white pillows whose feathers refused to support what felt like a lead weight. She recognized the weight to be her head. The "thing" digging into her sternum was nothing more than her own chin. Pia glanced downward to her hands. They were splayed wide, palms up, and beneath the multicolored woolen afghan blanket her legs were spread-eagled.

She wondered if she could—or dared—get up. Experimenting with one foot, she saw gratefully that the blanket began to move. Now she brought her eyes upward and began to examine her surroundings.

Directly to the right side of the bed was a small fireplace framed by huge stones. Above the mantel, a handmade Navajo blanket hung on the white stucco wall. On the opposite wall were two dark wooden doors. Several woolen throw rugs lay scattered across the terra-cotta tile floor. A voluminous chest of drawers stood to the left of the two doors, and an enormous rectangular mirror reflected the opposite wall, creating the effect of two fireplaces and two blankets identical to those on the right side of the room. The double image increased Pia's dizziness, and she quickly turned away.

Too quickly. The pain behind her eyes was so severe that she emitted a moan that could have carried all the way to the hills, to the very top of the "Hollywood" sign she so adored.

I must be dying, she thought. But the feeling was not accompanied by panic. It was too romantic a prospect to be frightening.

However, even in her agony, she had noticed a filled pitcher of water and a glass on the bedside table, and Pia's thirst took precedence over her drama. Cautiously, she pulled herself up on one elbow while trying to move with the slowest motion possible. She reached for the handle. So far, so good.

It weighed a ton. Water sloshed over the top and Pia spilled as much as she managed to pour into the glass. She downed four gulps and fell back exhausted onto the bed. The pounding pain resumed as her head hit the pillows.

She lay still for several minutes, then opened her eyes once more. For the first time came the sobering awareness that she was alone. Jeanne wasn't in the bed opposite hers. Of course not, she reasoned. This isn't our room.

Then where am I?

The panic that was absent at thoughts of death suddenly emerged full-force as she noticed the chair alongside the night table.

It was just an ordinary chair. A nice, cozy chair. Brown, overstuffed. But laid out neatly over the back was a familiar-looking dress. Folded on the cushion were a white rayon slip and garter belt—and next to them were . . . a bra and panties! Nylon stockings— with runs, she could see them now—were draped like limp wings over the arms of the chair. Leaning her head gently to one side, Pia saw a pair of shoes on the tile floor.

Those look exactly like my shoes, she thought. And my clothes. How strange. She blinked and focused more clearly.

Suddenly fear rose to meet her panic. She lifted the covers and saw that she was stark naked beneath the blanket and sheet. And then it hit her.

Those *are* my clothes! I've been kidnapped! Someone who knows I'm in movies must think I'm famous already! And Mama won't be able to pay the ransom! Maybe the studio, but—

She was stopped by the most horrifying thought of all. What had they done to her while she was asleep? She'd read stories in *Confidential*. She knew what kidnappers often did *before* they murdered their prey—

Pia screamed. Despite the hammering pain in her head and the deafening reverberation in her ears, she yelled as loudly and as long as her lungs would allow. Tears ran down her face as she threw off the covers and tore them from the bed. The empty water glass rolled to the edge of the mattress and fell, smashing as it hit the floor. Pia wrapped the afghan around herself and hobbled to the window.

There was no railing or terrace offering escape to the ground two floors below. A swimming pool shimmered in the morning light, and lush green shrubbery bordered the grounds as far as the eye could see.

But the luxurious setting of her prison mattered little to Pia. She rushed toward the chair and her clothes just as the bedroom door was flung open. The surprise caught her up short, and Pia tripped on the hem of the afghan. She reached out to break her fall, and in so doing, the blanket dropped. She opened her mouth to scream again, then stopped as she saw Wesley Guest standing on the threshold.

His expression of alarm changed as he saw that she was in no danger. "Pia! Are you all right?"

She broke into hysterical sobs as his comforting arms went around her. She shivered as he wrapped the afghan around her, then led her to the edge of the bed, while carefully side-stepping the shards of broken glass on the floor.

She was still shaking as he gently patted her matted hair.

"Okay, there. Everything will be all right now," he said.

"I thought—I mean, I didn't know what—I—" she stammered between sobs.

"I frightened you, didn't I?" he said. "I didn't mean to. But we heard screams, and—"

She nodded, sniffing and crying at the same time. Wesley leaned over to the night table and pulled several sheets of Kleenex from the tissue container. Handing them to Pia, who blew her nose vociferously, he said, "I'm sorry. About scaring you."

"My head hurts," she whimpered. "And I'm so thirsty."

Her head was leaning against his chest, and the terry-cloth fabric felt good against her cheek. Exciting, too, and somehow . . . intimate.

"I'm afraid you're having your first genuine hang-over, my dear. And it's a dandy!"

Through her tears, Pia managed to laugh, and Wesley joined in. She was feeling better, but she didn't remove her head from his chest. She could feel his heartbeat in her ear, and he smelled of soap and musky cologne and pipe tobacco, too. She loved it, and his voice was so kind and soothing.

Finally, she sat up and looked into his face.

"You are the prettiest child," he said. "Even with a hangover."

She smiled. Wes had called her the prettiest. He'd also called her a child, but somehow that word hadn't registered.

"How much do you remember about last night?" he asked.

She shook her head—slowly. "Not much at all . . . except . . . did something happen with a palm tree?"

"Sort of," he replied with a grin. "I'll fill in details later. Meanwhile, there's a robe and slippers in the closet. And a bathroom down the hall with anything you might need."

Pia squeezed his arms with all her strength. She didn't want to let go. She wanted him to stay here and soothe her headache away with his wonderful voice and smell and touch.

"You'll crush me to death!" he teased, breaking away.

She turned bright pink and released him. Wesley went to the night table and opened its single drawer. Withdrawing a bottle, he said, "Aspirin. Take two. And a shower will help. Then come downstairs and we'll have breakfast."

He was at the door when Pia called after him, "Wes! I almost forgot!"

"What's that?"

"Where's Mama?"

"She's here, too," he said. "Don't be worried."

After he'd closed the door, Pia lay back on the bed for a few minutes. Except for the lingering headache, she was feeling much better. She was safe, and Mama was nearby. But even if Mama were somewhere else, it would still be all right. Because Wes was here.

The aspirins helped. So did the shower. Pia immersed her head under the steady stream of cool-to-cold needles, and although she was shivering, her headache began to lift. She emerged from the glassed-in stall, toweled herself dry, and glanced at the wall-to-wall mirror in the guest bathroom.

She smiled at the play on words. This is also the Guest bathroom, she mused. Wes probably showers here, too. She leaned her face against the robe hanging from a hook on the inside door, but there was no trace of Wes's cologne or after shave.

Her eyes returned to the mirror, this time to assess

the morning-after damage. Slight circles beneath her eyes. They made her appear older. At least sixteen. But her hair! Pia blinked, wondering what to do with the mass of dripping ringlets whose carefully worked curls had lost their spring. Braids were one way out, but braids were for children.

And then she saw the little tray of bobby pins and knew. She'd put her hair up in a French twist, just the way Mama had worn hers last night. That would take care of the mess *and* make her look sophisticated at the same time.

By the time Pia came downstairs, only her squint at the daylight's glare gave away her agony of less than an hour before. All she needed now was coffee.

But Mama and Wes were drinking tea. "Sorry," said Wes as Pia entered the kitchen and plopped onto a chair. "My maid is somewhat absentminded. It's tea or milk with your eggs."

"It's all right, Wes," said Mathilde. "She's too young for coffee. Caffeine will stunt her growth."

Oh, Mama, thought Pia. I could strangle you! Aloud she said, "Tea is fine, thank you. There's caffeine in that, too." She patted the back of her head; the pins were holding her hair too tightly, but somehow she'd endure.

She devoured Wes's scrambled eggs and gulped down the tea. She noticed that Mama's hair this morning was loose, framing her face in soft waves. Mama looked quite pretty, in fact. They could almost pass for sisters—far more easily than she and Jeanne could. Except for one thing, amended Pia with her objective eye. I'm even prettier than Mama.

* * *

113

She was in paradise. Mama had insisted that Pia sit up front to avoid motion sickness during the drive home. Pia settled in beside Wesley and rolled down her window. Missing, of course, was the obligatory chiffon scarf that Grace Kelly or Kim Novak would have been wearing.

"We can stop for coffee on the way," offered Wes.

Pia's eyes lit up at the prospect of walking into a restaurant—even a roadside diner—on Wesley Guest's arm, but Mathilde vetoed the suggestion. "I have coffee at the house."

"You're sure?" said Wesley.

"My pleasure," answered Mathilde.

Pia couldn't figure out why Mama was suddenly blushing.

Jeanne felt the warmth of the morning sun on her face. From its heat and brightness, she knew she'd slept late. Still, she didn't open her eyes. Instead she lay in bed listening to the silence of the house.

Silence. She had awakened to it almost every morning since Pia had started shooting the movie. Mama and Pia were usually gone by the time she rose, except on weekends, when Jeanne tiptoed about the house to avoid waking them.

But yesterday the movie had finished filming—"wrapped," as she'd heard Pia announce with much self-importance. She and Mama must have returned home very late. They were probably still asleep.

Jeanne turned her head and opened her eyes. Pia's bed was made and empty. It wasn't like Pia to rise before her sister, much less to make her bed. Mama was always reprimanding her for that. No. Pia's bed hadn't been slept in. Hadn't she come home last night?

Jeanne sat up and as she did, something fell to the

114

floor with a thud. She slid her feet down onto the thinly piled rug and squinted against the light's glare as she bent to retrieve the borrowed library book. She picked up *Joan of Lorraine*, the play by Maxwell Anderson, which Mrs. Armitage had recommended.

Her heart beat a little faster as she recalled the beauty of the words, the purity and courage of the heroine. She had even dreamed during the night of the French saint; she'd imagined *being* Joan.

Jeanne slipped into her robe and, tucking the book under her arm, went into the hall. The door to Mama's room was open. She peeked inside and saw that Mama hadn't slept in her bed, either.

I'm alone, she realized, smiling. For an instant, she considered checking the closets to see if Mama's and Pia's clothes were gone. It surprised her that such a prospect was less than frightening. She'd miss Mama, of course, but Pia . . .

No, she almost said aloud, guiltily banishing the thought. Don't start behaving like Pia! Besides, they'd never have come home, packed, and left without waking me. After all, where could they go?

Jeanne waited for the coffee to perk and picked up her previous night's note to Mama and Pia, which lay unread on the Formica table. *Gone to bed. Hope the movie wrapped well.* She folded it and stuck it between two pages of her book.

The clock read almost eleven. Curiosity was giving way to worry. What if there'd been an accident? What if Mama or Pia had been hurt? Suddenly she wanted Mathilde nearby so she might tell her how much she loved her. She'd even be relieved to see Pia.

And then she did.

Pia was standing in the kitchen and smiling at her.

115

Her face had been scrubbed clean of the makeup she'd been allowed to wear last night, but her party dress was soiled across the bodice, and her skirt was a mass of wrinkles. There was a visible tear in her ruffled crinoline underslip.

"Oh, Pia!" Jeanne exclaimed, running to her sister. She stopped short of an embrace, but her eyes had filled with tears.

"Did you think I was dead?" Pia asked with a laugh.

"I didn't know what—" Jeanne's sentence went unfinished as Mama entered the room.

"Coffee! Thank God! Hello, darling," Mathilde said in a rush, hugging her younger daughter and then heading for the coffeepot.

Jeanne turned back to her sister. Behind Pia, his hands resting on her shoulders, stood a tall, tanned, breathtakingly handsome man.

He smiled, nodded, and glanced from Jeanne to the title of her library book on the table.

"*Joan of Lorraine*," he observed. "And is she you?"

Jeanne felt a flush of color rising in her face. She managed a tentative smile, though, and answered, "No, I'm just Jeanne."

"Well, it's the same name in French." He extended a hand. "Hello, Jeanne. I'm Wes."

"Yes . . . I . . . I know. I mean . . . I've seen . . . uh, I've heard about . . ."

"Oh, Jeanne!" Pia exclaimed. "What a wrap party! What a night! Lana Turner was there! And Joan Fontaine, and Debbie and Eddie, and . . ."

As Pia gushed on, Jeanne set out coffee cups and sugar. But her attention remained fixed on her mother. Wesley Guest had crossed the small kitchen to stand beside Mathilde. The tender squeeze he gave her arm was more than one of friendly affection, although Jeanne wasn't sure just what to call it. She saw her

116

mother shiver and gaze up into Wesley's eyes. Mama looked . . . radiant. It was only a split-second's glance before Mathilde turned back to the table, and as she did so, her eyes met Jeanne's. In that moment, Jeanne became aware for the first time of an unspoken understanding between them. Not an understanding between mother and daughter, but between two women. It thrilled yet alarmed Jeanne; she knew, without knowing, what had transpired.

The moment quickly passed, and Mathilde busied herself with pouring the coffee.

Pia hadn't stopped. ". . . and Robert Wagner was there, and Doris Day and Rock Hudson, and—"

"Pia!" scolded Mathilde. "That's enough name-dropping!" Then she remembered Wesley's admonition about mothering. "I'm afraid we're out of cream," she said nervously, "but there's milk—"

"No, no," he protested. "I can't stay. Really. But I wanted to apologize personally to . . . Jeanne . . . for keeping you both out until morning." To Jeanne he said, "There were . . . unavoidable circumstances."

Jeanne saw his eyes drift once more to her mother as Pia interrupted possessively, *"I'll* explain everything to her." There was giddy excitement in her voice.

Mathilde slipped her arm through Wesley's and said, "I'll see you to the door."

"Wes!" Pia called out. "I just want you to know what a great pleasure it was—working with you, I mean. Let's do it again soon."

Jeanne cringed with embarrassment over her sister's remark but was impressed by Wesley Guest's response, which was a simple bow. "With any luck," he said, "we'll be seeing a lot more of each other." He kissed her on the cheek and winked at Jeanne. Then he and Mathilde left the kitchen.

Pia stood motionless for only a second, then started

after them.

"Pia!" said Jeanne.

Pia stopped. "What is it?"

"There's . . . a smudge on your face," Jeanne lied. "Come here and I'll wipe it off for you."

Pia rushed to her. "My God! Was the smudge there all the time Wes was here?" she whispered.

Jeanne heard the front door open and then close. "Yes," she answered. "The whole time."

After forty-five minutes on the phone with Marybeth, Pia decided to go to bed.

Mathilde was grateful for the quiet. But from the kitchen she could hear Jeanne's voice in what sounded like a soft, one-sided conversation. Since the only telephone was in the hall and no one else was in the house, Mathilde grew increasingly curious. She tiptoed across the living room and down the hall, then peeked through the partially opened kitchen door.

She couldn't see Jeanne but was able to make out her daughter's hands. They were holding a book, and Jeanne was speaking in alternate attempts at an English, then French, accent. Neither was completely free of Southern California, and there was Jeanne's slightly adenoidal, thin tone to deal with.

If that's what she wants to be, Mathilde mused, she'll have to do something about her voice. The sudden thought stopped her. *Can* this be what she wants?

Back in the living room, Mathilde dismissed the idea. Jeanne loved the poetry, but she had shown no evidence—in fact, only reluctance—of a desire to perform. Nor had she displayed any of the "star" qualities that Pia seemed endowed with by nature. She must be reading the words aloud to further comprehend their meaning. One of my daughters a poet? She smiled to herself. But perhaps it was this poetic, romantic side that had kept Jeanne from prying about last night.

Mathilde appreciated—and had been touched by—her younger daughter's sensitivity, earlier. It seemed as though Jeanne had somehow understood her mother's desire for privacy. More important, she hadn't judged Mathilde. Jeanne's silence on the subject was entirely different from Pia's, which stemmed from total self-involvement and lack of awareness. So the interrogation Mathilde had feared from her daughters had been averted, albeit for diverse reasons.

Whatever, she was grateful, because if pressed for answers from either of them, what, she wondered, would she say?

For the fifth time Jeanne finished reading Joan's courtroom speech aloud. Well, she thought with a frown, I'm no Ingrid Bergman, that's for sure.

The doorbell rang. She hoped it hadn't wakened Pia. She listened. It was all right; Mama had answered before a second ring was necessary.

Jeanne left the book on the table and went into the living room. Only Mama was there.

Mathilde stood near the window holding in her arms a florist's box of long-stemmed red roses. There was a dreamy expression on her face. Jeanne, struck by how young her mother looked, felt suddenly like an intruder upon the scene.

But when Mathilde saw her, she smiled happily. "The roses . . . they're from . . . him," she said with amazement in her voice.

By the time Pia arose two hours later, Mathilde had

arranged the flowers in a tall glass vase. Pia came into the living room still rubbing her eyes awake.

She went immediately to the roses and picked up the card that was leaning against the bottom of the vase. It read: *The movie may be over, but the story has only just begun. Love, Wes.*

Mathilde was in the kitchen preparing lunch. Jeanne, observing from the hallway, saw her sister's eyes fill with tears as she read Wesley's message.

"Pia?" she said quietly, entering the living room. There was no reply. "Are you all right?"

Pia looked up and nodded. She placed the card back against the vase and sank into a chair. She leaned her head back and sighed deeply.

"Pia, what is it?"

"Can't you guess? It's Wes."

"What do you mean?"

"Oh, Jeanne," she said. "You're so . . . naïve. Didn't you read the card?"

"Well, yes . . . but . . ."

"Isn't it obvious what's happened? Isn't it . . . wonderful?"

Jeanne came over and sat on the arm of Pia's chair. Gently she stroked her sister's chestnut curls. A sensation of relief washed over her. Pia had understood after all. And was happy for Mama, too.

"Yes," Jeanne agreed. "It's wonderful."

Then, after a moment's silence, Pia murmured something. It was almost inaudible, but it sent a shiver down Jeanne's spine.

No, she thought. I *can't* have heard her correctly.

"What . . . did you say?" she asked softly.

"I said I love him. So very much," Pia repeated. "And he loves me."

Chapter Eight

Jeanne was flattered by the call. Perhaps it was why she agreed to read for the role. She wondered whether part of it was due to Mrs. Armitage's wanting to help her overcome shyness, but she also felt that the teacher's interest went beyond that of teacher-and-pupil and assumed more an aspect of mentor-and-protégée. Already at the hideous performance of *The Guardsman*—and before that at the library—Jeanne had sensed a kind of caring. That it was a caring without conditions made her all the more eager to please her teacher-mentor. And so she borrowed the Barrie play along with the others she'd been planning to read.

Peter Pan! Oh, not the title role—Jeanne recognized that she was far too awkward—not to mention frightened—to go flying through the air suspended by only a wire; she'd die first! It was true that Wendy Darling would also be required to fly, but it wasn't for long, and if Wendy appeared scared out of her wits—provided that Jeanne got the part—it might even add appeal to her interpretation.

Besides, she reasoned, it would give her something to do till summer was over. Mama was spending most evenings with Wesley Guest, and Pia was just lying around the house leafing through her movie fan magazines. A theatrical production, albeit nonprofessional community theater, would fill some of the time before school resumed.

Most of all, and this Jeanne confided to no one—not even to Mrs. Armitage—she was willing to audition because Wendy was only a *supporting* role. The show's success or failure would not rest on her shoulders but on whoever played the boy who wouldn't grow up.

She glanced at Pia, who was sitting cross-legged on the living-room floor surrounded by copies of *Modern Screen* and *Photoplay*. Her freshly washed hair was plastered to her scalp by minuscule pin curls and created a boyish cap. Jeanne was struck by the androgenous look of her sister's features. A beautiful face, yet because of its youth, she could easily be a strikingly beautiful boy.

Peter Pan! The realization stabbed Jeanne's chest and made her dizzy. She stared down at the spot where her sister sat unaware of scrutiny. Yes, she nodded to herself: Mrs. Armitage said the role is usually played by a girl. And Pia's perfect for the part.

Consciously she struck the thought from her mind and returned to the kitchen to study the role of Wendy.

Jeanne saw little cause for celebration, although Mrs. Armitage insisted they stop at the drugstore for ice-cream sodas. "You've landed the part," said her teacher as they settled into an initial-carved wooden booth at Hale's. "And you look as though you've just lost your best friend."

"I know," said Jeanne. "But I was the only one my age trying out for the role. They were desperate."

122

It was true. All the other girls had been too old to play Wendy and had been interested only in the role of Peter.

"Besides, I'll bet no one else *wanted* my part," she added as Bessie Hale handed them menus.

Mrs. Armitage sighed and ordered two of Hale's "super specials"—vanilla ice cream covered with hot butterscotch topping, whipped cream, toasted nuts, and chocolate sprinkles. Instead of the standard maraschino cherry, Hale's Pharmacy offered a bittersweet chocolate mint cookie at the center of the foot-high spectacle.

"Jeanne," cautioned the teacher when Bessie was no longer within earshot, "there's something you must do. Not for me, but for yourself."

"What's that?" she asked.

"You must stop being so self-effacing, dear. Whether you plan to go into the theater or to"—she glanced about—"to work in a drugstore. You must learn to appreciate your good qualities if you expect others to."

Jeanne understood immediately. She had practiced self-deprecation for so long that it had become a habit. Well, she decided as Bessie appeared with their sodas, habits can be changed. And there's no time like now.

Instead of daintily withdrawing the cookie from the mountain of whipped cream, she tore into the sundae with gusto, as though her table manners were an outward display of her silent vow.

The director of *Peter Pan* was a likable young man named Charles Goodman. A theater major on summer vacation from a university Jeanne had never heard of, he had decided that Wendy Darling must be blond. So, after countless previous, unheeded requests by

Mathilde, Jeanne submitted to a lemon rinse. However, it didn't produce the desired effect, so the allowance money that had been saved all summer toward books she wanted to own went instead for a professional "highlighting" at the local beauty parlor. Gladys, the hairdresser, convinced Jeanne that a body wave wouldn't hurt, either.

Jeanne emerged from the afternoon of torture—the shop wasn't air-conditioned—and glanced at her reflection in the drugstore window. She'd already seen herself in Gladys's hand mirror as well as in the round wall mirror in front of the hairdresser's chair. But inside the beauty shop she hadn't wanted to stare.

Now she did stare. A tall, slim—and yes, *pretty*—girl with a blond pageboy hairdo stared back at her. Can that really be me? she asked herself.

The image in the window nodded, and a gentle breeze blew against her waves. But the pageboy didn't lose its undercurl. Goodness! thought Jeanne, beginning to smile. I wonder . . .

She checked the coin section of her wallet. Even after a generous tip to Gladys, she still had a dollar and change left. That should be enough. A lipstick and a powder compact. Maybe a small container of rouge. After all, as Wendy she'd have to wear makeup, wouldn't she? May as well start getting used to it.

Mr. Emerson, the manager of the local Woolworth's on Pine Street, looked up in amazement as Jeanne entered the dimestore. "Why, if it isn't Jeanne Decameron, looking pretty as a picture!"

Her color rose at the unexpected comment. It reappeared on the way home as several neighbors stopped to compliment her on her "movie-star hairdo," then again when boys she didn't know gave out low wolf whistles. There was even a "Hey, doll!" with an inflection that she didn't particularly like.

By the time she reached the house, Jeanne was just as glad she hadn't bought the rouge. It would have been a waste of money; her cheeks were pink enough.

Charles Goodman was an efficient director who knew what he wanted to accomplish—and how to achieve those goals within the limits of rehearsal time and his amateur cast. He arrived the first morning and announced that although *Peter Pan* was essentially a star vehicle, everyone involved was important to the success of the production.

"Remember," he advised at the first read-through, "there are no small parts—only small actors." That seemed to infuse the entire cast with confidence, although Jeanne wasn't quite able to banish the butterflies fluttering in her stomach.

They increased as the days went by and Charles blocked each scene of the play; Jeanne hadn't realized just how long Wendy would have to be onstage with little or nothing to do.

"Just concentrate on listening to what the other actors are saying to you," Charles advised, echoing the words Jeanne had first heard from her teacher, Mrs. Armitage. "Being a good listener is the first step toward a truthful performance." Then, seeing Jeanne's pained expression, he added, "It's also the quickest way to overcome stage fright. Believe me, dear, I speak from experience. If someone had told me that before *my* first time, it might have saved me from falling into the orchestra pit."

"The orchestra pit? Did you really?"

Charles swore it was true; Jeanne, while impressed, couldn't help wondering if he'd made it up to calm her. Charles Goodman seemed so poised, so totally at ease, whether staging a complicated scene or discussing sets,

125

costumes, and the million other details connected with the show.

"I promise," he'd said in his welcoming speech the first morning, which now seemed light-years before, "that by the time we open, you won't believe your eyes. And we'll manage the whole thing in all of two weeks, just the way it's done in professional stock productions across the country."

His prediction had already proved true halfway into the second week. The huge, unpainted canvas flats that Jeanne had seen out back in the parking lot had been transformed into the inside walls of the Darling family's house. Up close they were paint-spattered and seemingly thrown together in haste; yet from the first row of the audience Jeanne could have sworn she was looking at the most elegant of old-fashioned flowered Victorian wallpaper.

The same held true for the greenery of Never-Never Land. Enormous rolls of chicken wire and giant barrels of glue had conspired and been magically combined with bits of colored paper and scraps of fabric to create the lushest setting for the Little Lost Boys—no wonder Peter didn't want to leave, thought Jeanne. I'd want to stay here, too.

In fact, she was beginning to enjoy being part of the "illusion," as Charles had called it; she'd memorized her lines by the third day, and now she had plenty of time to follow her director's advice. She listened constantly. And watched. Little escaped her eye. And all the while, she was learning.

She learned that Leonard MacEvoy, the actor portraying Captain Hook, as well as being the oldest member of the cast was also a member of SAG and another union named AFTRA. He had moved to California from New York and had appeared in the East on *Playhouse 90* and *Suspense*, two of Jeanne's favorite television shows. Leonard smoked a lot and coughed throughout rehearsals. His wheezing threatened to spoil his performance, but at every break he reached for his pack of Chesterfields.

The rest of his offstage time was spent admiring his own reflection in the floor-length mirror beside the stage manager's desk. Jeanne discovered that despite Charles's excellent direction, Leonard had already decided on *his* interpretation—and *he* never listened to anyone.

But Jeanne learned even from Leonard. He was a lesson in what *not* to do onstage. He constantly went up on his lines and, without apology, simply turned toward the wings and called, "Line!" It always arrived, spoken by the stage manager, but Leonard seemed not to care whether he'd ever be off book in time for opening night.

What annoyed Jeanne most, however, was "Captain Hook's" habit of addressing his most important lines to the now-empty auditorium of the converted vaudeville theater; Jeanne wondered if he would continue the practice once the five hundred seats were filled with people.

Five hundred seats filled with people! Jeanne broke out in goosebumps at the thought. I'll *never* get through this alive—and *I* was afraid of falling from those wires! I'll open my mouth to speak and I'll be worse than Leonard—I'll forget *all* of my lines! *Why* did I ever try out for this play in the first place? *Pia*'s the one who wants to be a star! She wouldn't die up here— she'd be wonderful! She'd stand up and face it, and—

"Wendy, please?" came Charles's voice. "Your entrance cue . . ."

"Oh! I'm sorry!" Jeanne exclaimed, immediately taking her spot upstage near the curtained "window" of the Darlings' nursery.

127

As she spoke her now-familiar lines and the scene continued, Jeanne responded to a newly learned lesson: in order to listen, she'd have to keep her mind focused on what was occurring onstage. To listen was not enough. Acting meant listening and *hearing,* watching and *seeing.* Not as herself, but as the character she was portraying.

I must *become* Wendy Darling! she told herself. And I must believe with all my heart that these two boys are my brothers, Michael and John. At that moment Laurie Martins, the actress playing Peter Pan, "flew" in the window in search of "his" shadow. With unaccustomed grace, Jeanne rose from her bed and greeted the "boy."

She spoke with a natural yet unaffected British accent that until now, despite all her practice, had eluded Jeanne completely. Her role was beginning to fit.

She had told neither Pia nor Mama about the forthcoming performances. This she rationalized as self-preservation. After all, Charles had said that an actor must come to feel comfortable in a part. At the theater, this meant leaving little to chance: studying lines until they were second nature; checking props to make sure they were placed in the correct positions; trying door handles to be certain they wouldn't come unscrewed from a flat and wind up in an actor's hand— or worse, on the floor.

Feeling comfortable in a part also involved practicing "flying" until Jeanne could soar after Peter without fear of crashing into the nursery furniture or knocking the "walls" to the ground. If she had once thought that fear might help her interpretation, Jeanne was beginning to discover the difference between *playing* fear

128

and the genuine article.

Well, then, she reasoned, both comfort *and* fear were why she had told a rather large lie at home. The prospect of having Mama or Pia anywhere near the theater was as terrorizing as the image of a fly-cable snapping or a sandbag dropping onto her head. Besides, a white lie wasn't the same as Pia's blatant brand of out-and-out prevarication. Jeanne had said she was working with an amateur theater group. All right, she *had* said she was working *backstage*. But there was truth in that. Studying lines between her scenes *onstage*—not to mention costume fittings, flying-movement rehearsal, and makeup practice—*did* occur *back*stage.

Nonetheless, Jeanne couldn't help feeling a twinge of guilt. Pia wouldn't have, but that didn't matter. It was one of the many differences between them. Jeanne knew when she was being less than honest—especially with herself. And in her heart she knew why she hadn't told Mama or Pia that she was *acting* in the play: there was always the possibility that on opening night—and through no fault of snapped cable wire—Jeanne would fall flat on her face. Despite all she had learned and absorbed and studied and rehearsed during the intensive two weeks of rehearsal, and even under Charles Goodman's expert, professional direction, there was no guarantee that Jeanne Decameron's stage debut would be anything but a flop. She understood, instinctively, that even stronger than her fear of failing or of letting Charles down was her greatest fear of all: having Pia there as witness.

While Jeanne was inventing an excuse to justify the late hours she would have to spend at the theater on the night of the technical run-through, Pia was looking for a way to manipulate—although she wouldn't have called it that—Mama and Wes into taking part in the surprise.

It isn't sneaky, she reasoned as she circled the news item advertising *Peter Pan* in the local paper. No sneakier than Jeanne's not telling us about her part in the play.

Pia smiled. I bet Jeanne didn't expect to see her name in the paper. But why lie? Did she think I wouldn't find out?

Painting scenery . . . *I* know why she didn't tell us—or me, at least. She was afraid *I'd* go to the audition and get the part instead of her!

Pia's nose wrinkled at the memory of the Disney movie. Oh, sure, it was cute, but it was just a fairy tale. As if I'd be willing to play Wendy, anyway; what does Jeanne take me for—a *supporting* player? I'd only accept the *leading* role, and *he's* a boy! Oh, Jeanne, you're such a dumbbell!

But Pia rethought her opinion. Maybe Jeanne *wasn't* so dumb; after all, for two whole weeks, she'd convinced them that she was part of the backstage crew, and they'd believed her—even Wesley Guest believed her!

Resolutely, Pia folded the issue of the paper and put it under the stack of fan magazines beneath her bed. She was forming a plan, and it pleased her. She would invite Mama and Wes to see the production of *Peter Pan*. But she'd never *dream* of ruining their surprise. Or Jeanne's . . .

Pia clapped her hands together in anticipation. This would be just like a mystery—one to which only she held the key. Saturday night would be such fun!

The technical run-through was a long and grueling

ordeal. The lighting crew was forced to improvise with the theater's antiquated equipment. Even Charles was heard to grumble, although his enthusiasm throughout the two-week period had boosted even the most flagging spirits among the company.

Exhausted as they all were, shortly after midnight on Thursday the show seemed to fall into place: the scenery, costumes, and lights suddenly merged to create the magical setting of Barrie's Never-Never Land. Jeanne marveled at the way in which the lights, shining through colored pieces of gelatin—gels, as she'd heard Charles refer to them—gave three-dimensional depth to the bookshelves and furnishings that had been painted onto the canvas flats. Everything appeared real—in many ways more real than the unlit areas offstage.

It was late, and a damp, late summer chill filled the musty air of the fifty-year-old theater. The wings and dressing rooms were drafty. But onstage, Jeanne was aware of a new sensation, one she couldn't name because she'd never experienced it before. It went beyond the warmth emanating from the footlights and the overhead bank glowing down on her with their pink and blue and amber gels.

For the very first time, Jeanne felt that she *belonged*. After two weeks of dreading her stage debut, she could hardly wait for Saturday!

Mathilde and Wes had probably agreed to attend the opening performance of *Peter Pan* if for no other reason than guilt. Pia hadn't had to lay it on heavily; she'd needed only to mention that they hadn't been out *together* since the night of the wrap party. She'd even laughed about the "morning after." That had made Mama blush, but it had done the trick.

The surprise part wasn't difficult, either. When Wesley had asked, "What about Jeanne?" Pia had innocently shrugged her shoulders. "She'll be there anyway. She's working backstage." She was pleased with the way she'd said *backstage*. No added emphasis. A throwaway phrase. That was the expression Montgomery Clift had used in a magazine interview about acting. Or was it James Dean? Whichever, they were both gorgeous.

But not quite as gorgeous as Wesley Guest, and he was escorting Mama and Pia to see her sister make an ass of herself. I wonder, mused Pia, what I should wear. After all, I'll be visiting Jeanne . . . *backstage*.

Charles Goodman was adamant on the subject. *"No one,* I repeat, *no one* other than cast or crew is to be admitted backstage until *after* the performance." He stationed an usher at the door to guarantee observance of his order and posted notices in the lobby.

Just the same, Pia tried. She managed to bypass the ushers leading to the stage entrance. However, the young man standing guard blocked her way. Pia tried flashing her most endearing smile, but he remained firm. "Sorry, miss. Mr. Goodman said *nobody's* allowed."

"And who is Mr. Goodman?" she asked indignantly.

"Our director, miss."

"Well, *I've* never heard of him," said Pia, turning on her heels. Just wait till I'm famous, she thought. You'll step aside, all right, Mr. Goodman or no. With her jaw set tight, she rejoined Wesley and Mathilde in the lobby and together the three were escorted to their seats.

Pia made sure she led the way directly behind the usher, who handed her all three of the printed programs. As she slid into her seat ahead of Mathilde and Wesley,

Pia allowed the folders to fall to the floor and hurriedly kicked them out of sight before anyone could notice the "accident." She'd kept her secret from them this far—only a few minutes more and they'd find out what a superb actress Pia was to not have even hinted at the truth.

But when the curtains opened and the play began, it was Jeanne's acting as much as the surprise of seeing her onstage that astounded Mathilde. It wasn't a matter of histrionics; Wendy wasn't a showy part. But Jeanne looked so poised, and . . . *lovely!* Such grace of movement, and a well-modulated voice—with a perfect British accent! Mathilde had to reach out and touch Wesley's wrist, just to convince herself that she wasn't dreaming.

She was close to bursting with pride. Wesley covered her hand with his own and smiled gently in the darkened theater. Then, as if reading her thoughts, he leaned over and whispered, "She's wonderful, darling. I mean *really.*"

Mathilde nodded and her eyes filled with tears. "Yes . . . she *is* good, isn't she?"

She could feel Pia staring—not at the stage but at her. Mathilde turned slowly toward her older daughter as the sudden flash of painful recognition gripped her.

In a low voice that she was unable to steady, Mathilde said, "You knew about it all along, didn't you, Pia?"

Despite a rising fury at seeing her sister looking prettier than ever before—stage makeup could do wonders!—it was, nonetheless, Pia's moment of triumph. Besides, Wendy wasn't the *important* role. The star was Peter Pan—the *girl* playing him. So Pia nodded, beaming in the dim light. "Yes, Mama. I knew. I've known for *days.*"

She couldn't understand why her mother's eyes

133

narrowed so coldly. Was that *all* Mama had to say?

Mathilde was incapable of saying more. Her hands were trembling and she clasped them tightly to stop. It was the first time she had ever acknowledged the existence—and the depth—of Pia's rivalry with Jeanne. Mathilde had always thought that if envy arose between the girls, it would be the other way around. She felt sickened by the child seated next to her, sickened by an overwhelming desire to slap her older daughter in the face. It required all the strength Mathilde could muster to force her attention away from Pia and return it to the performance onstage.

Mathilde watched, fascinated, as Jeanne flew weightlessly across the Darlings' nursery; at the same time she was aware of Pia's eyes still boring into her and trying to draw her back.

Peter Pan and Wendy and Michael and John, each of them suspended by invisible cable wires, bobbed merrily about the set, dipping low, then soaring upward and almost out of sight. Perhaps that was the cause of Mathilde's dizziness, she reasoned, wondering how long it would be until the act came to an end.

Chapter Nine

Mathilde opened the refrigerator door and had to wait two full seconds before the light went on. It was one more reminder of the run-down condition of everything in the house. Her only respite was being with Wesley Guest. Their evenings together were oases of elegance and, it seemed, mutual caring, in what was otherwise a desert of longing. Each of Wesley's calls brought with it the realization that Mathilde's world was capable of change.

She didn't dare to speculate beyond their evenings together, to wonder when he'd call again. That he always did call was not to be taken for granted; she'd learned the lesson of that danger from Hank. Instead she willed herself to enjoy each moment with Wesley, while casting no hopes toward an uncertain tomorrow.

The blast of cold air felt good as she picked up the iced-tea pitcher. Beside it was the beribboned clear plastic box that had been delivered earlier in the day. Inside it sat a crisp white orchid. Always a white orchid. "To go with whatever you wear," Wes had said.

He didn't know how limited was Mathilde's choice. Tonight she'd wear her last dressy outfit before starting to repeat her wardrobe.

135

She poured a glass of the tea and returned the pitcher to the asthmatically wheezing refrigerator. As its door swung closed, the kitchen's overhead fluorescent light flickered. But the sculpted perfection of the orchid had lifted Mathilde's spirits above mundane matters, and she headed down the hall with a spring in her step.

First she made a detour to the living room to retrieve the latest issue of *Look* from the magazine rack. On the coffee table were the roses Wes had sent three days before. Their petals were beginning to fall. She wondered if another dozen would arrive to take their place as these had when last week's roses had wilted.

Be practical! she warned herself. Stay in the present—in the here and now.

Mathilde overheard Pia's voice coming from the hall. From the gist of the one-sided conversation, she could tell that Marybeth was at the other end of the line. Talking about movies again. It was all they seemed to do.

Part of it, Mathilde reasoned, must be due to Pia's having nothing to occupy her time since the movie's wrap. Wes had promised to introduce her to the "right" people, but he felt it was best to wait until just prior to the film's release. "She'll be fresher in their minds, then. It'll carry more weight."

But the release was still two months off.

Mathilde wondered if she should do more to push Pia's career in the meantime—Pia had even intimated such on more than one occasion. Perhaps that was the rationale behind the episode with Jeanne and *Peter Pan*; boredom and frustrated ambition might account for Pia's bizarre behavior—although Mathilde suspected the reasons lay far deeper than that.

She sighed. If only I'd had Pia's drive at her age. I didn't even have Jeanne's . . . what? *Drive* wasn't the word. Mathilde was still awestruck over her younger

136

daughter's transformation—and similarly confounded by Pia's *offstage* performance the same night. Her cold premeditation bordered on frightening. And it rendered Mathilde helpless.

Wes is right, she reflected. I can't mother them forever. But there's something he can't possibly understand, because he's not their mother. I brought them into the world. I *am* responsible for them, at least until they're adults.

It was why, despite the temptation, Mathilde refused to stay an entire night at Wes's house. He was an ardent lover—she trembled at the thought of him and of the different woman she became when they were in bed together. But afterward, she always resumed her role of the mother of two teenage girls and insisted on returning home. She was grateful that Wes consented; if he hadn't, her dream would have already ended.

From the bedroom, she heard Pia say good-bye to her friend and hang up the phone. Maybe, thought Mathilde, she'd think less about movies if she were more interested in boys. At her age, it would be innocent dates—bowling, the roller rink, and ice-cream sundaes.

But Pia had expressed no interest in the boys she knew. And no wonder, thought her mother; she's constantly comparing the neighborhood boys with the photographs of those handsome Hollywood stars taped to her side of the bedroom wall. What teenage boy could compete favorably with Rock Hudson and Jeffrey Hunter? Or Tony Curtis and Robert Wagner? There was Joey Crane, the adolescent production assistant on Pia's movie. He'd developed a crush on Pia from her first day on the set. He'd called twice to invite her out—and Pia had turned him down both times.

"He's so . . . young, Mama," Pia had said.

"He's attentive and sweet," Mathilde had argued.

137

"And he's nice-looking."

"He's immature. And he wears his hair in a crew cut."

"That's unimportant. Joey's a very polite young man."

"Oh, Mama, he's only eighteen. Right out of high school. He didn't even apply for college. And besides, he's just a production assistant. What good will that do me?"

"Well, he'd be someone other than Marybeth to talk to about movies. It wouldn't hurt you to be around boys your own age instead of sitting home and daydreaming about being swept off your feet by some famous movie star."

"*You* can say that, Mama, because you've got Wes!"

"Pia, that's enough!" Mathilde's cheeks reddened with color.

The subject of movie stars—Wesley in particular—had dropped then, until several hours later and the arrival of the cashmere stole.

Mathilde had never owned anything made of cashmere. She recalled that once, a girl in her high school class had received a blue cashmere sweater for Christmas. Mathilde had secretly envied her. But such luxury had exceeded her parents' means, and, later, Hank's salary could afford no better than synthetics. Mathilde's dresser held sweaters made of nylon or Orlon, and blouses of rayon instead of silk.

She opened the bottom drawer and carefully lifted out the folded length of ivory softness that Wes had sent all the way from Bullock's in Pasadena. She wrapped the stole around her shoulders; the feathersoft wool caressed her cheek as it brushed against her skin.

When it had been delivered the week before,

Mathilde had wondered if it was correct to accept such a gift. A "nice" woman did *not* accept expensive presents from a man unless she was his . . .

I'm not *that,* she thought. If the stole were mink, I'd have to refuse it. But it isn't. It's cashmere, and it's perfect. I can thank him for it and not feel . . . kept.

She'd worn it both times she'd been out with Wes in the past week, and whether heads had turned because of the stole itself or because of the way she felt enveloped by it, she didn't know. She knew only that she loved it. And loved Wes for being so thoughtful.

But the stole wouldn't complement the outfit she was wearing tonight. She could try the dress without the bolero jacket, but the effect would lose its "ensemble" look. And the white background of the polished cotton fabric would make the ivory stole appear soiled.

Well then, tonight she'd wear the bolero jacket and save the stole until the next time, when it would disguise the start of repeat "performances" of her wardrobe. For a moment, Mathilde forgot that she was ignoring her own advice and letting her mind skip ahead to a next time.

She lovingly removed the stole and folded it neatly inside the tissue that she'd saved from the Bullock's box. Then she slid the dresser drawer closed and reached for her sewing kit; one of the buttons was missing from the bolero jacket she'd wear this evening.

Soft music wafted into Mathilde's room from the kitchen. Pia must have turned on the radio. Frank Sinatra was singing his new hit song, "Young at Heart." As Mathilde straightened her stocking seams, she began to hum. Young at heart. Her mood, lately. No wonder she liked the lyrics.

She was clipping on her button earrings when the

139

phone rang. "I'll get it," she called out, running into the hall. Wes always thought to call when there was a chance that he'd be late.

"Hello? Mrs. Decameron?"

It wasn't Wes's voice.

"Who is this, please?" she asked.

"It's Joey Crane. Remember me?"

"Why, of course, Joey! How nice to hear from you!" Her eyes darted toward Pia, who had come into the hall. She made a face when she heard Joey's name.

Pia was reading a copy of *Confidential*, but she'd looked up long enough to notice her mother's makeup and hairdo. Mama was wearing her new perfume. She must be going out with Wes again. It rankled her; even though she knew they were dating, she didn't like *seeing* them together. Not as a *couple*. As much as she looked forward to Wes's physical presence, usually she stayed around just long enough to greet him, then escaped to her room.

She heard Mathilde say, "Yes, she's home," before Pia could mouth the words, "Tell him I'm not here."

"I got a raise," Joey was explaining. "Well, actually, it's a promotion."

"A promotion!" exclaimed Mathilde, raising her voice for Pia's benefit. "What good news! Pia, turn down the radio and come congratulate Joey."

Pia threw the magazine to the floor. "Oh, Mama!" she hissed. But Mathilde stood holding the receiver out to her. One hand covered the mouthpiece as she said, *"Do* it, Pia."

Pia stomped into the kitchen and cut off Frank Sinatra in midphrase. Then she grudgingly trudged to the phone and took the receiver from her mother.

"Hi, Joey," she cooed sweetly, batting her eyelashes at Mathilde.

"Be nice to him," came the whispered command. "I have to finish dressing."

For *Wesley,* Pia thought, watching her mother walk down the hall and into her bedroom. And she isn't closing the door. That means she's listening. All right, then, I'll *be* nice to Joey . . .

Pia nodded and stifled a yawn as Joey Crane spouted a stream of inanities. The only cliché he didn't utter was one about the weather, and that, Pia surmised, was because he hadn't gotten around to it yet. His halting, reedy voice betrayed nervousness, which both bored and flattered Pia; the former showed a lack of self-confidence, the latter told Pia that she was important to him.

At last she interrupted him to say, "Joey, didn't my mother say something about a promotion . . . ?"

"Yeah," he answered shyly. "I'm not a production assistant anymore."

"You mean someone else will have to make the coffee?"

He laughed at that, and it lowered Pia's opinion of him even more.

"Well," he continued, "I'm a third assistant director now. I know it's still not much, but it's a step up, and I'm the youngest member of the union."

You sure are, she thought. It was the word *assistant* that annoyed her. Always . . . still . . . an underling. She'd never be *anyone's* assistant, and she'd bet money that Wesley Guest had never been one, either. "I'm very happy for you," she said aloud. "And very pleased that you wanted to let me know."

"You *are?*"

"Of course I am."

"Well . . . I got my first paycheck today . . . and I was kind of hoping you might help me celebrate. I know it's short notice, but something special's happening tonight that I thought you'd like. Maybe we could go together . . . ?"

Something special? thought Pia. With Joey Crane

141

that could be the opening of a new hamburger stand. On the other hand . . .

"I'd have to ask my mother. And before she'd say one way or another, I'd have to tell her where we're going. What's the something special you're talking about?"

Joey cleared his throat and said proudly, "I've wangled two passes to a screening of the new Hitchcock movie, and—"

"*To Catch a Thief*!" she exclaimed.

"Right! I knew you'd want to see that! It doesn't get released till next month. We'll be the first ones to *catch* it." His voice underscored the pun.

Pia restrained a moan and even offered the obligatory giggle at his joke. She'd read *so* much about the movie. And a theater meant they wouldn't have to do much talking.

"What time will you pick me up—if Mama says yes?" She knew Mama wouldn't say no.

"In an hour or so, if that's okay with you and your mother."

An hour. Mama and Wes should be gone by then. She could even offer Joey a drink. It might relax him. It had relaxed her on the night they'd gone to see Jeanne in *Peter Pan*, despite the fear of Mama's noticing the lower line of amber on the bottle of scotch. And this time she'd be more clever, to avoid the chance of being found out.

Into the receiver Pia said, "Will anyone important be there?" Then she quickly covered the question. "I mean . . . is it a fancy-dress occasion? So I'll know what to wear . . ."

"Gee," answered Joey. "I'm not real sure. I guess it'll be casual. Yeah. Casual but nice. Some agents and producers are bound to show up. And Hitch."

"Hitch?"

"The director of the picture . . . You know, Alfred—"

"Oh, yes—Hitch!" She wouldn't forget his nickname in the future.

But Joey had also said producers and agents would be there. That could prove useful.

"Say you'll go with me, Pia," he pleaded. "If I can't take Grace Kelly, I'd like to have *you* on my arm."

She paused just long enough to let him think that his compliment had convinced her.

Then, envisioning a theater packed with glamorous stars, she said, "Hold on a minute, Joey. I'll ask my mother."

Pia was watching her mother as Mathilde rummaged through the closet that her two daughters shared. Mama's polka-dotted dress smelled of sunshine from having hung on the clothesline to dry. The clean scent mingled with the Chanel No. 5 perfume that Wes had given her. What was wrong with the Elizabeth Arden Blue Grass cologne that Mama had always worn before? From the way she sprayed on the Chanel, you'd think it was going out of style! And yet when Pia had asked her to share some, Mama had refused. "I'll run out if we both use it, Pia. Besides, it's a grown-up scent. You're too young to wear Chanel."

Too young! she thought. Or is Mama just jealous that Wes always pays so much attention to me? Is that why she keeps talking about how *young* I am—to make sure I don't take Wes away from her?

A surge of resentment flashed through Pia. *That's* why Mama wants me to date Joey! she reasoned. To keep Wes for herself! Well, Mama, when *other* people think I'm "old enough" to wear Chanel, we'll just see!

For now, however, she had to find something appropriate to wear to "Hitch's" screening.

Mathilde had laid two of the three possibilities across Pia's bed. One looked too dressy, the other too

143

shabby. Pia was modeling the third alternative, a chocolate-brown cotton chambray that they'd found on sale at a church bazaar. It went well with her coloring, but with such thin shoulder straps, Mathilde wondered if it would do. The August nights brought with them a damp chill.

"Well," she said, "I suppose it's all right. You can take a sweater along for later."

"My pretty white cardigan?"

"I'm sorry, Pia, but I washed the white one this morning. It won't be dry. I didn't know Joey Crane was going to call—"

"I *can't* wear this alone—I'll freeze to death! And the screening room is probably air-conditioned, too!"

"Pia, must you whine? We'll just have to find something else for you to wear."

The cashmere stole! thought Pia as Mathilde left the room. Of course! She's going to let me wear the stole!

Pia's head was filled with her own image—she was swathed in the ivory cashmere and stepping from Joey's car. So the stole wasn't mink and the car wouldn't be a Rolls-Royce. And, she added with a frown, Joey wasn't Wes. But she'd still outshine everyone at the screening—unless she had to share the limelight with Grace Kelly.

But Mathilde returned to the bedroom without the stole. Pia couldn't believe her eyes as her mother held up Jeanne's pink sweater. "Your sister left it in the kitchen again," she said.

"That ratty thing?" Pia said with disgust.

"It's perfectly fine. And it's warm."

"It's—it's—"

"Pia, don't start with me. Put it on."

"It's horrible! It's ugly!"

"Well, it was good enough for your sister when you wouldn't let her borrow your white sweater, wasn't it?"

"It *is* good enough for Jeanne—just not for *me!*"

144

Quietly, Mathilde said, "I'm going to pretend I didn't hear you say that, Pia." She put the sweater on the bed and started for the door.

Pia's voice stopped her. "What about the cashmere stole Wes gave you?"

"What about it?" asked her mother.

"Can't I borrow that?"

"No," answered Mathilde. "You can't."

"*You're* not wearing it tonight, so why can't I?"

"Because you might spill something on it."

"That isn't the reason!" wailed Pia. "You won't let me wear the stole because I wouldn't let Jeanne wear my white sweater!"

"That's nonsense. And you'll wear the pink one."

"I will not! I want to wear your stole!"

"I said no," repeated Mathilde, her voice beginning to rise.

"But *why?*"

"Because"—she tried to keep from shouting—"because it's *mine!*" Then, trembling, she stormed from the room.

Wesley's car was just pulling away from the curb. Pia stood at the door and waved them off with her brightest smile. She saw Wes wave back, but Mathilde was facing forward and not looking at her daughter.

Pia closed the door and leaned against it with relief. Pretending that nothing was wrong in front of Wes had been as exhausting as her fight with Mama. She was still shaking with anger. She was glad that Jeanne had gone to the Armitages' house for dinner—she didn't need her sister to sit around gloating.

Mathilde's only words to Pia had been, "Make sure Joey gets you home early—before *we* get back."

Well, at least Wes knew she had a date with *someone.* She walked to the kitchen and caught a glimpse of her reflection in the shiny chrome surface of the toaster. Most of the puffiness was gone from her eyes, and a touch of powder, lipstick, and mascara had done the rest. She looked pretty and knew that her sundress, with its spaghetti-thin shoulder straps, was becoming. Wes had even commented on it.

Of course, Jeanne's pink sweater would ruin the effect entirely, she thought with a sigh. She had almost calmed down, but her hands were still shaking.

She noticed that the bottle of scotch still stood on the Formica table, where Mama and Wes had left it beside their empty glasses. Pia glanced behind her, even though no one else was home, then turned and poured an inch or so of the amber liquid into the glass with Mama's lipstick on the rim.

She took a sip and winced at the alcohol's bite. Then, after a deep breath, she downed the rest in a single, quick gulp.

She heard a knock at the front door and checked the wall clock. Joey's early, she thought. That figures. In one imagined scenario, she'd kept him waiting five minutes, then stepped into the living room and, wrapped in Mama's cashmere stole, asked, "Well, Joey, how do I look?"

Instead, using the toaster as her mirror once more, Pia adjusted her two "signature" spit curls and went to answer the door.

Joey seemed impressed when Pia offered him a cocktail. She joined him and they clinked their glasses together in a toast. It was remarkable, she mused, the way one drink had calmed her. The second helped her to regain control. And self-assurance. Pia could see in Joey's eyes the response to her bare shoulders. The spool-heeled sandals she wore caused her hips to sway

146

when she moved, and Joey seemed to appreciate that, too.

They drank their scotches in the living room, then Pia returned the empty tumblers to the kitchen. She opened the faucet and was about to rinse out the glasses, but thought again and put them back beside the bottle where Wes and Mama had left them. She was wearing Mama's lipstick, so the color on the glass's rim would match. And this time she remembered to add an inch or two of tap water to bring the whisky level to its previous mark. She didn't know whether Mama would notice such things, but there was no point in taking chances.

"I'll just be a second," she told Joey. "I have to get my wrap."

Pia went directly to Mathilde's room and opened the bottom dresser drawer. Then she lifted the cashmere stole from its tissue paper and shoved the drawer closed with the back of her heel.

She tossed the stole casually around her and pulled it high over one shoulder. She modeled a Suzy Parker three-quarter slouch and posed for the mirror as though it were a camera photographing her for the cover of *Vogue*. She lowered her chin, raised one eyebrow, and parted her moistened lips in a Marilyn Monroe pout. Deciding from all she'd read about *To Catch a Thief* that the evening called for ice-cool sensuality rather than overt sex, she abandoned Marilyn in favor of Grace. That meant she could still use the eyebrow as well as the hip-slouch.

Joey was standing facing the window, his back to her, when Pia made her dream come true.

Positioning herself against the arch that separated the hall from the living room, she licked her lips and asked, "Well, Joey, how do I look?"

Chapter Ten

The Mercedes turned off the main road and rolled over the now-familiar bump that signaled the last ten minutes of the drive.

Mathilde glanced at the clock on the dashboard. It was past one A.M. She was sorry to see their night together drawing to an end. It had been wonderful. He'd taken her to Mocambo, a chic club where they'd dined and danced and held each other closely while swaying in rhythm to the music. In a room overflowing with famous women, beautiful women, Wesley Guest had danced only with Mathilde. He wanted *her*.

After weeks of self-doubt, she had finally accepted the incredible fact. At first she'd been wary of the politeness shown her by Wes's friends and colleagues whenever they stopped to say hello—table-hopping, it was called—at Ciro's or Romanoff's. She'd speculated on their unvoiced curiosity: What could Wes possibly see in this post-thirty-year-old mother of two? Why this pretty but not spectacular woman of no visible gifts or talents—particularly with so many glamorous young girls to choose from?

Wes had sensed her insecurity and had sought to reassure her. She *was* special to him. More important than anyone. And his caring and tenderness had shown her.

Tonight he'd said, "I love you," and she knew that it was true. She knew also that she loved him.

Wesley had been unusually quiet after they'd made love, and he continued to speak very little during the drive home. It wasn't like him.

The car radio was playing the soft strains of "Love is a Many Splendored Thing." They'd danced to it only hours before.

"Butterfly," he said at last.

"What?" she asked.

"The first six notes of *'Un Bel Dì.'* Puccini."

"I . . . I don't know it."

He took her hand in his and squeezed it gently. "The story's about a man who . . . treats the woman he loves very badly."

Mathilde could tell something was bothering him. She returned the pressure to his fingers and said, "Wes, what's the matter?"

"I don't like having to . . . to make you do this."

"Do what? You haven't forced me into—"

"No, no," he interrupted. "I mean, having to take you home in the middle of the night like a sneak thief. As if we'd stolen away to some cheap motel for a few hours. I want more for you. For us."

She paused, then answered, "So do I. But we agreed . . . for the girls' sakes. And . . . I'm content with this. I love you."

"Well, *I'm* not content." He slowed the car for a stop sign and turned to look at her. Oncoming traffic bathed his face in light and accented the shadows and planes that Mathilde had come to know so well.

"You know, of course, there's only one way to solve the problem," he said.

Oh, God, she thought, please let him say what I think

he's going to say. "I . . . I . . ." was all she could stammer in reply.

"Will you marry me, Mathilde?"

"Yes," she answered, and he kissed her.

Thank you, God, she said silently.

They'd made a date for lunch the next day to discuss the girls. Although he hadn't mentioned it to Mathilde, Wesley wasn't blind to Pia's infatuation with him. Perhaps it was advisable to make some professional introductions for Pia now, instead of waiting until the film's release. With her adolescent self-involvement, it might divert her attention and thereby cushion the blow of her mother's news. Especially in view of what he had in mind for Jeanne.

Mathilde closed the door behind her and hurriedly entered the living room, where she parted the draperies to wave good-bye as Wes's car pulled away from the curb. She stayed at the window until the red taillights grew smaller and disappeared into the night.

But it isn't night, she reminded herself. It's early morning. Time for some sleep . . . and I'm too excited to be tired.

Nonetheless, Mathilde headed toward her room. On her way she stopped to check on the girls. She turned on the dim overhead bulb in the hallway and opened their door just far enough to see their beds.

Jeanne was sleeping peacefully, her blond hair catching what little light penetrated the room.

But Pia's bed was empty. The pink sweater still lay where Mathilde had put it earlier. So stubborn, she thought. Pia must have frozen on her date, without something to cover her shoulders. And just where is she

150

at this hour?

She felt a rising sense of futility, rather than anger. What *are* we going to do with Pia? she asked herself.

And then Mathilde realized that she'd used the word *we*. I no longer have to do all this alone, she thought. Quietly she closed the door and tiptoed down the hall to her own room, where she turned on the small milk-glass lamp on her night table.

Pia was asleep on her bed. Not under the covers but sprawled out on top of the spread with one arm tucked under her head.

Mathilde felt a rush of emotion welling inside her. Pia . . . her firstborn, yet still such a child. She barely looked her fourteen years, lying there in the innocence of sleep. Just like a baby. It hardly seemed possible; the years had flown by and Pia's childhood was already slipping away. Mathilde recalled the first time Hank had held the baby in his arms. Only yesterday.

No, she thought. Not yesterday. Almost fifteen years ago. The girls will soon be grown. Hank is gone.

And I have Wesley.

She wiped a tear from her cheek and bent to wake Pia. But she looked so comfortable, it seemed a shame to disturb her. Mathilde could spend the few hours until dawn on the living room sofa—or in Pia's bed.

Pia's bed. The pink sweater was still there. Why? wondered Mathilde as the image struck her. And why should Pia even *be* in my room, much less fall asleep on my bed?

That was when she noticed the bottom drawer of her dresser. It was closed, but a shred of tissue wrapping had somehow gotten caught and was sticking out over the edge.

Mathilde opened the drawer and immediately her heart sank. The cashmere stole was there, but she knew that Pia had removed it, because it was folded in threes;

151

Mathilde always folded it carefully in half, to avoid extra creases. Just as she always placed the tissue *over* it, not crushed *beneath* the stole, the way it was now.

She lifted the stole from the drawer to refold it—and saw the stain.

A large, dark red blotch covered one end—the bottom third. Her precious gift from Wesley had been spoiled by . . . ?

Blood? At first Mathilde reacted with alarm. But holding the fabric closer to the lamp, she understood. The stain had been made by red wine.

She fought the urge to shake Pia awake and demand an explanation. That her daughter had disobeyed was terrible enough. But to learn that she'd been *drinking* . . .

Unless someone *else* had spilled the wine. No. Mathilde knew Pia better than that. Pia wouldn't sip a Coke while everyone else was drinking wine or liquor. Just last week Mathilde had detected the faint smell of scotch in a glass that Pia had neglected to wash out with soap.

And there was irrefutable evidence of something more. In addition to Pia's rivalry with Jeanne, she was jealous of her mother—or, rather, of her mother's relationship with Wes. Mathilde had sensed it lately but had chosen to ignore it until now. She could no longer look the other way.

Had the wine spilled *accidentally?* Or had Pia deliberately set out to ruin the gift that Wes had given to her mother—even if she ran the risk of getting caught?

Mathilde glanced at the prone figure asleep on her bed. My own daughter, she thought. My lovely Pia is drifting farther away with each day that passes, only to be replaced by this . . . stranger.

Then, with a mingling of sadness and a strange, new detachment, Mathilde folded the stole—in half—and, smoothing the wrinkled tissue paper, replaced it inside the drawer.

Pia wrapped the cotton bathrobe around her body and rubbed the steam off the mirror with her towel. Her eyes were still red, but at least they weren't bloodshot. She felt much better, even though the shower had been a disappointment—as every shower had been since the needle jet-spray in the bathroom at Wes's house.

She walked barefoot down the hall to the bedroom. She could hear Mama and Jeanne laughing about something in the kitchen. *They've* become awfully chummy, she thought.

She entered the room and stopped in her tracks. The pink sweater was hanging over the closet doorknob. Had it been there when she'd come from Mama's room to get her robe? Mama had slept in Pia's bed; the faint hint of Chanel No. 5 still lingered on the pillow.

Pia cursed her carelessness. How stupid of me to forget about the sweater! Of course there's always the chance that Jeanne hung it there . . .

But what if it was Mama?

Pia considered the options until she settled on an answer. I'll just say I didn't need the sweater, she decided. After all, that's true . . .

Pia wasn't concerned about the stole. It was back in Mama's drawer, in case she should happen to check. There wasn't any reason to take it *out* of the drawer until Mama wore it again with Wes, and she wouldn't do that *two* days in a row. Time enough to have it dry-cleaned—a rush job—while Mama was out of the house. She'd never have to find out.

Unless, of course, the spot couldn't be removed. Mama's prized stole might be permanently ruined.

Pia weighed the possibility of punishment against a

curious satisfaction, the same satisfaction she'd felt just after the wine had spilled last night.

She ruminated over last night as she pulled a T-shirt over her head and tucked it into the waist of her pedal pushers.

I really looked fabulous, she mused, even if I *did* waste it on Joey. He was impressed, but who cares about that jerk? What happened to all the important people he promised would show up? Where were the agents and producers? Grace Kelly and Cary Grant? And "Hitch"? Just a bunch of studio nobodys, and those guys Joey said were newspaper reporters. *Sure* they stared—I was the prettiest girl there.

Her pleased grin turned to a frown as Pia recalled Joey's conduct after the screening. They'd stopped at a supper club, and Joey had ordered a bottle of wine to accompany their steaks. He'd also ordered a second bottle. The waiter hadn't asked her for proof of age. She'd obviously looked as grown-up as she'd felt.

Pia hadn't felt very grown up later in Joey's car. She endured his sloppy, clumsy kisses, even allowing his hand to stray to her breasts. Neither gesture pleased her—she felt nothing at all—but a few kisses and a quick feel were probably what he expected in repayment for the evening.

It was when his hand touched her knee and began moving up her thigh that Pia was overcome by a sickening wave of revulsion. She didn't throw up, but instead pushed him away with a plaintive request. "It's late, Joey, and I don't like having Mama worry about me."

He'd fallen for that and taken her home.

But honestly! she thought now. The nerve! I *should* have thrown up—it would have served him right!

*   *   *

"'Morning, Pia—'bye, Pia!" Jeanne called on her way out of the house.

God, she's chipper, Pia observed. Maybe that's what bleaching your hair does for you.

Mathilde was seated at the table when Pia entered the kitchen. A half-empty coffee cup sat beside her hand.

Mathilde took a drag of her cigarette, then exhaled and smiled. "Good morning, Pia. You're up earlier than I'd expected."

Pia yawned. "You and Jeanne were giggling so much out here, I couldn't sleep. Can I have a cup of tea, Mama?"

"Have some coffee. You may as well," Mathilde answered with a shrug.

A warning bell sounded in Pia's brain. Maybe it's nothing, she reasoned, but better play it safe. She poured herself some coffee, but instead of sitting she remained standing with her back to the sink.

Mathilde was studying her daughter. She was still smiling, but her eyes bored into Pia's, and it made Pia squirm.

"You're . . . dressed up, Mama. You . . . look nice," she offered, unsure of what to do or say. "Going out?"

"Yes," Mathilde replied. "With Wesley. Cigarette?" She extended her arm and held out the pack of Lucky Strikes.

"Uh . . . no . . . thank you," she answered, puzzled. "Mama—you don't think I *smoke,* do you?"

"Well, after all, Pia, I don't know, do I?"

Pia knew something was going on. Her mind raced. Joey had brought her home before Mama had come back, so it wasn't about her curfew. But her emotional antennae told her this could be a trap. Had Mama smelled wine on her breath last night? God, she thought, I shouldn't have . . . fallen asleep . . . in her bed. I'm smarter than that.

"How was your date with Joey?"

"It was okay, I guess. Nobody important showed up."

"How was the movie?"

"Pretty good. It's not scary or anything. Gorgeous clothes, though."

Mathilde continued staring at Pia while she crushed her cigarette in the ashtray. "That's all, Pia?"

"All? Oh, you mean Joey. He . . . took me out afterward. It was nice."

"Weren't you cold . . . ?"

The sweater! Now Pia understood the game being played. In a way, it was a relief. She knew where she stood.

"Mama . . . I hope you won't be angry . . . but I guess you will . . ."

"Not if I hear the truth, Pia."

"Oh, all right. I can't fool you, can I, Mama? I didn't wear the sweater."

"And that's the truth?"

"Yes," said Pia solemnly. "I'm sorry, Mama. You were right, too. I should have worn it. I *was* cold."

"And no one laughed at your bare shoulders?"

Pia shook her head. "No. I looked nice."

"I'm sure," Mathilde agreed. She was studying the well of coffee at the bottom of her cup.

"Where's Wes taking you?" Pia asked. Changing the subject was imperative.

"I don't know. Someplace for an early lunch. What are you doing today?"

"I'll call Marybeth. Maybe we'll go to a movie." Pia put down her cup and walked quickly to the doorway. "In fact, I'll call her right now."

She got as far as the hall and was half convinced that she was home free when Mathilde's voice stopped her.

"Pia," she called. "It's windy out today. Would you

156

bring me my cashmere stole? You know where I keep
it."

At first Mathilde's request met with silence. Then:
"It'll warm up later, Mama, and then you'll be too
warm."

"Thank you for your concern, dear, but I'd like to
wear it anyway."

Pia appeared in the kitchen doorway. Her face was
beet-red. Well, thought Mathilde, at least she has the
decency to be embarrassed.

"You've seen it, I guess," said Pia. "That's what this
is all about."

"Yes."

She couldn't control her own trembling and didn't
understand why. "I had to, Mama. Don't you see?"

"Did you have to drink?"

"No, but . . ."

"Did you have to spill red wine all over something
you know I love? Did you have to ruin it?"

"God, Mama!" Pia shouted. "It's not as if I did it on
purpose!"

"I wondered about that, too."

"Mama! *How* can you think that of me?"

"I don't know, Pia. But I did. And I do. I'm certainly
not proud of it. Nor of you."

"The stole can be dry-cleaned!"

"Pia!" Mathilde rose in a fury. "That isn't the
point—and it can't be cleaned—it's ruined!"

She tried to push past, but Pia blocked the exit and
grabbed her mother's arm.

"Mama, we can dye it—it'll be even prettier in
burgundy!"

Mathilde heaved a sigh. It was hopeless. "Pia, let me
go."

"It was an accident!" Pia screamed.

Mathilde stood still and looked directly into her

157

daughter's eyes. Neither spoke or moved. Finally Pia stepped aside and let her mother pass.

"What are you going to do?" she asked in a small voice.

Mathilde didn't reply. Instead, she disappeared down the hall that led to her room. Moments later, she returned with the cashmere stole.

"Here," Mathilde said, flinging it over Pia's shoulder. "It's yours. You've *earned* it."

Chapter Eleven

"I'll have to ask my mother about it," Jeanne was saying to Mrs. Armitage. They'd finished dinner and were sitting in the swing on the porch of the old white frame house. Mr. Armitage sat stretched out on a folding lawn chair. The curls of his aromatic pipe tobacco wafted gently upward and dissipated into the clear night sky.

"Well," said the teacher, "I should think that after your success in the play, your mother will be delighted."

They'd been discussing Jeanne's future, particularly the forthcoming year, and her participation in the school's drama club. "I'm sponsoring an experiment this year," said Mrs. Armitage, "and I admit I'm rather excited about it."

"Oh, Ellie," said her husband, "you're a frustrated actress *and* stage mother." But he chided his wife affectionately, and Jeanne sensed that he was behind her teacher one hundred percent.

"It's just that we're so near the movie community," she continued. "Why, you'd be amazed at the response —professional response—to *Peter Pan*. And that's *amateur* theater."

159

"But don't you think those agents you mentioned showed up because of Laurie Martins? I mean, *she's* been in three movies, and then there's Captain Crook—"

Jeanne burst into laughter. She and the cast of *Peter Pan* had invented the nickname for Leonard MacEvoy, because the actor had tried to steal every scene during the performances. He had inadvertently given everyone a crash course in the art of upstaging—and of surviving someone else committing that crime.

"Then why was Wesley Guest there . . . ?" teased Frank Armitage. "I saw him talking with *you,* young lady."

Jeanne recalled her shock at finding him backstage. Seeing Pia, she'd figured it out. But that was second only to the shock of Wesley Guest's words: "You're a natural onstage, Jeanne. A born actress." Pia had overheard and fumed, but it served her right for tricking them all.

Jeanne had repeated the words to her teacher. However, she'd neglected to explain Wes's presence at an amateur production, because she wasn't sure what to say.

Mrs. Armitage shook her head—Jeanne saw her— but there was no point in hiding secrets from the two people wo had offered her encouragement.

"My mother . . . and Wesley . . . uh, they're . . . friends." She was grateful that the porch was too dark for them to see her blush, even if they could read through her stammer.

"Well," said Frank Armitage, "speaking of friends, *I* heard Mr. Guest say to your mother that he was going to talk to some friends of his at the studio."

Mrs. Armitage nodded. "In a way, that's what gave me my idea." She outlined her plan. "We'll choose—by audition—ten or twelve students from the

160

drama club. We'll assign scenes to them, rehearse for a month, and then we'll invite agents and producers and directors to an evening of staged scenes. It'll be similar to a screen test but without the cameras. The students will be more relaxed because they'll be accustomed to working with their partners. And the atmosphere will be more that of a performance than of a test." She settled back against a flowered cushion. "It may be immodest of me to say so," she concluded, "but I think it's a wonderful idea."

"And so do I!" exclaimed Jeanne. "I nearly *died* at the thought of a screen test"—she winced, recalling her bout with hives—"but in *Peter Pan*, once the curtain went up and the play actually began, I felt so . . . *alive!* I was surprised, because when Charles called half hour, I was so nervous, I threw up—I'm not ashamed to admit that now—and yet I didn't want to leave the stage after the play was over! I wanted to stay there forever!" Her voice was feverish with excitement. "I could *feel* the audience—it was a kind of energy, like electricity!—I don't know how else to explain it!"

Mrs. Armitage smiled as the support chains of the swing creaked. "You've explained it eloquently, my dear. And someday you're going to be a great actress— if that's what you want to be."

"Yes . . ." answered Jeanne, half to herself. "That's exactly what I want to be."

Jeanne was glad that Pia wasn't home when Wesley telephoned. She would have insisted on joining them for lunch, and Wes had set up the appointment with Neal Genesco specifically for Jeanne's benefit.

Mathilde felt a moment's hesitation—shouldn't both girls be given an equal chance?—but the memory of Pia at her sister's performance, underscored by the fact

161

that Pia had already made a screen test for the same director, won out, and Mathilde had said nothing about lunch when Pia and Marybeth were leaving for their afternoon double feature.

In addition, she said nothing when Jeanne emerged from the bedroom wearing a simple navy cotton turtleneck with a white cotton piqué skirt. No jewelry, and simple navy-blue flats with neither stockings nor socks. She had continued to highlight her hair after the play, but had let the body wave grow out. The summer heat and sun had done the rest; now her hair fell to shoulder length, straight as before but silky in texture, thanks to the various creams and rinses Gladys had recommended.

Mathilde noticed that while one lock of hair fell over Jeanne's right eye and made her look like a young Veronica Lake, the total effect was natural. Jeanne wasn't posing as a sophisticated "starlet," nor was she dressed as a child. She looked her age, and Mathilde wanted to hug her for that.

Neither of them had ever been to the famous restaurant that was shaped like a hat. Heads turned as they entered the Brown Derby in the company of Wesley Guest. People smiled or nodded warmly at the trio, and Jeanne basked in the glow. Not because they were being greeted as royalty by the maître d' and his staff. Not even for the reason of the luncheon appointment. It was more from a feeling, a strange sensation, as they were escorted to a large, round booth. Seeing Mama so happy filled Jeanne with the same kind of overflowing energy she'd felt onstage in the play. There was an *aliveness* in Mama that Jeanne had never seen before. She silently prayed that Wes and Mama would be together forever. The strangeness was

162

that Jeanne didn't feel left out. As she slid into the tufted leather booth, the word that kept blinking in her mind was *family*. Even stranger was that these thoughts didn't include Pia.

Neal Genesco arrived moments later. An elegant woman of Mathilde's age, perhaps a few years her senior, stood beside him. She wore a beige silk shirtwaist and a beige straw hat.

Jeanne remembered the director but hoped he'd forgotten her awkwardness on their first meeting at the studio. She noticed that Lydia Genesco was the antithesis of awkward: her lustrous blond hair was pulled back neatly into a chignon at the nape of her swanlike neck, around which she wore a discreet strand of pearls, with matching earrings. The way she moved her body as she slid into the booth and the gracefulness with which she removed her beige gloves made Jeanne think of a choreographed ballet; indeed, Lydia Genesco could have been a dancer.

Her personality was as charming as her appearance. She put Jeanne and Mathilde immediately at ease while her husband and Wes discussed business.

"They always promise to leave studio talk for the studio," Lydia said, laughing. "But they always renege. Don't you notice that with Wes, Mathilde?"

Initially, Mathilde had felt self-conscious at being automatically linked with Wes—she wasn't sure of his reaction. Usually when she and Wes bumped into his colleagues on an evening out, the introductions were polite but brief and noncommittal. However, Lydia's openness, or acceptance, of Wes and Mathilde's relationship helped Mathilde herself to relax. And Wes, who had overheard Lydia, squeezed Mathilde's hand and said, "Guilty as charged, Mrs. G."

163

Soon it became apparent that pretenses were unnecessary. Mathilde liked Lydia for that.

So did Jeanne. She was included in the conversation and moreover was the subject of much of it.

"Wes told us about your lovely performance in *Peter Pan*," Neal was saying. "I'm sorry we were out of town. Otherwise, we wouldn't have missed it."

"Yes," agreed Lydia. "But I hadn't realized that you and my husband had already met."

"I recall that you were scheduled to test for me, young lady," Neal said kindly. "But you took sick."

Again Mathilde wondered if she ought to mention Pia, and again she did not.

"I was overcome by nerves," Jeanne admitted. "It seems so silly, now. But so much has changed." Then she considered the past few months and said, "Actually, it isn't that so many *things* have changed. I mean, not *outwardly*." How could she explain? "I guess it's me— I've changed."

Neal nodded. "So I hear—and see. You know, many actresses have failed miserably in their screen tests and gone on to have brilliant careers. But tell me, Jeanne. Wes says you have a feeling for the *stage*. Do you feel a tremendous difference between that and the movies?"

Before she could answer, he said, "Excuse me, but I must say that *I* do. Of course, I began in the theater. It remains my first love."

Jeanne waited to be sure he'd finished. Then she said, "You know, Mr. Genesco, I think it's because of the audience. A camera . . . well, a camera can't . . . *feel.*"

"No," he agreed, "but the camera sees what *you* feel. And records it *for* the audience. Do you understand what I'm saying?"

Jeanne was very thoughtful. Slowly, she replied, "I'm beginning to . . ."

"Excellent," said Neal. "Then we'll have to make

amends for the screen test you missed. You have only to promise me one thing."

"Yes . . . ?"

"You must call me Neal. I know I'm old enough to be your father, but 'Mr. Genesco' makes me feel like your *grandfather!* Promise?"

Jeanne nodded as a huge smile spread across her face. Neal turned to Wes and said, "You were right. She has something special. Her emotions show in her eyes."

As Jeanne shifted nervously in the booth, Lydia said, "There's time enough to talk more business. Why don't we all order lunch?"

By the time they said good-bye, the five of them were old friends. In exchange for Jeanne's calling Neal by his first name, he had promised not to schedule her screen test until *after* he and Lydia had attended Mrs. Armitage's evening of staged scenes. Jeanne felt if she could survive that—in a leading role—an audition in front of a camera would be easy.

In the car on the way home, Mathilde asked, "Have you decided what scene you'll do for the class?"

Jeanne, curled up in the backseat, shrugged her shoulders. "I don't know, Mama. I guess Mrs. Armitage will suggest something when school opens and she sees who to team me up with."

"Well, I have a suggestion," offered Wes. "That's if you're interested, of course."

"Sure I am—as long as it isn't Wendy!"

"Why not your namesake—*Joan of Lorraine?*"

"But it's so . . . difficult. I mean . . . do you think I'd be any good?"

"Doesn't hurt to try. You can use your mother and me as a kind of audition audience if you like. Is that okay, darling?" he asked, turning to Mathilde.

165

He called Mama 'darling'! thought Jeanne, her heart thrumming. "Oh, Wes, yes—and thank you—for everything!"

"I'm only offering because I believe in you." To Mathilde he added quietly, "In both of you."

And again, Jeanne felt the warmth of being part of a family. For an instant before they pulled up in front of the house, Jeanne speculated about Pia. She'll be furious when she finds out—about Neal, about lunch, about me.

But a moment later, when Wes opened the car door, a new thought crossed Jeanne's mind:

So Pia will be furious. *So what?*

When it came time to tell the girls, Mathilde was as nervous and uncertain as Jeanne had been backstage on opening night of the play. She understood the source of her qualms. Jeanne would be pleased, but an inner voice had warned Mathilde that Pia's reaction might be quite the opposite.

Each day Mathilde had procrastinated, and the more she put it off, the more difficult the prospect became. Sooner or later the news was bound to come out. Neal and Lydia Genesco had already accepted them as a couple. So had other friends and acquaintances, and Mathilde was aware that at any minute someone might guess as to their intentions. Wes was keeping his promise of secrecy until their plans could be announced to the girls. But he'd said he wouldn't lie. If a Hollywood reporter should begin asking personal questions, Mathilde knew that Wes would tell the truth. It was one of the reasons she had fallen in love with him; in an industry where illusion and deception ran rampant at every studio, Wesley Guest maintained his own code of ethics. He was direct and honest and refused to play games.

It was probably why Wes finally offered to tell the girls for Mathilde. She felt ashamed of her cowardice, but Wes didn't seem to mind. Perhaps he understood the reason for her reticence, although they had never discussed it.

Initially Mathilde suggested a threesome—Wes and the girls—at a fancy restaurant where Pia and Jeanne would be surrounded by movie people; in a celebrated public place, any objections to the announcement would have to remain understated, low-key. But Wes vetoed that.

"My God, we're behaving as though we have some terrible revelation to disclose, instead of wonderful news. I admit that Pia can be melodramatic, but for heaven's sake, we're *not* talking about a remake of *Mildred Pierce*!"

Mathilde tried to laugh, but she couldn't seem to shake her misgivings. Added to these was an imaginary black cloud: she hadn't felt such forebodings since Hank . . .

Now who's being melodramatic? she asked herself rhetorically, sitting down on the edge of her bed. That's past, and this is the present. And I'm going to marry Wesley Guest. I'm happy, thought Mathilde. For the first time in years. And no one—not even Pia—is going to ruin that.

She had to remind herself of her own words when she glanced toward the bottom drawer of her dresser—the drawer that had once held the wine-stained cashmere stole.

Wes told Jeanne later that week, on an evening when Pia was doing her homework at Marybeth's.

"Oh, Wes!" she cried, jumping up from the sofa and

167

running to him. Impulsively she flung her arms around his neck and then, realizing that she was behaving in a most unladylike manner, she stepped back self-consciously. "I didn't mean to—well, it's just that—"

But his smile disarmed her. "Jeanne, there's no need to apologize. I was hoping you'd be pleased, and—"

"Oh, Wes, I'm more than pleased! I think it's the most perfect thing that could possibly happen!" Tears welled in her eyes. "Oh, I *know* you and Mama will be happy, I just know it! And I love you both so much!"

Mathilde, who had been listening in the hall, uttered a silent prayer of thanks, then entered the living room. She hugged Jeanne and Wes, and the three of them went into the kitchen to celebrate with chocolate chip ice cream topped with hot fudge sauce.

Observing the domestic scene—the handsome Hollywood star, sitting at the table and listening to her younger daughter's animated chatter—Mathilde was touched by a wondrous, quiet tranquility. They'd be a family. The fancy house and cars and clothes—the things she'd previously thought so important—would be only the icing on the cake. All along, what she'd really dreamed of was love. To love and to be loved. And her dream was coming true.

That still left Pia.

"I tell you what," said Wes, rising from the table. "Let me have her friend's address, and I'll drive over and pick her up. We can have a little talk on the way back here."

"You'd better be careful," warned Jeanne. "Mary-beth is as star-crazed as Pia. You'll never get out of there alive!"

"Besides," said Mathilde, "it's only a few blocks' walk from here."

"Then I'll go on foot," he said, moving toward the back door. "What's the street and number?"

"Jeanne's right about Pia's friend," Mathilde put in. "And Marybeth's mother is the neighborhood gossip. I'd have that to contend with if she or anyone else sees you."

"I'm that notorious, hmm?" teased Wes. "Well, then, why don't you telephone and tell Pia that I'll be by with the car in five minutes. Have her come out when she hears two beeps of the horn." He glanced at mother and daughter, then added, "If that meets with the committee's approval . . . ?"

Mathilde nodded. "Yes . . . I suppose we may as well get it over with as quickly as we can."

Jeanne looked up. "Mama . . . you're not *afraid* of Pia, are you?" Her voice rose in disbelief as she heard her own words.

"Of course I'm not. Whatever gave you that idea?"

Jeanne didn't answer aloud. But silently she thought, You are, Mama. And if Pia finds that out, she'll use it to get what she wants . . .

Wes beeped the horn twice. The screen door opened, and Pia, carrying an armload of books, hurried to the car. In her haste, she almost tripped over the curb.

"Take your time," said Wes, leaning over to open the passenger door. "Nobody's chasing you."

Breathlessly, she sat down and swung her legs into the car, then let her schoolbooks drop to the floor. She glanced toward the porch of the house, but the inside door had closed behind her.

Pia leaned back against the velour headrest and sighed. "I was afraid she might be watching."

"Who's that?" asked Wes, turning the key in the ignition and starting the engine.

"Marybeth. I didn't want her to see us . . . together."

"Well, I don't happen to have any eight-by-ten glossies in the glove compartment, but I'd have been happy to sign an autograph, if that's what you—"

"No, no!" She cut him off. "I didn't *tell* her it was *you* in the car. I just said a friend of the family was picking me up because it was dark outside and Mama didn't want me walking home alone at this hour."

"That's true, too," said Wes. "But I also wanted to talk with you."

"I knew it!" said Pia. "We *are* on the same wavelength, Wes, I knew it!"

He stopped for the traffic sign and glanced at the girl seated alongside him. From the streetlight's reflection, Wes could see that Pia's eyes looked glassy.

"Move over here, Pia. I want to see something."

"Oh, Wes," she murmured, wiggling very close to him. Her thigh brushed his, and she giggled excitedly.

He could smell it on her breath. "You've been drinking, haven't you?"

Pia stiffened and bit her lip. After a moment, she said, "Only a little. But that'll help me relax, Wes." She didn't move away from him.

"Your friend's mother *let* you drink?"

"Of course not, silly. She wasn't home." She considered the next step, then, her heart fluttering wildly, Pia let her hand fall casually on Wesley's thigh.

Just as casually he removed it and placed it in her lap. "Your mother is going to be furious, young lady." He started to nudge her back to her side of the seat, but Pia seemed suddenly to have turned to stone. Icily she said, "I'm not *that* young, and we don't have to *tell* my mother . . . *everything,* do we . . . ?"

Wes pulled the car into the parking space closest to the Decameron house. He turned off the engine and withdrew the key from the ignition.

"Where're we going?" asked Pia.

"Inside," he answered. "We're home."

"Oh, Wes, not yet, please!" She grabbed his arm. "I'll do *whatever* you want, I *promise . . ."* She'd used her most seductive Marilyn voice and now was trying to purse her lips into a sexy pout.

"I drove over to meet you tonight, Pia, because I had something important to tell you. Something that concerns your mother and Jeanne and you and me. But I can see this isn't the right moment."

He sounds upset with me! Oh, God, don't let him be upset with me! "Wes . . . I'd never do anything that displeases you," she tried. "Don't you know that?"

He ignored her. "I'd have thought your hangover after the wrap party was a good enough lesson, but—"

"I slept in your house that night," she murmured dreamily.

"You passed out in my house, Pia," he corrected. Maybe this *was* the right moment. Say it and have it done with, rather than catering to a capricious child. "Speaking of my house, Pia . . . it isn't going to be just *my* house anymore. It's—"

"Oh, Wes!" she cried out, turning and flinging her arms so tightly around his neck that he could hardly breathe. "I've known it from the first! I *knew* you had to be feeling the same way about me that I feel about you. And when two people are destined for each other, age doesn't matter! Oh my dearest, I'll make you so happy, I promise I will!" Breathing scotch breath on his face, Pia's lips sought his mouth.

Wes grabbed her wrists and pried himself loose.

"Pia! For God's sake! Stop it!"

"Oh, Wes, darling, don't fight it—I *love* you! I have from the very moment we met, and—"

"Pia!" he interrupted. "I'm going to marry your mother."

171

"No—d-don't say that. Y-you must be j-joking!" But his eyes told her that he'd spoken the truth.

I've got to get away! she thought through blinding tears. Away from him! From them—from everyone! How could I *throw* myself at him—like a *fool*—when all this time it's been . . . Mama!

Mama! He wants Mama . . . instead of *me . . . !*

Her hands fumbled with the handle of the car door. Finally she flung it open and raced to the steps and on up into the house. She made a beeline for her room and yanked Mathilde's ruined cashmere stole from the dresser drawer. Then to the sewing box for the cutting shears. From there to the bathroom, where she locked herself inside.

Wesley had made his choice. "I'm going to marry your mother," he'd said.

Well, she silently vowed. I'll show you—*all* of you. Just wait and see.

Chapter Twelve

Jeanne sat with the opened script in her lap. She was trying to keep her mind on *Joan of Lorraine*, but the day's flurry of activity had made concentration next to impossible.

She had moved her script and jacket into the living room so she'd be ready when Mrs. Armitage arrived to drive her to the scene rehearsal at school. Jeanne was relieved to be out of the bedroom, which had been taken over by Mama and Pia, despite the fact that lately they'd been at each other constantly. Jeanne reconsidered. On second thought, it was Pia who'd been finding fault with Mama in small, subtle ways. Jeanne couldn't pinpoint one example in particular; nonetheless, she could feel the tension.

Still, tonight was the gala premiere of Pia's movie debut, and Pia was actually permitting Mama to help her dress. Maybe they'd called a truce. Jeanne hoped it would last beyond the one evening.

She was grateful to have a rehearsal scheduled. It served as a good excuse for not attending the premiere. It wasn't a matter of envy. This was, quite simply, Pia's night. And Wes's. I'll have my night, Jeanne reasoned, in a few weeks when I play Joan.

The bedroom door creaked on its hinge and she heard Mama's voice. "Pia, leave your spit curls alone, and put on your shoes. Wesley will be here with the limousine in fifteen minutes!"

"I'll be right there, Mathilde," answered Pia.

Jeanne frowned whenever she heard her sister call Mama by her given name, something Pia was doing more and more frequently. It seemed to amuse the neighbors, but Jeanne recognized it as another in a recent string of affectations. She sensed that it went even deeper, possibly an unconscious indication of the changes in the relationship between mother and daughter. Well, thought Jeanne, she's still Mama to me. Always.

The rustling of long skirts announced Mathilde, and Jeanne glanced toward the archway as her mother entered the living room.

"Oh, Mama!" she exclaimed. Mathilde looked beautiful.

"Do you really like it?" Her mother made a model's three-quarter turn in the gown of iridescent, dark blue-green taffeta with its matching bolero jacket. "I was afraid it was a bit extravagant, but Wes insisted, and now I—"

"Mama, you look wonderful! Just like a queen."

Mathilde smiled shyly through her nerves. Her hand went to her hair, and Jeanne noticed that Mama was wearing the enormous diamond engagement ring that Wes had given her. Then it's official, she thought happily.

She was about to embrace Mathilde when Pia's voice called from down the hall, "I'm coming out, now!"

Whether she had gauged it to upstage her mother's entrance didn't matter. Pia's timing was horrid—or perfect, depending on one's point of view. Mathilde shrugged her shoulders and said to Jeanne, "Well, you'll see in a moment—she *does* look gorgeous."

Mathilde stepped away from the arch as Pia made more than an entrance: she *appeared*.

Jeanne's breath caught. If Mama was a queen, Pia was every inch a fairytale princess, from the delicate, glimmering tiara nestled in her hair to the blue-sequined border of her paler blue chiffon gown. The only thing missing, thought Jeanne, are her glass slippers.

It didn't matter that Pia's role in the movie was little more than a featured support. She was dressed for stardom.

"Watch, Jeanne!" Pia laughed and spun dizzyingly around three times, showing off the gradations of swirling blue gossamer; tiny beads and seed pearls in varying shades of blue twinkled and captured the light as she moved. "There! Aren't I beautiful?"

"Yes," agreed Jeanne and Mathilde together. They laughed, and even Pia joined them in sharing the warmth of the moment.

The doorbell rang, and instantly they grew quiet. "Can it be Wes already?" asked Mathilde. But she peeked out the window and saw Mrs. Armitage's car instead of a limo.

"Am I early?" asked the teacher as she entered the house. Then she caught sight of Pia and Mathilde. "Why, Mrs. Decameron, you look absolutely lovely," she said.

Mathilde blushed. "Thank you. We're . . . going out."

"It's my sister's movie debut!" Jeanne explained in a rush. "Isn't it exciting?"

"It's my *premiere*," Pia corrected.

Spell it, Mrs. Armitage thought, remembering Pia's attempt to sabotage her sister in last semester's spelling bee. Still, despite her dislike for the girl, one fact was

175

undeniable: Pia Decameron was a beauty.

Aloud the teacher said, "Well, I hope your . . . premiere goes well. Come, Jeanne, we don't want to keep the other students waiting."

Jeanne collected her jacket and script from the sofa. "Oh, I *wish* Wes was here already so I could see him in his tux!" She kissed Mathilde. "Give him a hug for me. And memorize *everything* that happens tonight—I want to hear about all of it from start to finish!"

She turned to Pia, who stood posing at the arch. She touched her cheek lightly to her sister's. "I hope . . . I hope tonight is . . . a great beginning, Pia. And . . . the success that you want it to be."

Pia regarded her quizzically. "You really *mean* that, don't you?"

A smile formed on Jeanne's lips as she nodded. "Yes, I really mean it, Pia." The words cheered her. She wished her sister well, and it was a good feeling.

Five minutes later, the sleek black limousine pulled up in front of the house.

"He's here!" Pia called from her post at the window. She watched as neighbors paused to gawk at the car. Curtains in windows parted surreptitiously, and faces appeared in them to catch a glimpse of Wesley Guest as he emerged from the rear of the enormous automobile. Tall and striking in his black tuxedo and pleated white shirt, he straightened his satin bow tie and, with a jaunty spring in his step, trotted up the path to the door.

Pia flung it open before he could ring the bell.

She saw immediately that the pains she had taken with her clothes and makeup had not been wasted. She withheld a smile of self-satisfaction and closed the door behind Wesley, while wondering if his eyes were still on her.

He had remained in the foyer, and Pia moved closer, using the excuse of her greeting to kiss his cheek. He did not return the gesture.

But he smelled so good! "You look very handsome" was all she said.

"Thank you . . . young lady." He stepped past her. "Is your mother ready?"

"Almost. By the way, I suppose I should thank you, too."

"For what?"

She executed a smaller spinaround than she'd performed for Mathilde and Jeanne. "For this."

He nodded politely. "That's what charge accounts are for. Besides, we're going to be family."

Pia didn't have time to reply. Mathilde entered just then, pulling on the three-quarter-length gloves that ended at the very beginning of the black fox-trimmed sleeves of her jacket. Her mouth went dry when she saw Wes, always so magnificent-looking, but tonight so much a star. His eyes, which dazzled at the sight of her, seemed to say, "And so much in love."

There was an almost palpable silence in the foyer, a silence Mathilde had come to recognize; it was present whenever Pia was with them. She hoped her older daughter wasn't going to be difficult, especially on *her* night.

"Are you willing to be seen with me?" asked Mathilde, partly teasing, partly in need of reassurance.

Wesley turned to drink in her loveliness. He was as eager to show her off as he was to have her all to himself.

"Always willing," he said. "Forever."

"I'm nervous, Wes," she admitted.

"You'll put them all to shame, darling."

The purr of the idling motor mingled with the noise

177

of the large crowd, a noise that gradually increased to a roar with each halting, forward movement that brought them closer to the barricaded bleachers filled with screaming fans. Gigantic Klieg lights swept the evening sky; the flashing bulbs of cameras set sequined gowns and jewels to sparkling.

The limousine's fully stocked bar had remained closed without Mathilde's having to request it. A drink might have helped to settle her nerves, perhaps Wes's, too, but Pia was with them. Mathilde and Wes had discussed Pia's possible weakness toward alcohol and agreed. There was no point in tempting fate.

Pia peered out at the scene through the closed window of the limo. Beneath the pastel neon tubing that spelled "Pantages," Wesley Guest's name was emblazoned across the glittering marquee. Below it, the movie's title: *His Share of Heaven*.

Although her own name would appear only in the rolling credits of the film, this could be, as Jeanne had wished for her sister, Pia's great beginning. If she wasn't the star, at least she was in the picture and on the *arm* of the star.

Soon, she vowed solemnly. Soon it'll be *my* name above the title.

"By the way, Pia," Wes was saying, "most of the industry people I've introduced you to will be here this evening."

"I know," she answered without taking her eyes from the window.

"If a name escapes you, it's understandable. Just—"

"I'll remember their names. All of them," Pia replied. *"And* the names of their wives and husbands. And children, too." She turned and smiled. "I've read up on them. I even know their pets' names."

"That's . . . good . . ." Wes didn't try to hide his amazement. Taking Mathilde's hand, he asked, "How are *you* holding up?"

178

"I've forgotten my *own* name already," she answered with a tentative laugh.

"Try practicing with *Guest*," he said.

At last their limousine took the first position in line. An instant later, the passenger door was opened, although the driver was still seated behind the wheel.

Pia stepped out onto the red-carpeted pavement. A cool autumn breeze played with the filmy skirts of her gown and immediately set camera flashbulbs to popping. They temporarily blinded her; she blinked to red and green dots as the anonymous crowd murmured, "Isn't she gorgeous?" and "Who *is* she?"

When her vision finally cleared, Pia was looking up into the face of the tall, uniformed young man who had opened the door of the limo. He winked at her and she smiled in return.

More flashes popped as Mathilde emerged. The more ardent among the fans already recognized her from candid photos in recent issues of movie magazines. She was known in the captions as the "constant companion" of Wesley Guest. To much of the crowd, however, she was a stranger, no matter how stunning she might be, and the spectators were growing restless.

Two TV cameras and a newsreel team were gathered around a man standing at a podium near the entrance to the theater. Mathilde couldn't recall his name, but she'd seen him before, during coverage of events such as these for Fox Movietone News. She'd never dreamed of coming face-to-face with him. The man was announcing the celebrities' names as they passed, and, if famous enough, the stars were invited to "say a few words for our viewing audience." Mathilde knew Wesley would be asked to speak and hoped they'd ignore her presence alongside him; she'd never have known what to say.

Pia heard the announcer's voice over the microphone before she actually saw him. "And, if I'm not mistaken," he boomed, "we have with us—is it?—yes! The star of tonight's picture, Wesley Guest!"

Wesley appeared from inside the limousine at the very moment his name was pronounced. The crowd went wild. He acknowledged them with a wide grin and waved his left hand as his right reached for Mathilde's arm and held it tightly.

"You're . . . you're good at this," she said, her voice quavering.

"It's taken years," he answered through teeth locked in a smile. He could feel her trembling and strengthened his grip. "It won't take you long, I promise."

He glanced over at Pia, who was entranced by the mob and waving back at them as though she were the one for whom they had assembled and waited since dawn.

Then Wesley noticed the uniformed doorman who had been trying to catch his eye. The young man's face was familiar.

"Hiya, Wes!" he said quickly. "Rod Raynor—remember me? I did a bit part in your last picture . . . ?"

Wesley remembered. A bad actor who drank his lunch and was chronically late on the set.

"Yes . . . yes, of course," Wesley said politely. "Nice to see you."

They shook hands as a photographer yelled, "Hey, Mac, get outa the shot, willya?"

Raynor ignored the request and said, "Good luck in there tonight. And if you uh . . . happen to hear of anything I might be right for . . ."

"Certainly, Rod. Now . . . if you'll excuse us . . . ?"

"Oh, yeah, sure." He stepped back and allowed Wesley to lead Mathilde toward the announcer at the podium. Rod Raynor winked once more at Pia. This time Mathilde noticed.

"Do you know him, Wes?" she asked as they blinked their way through hundreds more popping flashbulbs.

"A beach bum masquerading as an actor," said Wes.

"But he's awfully cute," Pia noted, while smiling for the cameras.

"He's trouble," Wes insisted. Then he stepped up to the podium to say a few words to his screaming fans.

Wesley greeted with relief the dimming of the houselights and the start of the picture. Twenty minutes of smiling, handshaking, and introducing Mathilde and Pia to people he hardly knew or liked had exhausted him.

He was proud of Mathilde. She'd managed graciousness with an ease that belied the insecurity he knew she was suffering.

And he was impressed, though not surprised, with Pia. By instinct she seemed to understand the behavior required at a Hollywood premiere. She hadn't gushed over the stars he knew she adored; she never let it be known—nor even suggested—that she might feel less than their equal. Probably, he mused, because she doesn't. She'd commented on the number of luminaries in attendance. Wesley had explained that most were under contract to the studio and as such had been *ordered* to be there. Pia had nodded, accepting the custom as part and parcel of the industry she was preparing to conquer.

Fifteen minutes into the picture, Wesley realized that it could be in trouble. The editing was erratic, and for the first time he perceived himself as, if not old, definitely aging. To him, his performance seemed stilted and ill at ease with the character he was portraying.

Maybe *His Share of Heaven* hadn't been a wise choice. His swashbuckler films of the past decade were fading from vogue at the box office, but perhaps a leading role with less of a father image would have been better strategy. If *His Share* turned out to be a smash, the studio's lack of imagination would button-hole him to a series of "daddy" roles, and he wasn't ready to become Spencer Tracy, yet.

And if it should flop? That would mean a panicky scramble for decent scripts with genuine *acting* roles. His next picture was a light comedy, but that film wouldn't be released for ten months. His future career could depend upon the coming year.

The coming year. Mathilde was sitting beside him. He took her hand and pressed it gently. The coming year would find him married to this wonderful woman. Yes, and stepfather to two young girls on the verge of adult-hood. Pia was already more than enough to handle.

What about Jeanne? He smiled to himself. Fatherly roles might *not* be too far off the mark—certainly he felt a paternal affection for Mathilde's younger daughter, a fondness fostered by more than their mutual interest in acting on the stage.

Theater. How many years had it been since he'd done a play?

Broadway. Wes allowed his mind to wander. A play might help to reshape his image. He could afford to take some time off for a limited run in New York. Mathilde would love New York. He'd speak to her about it later tonight. From now on, his career moves would affect a family; it was no longer a matter of Wesley Guest's decisions alone. And somehow the prospect wasn't in the least disagreeable to him.

At that moment Olympia Decameron made her first appearance on the screen, and Wesley knew that very soon there would be more than one star in the family.

*　　*　　*

Mathilde's daughter stood before her, fifteen feet tall and glowing in the dark.

If asked, Mathilde would have been unable to describe her feelings. At first she attributed the emotion to maternal pride. But she dismissed that as the truth began to emerge: the celluloid image of Pia projected onto a CinemaScope screen was in many ways more real than the flesh-and-blood Pia seated in the auditorium. Her screen presence was formidable. She *belonged* there, larger than life.

Mathilde was overwhelmed by a deepening realization: that the offscreen world would never be big enough to hold Pia. Mathilde was aware of her daughter's effect on the audience. As earlier, the whispers of "Who is she?" buzzed through the air. But outside the theater the voices had been those of ogling fans; here, instead, the questions were being voiced by "insiders," the powerful and influential leaders of the movie community. They weren't being taken in by a capricious child named Pia; they were enthralled, they were falling in love en masse with a presence, and her name was Olympia Decameron.

As she watched, fascinated, Mathilde saw that Pia—the Pia to whom she had given life, nurtured, and tried to understand for fourteen years—was gone.

I couldn't do it, Mathilde thought, almost laughing to herself. Her former, private fantasies of stardom faded like smoke caught in the light of a movie projector. They drifted away, dissipating in the air, yet lifting from Mathilde an enormous burden.

I don't want this anymore. I never really did.

I want Wesley.

Pia studied her performance with objectivity, even to thinking in the third person: Her spit curls are a definite plus, but the set is too tight. She needs more mascara, a little less eye shadow. Her liner is too harsh, but better lighting would have helped. She looks best when her head is tilted to one side; she must never again allow them to photograph her in right profile; still, it's a good face. Her acting is adequate but a bit hokey. Liz or Natalie—the bitch—would have given it a lot less, which in this case would have been more. But in all fairness, when she's had as much experience as they have, she'll know better, too.

And it can't be all that bad; everyone's watching *her,* not Wesley. He does know how to make it look easier than it is, though. And God, he's handsome.

An older man, but handsome.

Mama's, but handsome.

Mama's.

In the lobby the endless—almost ten minutes— photo session was ending. Gerry Byrne, the picture's director, had posed with the leading lady, then with Wes, then with Pia, now all four of them together. No one seemed to take notice that Mathilde stood off to one side, alone.

She felt a hand gently touch her arm and turned to see Lydia Genesco.

"How are you managing?" she asked with a wan smile.

"Better than earlier," answered Mathilde. "But how are you? You look . . . a bit tired."

Lydia's face was pale beneath her makeup, and she was leaning against the wall as though for support.

"I *am* tired. My back bothers me if I sit for too long."

"But you're going to the party . . . ?"

"I'm afraid I'll have to. Neal's expected, so of course I'll go. It's part of the show. Anyway, I just wanted to say that you should be very proud. Pia really has 'it.'"

"Yes," answered Mathilde. "I suppose she does."

Lydia paused; she seemed to be choosing her next words carefully. "Mathilde . . . what if Jeanne . . . has it, too?"

"It" was beginning to sound like a contagious disease. She regarded Lydia with curiosity, then spoke. "Why do you ask that . . . about Jeanne?"

"Well, Wes seems to think she's quite gifted. I'd like to form my own opinion."

"May I ask why?"

"I stopped acting when I married Neal. But now and then I take a pupil to coach—if I feel he or she has special talent. Wes says Jeanne has and thinks I could help bring it out."

"And you want to see her do the Saint Joan monologue next week, don't you?"

Lydia nodded. "Wes suggested it, but he thought I'd better ask you."

"That's like him. Thanks. But isn't Jeanne the one to ask?"

"I think not," said Lydia. "It might make her nervous. Unless of course you mention it to her offhandedly. I'll leave it up to you."

After a pause, Mathilde asked, "Lydia, what if you see her and *don't* think she's . . . special?"

"Then I won't coach her. Simple. It's only *my* opinion, after all, and God knows I've been wrong before."

"Then . . . could you . . . help Pia?"

"It's not likely she'll need help," she answered with a slight smile. "Pia has an instinct for the camera that experience can only ripen. They shouldn't let an acting coach within ten feet of her."

"They," Mathilde repeated, gesturing to the crowd that completely enveloped Wes and Pia. "You mean all

185

of *them,* don't you?"

"Yes. Right now, Pia's future is being planned and charted. The whole town knows she has what it takes—including connections, thanks to Wes. She's being, as they say, 'discovered.'"

"I have no say in it, do I? In her future, I mean."

"Mathilde," Lydia said, drawing closer. "I . . . thought you wanted this for her."

"I thought I did, too. I'm just concerned. About what it may do to her. It's not an easy life, is it?"

Lydia shook her head. "It's posh. Lucrative. But even for the biggest and the best, no, it isn't easy."

Mathilde glanced from Lydia to Pia. Her arms were around Wes, but Mathilde could see that her daughter's main interest at this moment was in the collection of strangers who had suddenly become friends. Pia took no notice of Joey Crane, who stood at the perimeter of the circle. After a few minutes he turned and walked away. Pia was the birthday cake, from which everyone wanted a piece.

Is it already too late to help her? Mathilde wondered. The answer was there, in Pia's eyes and on the faces of the admiring throng.

But, Mathilde reflected, Jeanne still has a chance. Wes seems to have understood her sooner and better than I did. Perhaps Lydia has, too.

"Come with us next week," Mathilde said at last. "We'll do . . . whatever you and Wes . . . think best."

The bleachers and barricades had been taken down, the crowd of spectators dispersed. Mathilde, Pia, and Wes waited in the lobby until the car was brought around.

Every nerve ending in Pia's body was tingling. And the evening isn't even over yet! she thought. There's still

186

the party to come! She frowned at the prospect of having to sip ginger ale all night, but both Mama and Wes had been adamant on the subject. Well, probably with good reason; a clear head would help her through any business discussions concerning future contracts. *Some* sacrifices were necessary on the road to the top.

Pia had seen Joey Crane out of the corner of her eye, but she'd had no time for him—not with all those important people dying to meet her. Too bad so few of the men fell into her "eligible" category. Most of the studio bigwigs were either ugly and fat with cigar-stained teeth or old enough to be her grandfather. And the really handsome actors—Tab Hunter and Robert Wagner among them—had brought dates.

In fact, Pia reflected, the only cute guy without a girlfriend was the doorman who had winked at her earlier. True, he was *only* a doorman, but she'd liked his attention; there was something about the way he'd looked at her . . . Even now, as they waited for the limousine, she found her eyes searching for him among the other red-capped, uniformed attendants.

She spotted him leaning against the box-office window and smoking a cigarette. His too-full lips drew in the smoke, but the cigarette remained dangling from his mouth. From beneath heavy lids, his gray eyes strayed to Pia and he grinned the way he had before. Pia noticed that he needed a shave; otherwise his features might have given him a baby-faced quality. Now he offered Pia that look—half wink, half come-hither—and she found herself winking back. The off-limits aspect of his gaze, and the seductive manner with which he ran his fingers through his greased, dirty-blond ducktail hair, seemed to flash a sign that read: FORBIDDEN. It transformed an otherwise ordinary, everyday face into the fabric of which Elvis and Fabian had been fashioned.

And Pia found him . . . tantalizing.

"There's the car," said Wes. He pushed open the lobby door before any of the doormen could hop to attention.

Rodney Raynor put on his hat, flicked the cigarette butt into the gutter, and ran forward to the redcap at the curb.

"I'll get this one, Jack. Take your break," he said, rushing to open the rear door of the limo before Jack could protest.

He's here again, Mathilde thought, remembering Wes's dislike of the young man. She quickly climbed into the car.

"Thanks, Rod," said Wes, handing him several bills' tip.

"Thank *you,* Wes! And . . . hey, I heard it went great!" Rod turned then to Pia. "And especially for you."

"Thanks."

"Get into the car, Pia," said Wes.

She looked up at him as though she'd been challenged. Then, ignoring the order, Pia turned to face Rod again. "Go see it," she said. "It's a good picture."

"I might," answered Rod. "Maybe I'll take you with me."

"Maybe you will. I'd see it twice."

"What's your phone number?"

"Pia!" Mathilde leaned out from the backseat. "Get *in!*"

Pia obeyed but, stepping from the curb, she said to Rod, "My number? That's for me to know . . . and for you to find out."

Wes followed her into the cavernous limo, and Rod slammed the door. Before the driver pulled away, Rod managed to wink at Pia through the window.

As the car entered the stream of traffic, Wes asked, "Was that really necessary?"

"There's no harm done," answered Pia indifferently.

"If he calls you, you are not to have anything to do with him."

"Wesley," Pia replied in a matter-of-fact voice, "you are *not* my father." She turned toward Mathilde and waited, expecting her mother to countermand the order.

But Mathilde remained face-forward, avoiding her daughter's eyes. To ignore Joey Crane was rude enough. However, to actually be interested in Rod Raynor—to prefer him over Joey—was beyond comprehension. *Pia* herself was beyond comprehension.

"Mama . . . ?" Pia asked with a petulant whine.

"You heard Wes," replied Mathilde. "And his word is the same as mine. Do you understand, Pia?"

"Completely, Mama . . ." was all she said.

Chapter Thirteen

"Mama will kill you if she sees you like that," said Jeanne as she sat brushing her hair.

With the tip of her pinky, Pia rubbed in another layer of blue eye shadow from the tube in her hand. Then, spitting onto the mascara cake to moisten it, she ran the little brush back and forth until it was loaded with black.

"Mama won't kill me, because Mama won't know," she answered without looking up from her work. She blinked several times, careful not to let her wet upper lashes dot the ridge of skin beneath her brow. Her pursed lips and wide-eyed expression gave her the aspect of a Kewpie doll.

"Are you going out with that guy—what was his name—Joey?" asked Jeanne.

"Don't be silly," Pia scoffed. "He's just a child." She leaned closer to the mirror to check her handiwork and added, "I have a date with Rodney Raynor." She turned to her sister. "I've been seeing him since the premiere party. He's an actor. Gorgeous. Even handsomer than Wesley." She had stopped using Wes's nickname since he'd announced his plans to marry Mathilde.

190

Jeanne had braided her hair and now pinned the braids close to her head. Pia glanced at her and frowned.

"That's an ugly hairdo. You look like a country bumpkin."

"But it makes me *feel* more like Joan of Arc," answered Jeanne. "It'll help me concentrate when we do the scene in front of an audience."

"God, I wouldn't be caught *dead* with my hair like that. Don't you want to look pretty—especially with people watching you?" That reminded Pia to add extra rouge to her cheeks. "You can borrow some of my makeup if you want," she offered.

"Thanks, but Joan wouldn't wear color. I'll just use a pale base and powder."

"God, you'll be invisible! You call that *acting?*"

Jeanne shrugged. Her mind was on the script, on the blocking of the scene, and not on the polemics she and her sister had gone over many times in the past weeks.

"Well, you won't have to worry about being compared with Ingrid Bergman," Pia said, exhaling audibly. *"She's* beautiful."

Jeanne ignored her sister's remark and the two of them continued applying their makeup: Jeanne sponging palest Pan-Cake on her cheeks, Pia adding more rouge to hers.

Finally Pia said, "By the way, you won't mention to Mama that I'm out with Rod, will you? I mean, in case she calls."

"Does Mama know him?" asked Jeanne.

Pia nodded. "Yes. And I don't think she approves. I *know* Wesley doesn't."

"What do they have against him?" asked Jeanne.

Rather than repeat Wes's assessment of her boy-friend, Pia shrugged. "I guess it's the difference in our ages. As if *chronological* age has anything to do with

191

maturity. After all, it's *not* as if he's *old.*" More and more Pia's speech pattern was adopting mannerisms that stressed the words she thought important in a style that sounded like voiced italics. Jeanne wondered if her sister was consciously or unconsciously imitating Bette Davis.

"Just how . . . mature . . . is this Rodney?" Jeanne asked.

Pia beamed, delighted at her sister's question. With a practiced, nonchalant wave of her hand, she replied, "Oh, I can't be *sure.* But I'd *guess* that Rod is twenty-five . . . or twenty-six . . ."

Jeanne regarded the image in Pia's mirror. With all that makeup and her hair waved and held by combs on each side of her temples—except for the trained "trademark" spit curls—Pia could pass for seventeen or eighteen, especially on the arm of an "older" man.

But what on earth, Jeanne wondered, will they *talk* about . . . ?

Joan of Lorraine was last on the evening's program. Earlier that month, Mrs. Armitage had decided to present her prize pupil in a monologue, rather than in a scene with someone else. Together she and Jeanne had selected the "Light your fires" speech. Few of the other students in the school's drama club possessed more than minimal talent, and even those with promise seemed eager to be assigned "easy," undemanding scripts. In this way, the boys were unhampered by rehearsal schedules that might conflict with football practice, and the girls could spend more time at primping with costumes and makeup than with working on interpretation.

By contrast, Jeanne was determined to explore every facet of the character she would portray. Each day she pored over other plays on the subject of the young maid of Orléans. She read Shaw and Anouilh and went over and over Anderson's words for their inner meanings. She used each rehearsal to try different approaches, to experiment with the role. Learning the lines would never be enough.

So immersed was Jeanne in her heroine that she'd only half heard Mathilde's words that afternoon. Mama and Wes would be at the performance, and . . .

For the life of her, Jeanne couldn't recall what else her mother had said.

Now she was sitting "backstage" in the school orchestra's practice room, which was doubling tonight, so read the sign on the double wooden doors, as MAKEUP and WARDROBE. A hall guard stood outside to make certain no one disturbed the "actors'" preparation.

Mrs. Armitage had given the dozen students a pep talk at the start of the evening. Most had chewed gum or rolled their eyes heavenward, and Jeanne had wondered whether she was the only person there who cared about the evening or about the sacrifice of Mrs. Armitage's time and energy.

Two by two they had gone downstairs to the auditorium, and two by two they had performed their "safe" duets from the dated staples of the school's repertoire, plays that required nothing more than recitation: *Harvey*, *Oh to be Sixteen Again*, *Junior Miss*.

A squawkbox intercom had been installed so that the next students scheduled on the program could reach the stage on cue. Jeanne had listened as the boys raced through or mumbled their lines, and the girls all seemed to be going for a breathy Kim Novak or

Marilyn Monroe, a perky Sandra Dee, or in a few more ambitious cases, the sophistication of Greer Garson and Irene Dunne.

Then, after nearly two hours of waiting, the scene from *Sabrina Fair* ended and it was Jeanne's turn. The adrenaline butterflies, which had been absent until now, suddenly appeared and made up for their late arrival.

"Don't worry," Mrs. Armitage reassured her as she reached the dark wings offstage left. "Nerves are a good sign. Now just go out there and . . . break a leg!"

Jeanne had read enough biographies of famous actresses to recognize the good-luck wish long before Charles Goodman had said it to her on opening night of *Peter Pan*. And she'd been a hit as Wendy. But that hadn't been due to luck. She'd worked hard for that "luck." Remember that, she reminded herself as her knees began to wobble. You've worked hard for this, too.

"Just breathe and relax," encouraged her teacher, gently shoving her protégée toward the stage.

Jeanne nodded and inhaled deeply as she strode to the center. Find the light, she told herself. The warmest spot. And exhale. In, out. Again.

She almost panicked at first sight of the auditorium filled with people. Oh, no! she thought as her mind went blank. I can't recall a single word! Not even my opening line!

Inhale, exhale. *"King of Heaven . . ."* she began. Oh, yes . . . it's there. I haven't lost it. Inhale, exhale. *"I come to fulfill a vow."* As the words returned to her, she began to relax.

"But don't relax too much," whispered Mrs. Armitage from the wings.

*　　*　　*

Only when it was over, and she saw Mama and Wes coming toward her with Neal Genesco and his wife Lydia, did Jeanne suddenly recall the rest of what her mother had said.

"I forgot you were coming!" she blurted out as the director's wife embraced her.

"My dear child," said Neal Genesco, taking her hand. "My dear, dear child." He was shaking his head, as though in bewilderment.

"Is something wrong?" asked Jeanne, terrified that he had hated it, that she'd been a disaster.

"Wrong?" He laughed softly and turned to Wesley, who was standing alongside him. "I regret only that André Bertrand could not see this vision before he cast that poor little Corinna Sedgewicke at Edinburgh last year."

"André Bertrand?" said Jeanne. "Corinna . . . who?"

"Sedgewicke," explained Wesley. "She played Joan at the Edinburgh Festival. And she wasn't very good."

Genesco said, "It wasn't her fault. It was too much for her. She'd never acted before." Then he considered his words. "Of course, except for *Peter Pan*, neither have you . . ."

When a crestfallen expression crossed Jeanne's face, Lydia Genesco offered, "Didn't you hear the applause? You were splendid! Remarkable, in fact. As touching as Ingrid Bergman."

That reminded Jeanne that her sister was nowhere in sight. "Mama," she said, turning to Mathilde, "where's Pia? I thought she was coming."

"She was complaining about a headache," said her mother. "I gave her some aspirins, and she had fallen asleep when we left." Mathilde wasn't concerned; Pia's headache was most likely an excuse to avoid having to watch her sister as the center of attention. "She'll be sorry to have missed your performance," added

195

Mathilde for the Genescos' benefit.

"But you're sure Olympia's all right?" asked Lydia.

"I'm sure she is," said Mathilde. "It's that extra homework. Now that Pia's in high school, she spends all her time reading at the library. I think she's having eyestrain headaches. She may even need glasses."

Jeanne was struck by Mama's remark. Pia would *never, ever* wear glasses—not in public, anyway. But suddenly her mind flashed to Mama's first comment. About Pia's spending all her time at the library.

That's really strange, thought Jeanne. Except for the past week's rehearsals, *I've* been at the library every afternoon since school reopened. And I've never once seen Pia.

But speculation on her sister's afternoon whereabouts would have to wait. Jeanne found herself at the very apex of a crowd of "industry people"—agents, directors, and producers who had been invited to the performance. She was amazed at the turnout—and that they'd stayed through to the end. Two newspaper reviewers had even come.

In Friday's paper, one of them would write: "Jeanne Decameron left a California schoolgirl in the wings and, as her namesake of another time and of another place, soared to unexpected glory."

It would be her first review.

Rod's secondhand Cadillac convertible was an unfortunate shade of bilious green; however, Pia reasoned, it's still a Caddy. And *anything* was preferable to Joey Crane's ugly black Studebaker, with its lookalike back and front. Just as Rod was preferable to Joey—or to any of the *boys* she knew.

He stopped at the deserted beachfront but didn't come around to open her door. Instead, he reached across her to unlock it. Pia knew he'd done it on purpose so his arm could brush across her breasts; she'd seen it in countless movies.

She'd also seen actresses sigh in response, their mouths slightly parted, their eyelids fluttering. She could do that. *Any* actress could do that.

"Ohh," she murmured softly.

Rod looked up at her and whispered, "You like that, baby?"

"Mmm," she replied.

"Good. There's more to come." He leaned over, placing his right hand on her knee for leverage, and opened the glove compartment. "Thirsty?"

"That depends on what you're offering," said Pia.

"Well," he answered, "it's stronger than that watered-down stuff we were drinking at the roadhouse."

"Oh, then I'll try some . . ." No wonder I'm not feeling high, Pia thought, disappointed. She hadn't realized that a bar might dilute the whisky.

"Let's take the bottle and go for a walk," Rod suggested. Before she could reply, he was out of the car. This time he did come around to Pia's side to open the door for her. He also leaned over the backseat and pulled out a beach blanket.

"C'mon," he said, taking her hand. "Take off your shoes and let's have a look at the moon."

The silvery reflection on the water and the cool sand under her stockinged feet made Pia think of the scene between Deborah Kerr and Burt Lancaster in *From Here to Eternity*. Of course, she and Rod were younger than their screen counterparts, and the beach in the movie didn't have pebbles and shells stubbing Deborah Kerr's toes every few yards. Still, the settings had their similarities.

"Let's sit here," said Rod, bending down to spread the blanket over a relatively smooth patch of damp sand.

Pia dropped her sandals, then joined him. "It's nice

here," she said. "So quiet."

"And secluded," he added. "Here." He unscrewed the cap of the bottle and handed it to her. "I didn't bring glasses."

"That's okay," she said. "It's more like a picnic."

"Yeah . . ." While Pia took a swig of scotch, Rod pulled a comb from his shirt pocket and smoothed the sides of his hair. Pia thought it was rude to do this in front of her, but she said nothing. Instead, she took another swallow.

"Here, it's my turn, baby," said Rod, taking the bottle from her. "I mean, relaxing is one thing. But we don't want you passing out on me, do we? That would spoil the fun."

Pia almost giggled at the way he'd pronounced *fun*. He's trying so hard to play the big, strong hero, she thought.

A moment later, though, she didn't find it worth giggling over. Rod propped the whisky bottle into a well of sand and moved closer to her. She didn't like the smell of scotch on his breath. Some of the liquor had spilled on his plaid shirt, and Pia realized that if she came home with any telltale signs of scotch on her own clothing, there'd be hell to pay.

Wait a minute. Mama wouldn't *be* there when she got home. Mama and Wesley had gone to Palm Springs with the Genescos and wouldn't be back until tomorrow afternoon . . .

Rod broke into her thoughts then. "C'mere, baby. Don't be a stranger."

"I'm not. I'm thinking."

"What about?" His fingers began tracing the outline of her features.

"Stop it, Rod, you'll ruin my spit curls," she said.

"Oh, sorry . . ." He pretended to draw away, although he didn't move an inch. "We need to loosen you up." He pulled the bottle from its sand-coaster and handed it to her.

Maybe another drink would take her mind off Mama and Wesley. She took a long swallow.

"Boy, you sure can put it away," said Rod. Then, teasingly, he added, "Does your mother know?"

"It's none of my mother's business," said Pia. "I'm old enough to take care of myself."

"Well, I *do* believe that," said Rod. "It must run in the family."

"Huh?" She bristled slightly.

"Hey, baby, no offense. I can't blame Wesley Guest—your mom's a real looker. Probably knows it, too—like you. And you should be happy. With Wesley Guest around to pay the bills, you'll *all* be on Easy Street."

Pia didn't understand why in that moment she wanted to strike him, to jam Rod's words back down his self-satisfied, presumptuous throat. Inadvertently, her hand reached out to slap him.

But Rod caught her wrist in midair. "What's the matter, baby? It's no secret, is it? She's even got him promising to marry her, if what I read in *Photoplay* is true."

Tears began welling in Pia's eyes. She didn't care, even if Rod misinterpreted the reason.

"Hey, c'mon, I'm sorry. But you've got to face facts." He brushed her hair with the hand that had gripped her wrist.

She tried to resist, but he laughed quietly. "Take it easy, I won't touch your spit curls."

"I want to go home."

"No, you don't," he coaxed. "Not really. You want to stay here with me. C'mon, admit it."

"I want to go home," she repeated, her phrase as unconvincing to herself as it was to Rod.

"No, what you want is another drink. And then you want to do with me what your mom is out doing with

199

Wesley Guest."

Pia tried to block his words from her mind, but in their place appeared the image of her mother in Wesley Guest's arms. Her heart began to pound furiously; she could feel the pulse beating against her temples, just beneath the spit curls she wouldn't let Rodney touch.

Suddenly she stiffened and sat up straight. "You're right, Rod," she said. "I *don't* want to go home. And I want . . . more . . . than another drink."

He nodded knowingly. "That's my baby," he murmured, stroking her cheek. "I like a gal who plays hard to get in the beginning. But it's been a month. Don't you think it's time we . . . got to know each other . . . better?"

Before Pia could reply, Rod lowered his face to hers and began kissing her. His lips tasted like scotch, and the odor mingled with his perfumed hair tonic. It turned Pia's stomach.

"Oh, baby," he said, blowing into her ear as his hands unbuttoned her blouse. "Oh, I've wanted you since the first time I saw you."

Pia sighed with boredom, but evidently Rod mistook the sigh for increasing arousal, because now he reached inside her blouse and began fondling her small, round breasts through the lace of her bra. She felt nothing, but when her blouse fell away and Rod commanded her to take off the bra, she complied.

"It's cold," she said, shivering.

"It won't be for long," he said, lowering his head. As Rod's tongue moved in circles around her pointed nipples, Pia's eyes gazed up at the moon.

"Oh, baby, baby . . ." Rod's hand went beneath her flowered skirt.

Pia hated his calling her "baby," but she didn't have a chance to tell him. His fingers were unfastening the garters from her stockings, and Pia wanted to be the one to roll down her nylons; this was her last pair without runs, and Rod wouldn't think to remove them carefully.

She slid them off and laid them neatly at the edge of the blanket.

"Take off your garter belt and panties, too, so we can get to the good stuff," he said.

God, thought Pia. I'll bet he thinks I find that kind of talking sexy. He's a lousy actor.

Aloud she teased, "Why don't you help me, Rod?"

"Sure. Why not? Lie down."

She lay back on the scratchy blanket and tried to land in a position that wouldn't ruin her curls. Earlier, in her haste to be on time for their date, she'd forgotten to spray her waves in place. Now she hoped her hair was fanned out the way she'd seen in the Lustre Creme Shampoo ads. Well, if not, it was dark out . . .

Rod undid her garter belt and slid her panties down to her ankles, where Pia slipped her feet out of them.

"There we are," he said. "All done . . . and ready."

Pia was covered with goosebumps. The breeze was cold against her body. She shivered as Rod's warm hand went between her thighs.

"It won't be long, baby," he said. "I promise."

She hoped he'd hurry. She didn't want to catch pneumonia out here.

Rod's fingers parted her mound of pubic hair and found the lips of her vagina. He began massaging them, and Pia felt a slight twitch as he played with her clitoris, but the feeling quickly passed. She closed her eyes. An image of Wesley appeared then, and its suddenness made Pia's entire body jerk.

Quickly Rod rose. "You're fast, baby. I'll be right there," he said, tearing off his clothes.

Soon he stood over her, straddling her with his legs, his tall, naked body shining in the moonlight. Pia looked up at his muscular limbs, his flat stomach, his erect penis.

"Oh, baby, have I got something for you," he said, moving to a position over her.

Wesley wouldn't have said it like that, whispered a voice inside Pia's head.

"You'd better not get me pregnant," she warned.

"Christ, baby, you mean you're not wearing a diaphragm?"

"It isn't up to me," Pia snapped. She wasn't going to admit that she'd never done this before.

"Shit. Just a sec." Rod rose and hurried back to the car. A moment later he was back. Ripping the tiny packet open, he took out a condom. "It's all right this time, baby," he said, placing it on his erection. "But next time, it's your responsibility. You're the lady."

Then he lowered himself and entered her.

"Owww," she wailed softly. "That hurt!"

Rod didn't speak. Pia thought he looked like someone doing push-ups as he plunged in and out. She stared at the stars to keep from laughing. She could almost see the Big Dipper among the passing clouds.

Rod's face became contorted as he approached climax. Pia hated the grotesque sounds he made during his final thrust. Earlier, she'd cried wolf; now she wanted to go home.

"How was it, baby?" asked Rod, rolling off her and onto the blanket.

"Wonderful," she lied, forcing a sigh.

"Next time it won't hurt," he said.

"Why not?"

"Because next time you won't be a virgin. Didn't your mother teach you *anything?* I mean, she's *gotta* know what it's about—after all, she's had two kids."

Pia tried to envision her father and Mama doing . . . what she and Rod had just done. She couldn't; Hank's face was superimposed by another image: Mama and Wesley again. Pia couldn't bear it. She had to do something to drive them from her mind.

She reached out to touch his shoulder. "Rod . . ."

He had rolled over to his shirt pocket for his comb, which he ran through his hair and then exchanged for a pack of Camels and a book of matches.

"Yeah, baby, what's up?" He lit the cigarette and took a puff.

"I was wondering . . . since it won't hurt again . . . do you have any more of those . . . those rubber things . . . ?"

"I've got a whole box—in case of emergencies." The corners of his mouth curved into a sly grin. "You *do* like it, don't you, baby . . . ?"

"Yes . . ."

"Well, it'll be even better the second time. You'll *love* it. So stay there—I'll be right back." He stubbed out the cigarette in the sand and hurried to the car.

This time, Pia wasn't bothered by the bumpy, cold sand beneath the blanket, nor by Rod's whisky breath and Vitalis. She didn't mind the damp chill in the night air, or even the wet stickiness between her legs. She lay back and let her mind go blank.

Rod was right about one thing: this time it didn't hurt. But he was wrong about something else. It wasn't better. She didn't love it. She didn't even like it. It would have been different with Wesley, but Mama was going to be the one to find that out. If she hadn't already.

And what if she had? Maybe Mama didn't like it, either—*even* with Wesley. That particular thought appealed to her, even if it did add to the ambiguity of her feelings.

By the time Rod drove her home later that night, Pia was certain of only two facts: that she was no longer a virgin, and that sex, at least with Rodney Raynor, wasn't all that it was cracked up to be.

Chapter Fourteen

Planning the wedding wasn't the complicated ordeal Mathilde had anticipated. She felt that eloping might have been still easier, but the studio wouldn't hear of that, and since they were handling most of the preparations, her own participation was minimal.

Every ounce of publicity would be wrung from the occasion. Mathilde cooperated fully, although she couldn't help feeling that her wedding to Wesley Guest was adopting the atmosphere of a carnival side show. She only hoped that the girls would be spared a center-ring spotlight.

Of course Pia was a studio commodity now; therefore, her presence at interviews, parties, and photo sessions was unavoidable. Because Jeanne was unknown to both the studio and the public at large, her very existence was played down. The stunning young mother—a policeman's *widow!*—of a budding star was marrying one of Antaen Pictures' major box-office names. That the bride-to-be had given birth to a second daughter was tacked onto articles as an afterthought. Mathilde hoped Jeanne wouldn't feel excluded, although she sensed that the "starlet's sister" would feel relieved, rather than left out.

With the studio supervising the "choreography" so efficiently, Mathilde had only to oversee the smaller, more personal details. She insisted on choosing her own trousseau. The head of publicity, Nathan Schutz, tried to veto even that, but when Mathilde described the wardrobe she had in mind, he was forced to admit that the lady possessed taste.

It was the single point he conceded. "We're experienced in these matters, Mrs. Decameron," he explained. "Antaen Pictures has been arranging marriages since the beginning of the star system."

Mathilde corrected him with a smile. "Arranging *weddings,* Mr. Schutz, not marriages."

He squinted. "Both. Besides, is there any difference?"

The studio had urged her to make Pia the maid of honor, but on this Mathilde stood firm. "I don't mind my younger daughter being relegated to the background for reasons of studio publicity," she told Nathan Schutz, "but I will *not* favor one daughter over the other at my own wedding." She was adamant, and finally Schutz gave in.

"On one condition," he said. "That you pick someone who photographs well and is *not*—you'll forgive the expression—one of your . . . uh . . . neighbors."

Mathilde offered no argument; she wasn't that close to any of her neighbors. But who was left?

Then it came to her, and Schutz was jubilant. Since Neal Genesco would be Wes's best man, Lydia Genesco could be Mathilde's matron of honor.

Nathan Schutz had devised a plan for press coverage not only of the wedding but of the honeymoon as well. A photographer and two reporters would accompany the bride and groom for the first two days of their trip, following separate private "audiences" with Louella and Hedda. After that, the newlyweds would be free until Wes was due back to begin his next picture.

What to do with the girls was the major decision to be made. "It would be adorable—and good publicity—to have Pia along," Nathan Schutz suggested. "Oh, and Jeanne, too . . ."

"Absolutely not," said Wes. But leaving them alone was out of the question, and at first it seemed as though there'd be no other alternative.

New York. It was Wes's idea, and Mathilde eagerly agreed. She'd never been farther east than Chicago.

"I'll admit to an ulterior motive," said Wes. "I'd like to find out if you take to the town."

"Are we planning to move there?" she asked.

"That depends." He explained his thoughts about doing a play, despite the fact that the reedited version of *His Share of Heaven* was doing well at the box office. "If you like New York, I'll have my agent start submitting scripts to look over."

"Wes . . ." Mathilde ventured, ". . . what if I hate it?"

"Then Broadway's out. I wouldn't have it any other way." He took her hand and kissed it. "But it'll be after Thanksgiving, and there are few places more charming than New York dressed up for Christmas. I also have a little cottage 'getaway' in Connecticut that we can sneak off to."

She laughed. "Wonderful. Just you, me, Pia, Jeanne . . . and Mr. Schutz?"

He burst into a wide grin, and Mathilde felt a warm tingle; she loved to make Wes smile.

Mathilde's wedding day began with the arrival of a legion of studio personnel. Experts in each of their

206

particular fields, these professionals descended upon the Decameron house in a caravan of sleek black limousines.

"It'll entertain the neighbors for a week," Mathilde observed, unsure whether that held appeal or not.

An assembly line was formed: the makeup man finished with Mathilde in her bedroom and moved down the hall to Pia, while the hairdresser took over with Mathilde. By the time Jeanne's makeup was powdered down in the kitchen, Pia's hair—with spit curls intact—was being Adorned and Mathilde was being zipped—and pinned—into her taupe silk knit Chanel suit. The production was a far cry from preparations for her first wedding, with the bargain-basement white nylon lace dress, the homemade veil, and stiff white pumps that didn't fit because they belonged to a friend. They'd been the "something borrowed," but not for superstition; there'd been no money for new shoes of her own.

Today, instead, the shoes were buttersoft kidskin in a shade of taupe that matched her three-quarter-length kid gloves. Both were slightly lighter than the suit. Her hat was a silk shantung cloche cut from the same fabric as her jacket and trimmed in brown mink. Diamond earrings sparkled from just beneath the fur; they'd been a present from Wes. "To go with your ring," he'd said.

When she looked in the bedroom mirror, Mathilde was almost tempted to ask, "Is this really me?"

The reflection smiled back as if to say, "You know it is, Mathilde. And it's the happiest day in your life."

Jeanne entered Mathilde's room to model her beige silk shirtwaist dress for Mama.

"Who was on the phone?" asked her mother, adjusting her hat for the third time. A woman from

Wardrobe was removing the suit jacket from a plastic-covered hanger and examining it for wrinkles.

"It was Mr. Schutz, Mama. I told him everything was all right but that you couldn't come to the phone."

"Thank you. I couldn't. Are you almost ready?"

"They just have to do my lipstick. And probably more powder so I won't shine like a light bulb."

Mathilde smiled. "You're being wonderfully patient, dear, and I appreciate it."

"Oh, Mama," said Jeanne, "I'm so excited for you—I'll do anything to help make it go smoothly."

"Well, just let them finish up, then, so we'll be ready."

Jeanne left her mother's room and started back to the kitchen. On her way there, she heard Pia's voice coming from their bedroom. "The makeup is *fine*. And this is all taking too long!"

"We just want you to look—"

"I *know*. My *best*. And I *do*. But *I* have an appointment—"

"Now, now," said the makeup man. "The wedding isn't for an hour and a half."

"I'm not talking about *that*. Just hurry, would you?"

Poor Pia, thought Jeanne as she reentered the kitchen. The studio must have scheduled an interview or a photo session to fill the time *before* the ceremony.

Jeanne was seated on a Formica and chrome chair facing the kitchen doorway when Pia hurried by ten minutes later.

"Pia!" she called.

Her sister turned to face her. But she wasn't dressed in the pink chiffon frock the studio had sent. She wore a white angora sweater and a circular black felt skirt with a large white poodle appliquéd on it.

"Pia—where are you going?"

"It's a . . . secret. Have fun . . ."

208

"But . . . the wedding ceremony . . . ?"

"Well . . . they'll just have to start without me!"

Jeanne couldn't believe her sister. "You'll . . . you'll be back in time for the reception, won't you? I mean, what will Mama and Wes say? And Mr. Schutz! Everyone's depending on you!"

"Oh, don't worry," answered Pia. "I'll *definitely* make the reception. I wouldn't miss *that* for the world!"

And, using it as an exit line, she was out the front door.

When Nathan Schutz arrived and found Pia gone, he exploded in near hysteria. "We're running way behind schedule," he said. "There's no time to go looking for her." To Jeanne his question carried an accusation. "Are you *sure* she didn't say where she was off to?"

"If she had, I would have told you."

"Jeanne isn't in the habit of lying, Mr. Schutz," said Mathilde indignantly, at the same time feeling both concern and a rising anger. Her own bridal nerves, and now this! Pia had managed to take center focus by her absence. And just where *was* she?

Nathan Schutz rushed Wes and Mathilde past the photographers they were to have posed for. Some excuse was made as he ushered them out of the house before anyone could ask why the bridal party was incomplete.

Mathilde fully expected Pia to stage her entrance by the time they reached the chapel—indeed, she half envisioned her unpredictable daughter rushing in and protesting at the instant it was asked "if there be anyone present who sees why this man and woman should not be wed . . ." The prospect terrified Mathilde throughout the ceremony.

But Pia did not appear.

Fear and worry vanished momentarily as Mathilde and Wesley were pronounced man and wife, and no thought of Pia crossed her mind as Wes bent to kiss his bride. But seconds later, as Nathan Schutz hurried them down the aisle and fairly pushed them into the waiting black Cadillac, Mathilde realized that something had to be done. Mother's instinct told her that no harm had befallen her daughter, but instinct did nothing to quell the uneasiness that had begun churning inside her.

The main floor of the private supper club had been taken over for the reception. As Mathilde and Wesley entered, George Jessel, standing on the raised musician's platform, announced through the microphone: "Ladies and gentlemen, Mr. and Mrs. Wesley Guest!"

The band struck up the opening chords of *Lohengrin*'s bridal chorus as bride and groom strode through the center of the applauding well-wishers. Mathilde and Wesley kissed, everyone cheered, and the photographers finally got their pictures.

Then the newlyweds led off the dancing. Wes had chosen "Love is a Many Splendored Thing." They waltzed to "their song," and it was their secret. Other guests soon joined in, and Mathilde, floating and whirling in Wes's arms, began to feel as though she were dancing to the musical score of her own life story, for which this moment was the happy ending. Better yet, the new beginning.

Neal Genesco, as best man, led the crowd in a toast. The room grew still as he raised his glass. "To Mathilde and Wes, the two brightest stars on the horizon—"

But before he could finish, a voice called out, "Make that four!"

Mathilde wheeled about. Her eyes searched the hushed, whispering crowd until at last she spied Pia, who stood with Rodney Raynor just inside the door.

Together they moved forward, laughing and waving people aside all the way to the head table. There they lifted two just-poured glasses of champagne, clinked them, and drained the contents.

Jeanne could feel her mother trembling beside her. It was obvious that Pia had been drinking; she wondered if it was as evident to the guests. Her eyes darted to Nathan Schutz. His face had turned ashen, his brow was covered in sweat. Quickly he rose, heading for the bandstand.

"Sorry we're late, everybody!" Pia announced. She held Rod's hand up overhead and they executed deep, clumsy curtain-call bows. "But you see, there's more than *one* bride here today!" Then, looking directly at Wesley, she added quietly, "And there's more than one groom."

Wes's face reddened with anger. He threw down his napkin and stood. Unsteadily Mathilde rose from her chair and clasped her husband's hand so tightly that her fingernails dug into his palms. Neither of them took their eyes from Pia, who stared them off as though daring them to play out the scene.

Nathan Schutz's voice crackled over the mike. "A little surprise, folks!" A nervous throat-clearing and then, "Two for the price of one!" Embarrassed laughter managed to relieve some of the tension.

"Now," continued Schutz, "I'd like us all to give a big round of applause to Antaen Pictures' newest star—and her handsome groom!"

The guests applauded politely, and the band played a few phrases of Mendelssohn's "Wedding March." Schutz, meanwhile, raced down from the bandstand and motioned the newspaper people to follow him.

Within seconds, he had maneuvered Mathilde and Wesley out onto the floor beside Pia and Rodney. He grabbed two floral centerpieces from a nearby table and shoved one each into the women's hands. The quartet stood motionless, set smiles plastered on their faces, as a battery of press and studio photographers surrounded them.

Exhausted, the publicity manager sank into a seat beside Jeanne. He picked up a linen napkin and, ignoring the red lipstick left on it, mopped his brow. With his free hand he reached for the nearest glass.

"What's in this?" he asked.

"Bourbon, I think," answered Jeanne.

"That'll do." He downed the drink in a single gulp, burped, and leaned back, staring at the foursome standing center stage. Pia's smile flashed as brightly as the cameras' bulbs. "Spiteful little bitch," said Schutz.

The last photographs had been taken. Rod Raynor released his grip from around Mathilde's waist, but on her right, Pia still held tightly. Mathilde looked pleadingly toward the head table and Nathan Schutz. When she caught his eye, the gallant knight nodded, helped himself to an abandoned glass of champagne, and rose. "Excuse me, dear," he said to Jeanne. "Into the breach once more. It's time again to save the day."

Hurry! thought Mathilde as the publicity man approached. I don't know how much more of this I can take. She'd begun to feel queasy, not the least helped by the combined odors of Rodney Raynor's beer breath, hair cream, and sweat. His brown corduroy suit smelled as if it had been taken out of mothballs in honor of today's . . . performance.

The photographers were dispersed, and Nathan Schutz assured the reporters that a press conference would be scheduled for the moment the two couples returned from their respective honeymoons. He then drew his two stars off to one side as the band resumed playing and guests returned to the dance floor.

That left Mathilde alone with Rodney. After an awkward pause, he said, "Sorry if this was a shock."

"Are you?" she asked.

"I just said so. Hey, lady, don't blame *me* for—"

"Don't blame you?" Mathilde interrupted, trying to keep her voice low. She forced herself to think calmly, clearly. What, after all, did this boy know about Pia? Suddenly she almost felt sorry for him. He was the one who was in for the shock. In an even, controlled tone, she said, "Tell me something."

Rod seemed to sense her change of attitude toward him. "Sure," he replied.

"Is Pia . . . pregnant? Is that . . . why?"

Color rose from his neck to his forehead. "No. Leastways, I . . . I don't think so."

So it *wasn't* the reason.

Mathilde felt a tap on her shoulder and turned to find Pia smiling at her. "Happy for me, Mama?"

There was so much Mathilde wanted to say, but nothing she *could* say. Not with so many people around them.

Rod said uncomfortably, "I . . . guess you two wanna talk." He moved away in search of a champagne tray.

Tears spilled down Mathilde's cheeks in spite of her effort to contain them. "Why, Pia . . . ?" she asked in a voice choked by emotion.

"Simple. I had to get out of the house."

The years flashed by in Mathilde's mind. How could Pia's childhood have ended so abruptly, and like this? "Oh, Pia . . . what's to become of you?"

"It's a little late for that," she answered.

213

"But to do . . . *this. Today!* Do you hate us that much?"

Pia paused before she said, "Not *you,* really . . ." Then her eyes moved from Mathilde toward the direction of the bar, where Wes stood talking to Nathan Schutz. "But *Wesley* . . . yes."

Mathilde's face drained of its color at hearing Pia reply so simply and so coldly. She felt her voice quavering as she spoke. "Pia . . . Wes has helped you— given you a start. W-what *more* could he have done . . . ?"

Pia stared at Mathilde. "Don't you know, Mama?"

Suddenly it didn't matter who was watching or what anyone thought. Mathilde's opened palm rose to strike her daughter across the face.

But another hand gripped her wrist. She looked up into Wes's tense face.

"Not here. Not now. No matter how much I'd like to see it." To Pia he said, "You're a minor. We can have this . . . this farce annulled."

"What?" she cooed. "And ruin my career, Wesley? Maybe even your own? I doubt it."

Wes's arm was around Mathilde's shaking body. In a quiet but steely firm voice, he said, "Leave, Pia. Do whatever you please. Just . . . go away."

An expression of incredulous surprise crossed Pia's face. She looked at her mother. Their eyes held for only a moment, but neither uttered a sound. Then Pia turned on her spindly heels and, never glancing back, strode from the room, with Rodney Raynor following behind like a mongrel puppy dog.

Lydia Genesco joined Mathilde an instant after they'd gone. "Wes," she said, assuming command, "Nathan Schutz has some ideas he wants to talk about

214

with you. I'll take care of Mathilde."

Wes hesitated, then decided that perhaps Lydia might know better what Mathilde needed to hear.

"All right," whispered Lydia, gripping Mathilde's arm, "just hang on till I get you to the powder room."

Lydia gave five dollars to the matron on duty. "I've . . . got a nervous bride here," she explained quickly. "Can you bring her a scotch—neat—and then take a break for about five or ten minutes?"

The matron pocketed the bill and disappeared. As soon as she was gone, Mathilde sank into the chaise longue and began to sob. Lydia handed her a box of Kleenex from the mirrored counter.

After the matron returned with the scotch and left on her break, Lydia locked the door from the inside.

"Drink it all down," she ordered, taking a seat beside her friend.

Mathilde took a sip, shivered, and wiped her eyes. The tissue came away streaked with black.

"Oh, God, my mascara," she moaned. "I must be a fright!"

Lydia chuckled. "Well, I wouldn't peek in the mirror just yet. But we'll fix you up fine in a minute. First, though, you're going to get it all out of your system."

Mathilde shrugged. "Oh, Lydia . . . somehow I feel as if I could have avoided this . . . if . . ."

"If you hadn't married Wes?" The expression of surprise on Mathilde's face made Lydia smile again. "Pia's . . . crush on Wes was pretty obvious. At least to Neal and me."

"But . . . she could be ruining her life."

"Mathilde, darling, what's done is done. The point is not to let it ruin *your* life with Wes."

"She's my *daughter,* Lydia! How can I go on a

honeymoon trip now, when . . . ?"

"You've *got* to. You're married to an important man, and like it or not, certain things are expected of you."

"By whom? Nathan Schutz?"

"For one. He may be an annoying little man, but he knows this business."

Mathilde didn't like him, but she had to admit that he'd saved them all a short while before. "What's Schutz's plan?" she asked, still hesitant but more resigned.

"He told Neal he thinks he can talk Antaen into some kind of a contract for Pia's . . . husband. Pawn him off as a beefcake pinup with a great future. Publicize them as so much in love they couldn't wait . . . two young stars . . . that sort of thing . . ."

"But, Lydia, it's all a lie! What kind of a mother would I be if—?"

"Darling," Lydia interrupted, "compared to some of this town's leading ladies, *you're* mother of the year. Now listen to me. Pia will start a picture as soon as she gets back . . . from wherever . . . The studio will make certain that she stays far away from Wes on the lot. When the two of you return from New York—"

"I can't! Not now—not with all those newspaper reporters!"

"You can and you will. Schutz is calling off the honeymoon coverage. You'll be alone with Wes."

"But what about Jeanne?"

"She can stay with Neal and me. We'll take care of her."

"You . . . you'd do that?" Mathilde asked in a tiny voice.

"We like Jeanne. It'd be one thing if her grandparents were alive. But they're not, and Neal and I have no children of our own. We'd enjoy it. I think Jeanne would, too."

"Yes," said Mathilde. "I know she would."

"Then it's settled. And one more thing I want you to remember. If you need anything—anything at all—I'm here. So is Neal." She took the Kleenex box from Mathilde and replaced it on the countertop. "Okay, time's up. Down the hatch."

Mathilde finished the scotch in several sips and a final, long swallow. The liquid burned her throat, but it did relax her. "Lydia . . . I don't know what to say, except . . . thank you . . . for everything."

"Forget it. I was new to all this myself, once. C'mon, now. Let's see what we can do about fixing your makeup."

Jeanne sat on the edge of Mathilde's bed while her mother packed the two new matching suitcases. Then they moved to the room she had shared, until today, with Pia.

The place was still a shambles after that morning's studio invasion, but it didn't matter; the house in which the girls were born seemed to have already been abandoned.

Jeanne had packed her own suitcase with her favorite books. The nondescript clothing in her closet was unimportant to her. But Mama was rummaging through Jeanne's dresser drawers—the top two—to pack the best of her daughter's wardrobe for her stay with the Genescos.

Jeanne was happy that Mama and Wes would spend their honeymoon alone together and was delighted at the prospect of staying with Lydia and Neal, even if everything had been brought about by Pia's ugly scene at the wedding.

"Where's your new blouse?" asked Mathilde. "It isn't in your drawer."

217

Jeanne looked up and shook her head. "I don't know. Pia borrowed it last week. Maybe she forgot to put it back." No one had mentioned her sister's name on the way home after the reception, but Jeanne knew that Pia was very much on everyone's mind. Right now, her presence lingered over the bedroom like a malevolent spirit.

Mathilde checked the closet once more, then returned to the dresser and opened the third drawer, the first of two occupied by Pia's clothes.

She shook her head, shoved it closed, and pulled open the bottom drawer. Jeanne wasn't paying particular attention until she saw Mathilde withdraw a large brown paper grocery bag from beneath several layers of sweaters.

She watched as her mother opened the bag.

Mathilde's face went purple, then white, as she sank down onto the edge of the bed.

"Mama . . . Mama, what . . . is it?" Jeanne asked, suddenly frightened.

Mathilde was unable to speak. Instead, she overturned the paper bag and let its contents fall to the floor.

The wine-stained cashmere stole that Wes had given to Mathilde.

It had been cut to ribbons.

Part II

1963–1964

Chapter Fifteen

Mathilde glanced up at the clock on the brick wall in the kitchen. Lydia Genesco, standing in the doorway with her cup and saucer in hand, noticed and said, "With all of last night's excitement, she probably never got to sleep. I'll bet she's decided to take a later train."

Mathilde nodded and reached for the large wooden spoon. She went to the stove and began stirring the ingredients in the large cast-iron pot. "Jeanne generally phones if she's going to be late."

"You're making mother sounds," teased Lydia. She refilled her cup from the coffeepot on the round glass breakfast table and added, "That's going to be the most-stirred chili the state of Connecticut has ever seen . . ."

Self-consciously Mathilde removed the spoon from the pot, pretending to sample a mouthful of the sauce. "It may need a little more cumin."

"Mathilde," said Lydia, "you're talking to an old friend. So stop trying to pull the wool over my eyes. And while you're at it, stop worrying. Jeanne is a grown woman of twenty, and if she weren't intelligent, Ted—" Lydia interrupted herself and nervously tried to change the subject.

"Ted . . . who?" asked Mathilde.

"Uh . . . where's the sugar?" Lydia opened a cabinet and pretended to be looking for the bowl.

"Speaking of old friends," said Mathilde, "since when do you put sugar in your coffee? In seven and a half years, I've never seen you drink it any way but black . . ."

Lydia threw her hands up in resignation. "All right, you may as well know. Jeanne has a young man. An understudy in the play. He's actually very nice."

"Then why hasn't she mentioned him to me?" But it was a rhetorical question. Mathilde saw her daughter only on weekends; Lydia, as Jeanne's drama coach, saw her almost every day.

Lydia hastily explained, "Look, darling, she isn't trying to keep things from you. You have to remember that Jeanne . . . well, that Jeanne *isn't* her sister . . ."

At the thought of Pia, Mathilde inadvertently flinched. She opened the cupboard and took out a cup and saucer for herself, poured it two-thirds full of coffee, and sat down at the table. Half to Lydia, half to herself, she said, "You know she's filed for divorce again."

Lydia nodded. "It was in the Hollywood trades." Sensing Mathilde's discomfort, she added, "With this damned newspaper strike, my only source of information seems to be the trades. I don't think I could carry on a conversation that didn't involve theater or movies these days."

Her remark seemed to pull Mathilde away from Pia and back to Jeanne. "Will those papers carry reviews of the play? I mean, it's so unfair to have an opening during a strike—"

"There'll be write-ups in the trades by next week and there will probably be reviews on the news tonight. We'll find out for sure when Wes and Neal get here."

"And just where are they?" asked Mathilde. "Everyone said they'd be here by three, and if you hadn't driven over . . ."

"Relax. Rehearsals never end on time. Not for the director, anyway. And then Neal and Wes are probably having a drink so they can argue politely with one another. They'll be here." She patted Mathilde's hand. "And Jeanne will be here. *And* . . ." But she stopped herself once more.

"What were you going to say?" asked Mathilde. "It drives me crazy when anyone does that."

"I was going to say something bitchy. About Pia. But I changed my mind."

"Lydia . . ."

"I'm sorry. Sometimes I forget she's your daughter. You're so . . . unalike."

"Well . . . ?"

"All right. I was about to say that this divorce may be trickier than the ones before and she may have to pay through the nose."

Mathilde sat quietly, waiting for Lydia to continue. Her friend seemed reluctant but finally said, "Well, the annulment from what's-his-name . . . Rodney . . . was easy because she was under age. And that Emerson Whatever was happy to get off without assault charges being filed against him. Not to mention that he had money of his own. But *this* time . . ."

"I read that he'd been playing around," said Mathilde, feeling uncomfortable about defending her estranged daughter, yet even more uncomfortable about *not* defending her. "Surely Pia has grounds . . . ?"

"Maybe. But they live in Beverly Hills, darling, and that's in the state of California. Your Pia had better read up on community property laws if she plans to marry and divorce on a regular basis. *And* keep her cash flowing, that is. Bigger stars than Pia have lost every dime they ever made. She's not as savvy as she may think."

"For someone who hardly knows her, Lydia, you really have her pegged." And Mathilde couldn't argue.

"It's my job to explore characters. In plays, on film. It's really no different in life. I'm always observing." Lydia rose to rinse out her cup, and in doing so, she glanced through the window over the kitchen sink. In the distance, like a black dot on the high snowdrifts, was something moving. As it grew larger, Lydia recognized Neal's black Lincoln.

"See, all that worrying for nothing. The men are here." She was relieved to be off the subject of Pia, which she knew must be painful for Mathilde.

Mathilde gave one final stir to the chili—this time for a legitimate purpose—and followed Lydia to the door.

The two couples now sat in the cozy, rustic living room of the small weekend "getaway" house. Flames rose in the fireplace, and logs crackled, while the afternoon sun cast pink shadows on the pristine snow.

Lydia had been right. Jeanne had telephoned to say she'd be taking a later train. No, amended Mathilde. Jeanne had said *they'd* be taking a later train. She'd sounded breathless, in a rush, and Mathilde hadn't had time to ask who was coming with her.

When she'd settled beside Wes on the sofa, he and the Genescos were already talking about the previous night's opening. Lydia and Mathilde had returned to the country after the reception at Sardi's, but Wes and Neal had stayed overnight in the city so they could be at the theater in time for a ten A.M. rehearsal.

"She's come a long way since her monologue as Saint Joan," Neal was saying. "I wish Preminger had waited for her to grow up before doing the movie."

224

"She had a special gift even then," Lydia recalled.

Mathilde smiled. "A lot of the credit goes to you, Lydia. You've helped her so much."

"I've only brought out what's always been there. A teacher or coach can't do more."

"She'd be a pleasure to direct," said Neal. "I'm sorry there wasn't a role for her in our play."

Wes's arm was around his wife's. "I'd love to do a play with her. But not for her first Broadway show."

"Afraid of being upstaged?" Mathilde teased.

But he wasn't joking. "No. I don't want anyone to cry nepotism. She's done it on her own, and the public ought to know it."

That reminded them all of the newspaper strike. "Neal," said Mathilde, "is it true that there'll be televised reviews tonight?"

He nodded. "At eleven o'clock. We ought to set your kitchen clock."

"As if anyone is likely to forget the time!" said Lydia.

That reminded Wes that Jeanne's train was due in fifteen minutes, so he excused himself and headed for the station wagon. "Start a fire under the chili," he said. "They'll be starving by now."

Mathilde noticed that Wes, too, had used the word *they*. Did everyone know that Jeanne was bringing someone?

Within half an hour, the crunching gravel, muted by the snow, announced the station wagon's return. Mathilde peeked through the kitchen window and saw Wes emerge from the driver's side of the car and open the rear door.

Jeanne stepped out, her camel hair coat turned up at the collar as protection from the cold Connecticut air. She was followed by a tall young man with longish

225

dark brown hair. He wore a pea jacket, also with an upturned collar. A plaid scarf was wrapped around his neck and the lower half of his face, hiding his features from view. He wore lumberjack boots and woolen mittens.

Mathilde smiled. A sensible young man, dressed for the weather and fashion be damned. Jeanne, too, wore high boots—shiny black rubber boots—and fuzzy earmuffs with matching gloves. So this Ted person must be just a casual friend; Jeanne wasn't dressing to impress him.

She watched as her daughter straddled Wes's larger footprints to avoid slipping along the path. In the suburban setting, Jeanne looked far more the part of a Vassar or Wellesley freshman than she did the role of a Broadway star.

The phrase sent a thrill through Mathilde. The semesters at Performing Arts, juggling theatrical studies with algebra and biology, while taking minuscule roles in TV soaps, series, and theaters so far Off-Broadway that they qualified as out of town. All of it had paid off. Last night.

Mathilde had no need to pinch herself. They'd worked long and hard to make the dream come true. So had Lydia. And none of it had been for vicarious reasons.

She couldn't help wondering if Pia's need to shock those closest to her might be due to Mathilde's pushing her as a small child. Perhaps it was why Pia felt compelled to constantly seek attention. She might be confusing attention with love.

Mathilde had. During the years between Hank and Wes, she had made the same mistake. Could she have passed this on, not unlike a legacy, to Pia?

The question had appeared with frequency as Pia's offscreen behavior grew more and more notorious with

226

each new film, each new leading man. At times Mathilde marveled that she had spawned such a creature. But she also knew that Pia had been different from birth. She'd always told lies and believed them as gospel. Maybe that didn't make her immoral but *amoral;* perhaps Pia couldn't tell the difference.

Mathilde had learned to live with the unanswerable questions; however, every now and then—as with Lydia's comments earlier in the kitchen—thoughts of Pia were accompanied by a sad, persistent twinge. The pain came just below her heart. Or inside it. Sometimes Mathilde couldn't tell the difference.

Ted Sayers was a likable young man whose hobby was cooking. "Helps to calm pre-performance nerves," he explained to Mathilde when he commented on the aroma coming from the kitchen. She allowed him a sampling, and he immediately headed for the stove.

"It's the best chili I've tasted outside of Texas," he said, his mouth still full. "And I practically lived inside Tolbert's Chili Parlor when I was on tour in Dallas."

He'd done small roles and understudies in bus and truck companies for several years. *All in Good Time* was his first show on Broadway. "Of course, Ralph Allen will have to *really* break a leg if I'm going to get onstage with the role, but—"

He stopped to glance at Jeanne, who was seated on a chair and slowly removing layers of sweaters, leg warmers, and socks. "I'm having a great time, though. I'm meeting *very* interesting people, and—if we run— the rent gets paid. What more can an actor ask?"

Mathilde was certain her daughter's cheeks reddened then, but she went on setting the table.

*   *   *

Dinner conversation centered around theater, mostly about Jeanne's performance in the play, and an occasional reference to something Wes or Neal had worked on during their day's rehearsal. For dessert they had coffee and the huge strawberry cheesecake Ted had brought from Lindy's. They moved to the living room around nine-thirty, where they talked more about the current theater season and the problems caused by the newspaper strike. And again, the subject turned to reviews.

"Who needs the papers?" asked Ted. "Everyone who saw Jeanne last night knows how terrific she is."

"That's supposed to be Mama's line," she teased.

"Well, I'll second it," offered Mathilde. "Darling, I'm so proud. We all are."

Jeanne seemed embarrassed by all the attention. "I . . . I received a telegram from Mrs. Armitage, did I tell you? And from some of the kids I went to school with. It's funny . . . I didn't think they knew I was alive."

"Don't be so surprised," said Ted. "Get used to it. You'll be hearing from friends—and people claiming to be friends—now that you're a star."

"Please, Ted—one play doesn't make a star. Besides, that word seems so . . ." She was at a loss for a substitute.

"Well, Jeanne, you were marvelous last night," interjected Lydia. "And you carry the show. What would *you* call yourself?"

"An actress," she answered. "And that's just what I want." Then, to lighten the mood, she added, "But it's not *all* I want. Isn't anyone going to offer me a second piece of cheesecake?"

The six of them tried to avert their eyes from furtive

glances at their watches or at the clock over the mantel of the stone fireplace, but it was no use. As the hour and a half ticked by, awkward silences crept in, or conversation began, only to halt in midsentence. Everyone seemed to be trying—unsuccessfully—to fill in the lapses until the news came on at eleven.

"God!" Jeanne exclaimed at ten fifty-five. "Is it always like this? I mean, does the waiting get any easier?"

Wes laughed and shook his head. "You'll learn that firsthand. It gets worse. Especially when the reviews are *printed.*" He closed his eyes, pretending to drift off in thought. "Ah, yes . . . the interminable waiting in Sardi's fishbowl. You sit and half listen to the chitchat, half reply to questions you didn't hear, toy with your champagne till it's absolutely flat, and pick at your cannelloni till it's stone-cold—and all because you're waiting for that moment when the *Times* and the *Tribune* and the other members of the jury turn in their verdicts. At least in a court of law you have twelve chances. We have only seven." Wes reached for his cognac and concluded, "Ah, yes . . . the power of the press."

"Bravo, Wesley!" said Lydia.

He rose, bowed, and said, "And now, ladies and gentlemen, since timing is everything in both the theater and television, I duly note that the hour . . . is eleven."

Jeanne's heart began pounding rapidly, not for what the reviewer might say about her performance—she was pleased with it and was only eager to grow in the role. But the very existence of the show depended on the three or four minutes of opinions—verdicts, as Wes had joked—that would be heard throughout the city within the next thirty minutes. She'd seen rave reviews establish long-running hits. And she knew that poor reviews—written or spoken—could kill a show before word of mouth had a chance to ensure even a modest run.

All agreed that the three networks would be watched by more viewers than would the local stations. For this reason, Neal stationed himself on the hassock closest to the TV set.

"The two of you have to get one of those new remote-control sets," he said. "But for tonight, *I'll* do the honors."

"Always the director," Lydia commented to Mathilde.

The anchorman announced the top stories: an attempted bank robbery in Queens, a mob hit in Brooklyn, a civil rights demonstration at City Hall. Ted had moved closer to Jeanne on the sofa.

Commercials. Four of them—Mathilde counted—back to back. Kitchen cleanser, instant coffee, laundry detergent, and soap. Then back to the news.

A clean-up campaign for city streets—"Children Before Dogs" read the banners—had turned into a brawl between two grandmothers. A health warning about flu shots. Four more commercials.

Mathilde exhaled audibly. Wes leaned over to kiss her, and Neal switched to Channel 4. More commercials. It was the same on Channel 7, so he quickly switched back to 2.

"The ads are timed. All the stations are in cahoots," Ted said to lessen the tension.

"They are?" asked Jeanne.

"No, silly," he said, cuffing her affectionately on the chin.

"Shh!" commanded their channel director. "Here it comes!"

The photo inset behind the anchor's back showed a picture of the Booth Theater and the glittering opening

230

night crowd. A balding middle-aged man wearing a vested suit and a bow tie moved into the camera closeup.

"*All in Good Time* opened at the Booth Theater earlier this evening," he began in a lispy, nasal voice. "Although the play, by Arthur Kornitz, has its flaws, I would say that in a theater season thus far distinguished by its *lack* of memorable opening nights, this two-acter deserves a run.

"Mr. Kornitz has earned a reputation for creating characters of great emotional depth and range—second only to those created by Tennessee Williams and Edward Albee. With the role of Margaret Ellsworth, credit must go not only to the playwright, but also to the director, Daniel Evans, for a stroke of genius. I speak not of his staging but of his casting. I speak of a young actress whose name and face are new to me, new to Broadway. But not for long. I speak of an essence, a presence, a spark of magic, touched by the muse. I speak of Jeanne Lorraine, and I speak her name with joy."

Jeanne sat beside Ted as the words sank in. She felt as she had during her standing ovation the night before—as though the cheering were for someone else, someone she didn't know and had never met. Even her name sounded unfamiliar. Lorraine. It had been Lydia's idea, but wasn't it too much? All right, Mama's maiden name was Loran, and Lydia hadn't known that. Jeanne had agreed because of her love of Maxwell Anderson's play. But now . . .

And then she saw Mathilde, who was trying to hide her tears behind Wes's sleeve. Lydia, too, reached for her handkerchief. Ted was applauding, while Neal flicked the channel selector to the other networks.

But critics' reviews were not so well timed as commercials, apparently; the weather report was in midforecast on 4, and the earlier dog-cleanup segment was airing on 7.

"Well," said Neal pragmatically, "with a rave like that, who needs to hear more?"

No one replied. At that moment, the anchor was saying, "And finally tonight, in a related story: It's getting closer to Academy Awards time again, and in Hollywood today, the Oscar nominations were announced. Olympia Decameron, sister of Broadway's brightest new star, Jeanne Lorraine, has been nominated for Best Actress. Her performance in—"

The anchor was cut off by Neal, who pushed the OFF button and stood, his jaw set firmly. "This is Jeanne's night, and *nobody* is going to upstage her." He reached over to the table and lifted his brandy snifter in a toast.

"Ladies and gentlemen," he said with false gaiety, "I give you Jeanne Lorraine."

The others lifted their glasses, but, not unlike the opening-night champagne Wes had spoken about earlier, the scene had suddenly gone flat.

Chapter Sixteen

The newspaper strike ended in April, but it was too late to save Wes's play, *Final Stages*, or *All in Good Time*, despite excellent reviews from the television critics. Word of mouth had ensured mostly runs of musical comedies, but it was next to impossible to attract Hadassah audiences and Lions or Elks Club theater parties for an evening of straight, serious drama.

On both coasts, all members of the Decameron-Guest family were passed by when awards were handed out. Pia lost the Oscar to Anne Bancroft, and neither Jeanne nor Wesley was nominated for a Tony. Wes reminded her that it was all just part of the business, but Jeanne suspected that he was as disappointed as she was, especially coming on the heels of their respective shows' closings.

"After all those weeks of rehearsal," she remarked to Ted. "I feel suddenly . . . like a fish out of water."

They were standing in line at the unemployment office near Ted's apartment in Chelsea. Jeanne hadn't filed a claim; she felt that collecting money when she didn't need it would be dishonest, as well as contributing to the already overburdened welfare system in

233

the city.

Ted still didn't understand her attitude. "It's tax money that you've paid out of your salary," he insisted.

"But Mama's helping me out till I land another show," she said. "I wouldn't feel right."

It felt right to Ted, though, whose past six years had been divided regularly between Broadway, the road, and these same green-gray premises at the corner of Twentieth Street and Sixth Avenue. "Well," he joked, "if your landlord decides to kick you out as a deadbeat, you can always stay with me." He nudged her playfully with his elbow just as the clerk behind the high green counter called out, "Next!"

Jeanne quickly stepped off the waiting line while Ted signed for his check. She'd gotten dirty looks the week before from another clerk who muttered words about "lousy bum actors" under her breath, and Jeanne didn't want to jeopardize Ted's receipt of money he'd already paid out in state withholding taxes.

She reflected on his offer. They could easily squeeze his tiny one-room apartment, with its Pullman kitchen and minuscule bathroom, into her three rooms on West Fifty-third. Her brownstone was down the street from the Rehearsal Club, where several of Jeanne's friends had rooms, but what she loved most was the proximity of the Museum of Modern Art several doors east, and the theater district just across and west of Sixth Avenue. An added bonus was that Wes and Mama, when they were in New York, lived only ten minutes north on Sixty-sixth Street and Central Park West.

Right now, though, Wes and Mathilde were in Hollywood, and Jeanne missed them dearly. Neal and Lydia Genesco were still in town, and she saw them, Lydia in particular, several times during the week for coaching lessons. But it wasn't the same as having

Mama and Wes close by.

They'd invited her to return to California with them after the show had closed, but Jeanne had declined. "I've got to stay here and find work. The movies don't really interest me that much," she'd said. It was true, but unemployment appealed to her even less. Ted might be more in need of money than Jeanne—a fact whose irony did not escape her, considering the years when she had gone without—but now that she'd tasted the sweetness of triumph in a role she had loved, Jeanne recognized her need to act onstage. Perhaps it was why she wasn't jealous of Pia's success in film. And perhaps it was why she understood Ted's need of financial security; her desire for artistic fulfillment was no less strong.

For this, they checked the casting notices at Actors Equity every day. Jeanne had acquired an agent as a result of her glowing performance in *All in Good Time*, but it was the beginning of summer—the slowest months of the theatrical year.

Neal and Lydia had been looking at scripts, both for Jeanne and for the director, who was suddenly "at liberty." Unlike Wes, who had flown back to the West Coast to star in a new film, Neal Genesco's return to Broadway had reminded him how deeply he'd missed the theater.

"It makes him feel young again," Lydia commented to Jeanne one afternoon. "You know, he began his career as a stage actor before he came to the States. I don't think he's ever gotten the bug out of his blood."

Jeanne smiled. She understood exactly. "But don't you ever miss it, Lydia?" she asked.

Her teacher-friend shook her head. "I love uncovering the facets—I call it unlayering—of a character in a play. But for me the fascination is in the discovery itself—not in *playing* it." She swirled the lone ice cube

235

at the bottom of her glass of iced tea. "There's another reason, too," she confided in a whisper as if someone else might hear, although she and Jeanne were alone on the terrace of the high-rise apartment. "I never fully overcame stage fright. Something constantly got in the way and blocked all those 'revelations' I'd found from coming through. I was always better in rehearsal."

"But . . . why? The audience seems to . . . ignite . . . me," said Jeanne. "I mean . . . well, *I* always feel that something's missing during rehearsal. But then . . . when I get onstage . . . I understand. It's the *audience* that's been missing . . ."

Lydia nodded. "And that, honey, is why you act . . . and I teach. It's no more complex than that." She rose and crossed to the balcony that overlooked the rush-hour traffic on Third Avenue. "And that's why we have to find you a suitable script."

"My agent's been looking, too, but . . ."

"With all of us hunting, the right one'll turn up, don't worry." Even on the fifteenth floor, the backfiring of trucks, coupled by three police squad cars with screeching sirens, became ear-splitting. "Let's go inside where we can hear each other," suggested Lydia.

As they settled on the sofa, Neal entered the room. He kissed his wife on the cheek, then Jeanne. Lydia said, "We didn't hear you come in. How'd your day go?"

He shrugged. "Well, in some circles I'm considered crazy, but I can't direct a play I don't believe in, so I said no."

"Good for you!" said Lydia.

Neal went to the bar and poured himself a vodka and tonic. Then he asked Jeanne, "And what about you? And Ted? Any auditions—for good plays—on the horizon?"

She sighed. "By the time our show closed, all the

236

decent stock packages were cast. I mean, there was a company somewhere in Michigan, but two months of *The Gazebo* and *Who Was That Lady I Saw You With?* won't exactly help a career *or* a résumé."

"That's true," said Neal, joining the women on the circular sofa.

They were trading gossip about shows, actors, and mutual acquaintances when the telephone rang. Lydia went into the den to answer it and returned a moment later.

"It's Ted," she said, "and he sounds excited about something."

Jeanne hurried into the den and a few minutes later reentered the living room with glistening eyes and a wide grin. Clasping her hands with the news, she said, "You'll never guess."

"Well, then you'd better tell us—before you burst!" said Neal.

"It's *All in Good Time*! The show is going on a national tour this fall, and they've offered us the leads—I mean, they want me to repeat my role, and they've offered Ted the *part,* not the understudy this time! Isn't that *fabulous?*"

"Oh, honey, that's wonderful!" agreed Lydia, coming to Jeanne and embracing her.

But Neal was less enthusiastic. "How long is the tour?" he asked.

"Fourteen months—we play all the major cities!"

"That's more than a year away from New York," said Neal. "It's fine for Ted. He should have played the part all along, instead of just understudying. But we all know that talent doesn't always win in this business."

"Well, then . . . ?"

Lydia said slowly, "Jeanne, dear, I know it's an awfully long time for you and Ted to be apart, but . . . Neal is right. You've already played the role *here*. On

237

Broadway. You don't *need* the credit. What you need is a *new* role—in a new play."

"But all the big stars go out on the road—" Jeanne protested.

"That's just it," Neal put in. "Big stars can afford to. Carol Channing or Mary Martin can spend fourteen months away from New York and nobody forgets who they are. But you're at the beginning of an important career. You need to follow one leading role with another—especially for the new season. You go out on the road for that long at this juncture, and you'll have to start all over again when the tour is over. Broadway producers—even with my help—will say, "Jeanne *who?*"

She looked at Lydia for help, but her coach's expression clearly showed that she agreed with her husband.

"It just wouldn't be a good career move for you," Neal repeated. "No matter how you and Ted feel about each other."

"Maybe you can join him on weekends," Lydia suggested. "If it's a national tour, there'll be long runs in Boston and Philadelphia and Washington—"

"Yes . . . I suppose." The thought of sneaking up to Ted's hotel room in a different city every week held no appeal. The Puerto Rican super at Ted's apartment building on Seventeenth Street had already made Jeanne feel as though she had no morals; whenever she and Ted came downstairs together in the early morning, José never failed to offer a derogatory smirk. How then would she deal with snoopy hotel front desk clerks?

But she knew that was only part of it.

"I'd better be going," she said. "I promised to meet Ted at Downey's to celebrate. And . . . I guess we'll have a lot to talk over . . ."

Lydia walked her to the elevator. "Honey, he'll understand. You have two careers to think of." In a lower voice, she added, "That's the third reason I gave up acting. I don't for a minute regret my choice. But if you were to do as I did, you'd regret it for the rest of your life. And so would Ted, because eventually you'd start resenting him."

The panel above the elevator lit up, and as the doors slid open Lydia kissed Jeanne on the cheek. "I don't want to spoil your celebration, honey. But you and Ted talk it over . . . and think about what I've said."

As the taxi sped through the underpass of Central Park and then made its way downtown through the pre-theater traffic, Jeanne's thoughts were centered on more than Lydia and Neal's advice. On the phone Ted had mentioned something he wanted to discuss with her. Something important, he'd said. Jeanne intuitively knew—and dreaded—what that something was probably going to be.

Most of the dinner crowd had left for theaters dotting the West Forties east and west of Eighth Avenue by the time Jeanne entered Jim Downey's Steak House. The remaining patrons—the "regulars" who frequented the landmark restaurant—were producers, directors, or agents. They wolfed down enormous portions of Swiss steak in the "show biz" section at the rear of the famed eatery, and spoke in low, confidential whispers among the framed caricatures and photographs of famous Broadway stars and personalities.

Usually Jeanne and Ted sat in the back area as well. Tonight, however, Jeanne found Ted seated in one of the booths up front near the bar. The walls here were covered with framed photographs of prize-winning racehorses and their jockeys. Each time she entered the premises Jeanne wondered about the racetrack/theatrical connection. Tonight it didn't once cross her mind.

A small package rested beside Ted's Bloody Mary. Its contents were concealed by an ordinary brown paper bag. Jeanne hoped the unglamorous wrapping was indicative of something *other* than a ring. Otherwise, the evening would prove even more difficult than she'd anticipated.

Ted noticed her eyes on the parcel, and she saw that he'd noticed. To cover any awkwardness, Jeanne smiled, slid into the booth opposite him, and asked, "Plain brown paper . . . is it pornographic material?"

He broke into a laugh. She loved his slightly crooked grin and the fact that his teeth weren't Hollywood perfect. He was good-looking without being *too* good-looking.

He shook his head. "I came here from my optometrist's. Otherwise you'd never know." He reached inside the bag.

"Eyeglasses?" she exclaimed, relieved to see the oblong shape of the case.

"Shh!" he cautioned. "They're only for reading." He modeled them for her. "Still love me?"

She smiled. "They make you look . . . distinguished."

"Hmm. You didn't answer my question, though."

"What question was that . . . ?" She didn't like herself for playing coy. He'd asked it lightly—he always asked it lightly—but she could read him well, and he wanted a serious answer. Still, she felt that evasiveness was preferable to an outright lie.

Ted could read her, too. He knew he was her first lover—it had come as a surprise last January and it had convinced him further that she cared for him. But how

Get a Free
Zebra
Historical
Romance

*a $3.95
value*

— FREE —

B O O K C E R T I F I C A T E

ZEBRA HOME SUBSCRIPTION SERVICE, INC.

YES! Please start my subscription to Zebra Historical Romances and send me my free Zebra Novel along with my first month's Romances. I understand that I may preview these four new Zebra Historical Romances Free for 10 days. If I'm not satisfied with them I may return the four books within 10 days and owe nothing. Otherwise I will pay just $3.50 each, a total of $14.00 (a $15.80 value—I save $1.80). Then each month I will receive the 4 newest titles as soon as they come off the press for the same 10 day Free preview and low price. I may return any shipment and I may cancel this arrangement at any time. There is no minimum number of books to buy and there are no shipping, handling or postage charges. Regardless of what I do, the FREE book is mine to keep.

Name _____

(Please Print)

Address _____ Apt. # _____

City _____ State _____ Zip _____

Telephone (____) _____

Signature _____

(if under 18, parent or guardian must sign)

Terms and offer subject to change without notice.

4-89

ACCEPT YOUR FREE GIFT
AND EXPERIENCE MORE OF
THE PASSION AND ADVENTURE
YOU LIKE IN A
HISTORICAL ROMANCE

❧

Zebra Romances are the finest novels of their kind and are written with the adult woman in mind. All of our books are written by authors who really know how to weave tales of romantic adventure in the historical settings you love.

Because our readers tell us these books sell out very fast in the stores, Zebra has made arrangements for you to receive at home the four newest titles published each month. You'll never miss a title and home delivery is so convenient. With your first shipment we'll even send you a FREE Zebra Historical Romance as our gift just for trying our home subscription service. No obligation.

BIG SAVINGS
AND **FREE** HOME DELIVERY

Each month, the Zebra Home Subscription Service will send you the four newest titles as soon as they are published. (We ship these books to our subscribers even before we send them to the stores.) You may preview them *Free* for 10 days. If you like them as much as we think you will, you'll pay just $3.50 each and *save $1.80 each month* off the cover price. **AND** *you'll also get* **FREE HOME DELIVERY.** There is never a charge for shipping, handling or postage and there is no minimum you must buy. If you decide not to keep any shipment, simply return it within 10 days, no questions asked, and owe nothing.

deeply she cared was the source of his constant speculation. He just didn't know.

Jeanne didn't know, either. She liked him—*more* than liked him . . . and yet . . . was it *love?* Whatever they shared, however passionate was Ted's behavior or her own response, there seemed to be something missing. She couldn't identify it, but she'd seen enough of Mathilde and Wesley together to know that what *they* shared was love—the head-over-heels kind of love that she didn't feel for Ted. To tell him would hurt him; therefore, she opted for evasion.

". . . so I came up with a terrific idea to *uncomplicate* matters," he was saying. "At the same time, we'll save on expenses and come back to the city with some money to put in the bank."

"I . . . I'm sorry, Ted . . . my mind was distracted. I . . ."

"Here I'm mustering up the courage to propose to you," he said, "and now I have to run the dialogue all over again . . ."

It was as painful as if the package *had* contained a ring. "Ted . . ." she began. But the words didn't come.

"Maybe we'd better get you a drink before I try again." Nervously he signaled for John, their regular waiter.

"Ted . . ."

He caught John's eye and held up two fingers. "I need another one, too," he said. "God, this proposing bit isn't easy in real life, no matter how often you've rehearsed it."

Still trying to keep it breezy, she thought, grateful but no less uncomfortable. "Ted . . ."

"Uh, oh," he said. "Three *Teds* in a row. This sounds serious."

She reached across the table for his hands, which were loosely clasped over the menu. "This isn't easy for

241

me, either," she managed at last. "Maybe we ought to change the subject . . . ?"

He was studying her through his reading glasses; the lenses' magnification enlarged his deep blue eyes and increased their intensity. Jeanne felt as though she were under a microscope.

"I just thought . . ." It was his turn to falter. "I figured with the good news about the tour . . . well, as I was saying a minute ago, we'd save on hotels by sharing the same room, which I wasn't sure you'd want to do if we weren't already Mr. and—"

She had to stop him before he went too far; if she didn't, they'd be unable to salvage their relationship. It was clear that after tonight they could never return to the same status of the past five months.

So she cut him off and blurted it out in a single line: "Ted . . . I'm not going to do the tour."

At first he offered no reaction. Then the actor in him assumed direction and he removed his glasses. He wiped a nonexistent smudge from the lenses with his napkin, put the glasses into their case and the napkin back on his lap, and took the last sip of his drink before saying, "I see . . ."

Then he looked up into Jeanne's eyes and gave a self-deprecating laugh. "Actually, I *don't* see . . . Scenes like these always work better onstage, when you're not playing opposite . . . the woman you love."

John's arrival with a second round of Bloody Marys caused a momentary interruption. The burly Irishman looked from Ted to Jeanne and said, "Will you be wantin' to order anythin' to eat . . . or are the two of you skippin' dinner t'night?"

Ted handed John his menu. "I don't know about the lady, John, but I'm not very hungry this evening."

Jeanne placed her napkin on the table. "Neither am I. It's been a very long day, and . . ." Her voice trailed off and John took the hint. "Well, if you'll be needin' another round, just let me know. I'll be over by the bar, mindin' me own business, then." He seemed eager to escape.

When they were alone again, Ted said, "Jeanne . . . all you need to tell me is . . . why. If I can understand, maybe . . . well, maybe I won't feel so damned rejected."

Jeanne couldn't keep tears from welling in her eyes. "Oh, Ted," she said, "I wish *I* understood. I know it has *something* to do with wanting to stay in New York—*needing* to stay here—but it's more than that. And I do care a great deal about you. Maybe I just need time. The thought of . . . of getting married and settling down—even if it's settling down in one hotel after another—scares the hell out of me. I'm afraid of . . . of being . . . smothered." She said the last word in a small, barely audible voice.

"By me?" he asked. "Or do you think fourteen months on the road would . . . smother . . . your chances for a new show?"

Jeanne searched his question for sarcasm or bitterness but found none, so she replied with candor. "I . . . I've considered that aspect, too, Ted."

He nodded. "I guess it was presumptuous of me to expect . . . well, to expect that you'd be thrilled about the tour simply because we'd be . . . together."

"It's just . . . too soon. For all kinds of reasons, Ted. My mother gave up all hopes of a career. I know you're not asking me to do that. But she did it for the man *she* loved, and . . ." Thoughts of her father, even after so many years, never failed to dredge up emotions she'd thought to have under control.

"What happened?" asked Ted. "I mean, I know your mother is married to Wesley Guest, but what happened to your father?"

243

Jeanne gazed up at the photographs of prize-winning horses and their jockeys. In a faraway voice, she said, "It was a stupid accident. He was a policeman. When I was a child, I thought he'd been shot in the line of duty. I guess that made it easier to bear—you know, a hero's death, the kind of thing kids need. But . . . later, my mother told me the truth."

She paused for a deep breath and another sip of her drink. "The senselessness of it is the part I have trouble with."

Ted was listening so intently that it seemed as though they were alone in the restaurant. He wished they were.

"My father was alcoholic. Apparently he couldn't stop drinking even while he was cleaning his service revolver." Her vision blurred by tears, her voice choking inside her closed throat, Jeanne said, "One day his finger slipped and the gun went off. It's why I forgive my sister's . . . aberrant behavior. Pia . . . saw it happen."

Ted shook his head. "That explains a lot . . . But not about your fear of being suffocated. Jeanne, I swear I'd never ask you to give up anything for me. For us. You've got to understand that."

She used her napkin as a handkerchief and wiped away her tears. "Then *you've* got to understand why I can't accept the tour, Ted. And . . . and why I need room . . ." She couldn't finish the sentence.

If he pressed the issue, he'd lose her altogether. At least she hadn't completely closed the door. He'd try to see it her way for now.

"Fourteen months ought to give you some room," he said. "And . . . if you like, maybe you can come up on weekends." He signaled John for their check and concluded, "We'll find out if there's any truth to the old cliché."

"What cliché?"

244

"That absence makes the heart grow fonder . . ."

Jeanne managed a weak smile. She and Ted were leaving the restaurant together, heading for his apartment together. Yet she felt something—that familiar, intangible tugging—which she knew would ultimately drive them apart. She didn't understand why, but as they exited onto Eighth Avenue, she recognized that their impending separation had nothing to do with the tour.

Chapter Seventeen

"Do you *believe* it!" Pia exploded, throwing that week's copy of *Variety* onto the wet tiles beside the pool.

"Believe what?" asked the slightly bored voice of the muscular blond lying on the chaise next to Pia's.

"This!" She leaned over to retrieve the paper, but the wet ink smudged as she touched it, and rather than soil her white swimsuit, she recited the quote. "Jeanne Lorraine is going into rehearsal for a new Broadway play—*the* newest, hottest play of the fall season, to be exact. *The* best-written role since Blanche in *Streetcar!"*

Brad Morrow's eyes were closed behind his mirrored sunglasses. "Isn't Jeanne Lorraine your sister?" he asked lazily.

"Damn right she is! *She* wasn't even nominated for a Tony, and *she* gets a role that major stars would *kill* for. *I* had the rotten luck to be nominated for an Oscar in the same year as that Bancroft woman—"

Brad interrupted. "She's one hell of an actress, Pia. And *The Miracle Worker* is one hell of a picture—"

"Oh, shut up! Anyone could win by pretending to teach a blind deaf-mute to say *wa-wa."*

"Hey, lady, *you're* not blind. Give her *some* credit—"

Pia turned over on her side and pulled off Brad's glasses. "Since when are *you* such an authority on acting?"

Looking into her eyes, he said lazily, "Well . . . I suppose since *you* discovered me, beautiful . . ."

"And don't you forget it!" she snapped, rising and smoothing the lines of her uncreased maillot. "I'm going inside. The afternoon sun isn't good for my skin."

She started for the glass doors of the patio, but Brad's voice stopped her. "Pia . . . don't you think you've had enough to drink for one day?"

Fuming, she opened the doors, disappeared inside, and headed straight for the bar.

Brad joined her while she was sipping her second martini. She watched him standing in the curved archway between the patio and the living room. Why do I put up with him? Pia asked herself. Sure he's gorgeous. They're *all* gorgeous. She gave him a once-over. His tanned body still glistened from perspiration and the lotion he'd so carefully worked into his chest, arms, and legs.

Well, Pia mused, this is one scene Jeanne can't play. She's probably holding virginal hands with some skinny, balding theatrical genius who wears horn-rimmed glasses and boxer shorts.

She glanced at the outline of Brad's skintight bikini swimming trunks. He had removed the mirrored glasses and was looking directly at her now, watching her as she watched him.

"Why don't we change into something . . . else?" he suggested, coming toward her at the bar.

"You need a shower." She drained her glass and popped the olive into her mouth.

"You need more than that," he said in the sleepy, languid way that made women swoon when they saw him onscreen.

"Think I'm one of your fans, do you?" she teased.

He shook his head. "I *know,* so what are we waiting for, hmm . . . ?"

Pia swallowed the chewed olive and placed the glass on the marble top of the bar. When Brad held out his hand, she took it and followed him up the six steps to the bedroom.

"I'm really not in the mood, Brad," she said as he drew the draperies closed.

"Darling, if I'd waited for you to be in the mood, we'd never have gotten to know each other in the first place, would we?"

"Why do I let you insult me instead of throwing you out?" she asked, half rhetorically.

He was beside her now and slowly unzipping her swimsuit down the back. "Why? Because, lover, we both know the meaning of publicity, and our 'hot affair' is a big help at the box office, isn't it?"

"It's a big help for *your* career, Brad. I'm *already* a star. Don't forget that."

He pulled her swimsuit down to her ankles in one movement and said, "I won't. And don't *you* forget that Anne Bancroft won the Oscar. Nobody's indispensable, darling . . ."

Brad had insisted upon driving Pia to her appointment with Nathan Schutz. She was convinced that it was to dispel rumors of their rocky relationship, but she hadn't argued. Even after two cups of black coffee, she felt too unsteady to take the wheel. Brad had further insisted on using his aging Olds convertible, with the top down, rather than Pia's sleek Lincoln Continental with its air-conditioning and automatic everything.

"I don't need to breathe in all that pollution," she'd said.

"Maybe not, but you *do* need the open air. You don't want to give truth to all the gossip."

She was furious because he was right. He usually was. That's a strange reason for keeping him around, she thought.

Nathan Schutz greeted Pia warmly, although he didn't like her. He hadn't liked her since her surprise performance at Wesley and Mathilde's wedding almost eight years before. But he was a Studio Man, loyal to Antaen Pictures, and if that meant treating Antaen's top stars with kid gloves, well . . . no job came without its drawbacks.

"Olympia, my dear!" he gushed, rising and coming from around his desk to greet her. "And Brad. So nice to see you, too." Schutz actually had nothing against Pia's latest leading man *except* for his involvement with a notorious lush. The publicist had given Brad Morrow credit for more intelligence. Then again, maybe it was a smart career move to be linked with Olympia Decameron. It couldn't last forever. They never did . . .

"You wanted to see me, Nathan?" Pia had never tried to hide her contempt for the man whom she called The Little Yes Man.

Schutz swallowed and returned to the safety of the high-backed leather chair behind his desk. With a nod he indicated the two French provincial chairs on the opposite side of his domain, and his two guests seated themselves.

Glancing at Brad then to Pia, Schutz cleared his throat and said to a spot somewhere between the two of them, "This is a somewhat . . . personal matter, Olympia. We can discuss it later if you like. Perhaps—"

"Anything that concerns me concerns Brad," Pia said, pronouncing her words with the utmost of care to avoid slurring her consonants.

Schutz looked down at the papers on his desk, none of which pertained to the appointment with Pia.

"Well . . . um . . . it's about your next picture," he said.

"You must know something I don't, Nathan. I haven't been assigned to a new picture since ours"—she glanced adoringly at Brad—"wrapped."

"But you've turned down several screenplays, and I've run out of stories to give the press—except, of course, uh . . . the ones . . . er . . . about . . . ah . . ."

"My personal life?" she finished for him.

Schutz was grateful for that. It was the single factor about Olympia Decameron he could count on. Hem and haw long enough, and she'd say the words for him. It was always a load off.

Pia laughed now and began to relax. She'd expected another reprimand about her drinking, although these usually came from Joe Sanchez, a studio higher-up, not from one of The Little Yes Men.

"Well, Nathan," she said, "your worries will soon be over. I've been looking for a new property, and the moment I've found it, I promise you'll be the first to know. In the meantime, I have an idea for a lovely story." She shot a glance at Brad and a broad smile crept over her face. "It's a family kind of story, Nathan. The heartwarming stuff my fans clamor to read . . ."

Schutz, too, turned to Brad. If this good-looking blond actor was about to become husband number

four, the only news would be that Olympia Decameron's marriages no longer made news.

But Pia was never lacking for surprises. "I've
decided," she said, inventing as she spoke, "that during
this . . . hiatus, and since they're in California again . . .
it might be the right moment to visit my mother. And
my stepfather. We've been estranged for too long.
And . . . I think Brad and Wesley will get along just
fine. They have a lot in common . . ."

Schutz opened the pillbox next to the phone. Then,
reaching for the water pitcher on his desk, he hastily
filled a glassful. One of the most difficult jobs of his
past seven-going-on-eight years had been and still was
keeping Wesley Guest and Olympia Decameron apart.
What in God's name did she have up her sleeve this
time? Schutz hurriedly washed down two green tablets,
after which he asked, "Olympia . . . it's been such a
long time. Why . . . *now?*"

Pia's smile suddenly changed to a Cheshire cat's grin.
"Well, Nathan . . . why *not . . . ?*"

Brad was quiet during the drive back to Laurel
Canyon. He drove, and Pia stared straight ahead at the
tiny houses dotting the hills and growing larger and
larger as the car approached the turn. She could spot
her own house, its angular structure of tinted glass and
redwood visible from the road below. The falling late-
afternoon sun cast dramatic shadows along the way.
Within half an hour it would be dusk, and Pia loved
that time of day—as long as she wasn't driving.

She was glad to be seated on the passenger side now,
but not because of the hour. Nor because she'd been
drinking. She hadn't touched a drop since they'd left
the house for her meeting with Nathan Schutz. Her
mind was far from the flask of scotch in the glove

251

compartment; it was centered on a new game, the one she'd begun in the publicist's office.

A family reunion. Mathilde and Wesley and Brad and Pia. Too bad Jeanne can't be included, she mused, but *she's* busy in New York with her new play . . .

The thought of surprising Mathilde and Wesley gave her an adrenaline rush. She hadn't felt that in quite some time. Not since her anticipation on the night of the Academy Awards. But this time there wouldn't be an aftermath of letdown.

Nathan Schutz made every attempt to have a studio photographer and reporter accompany Pia on her surprise visit—and with each attempt he had to remind himself *not* to call it a surprise *attack*.

When Pia refused, Schutz took the only other safeguard left to him. It could be attributed to studio loyalty—the protection of one of its stars. But Schutz's main purpose in warning Wes and Mathilde of Pia's impending visit was due to his respect for the actor and admiration for his wife. Never had either of them spoken a critical word against Olympia Decameron— and they'd certainly had ample opportunity, considering the fiction they must have read in fan magazine interviews with the beautiful star of Antaen Pictures.

When it came down to it, Schutz was forced to admit that Olympia Decameron had one hell of an imagination. On the other hand, she was no more than a stunning, pathological liar. His own careful editing of her "confessions" for the press had transformed certain references to her family—especially where Wes was concerned—into ambiguous reading. If it resulted in the public's being misled, well . . . so be it . . . Schutz was only doing his job.

* * *

"I suppose it's silly," said Mathilde after Schutz's call, "but I can't stop wondering *why* she's coming . . . after such a long time."

Wes's reply offered no answer. "Pia may not know why, either. We're probably all just stumbling in the dark. But I'll never let her hurt you again, darling. I promise you that."

They took Pia's Continental to Pasadena, but Brad drove. He didn't trust Pia behind the wheel even when she hadn't been drinking, and although she'd sworn she was cold sober, he'd caught a glimpse of her at the bar shortly after lunch. He wasn't going to take any chances.

Brad hadn't counted on the glove compartment. By the time he'd turned off the freeway, Pia had taken more than a few gulps from the flask.

"That'll ensure a great entrance," said Brad, glancing sideways through his reflecting sunglasses.

"Keep your eyes on the road, will you?" she retorted. "I haven't seen my mother . . . or her husband . . . for ages. This helps to settle my nerves."

"The way you're belting it down, anyone would think you don't *want* to see them."

"Maybe I don't."

"Then what the hell are we doing . . . ?"

When Pia didn't answer, Brad asked, "Just how long has it been, anyway?"

She was facing the window on her side of the car. "I saw my mother after my last divorce. Briefly."

"What about your stepfather?"

"Well, we've *seen* each other—after all, we live in the same town, don't we? We work at the same studio, go to the same premieres. We can't exactly *avoid* seeing one another, can we?" As an afterthought, she added, "I'll grant you, though, Nathan Schutz earns his salary

253

by trying to keep us apart, especially on the lot . . ."

"What have you got against Wesley Guest? I've met him. Seems like a down-to-earth guy for such a big star."

Pia took another swallow, then capped the flask. "It goes to show you that your judge of acting talent is as lousy as your judge of character." For emphasis, she replaced the flask in the glove compartment and slammed it shut.

Her pulse began to quicken as Brad took the turnoff up the road to the rambling two-story, ranch-style house Pia remembered from the time of her very first film. And her first hangover. So long ago. She'd passed out and awakened in Wesley's house. In Wesley's arms.

No. She knew better now. Her *mother* had awakened in Wesley's arms. That was when I lost Wesley to Mama, she thought, her rising anger mixing with nerves and too much scotch.

Pia pressed the automatic window button and a rush of wind entered the car. She inhaled deeply, but the exhaust from the truck directly ahead of them caused her to cough. Brad pressed a button on his side of the car and Pia's window rolled back up. Neither of them looked at the other.

Two more turns, and a wrought-iron mailbox appeared at the foot of a steep incline. Beneath it, in brass, were the letters G-U-E-S-T, and an arrow pointing to the left.

"Sober up, beautiful," said Brad. "We're almost there."

Pia's stomach was churning, and her head was dizzy. It must be from the confined quarters of the car, she thought.

The road swerved right, allowing a glimpse of the

house hidden among the dense shrubbery and tall palms.

Pia reached once more for the glove compartment, but Brad's right hand stopped her. "If you want to make a drunken fool of yourself," he said, "that's fine. But do it on your own time."

"Don't talk to me as if you own me!" she cried. "And pull over here. We'll walk the rest of the way."

"*You'll* walk," he said, his foot on the brake.

She was glaring at him. The mirrored lenses of his sunglasses suddenly seemed to be mocking her. "Just what the hell does *that* mean?"

"What I said, beautiful. *You'll* walk. I'll wait here." He leaned across her lap and unlocked the passenger door. "This is your show, not mine."

"You didn't tell me that before we left the house!" she yelled.

"You didn't tell *me* you were going to get drunk."

Pia had expected him to shout at her, but his voice was calm and cold, like steel.

"Get out, Pia," he said. "We're here."

"You—bastard!" She flung open the door on her side of the car, not bothering to close it, and headed resolutely up the path.

Pia didn't turn to see if Brad was watching her. She knew he had to be. Her throat felt tight and dry, and her spindly heels kept catching in the gravel on the walkway.

Finally she reached the front door. Her head was swirling as her hand went out unsteadily to ring the bell.

She could hear the chimes from inside.

And then footsteps on the tiled floor. Coming closer. Oh, God! she thought. What have I done? I must be crazy!

There was the loud click of the lock as it was

unbolted. Then the massive redwood door began to open.

Pia was now on the verge of hysteria. Without thinking, she turned and ran.

Brad sat watching from the car. He saw Pia trip and almost fall. He saw a squirrel dart across the path.

And he saw Wesley Guest's tall silhouette appear in the arched doorway. He stood there without moving or calling her name, and returned inside a moment before Pia reached the car.

"Let's get out of here!" she said breathlessly between gasps.

Brad started the ignition and stepped on the gas pedal. He didn't speak. But he had removed his sunglasses, and the expression in his eyes when Pia looked at him made her wish he was still hiding behind the mirrors. That way she wouldn't have seen his contempt.

Chapter Eighteen

The taxi moved forward at a steady pace in the downtown lane of Central Park West. Neal Genesco yawned and covered his mouth as he glanced to the left. Beyond and above the stone wall bordering the park, patches of red and gold in the trees bore evidence of winter's approach. Beside him a muffled yawn responded to his own.

"It's catching," Lydia said with a laugh.

"Sorry." His attention remained with the passing scenery.

Lydia would have preferred to stay in bed all morning. Last night they'd both been reluctant to leave Connecticut. Their late departure and bottleneck traffic had delayed their return to the city, and it was past midnight by the time they reached their apartment on the Upper East Side. Then they'd set the alarm clock for seven.

"Hey," she said, looking up at him now. "Hey!" She gave him a playful poke with her elbow.

"Hmm?" Neal mumbled absently.

"Something especially interesting out there?"

"I don't know. The time of year, I suppose."

"What's on your soundtrack? 'Autumn Leaves' or

'Autumn in New York'?" she asked.

Grinning, he replied, "'Ole Rockin' Chair's Got Me.'"

Lydia sat up, fighting the gravity of a right turn around Columbus Circle.

"Neal," she said, "you can't be serious."

He shrugged. "I'm not as young as I was yesterday."

She put her arm through his. "If you were a woman, I'd say this was hormonal."

"Maybe it is, anyway," he said with a short laugh.

"Listen. I should be through at the Actors' Studio around one. I can walk over to the theater and meet you for lunch."

"Can't," he replied. "The producers want to discuss Act Two. They're worried."

"The love scene?"

He nodded. "It's not working. Herb wants to talk with me about a possible rewrite before he suggests it to the playwright." He turned to her. "How did you know it was the love scene?"

"Jeanne's mentioned it during our coaching sessions."

"I'm not surprised," he said. "Oh, well . . . maybe we can work out the kinks today. I want to run the scene after the meeting."

The taxi slowed and came to a stop at the corner of Broadway and Fifty-second Street.

"I'll get out here," said Neal. "I want to pick up some coffee. You go on." He kissed her on the cheek. "See you at home tonight."

"Maybe I'll drop by this afternoon anyway!" Lydia called after him as he dashed into the coffee shop. She wasn't sure whether he'd heard her.

Men! she thought with a grin as the cab pulled away.

Almost four hours later when the acting class was

over and Lydia had lunched alone, she decided to walk for a while. The crisp late-November air was clear—and clean, for New York. The pleasant surprise invigorated her as she strolled uptown along Eighth Avenue. At Fifty-second Street she stopped and checked her wristwatch. Neal's rehearsal ought to be resuming about now. Maybe she could watch unobtrusively from the back of the house and see what all the fuss was about.

She waited for the traffic light on the corner in front of Howard Johnson's. Fifty-second was one of Lydia's favorite blocks in New York, its show business atmosphere never failing to envelop her. Just ahead was Jilly's bar, and beyond it her destination, the Alvin Theater. Across the street Roseland was still there, standing like an old friend. The marquee of the ANTA announced "June Havoc's *Marathon '33* starring Julie Harris." From a narrow building next door, a flapping banner extended over the street. White letters on a field of black read: "The American Academy of Dramatic Arts."

Perhaps it had been Neal's comment in the taxi that morning that now made Lydia stop to watch a group of Academy students huddled in front of the glass-and-iron door. Overweight or skinny, gawky or poised, they all possessed the same, unchanging exuberance that came from great expectations. Except for the modern sixties' cut of their clothing, Neal and Lydia might have been standing there among them in the cold of a November twenty years past. She envied these students their adventure, but not their struggle. Even if I *could* go back, she reflected, I wouldn't. Not for a minute.

The group's laughter faded as they entered the school and the door closed behind them.

Onstage at the Alvin, the afternoon rehearsal had already begun. Lydia waited until her eyes had adjusted to the darkness and then tiptoed to the center of a row at the rear of the orchestra section.

She slid out of her mink coat and, draping the sleeves over the velvet arms of the seat, settled back to watch.

Only a string of work lights illuminated the stage. From their spill she could see the back of Neal's head in the center of Aisle 5. Beside him sat the playwright, Steven Day, and two rows farther back, Herb and Carol Scofield, the producers.

Onstage, a tattered sofa, two tables, and one folding chair represented the set pieces that would be put in later. The only actors on the set were Jeanne and her leading man, Andrew Thorne. Three seasons before, Lydia had seen him in the performance that had brought him Broadway recognition. He was highly accomplished, respected, and possessed of a matinee idol sexuality that carried over the footlights in the way that Wesley Guest's transcended the screen. As he started to speak, Lydia was again reminded of how lucky they were to have him in the cast.

During coaching sessions with Jeanne, Lydia had tried breaking through the barriers her young pupil seemed to have erected. In the title role of Alice, Jeanne was playing a promiscuous alcoholic. Surely it was far from her experience. But something more was holding her back, particularly at the pivotal moment in Act Two—the drunken love scene between Alice and Bernard, her secret love of many years. Actresses waited decades for such a plum role, yet, despite her commitment to the part, Jeanne had continued to avoid—or block—the emotion that would bring Alice to life.

Until today. Lydia could tell as soon as the scene began. Something was different.

*   *   *

Jeanne picked up the prop glass and downed its contents in one gulp. It was water, meant to be vodka.

It *became* vodka. She became Alice.

Her feet were cramped inside the pointed-toe, three-inch-heel pumps she'd chosen to wear. She poured more "vodka" into the glass and spun lazily around on one of her steel spikes to face Andrew Thorne, who in a moment had to become "Bernard," the man whom "Alice" wanted.

Phrases from coachings prompted her: "Substitute," Lydia had said. "Use the image of a man you love. Use Ted." She had tried, but it didn't work. She wasn't in love with Ted. Still, finding the key to Act One had infused her with a fire. For the first time, Alice was filled with a command and authority that had been missing before. It brought with it a sense of daring.

Jeanne closed her eyes and let her mind go blank. She wasn't trying to substitute. Previous attempts had met with resistance, but to what or whom, she didn't know.

Now, relaxed but aware of every nerve ending in her body, an image appeared. A face she had never consciously expected to see, yet the instant she saw it, she recognized exactly what she'd been fighting since rehearsals had begun.

Shrinking back and opening her eyes, Jeanne found Andrew Thorne enfolding her in his arms. As she tried to erase the other face her mind had seen, the image kissed her.

Think! she commanded herself. He's Bernard! He's Andrew! He's *not*—

The image grew stronger as she tried to shut him out. Unable to resist, she closed her eyes once more and gave her heart to him. She knew it was wrong. He wasn't hers to love.

He belonged to Lydia.

"Alice" broke the embrace to take another sip of vodka. She moved two steps forward, spoke her line, and offered him the glass.

Andrew held it to her lips and, drawing her to him once again, said, "Drink." Jeanne felt the familiar barrier rising between actress and role, one that had kept her thus far from givng in to Alice's obsessive addiction.

And then, as though viewing an instant flashback, she saw the answer. Another image: a drunken, adolescent girl disrupting a wedding; a tipsy actress trying to hide her trembling hands from the television cameras; a striking face staring out from covers of magazines.

The obstacle was the key.

Then, as suddenly as it had appeared, Pia's image was gone. "Alice" gulped down her second vodka and crossed into "Bernard's" arms. And once more, as her arms closed and their lips met, he became Neal and she was helpless to stop him.

Their lips met as her fingers crawled across his chest and tore at his shirt. His arms held her in a viselike grip while his hands explored her back and moved over her breasts and buttocks. She dropped her glass and heard it smash upon hitting the floor. They were kissing, embracing, caressing passionately now, oblivious of their audience, of anyone but each other. The single sound in the theater was coming from the stage; the people out front were breathing as one.

Until the director cried, *"Stop!* Cut! This is a *play—* not *pornography!"*

The outburst startled everyone. Even from so far back, Lydia could see that Neal was bathed in perspiration. And she'd heard his rolled *r's* in the last word; it was a remnant of his European childhood and returned only in moments of rage. She had witnessed

262

that *r* twice in all their years together.

Lydia watched as her husband threw his script at the stage and stormed up the aisle past her toward the lobby.

She didn't follow. It was wiser to leave him alone when he was in one of his furies.

But what had gone wrong? Lydia wondered. The scene had finally played the way it needed to play. After all their work on it, Jeanne had broken through.

"Neal!" Jeanne called out from the stage. Lydia turned to see her pupil jump from the apron. "Neal!" she cried again. "I'm *sorry!*"

She raced up the aisle and Lydia hurried to intercept her. Jeanne paled as her friend's arms went around her.

"Darling, it was wonderful—"

No! Jeanne thought, too weak to pull away. Not you . . . not now . . .

But before she knew it, Lydia had helped her into a seat. Jeanne buried her face in her hands and began to sob.

The stage manager called a fifteen-minute break. Lydia rummaged through her purse until she found a handkerchief, which she handed to Jeanne.

This makes no sense, thought Lydia. Surely it's because she hasn't come down from the intensity of such a highly charged scene. And she's upset about Neal's disapproval—especially considering how close we all are to each other.

When Jeanne's tears at last subsided, Lydia asked gently, "What happened up there?"

"I . . . I don't know. I *thought* it was working, even that it was . . . good, until Neal—"

"It was better than good," said Lydia. "I don't understand what got into him."

Jeanne said, embarrassed and half to herself, "I . . . don't completely understand what got into me."

263

"That's easy. You opened a door and walked through."

Jeanne shook her head. "Neal . . . hated it."

Lydia managed a smile. "Neal may be my husband, and he's a fine director. But in this case, he needs to have his head examined. Now tell me, what happened?"

Jeanne shrugged her shoulders, then said simply, "It was Pia. Alice . . . is so much like Pia . . . I . . . I guess I've been afraid of the character." She blinked away the last of the tears. "My sister was keeping me from playing it full out . . . until . . ."

"Until what?"

An expression of incredulity crossed Jeanne's face, as though she were realizing it as she spoke. "Until I *allowed* Pia to help me *find* Alice . . ."

"Oh, Jeanne," Lydia said softly, "you've been letting your sister stand in your way all this time—and she's three thousand miles away."

Jeanne nodded. "Well, I've *used* her now. And . . . I guess if it helps me as an actress, I shouldn't care."

"What about Jeanne-the-woman?"

"There isn't any difference," she answered.

"You're wrong," said Lydia. "What I saw up there a few minutes ago was a woman in the arms of the man she loves. Unless you're falling for Andy Thorne . . ."

Jeanne swallowed guiltily. What could she say to her friend and coach who knew her so well? She couldn't come right out and tell the truth. At the same time Lydia would recognize a lie.

Taking a deep breath, she said, "It's just acting. I took your advice and . . . found a substitute image . . . for Andrew. Someone I—" She stopped herself short, and Lydia supplied the word.

"Someone you love?"

Color turned Jeanne's face crimson, but she didn't answer.

"Is it Ted?" Lydia asked. But she knew as she pronounced his name that it was someone else.

A calmer Neal Genesco returned to the auditorium. Now he saw his wife from across the row of plush seats.

"We'll talk about the scene tonight," he said, coming down the aisle. "Don't worry. She'll be fine."

"Yes . . . I know she will," said Lydia.

He waved and moved on to the stage manager. Seconds later, Jeanne and Andrew Thorne were called back and the rehearsal resumed.

"He won't touch the scene," said a voice behind Lydia. She turned to find Herb Scofield.

"Neal's the director," she replied. "He might."

"It's my money, Lydia. And we both know he's wrong. That scene—if she can repeat it opening night—will win her a Tony. And make her a star."

She didn't disagree, but instead said, "Then I take it you've changed your mind about those rewrites you wanted."

"*I* wanted?" Scofield seemed genuinely surprised. "*Neal* wanted the rewrites, Lydia. We're more than happy with the way it's going. Especially after today."

Lydia nodded as the meaning became clear. "Oh," she said at last. "My mistake." Then she picked up her coat and left the theater.

"Lydia?" Wesley said into the phone. "We're just leaving the house. We'll be by to pick you up in about fifteen minutes."

"Oh . . . Wes," said Lydia. "I . . . don't think I'm going to be able to make it this afternoon."

Wesley paused. "It's the dress rehearsal. They'll miss you."

He heard a rush of breath into the receiver. "I know. It's . . . my damned back again. If I try sitting for two solid hours today after the ride into Manhattan, I'll never get through the preview tomorrow night."

"Well," he said, "you know what's best. We'll call you this evening."

"Good. And tell Neal not to worry about me. He's got enough on his mind with the show. I don't want him to rush all the way back to Connecticut tonight just because of my silly aches. I can take the train in tomorrow, late morning."

"Do you need anything in the meantime?" asked Wesley.

"Not a thing, thanks. And tell Jeanne to save her energy for tomorrow night."

"It's only the first preview, Lydia. There's still a week till the opening."

"Jeanne hasn't had your years of experience, Wes. For her, tomorrow night *is* the opening."

"You're right," he said. "Well . . . you get some rest and feel better."

"I do already. Kiss Mathilde for me."

"What do you think?" Mathilde asked, when they'd settled into the car.

"About what?"

"Whenever you answer a question with another question, I know you're stalling."

Wes grinned. "You've got me. I think she's telling the truth. She sounded tired."

"Well, either way, I don't like it. Whenever her back goes out, it's painful for her. But she uses it to avoid things, too."

"What's she trying to avoid this afternoon?" he asked, leaning over to turn the heater to maximum.

266

"I'm not sure," said Mathilde. "She's been . . . well . . . distant, I guess. For weeks now."

Her hesitation fueled Wes's speculation. "You have some idea . . . ?"

"No . . ." she said slowly, pulling the collar of her mink coat up around her neck. "It's . . . just a . . . a feeling."

They dropped off the car at the garage adjacent to their apartment building and took a taxi to the theater.

"Oh, darling!" Mathilde exclaimed as Wes paid the driver and they stepped out onto the sidewalk. "You didn't tell me!"

The name *J-E-A-N-N-E L-O-R-R-A-I-N-E* was spelled out in blazing red letters above the title of the play, *A-F-T-E-R A-L-I-C-E*.

"I wanted to surprise you," Wes said, feeling as happy and proud as he knew his wife must be.

Once inside the Alvin, Wes and Mathilde became part of a select, intimate audience of forty or fifty invited guests, all friends or associates of the cast and production personnel.

The lights dimmed, the curtains parted, and the dress rehearsal began.

Wes watched, and as he did, he smiled to himself. He had been right about Jeanne. Her natural gifts, brought out further by Lydia's insightful coaching, Neal's strong direction, and the power of Andrew Thorne's presence, came together and resulted in an electrifying, breathtaking performance.

Wes had read the script. And he'd heard about the controversial love scene in Act Two. Now he recognized Neal's subtle changes, changes brought about without rewrites. The scene as played was still overwhelming, almost too . . . real. Too . . . familiar.

267

As the second act drew to its climax, a sound, not unlike a strangled cry, broke out from the wings. Andrew Thorne stumbled over a line of dialogue, his concentration temporarily thrown off. Wes saw Neal suddenly bolt from his seat and rush through the side door to the backstage area. A flurry of curious murmurs rippled through the auditorium, then diminished and died away with Jeanne's final entrance.

"Alice," having experienced a metamorphosis during the course of the play, should have been calm and self-assured by this point in the drama. Instead, she was visibly trembling and barely able to control the shaking of an already inaudible voice.

Mathilde gripped Wesley's arm. "Something's wrong," she whispered.

Mercifully, *After Alice* came to its end. Despite their applause, the members of the audience were clearly confused by what they had just seen. They rose for Jeanne's curtain call, but their applause faded immediately at sight of her.

She bowed deeply, momentarily in control, and then her hands came up to cover her face. Andrew Thorne entered the stage and led Jeanne off into the wings. At the same instant Neal opened the side door and returned to the house in search of Wes and Mathilde.

"Neal!" said Mathilde. "What's happened?"

"The . . . radio," he replied in a choked voice. "The news report—"

He was interrupted by the stage manager's appearance center stage.

"Ladies and gentlemen," he began. "I regret to tell you—that we have—just received confirmation"—he struggled to control his emotions—"President Kennedy has been shot."

*   *   *

Despite traffic and subway noises that continued with indifference to Friday's tragedy, a pall had fallen over the city. As dusk gave way to darkness, the quiet became almost palpable.

Mathilde could sense it even before they stepped out of the theater onto the pavement. From car radios blaring relentlessly, Governor Nelson Rockefeller proclaimed a state of mourning to a numbed populace. Pedestrians passed one another with stunned expressions. If strangers' eyes chanced to meet, each mirrored the other's shock and disbelief.

Under the Alvin's marquee, Neal strengthened his hold on Mathilde's arm and tried to force a smile.

"What will you do?" she asked him. "About the play, I mean?"

"As of right now, unless Herb decides to postpone, we'll start previewing tomorrow night. That's if Jeanne's up to it, of course."

"She will be," Mathilde assured him. "If she has to, she'll go on."

They waited for Jeanne and Wes at the corner of Eighth Avenue.

"Would you like to come back to the apartment with us?" Mathilde asked when the four of them were together. "Dinner . . . or a drink? We could probably all use one about now."

"Not me, thanks, Mama," said Jeanne. "I wouldn't be very good company."

"Well, if you change your mind, the sofa in the study opens into a bed." Turning to Neal, she said, "Will you come up and join us for a drink?"

He shook his head. "I can't. Lydia sounded upset by the news. I couldn't really tie up the backstage phone with everyone waiting to use it. I promised her I'd call again as soon as I get to the apartment."

"You can phone from our place," Wes offered.

"Thanks . . . but I'll head uptown. You two go on home."

A checker cab pulled up at curbside. Mathilde hugged Jeanne, then climbed into the backseat with Wes.

"I'll let you know what Herb decides about tomorrow," said Neal.

He closed the door of the taxi and the car sped off.

Their own breath created clouds around them as Neal and Jeanne stood shivering, neither sure of what to say. At last Neal ventured, "Will you . . . have a drink with me?"

"As long as we don't have to talk. I'm feeling kind of . . ." She didn't finish the sentence.

"I know," he said, putting a protective arm around her as they started down the block.

After ten minutes' wait they managed one drink at Jilly's. The bar was always crowded at this hour, but tonight people were jammed three-deep. Cigarette smoke blanketed the air and fogged the television screen over the bar. All eyes were glued to replays of the horrifying moments in Dallas. Jilly's was known as a favorite Sinatra haunt, and every so often someone's voice could be heard speculating on how "Frank" was taking the news.

Neal elbowed his way through the mob until he located the pay phone. It was in use, and a line had formed behind it. He made his way back to the bar without having called home. He noticed that Jeanne smiled—a very slight smile, but it was the first one he'd seen from her in hours.

"That's better," he said. "You're prettier without a frown."

270

"What?" she yelled over the din.

"I said let's get out of here!" he shouted.

They settled on the Chinese restaurant at the corner of Fifty-second and Seventh. Neither of them was hungry, but it was refuge from the cold. Jacket and tie were supplied to Neal by the maître d'. Jeanne laughed as he slid the black checked blazer over his blue plaid flannel shirt and V-necked navy sweater. The all-purpose jacket was big enough for two Neals to fit inside, and the bow tie hung lopsidedly from the clip at his neck.

"You see," he whispered as they were shown to a table, "I try for Ronald Colman and end up Jerry Lewis."

They lingered over two more cocktails, comforted by the alcohol and by each other's presence. They hardly talked at all.

Their meals went largely untouched. Jeanne wondered if the restaurant's staff was as uninterested in food tonight as most of the patrons seemed to be. A glance at other tables only served as a reminder that the President's assassination was a fact, not a scene in a play. She tried to turn her mind to other subjects. In doing so, she brushed her long hair off her face.

"I'm glad you left your stage makeup on," Neal said, breaking the long silence.

"I'm not," she said. "But everyone was in such a hurry to find out what happened, and—"

"You look wonderful. Very grown-up too."

"I *am* grown-up."

Neal smiled. "I know. I meant . . . I don't care how silly I look." He touched the knot at the center of his borrowed tie. "And I must look quite silly."

271

"Why silly?" she asked.

"Well . . . this getup. And the sight of an old man with such a young girl."

"Neal . . . you're hardly forty."

"Forty-five, thank you. I could be your father."

Jeanne averted her eyes.

"Have I said something wrong?" he asked, placing his hand on hers.

Some unknown reflex action made her pull her hand away. "No. It's just . . . my father's been on my mind."

"He's dead, if I'm correct . . . ?"

She nodded. "I've barely thought about him for years, but lately . . . and especially tonight, with the President—"

"Violence can . . . change us all," said Neal softly, sipping his cognac. "I lost a brother in the war."

"How awful. I'm sorry . . ."

He shrugged. "Actually it was just before the war. In Bucharest. We were young, not much older than you. They beat Leon to death—"

"But *why*? And who were 'they'?"

"'They' were members of the Iron Guard. As to why"—he paused reflectively—"no reason. Except that we were Jews."

Jeanne had never known anything about Neal's personal history. His brother's death seemed as wasteful and senseless as the President's assassination. "What about the rest of your family . . . ?"

"Friends helped us to get out. If it was no longer safe to go into the street—that's where Leon was when it happened, a stone's throw from the king's palace— then it was no longer safe to remain in the capital."

Neal's eyes met Jeanne's. "I haven't thought about that in quite some time, either."

Once more his hand reached out to cover hers, and this time she didn't draw it away. "It's a strange night,

272

isn't it . . . ?"

"Yes . . ." she answered, not immune to the effect of his touch. "I . . . I think we should probably get the check, don't you?"

While Neal paid the bill, Jeanne went to the ladies' room and washed off most of her stage makeup. She had hoped that a scrubbed face and a splash of cold water would help her think more clearly, but she found herself still confused. Too much had happened that afternoon—the play, followed by the tragic news. And the night—this strange night, as Neal had said—wasn't over.

On their walk east, Neal noticed but didn't remark about her clean, shiny face, although the absence of makeup made him painfully aware of just how young she was. He and Jeanne were both conscious of the extra care being taken to avoid physical contact with each other. Only when they crossed Sixth Avenue did he take her arm, and then lightly and briefly. Their conversation had become forced and polite as well.

Jeanne stopped in front of the old brownstone. "This is home," she said. "Thank you for seeing me to my door, Neal."

"It's on my way. I can walk up to Fifty-fourth, and a taxi will get me across town and straight up Third Avenue. At this hour it shouldn't take more than fifteen minutes."

A sudden gust of wind sent Jeanne's long hair swirling around her face. She laughed, peeking out as she brushed it behind her ears. "I should be wearing a scarf," she said self-consciously.

"No. It's lovely, free like that . . ."

She tried to look away, tried to find something—*anything*—that wouldn't sound idiotic. "You'll call

273

me—about tomorrow's schedule . . . ?"

"Damn!" he cried.

"What's the matter?"

Neal checked his wristwatch. "I'm a fool. It's nearly eight—and I promised to phone Lydia before seven!"

"Well . . . it's not as if you hadn't tried," Jeanne answered.

"No, that's true . . ."

"And you'll be able to call her . . . as soon as you get home."

"Yes."

"And . . . that won't be long—"

"No," he said on impulse. "Not if you'll let me use your phone."

Jeanne thought it might be prudent to say, "Don't take off your coat," but it was too late for that. Neal had slid out of the tan trenchcoat and let it drop onto a chair.

"The phone is over there," said Jeanne, gesturing toward a small table next to the sofa.

She hung up her own coat and suddenly felt immodest as she saw that Neal was watching her. Meeting his gaze, she said, "I . . . I'm not offering to make coffee . . ."

"I understand," he answered. He was standing beside the table but hadn't yet touched the phone.

"Neal . . . your call," she reminded him.

After a beat, and still looking at Jeanne, he picked up the receiver and dialed.

"No," he was saying over the line, "I'm not at the apartment."

Jeanne was about to pantomime her regards when

274

she heard Neal say into the phone, "I'm ... at Herb Scofield's. We ... needed a drink."

His eyes darted to Jeanne, who stood frozen to the spot. Then he continued. "Yes, it's horrible news ... everyone's still shocked ... No, I think we'll go ahead with the preview tomorrow ... Is your back feeling any better?... Good ... Jeanne? Well, she's ... upset, of course, but she's all right ... no, she ... isn't here. She ... went home. Wanted to be ... alone."

Jeanne was growing increasingly nervous. Neal smiled tentatively at her and said into the receiver, "Darling I'll meet you for lunch tomorrow. As soon as you get into town. Meanwhile, try to get some sleep ... Yes, I will, too ..." He hung up and stared at the blank plastic cradle as the line went dead.

After a long pause, he glanced up at Jeanne. "I ... don't know what made me ... lie."

But he did know, and the fact that Jeanne also knew made her feel guilty of complicity without having uttered a word.

"I think ... you'd better go, Neal."

"Jeanne—"

"Please," she said.

He went to the chair and picked up his coat without taking his eyes from hers.

I'll be okay, she thought, if he leaves right this minute.

But downstairs, out on the street, she'd known she was tempting fate. He could have waited fifteen minutes and called Lydia from uptown.

They both knew that.

Neal came toward her now, and Jeanne backed away, retreating toward the door. Her hand went to the knob. She was determined to turn it when Neal gently grasped her shoulders.

"I'm sorry," he said quietly.

Her whole body began to tremble. Her fingers slipped off the doorknob and touched his wrists.

"So am I," she whispered.

Neal wiped a tear from her cheek and with his fingertip tenderly traced the outline of her lips. The fine hairs across the back of his hand caressed the soft down of her jaw. She could feel his staccato breathing, his own hesitation. They stood motionless, looking deeply into each other's eyes. There was still time to break away, to smile and say that nothing had happened between them.

But something *had* happened, and no amount of pretending would ever erase or cancel the moment.

He lowered his face to kiss her parted lips.

She tried to withdraw from his embrace. "No . . . !" she pleaded, shaking her head.

This can't happen! Mustn't happen! She shut her eyes tightly and commanded herself to regain control of her senses.

NO! reason silently cried out. I *cannot* love this man! Not Neal!

It was wrong. He wasn't hers to love.

Suddenly her eyes flashed open and Jeanne looked into the face of the man whose image had made love to her onstage that afternoon.

He's here. I'm not pretending. This is real. He is real.

Jeanne's legs gave out from under her, but Neal's arms kept her from falling. Her neck arched as he pulled her closer, and this time she made no effort to pull back. They began kissing each other with ravenous abandon, their appetites only heightened by their previous restraint.

And the phone rang.

It startled them for an instant, then Neal whispered breathlessly, "Let it ring."

"N-no. Neal . . ."

276

At the second ring she tore her mouth away from his lips. "Neal, please stop . . ."

"Why?" He didn't release her from his embrace.

The third ring sounded in Jeanne's ear like an alarm bell. "Because, Neal . . . we both know who's calling."

She managed to break free and reach the phone. She picked up the receiver. The voice at the other end sent a shooting pain across her chest and made it difficult for Jeanne to find her voice.

"Lydia . . ." she said at last.

"Neal said you were upset, darling. Are you feeling any better?"

Jeanne cast a glance at Neal. "I'm . . . all right, now." The tears began to flow freely as she spoke. "I . . . I can't tell you, Lydia . . . what your phone call . . . has meant to me . . ."

Neal was at the door, his coat slung over one arm. His fingers touched his lips and he blew her a tender kiss. Jeanne saw tears in his eyes, too, but he turned the knob, went out into the hall, and closed the door behind him.

Chapter Nineteen

Pia stood naked in front of the full-length hotel-room mirror in the pose she had held for nearly fifteen minutes. She took a final turn and sat down on the overstuffed loveseat, where she began to examine the shape of her legs. She lit a cigarette and inhaled deeply as a smile crept over her face.

Once again she had reassured herself that her breasts and buttocks were still high, her tummy flat, her thighs firm. Her face would undergo similar scrutiny only after she'd applied makeup. Others might consider her concern about aging as neurotic for a girl of twenty-one, but others weren't *stars*. Olympia Decameron wasn't going to wait until the cameraman had to shoot through forty filters of gauze to make her appear youthful; she'd have cosmetic lifting before that!

She picked up the screenplay lying beside her. Next Monday would be the first day of principal photography, and she'd have to look good. Better than good. *Great*. It might not be the world's best-written script, but by the time the film was shot and released, she'd have suffered a year's absence from the screen. Too long—she didn't need the industry people's advice to know that. And at least it was better than most of the screenplays Antaen Pictures had submitted to her agent. Besides, the studio was making noises about another suspension, and she couldn't afford that—career-wise *or* otherwise.

One more year on this stupid contract, she thought. And then? The studio had better come up with a better offer—and better roles. Of course, there's always the possibility they might not renew . . .

No, she decided, they wouldn't dare! I may not be Number 1 at the box office, but Number 6 is still money in Antaen's coffers. They need me . . .

But what if . . . what if *I* decide *not* to sign again? Other stars are branching out now that the studio system is on its last legs. Maybe Barney's suggestion about my buying and producing a property on my own isn't such a bad idea . . .

To the press, Pia had intimated that her Oscar nomination had whetted her appetite for strong drama—she constantly used the phrase "something to sink my teeth into"—but the truth was that it had made her lust after the golden statuette. Antaen Pictures certainly wasn't much help to that end.

Oh, well, she reasoned philosophically, at least they're footing the bill for this trip east, even if they *have* sent Hilda.

Hilda was "billed" in the gossip columns as Pia's secretary. She was actually a chaperone—or, as Pia more accurately put it, a "watchdog." It was convenient to have the woman answering the door and taking phone messages. But Nathan Schutz had lied in calling her a studio liaison. Her presence at Pia's interviews in New York was not only to ensure that Olympia Decameron be given the "star treatment"; Hilda's presence also ensured that Pia would be given nothing but water to drink.

Antaen Pictures' watchdog attitude added to Pia's

279

eagerness to be free of the slavery that the studio called a contract. More immediately, however, she wished to be free of Hilda.

There was a knock at the connecting door between their rooms.

"Come in if you have to," Pia called as Hilda entered. The woman, who resembled a middle-aged English bulldog, was carrying an armload of newspapers. "California's on the phone. It's your agent. Here are yesterday's interviews. You're due at the RCA Building in an hour for the NBC taping, and curtain time for the theater this evening is eight-fifteen. Oh, and I've ordered a sandwich from room service. You might want to put on a bathrobe, unless you like being ogled in the buff."

At the end of her speech, Hilda returned to her own room. Pia was constantly put off by the woman's abruptness. Anyone *that* homely, she reasoned, can't afford to be so rude

She picked up her phone extension. "Hiya, Barney," she said into the receiver.

"Hiya, gorgeous. Just thought I'd let you know what I found out."

"About what?"

"About the rights to the play. They're still clear, but a few studios have already made bids, plus the fact that Woodward and MacLaine have put out feelers to personally option it. We're gonna have to move fast, and it won't come cheap, with all those other bidders in the ring."

"Shit," Pia hissed through clenched teeth. "How fast? I don't even know yet if I want the damn thing."

"Call me at home tonight after you've seen the show. I can put in an offer tomorrow morning."

"What studios have made bids, Barney?"

"Uh . . . lemme see . . . Metro, Fox, Universal, and—"

"And Antaen Pictures?"

"Yeah."

"Goddammit, Barney! I've got to bid against my *own* studio!" she yelled. Then she remembered the spy in the adjoining room and lowered her voice.

"Pia, honey, you gotta face facts. If you decide you want it, it's gotta be on your own, 'cause Antaen sure as hell won't buy it to star *you.*"

"Why, in God's name?" she whined.

"They think you're too young for the part, gorgeous."

"I'm a year *older* than Jeanne!" she cried.

Barney's voice broke into a laugh. "I never thought I'd hear you admit that."

"Well," she countered, smiling, "maybe I'm really younger than she is—and just lying to get the role."

"Right. And maybe your last husband will give you back all the money. Call me—and do it *before* one in the morning, or I'll hang up."

"Good-bye, you bastard," she said, replacing the receiver to its cradle. Then a grin formed across her face. Barney was one of the few people who understood her. His ruthlessness equaled her own, and although he could be too brutally frank, he never failed to make her laugh.

I'd marry him if he wasn't so much like me, she mused, picking up a copy of the first newspaper in the stack and turning to her interview.

"Prodigal Pia" didn't please her as a headline—she wasn't entirely sure what the word *prodigal* meant—but above it was an excellent photograph of Pia sitting in a booth at Sardi's, where she'd given yesterday's interview. She looked happy and glamorous. Pia stared at the picture for some time and tried to connect the serene black-and-white image with her own current, tense jangle of nerves. Other women would see the picture and wish they could trade places with the face in the photo. I'd like to, too, Pia reflected.

Then she noticed something else. On the wall behind her were framed caricatures of the restaurant's celebrity patrons. Directly overhead was a rendering of Jeanne.

I suppose they think that's cute, she fumed. She hadn't seen it during the interview. Well, may as well read what I've said . . .

"Olympia Decameron. A romantic name that defies the rules of brevity dictated by marquee space. A name that has become synonymous with the word *star*. But what of the woman behind the name? your reporter asked. 'I'm basically uncomplicated,' Miss Decameron replied, leaning back in her chair. 'My wants . . . my needs . . . are humble.' Asked to comment on the diamond bracelet she wore, the beautiful Oscar nominee answered, 'This! A . . . token of appreciation from . . . a dear friend.'"

Pia smiled, crushing her cigarette into an ashtray. She'd bought the bracelet for herself—wholesale.

"Dismissing rumors of a rift between her and Broadway stage star and sister, Jeanne Lorraine, Miss Decameron laughed. 'They're only that . . . rumors. We merely work on two different coasts. We don't often see each other, but Jeanne and I are in constant touch. She just decided on a career in the East.'
"And the purpose of her own visit to New York?

'Some Christmas shopping, and of course, to see my mother and Wesley in Connecticut. We're all very close.'"

The interview explained Wesley's marriage to Mathilde and went on with a further quote:

"'I wish I'd been able to see his last play,' she said with regret. 'But it didn't run long enough . . . Jeanne's, either. And I was *so* busy at the time. The nomination, you know.'

"Mention of a possible—some say probable—Tony Award for Miss Lorraine's triumph in the current hit, *After Alice*, was greeted with a beaming smile. 'I'm *sure* she's marvelous in it. Such a shame it's sold out . . . I mean . . . I might not be able to get a seat!'"

The reporter had fleshed out the rest of the page with the usual facts or inventions about the "much-married Miss Decameron." But Pia was satisfied. With this, plus the week's TV and radio interviews and talk shows, knowledge of Pia's presence in town couldn't possibly escape Jeanne. Tonight's appearance at the play would come as a complete surprise to her sister, while Pia sat and watched Jeanne squirm. She hoped only that Wes and Mathilde wouldn't be there.

Jeanne folded the magazine section of the *News*. If she'd thought there might be any truth in Pia's interviews, she'd thought in vain. Each paper carried similar lies—fairy tales, as Mama called them. Maybe Mathilde was right and Pia didn't know where truth left off and her fanciful stories took over.

Well, at least this time she'd had the grace to leave

283

Jeanne out of it—almost. Being ignored was preferable to reading that the two actresses were the best of friends and constantly together whenever they found themselves in the same city. Jeanne wouldn't have even known that Pia was in New York if it hadn't been for the tabloids. They hadn't seen each other since Wes and Mama's wedding. On an impulse, Jeanne had sent a note of congratulations on the occasion of Pia's Oscar nomination, but it had gone unanswered. They hadn't communicated since.

She glanced at her image in the makeup mirror on her dressing table. Jeanne had arrived at the theater early, which was her customary habit, and the bulbs framing the mirror were still off, except for the right-hand bank that she used as reading lights.

With the rest of her dressing room cast into semi-darkness, Jeanne allowed her thoughts to roam. This half hour of random mind wandering each night had also become a habit; it helped her to shed her daytime persona and whatever cares were part of the outer world, and enter into the fictive realm of *After Alice*. As the minutes ticked by, her breathing became slower, and her mental screen filled with Alice's needs and wants, Alice's problems, Alice's joys and sorrows.

At first this time alone had been no more than one actress's nightly preparation. In recent weeks, however, it had become salvation, as Hollywood star after Hollywood star traipsed backstage to kiss her cheek and rave over her performance—only to march back to her respective studio and demand a contract to portray Alice in the film version of the play.

So far no studio had formally announced victory over a rival, but it was common knowledge on both coasts that *After Alice* was the prize catch of the season—and the title role would almost certainly garner an Oscar for the actress who was lucky enough to be cast.

No, Jeanne amended, luck has nothing to do with it. The role will go to the actress who's *famous* enough to play it.

An inadvertent sigh escaped as she realized that her concentration on the business aspect of Alice was keeping her from *becoming* Alice. But Jeanne had learned that she had to "let" Alice arrive; if she tried too hard, her own trying got in the way, with all of her energy wasted on effort.

Well, then, she mused, I wonder who'll be here tonight. Have any big studios or stars *missed* the play?

She knew her attitude was less than magnanimous, but at times the unfairness of the Hollywood "system" overwhelmed her. To have *created* the role—from nothing but words on a page—and not be in the running simply because she wasn't famous enough, struck a sour chord. When friends or colleagues reminded her that Anne Bancroft had gone from playing Annie Sullivan on Broadway to the same role on film, Jeanne had to remind herself that Bancroft's case was the exception. Hollywood "tradition" dictated that major stars were cast in major roles. To wit, Mary Martin in *South Pacific*—onstage; Mitzi Gaynor, on film. Period, end of hope and speculation.

Jeanne had finally "entered" Alice—or, rather, Alice had entered Jeanne—when Roger Dalton, the stage manager, came by. He knocked at her dressing room door, although he knew that Jeanne was inside; she was usually the first cast member to arrive at the theater. Jeanne appreciated Roger's thoughtfulness at not bursting in on her thoughts. He always stood outside her door until she called out, "Come in."

His enthusiasm was contagious, as was the company's. It stemmed from being involved with a hit

285

show. Guaranteed employment for months. The limelight. A good feeling shared by cast and crew. "Outsiders" seemed to sense it. Those who were envious stayed away; others basked in a reflected glow.

Unfortunately, Ted Sayers fell into the former category; his road company tour had separated him physically from Jeanne, while her triumph on Broadway created a greater distance between them. What might have been a beginning had, by tacit consent, come to an end. It saddened Jeanne, but in another way, she was grateful. She had been since the night of the President's assassination. The night of Neal's lie.

During the week of previews, then for the two weeks following the official opening, they hadn't been alone together for a moment. He was seldom out of her thoughts, and admittedly she used her feelings for Neal onstage at each performance, just as she used her sister's nature to penetrate Alice. But she wasn't going to do *anything* that might encourage a repeat of the night in her apartment. He must never know how close her resolve came to weakening when they passed each other backstage or were forced to be in the same room during a brush-up rehearsal. Some things just weren't meant to be, and this was one of them.

And every coaching or luncheon or conversation with Lydia Genesco confirmed to Jeanne that no other decision could have been made. Not if she ever wanted to face her close friend and mentor without guilt or shame.

But each evening, with the exception of Monday when the theater was dark, and each Wednesday and Saturday afternoon, Neal was here to love for two full hours, and she could still look Lydia in the eyes. The heartache was in Neal's not knowing.

And yet she felt that somehow he did know, had to know. If he didn't, it would be Neal at her dressing

286

room door each night at seven-thirty, instead of Roger Dalton.

"My God, Roger!" Jeanne exclaimed, realizing that he'd probably been waiting there for five minutes or more. She jumped up and opened the door.

He didn't seem perturbed. He handed her a heavy vellum envelope. "It's an invitation to *another* party," he said. "Isn't it wonderful to be popular?"

Jeanne laughed and added the invitation to a mounting stack in her dressing-table drawer.

"Do you think we'll grow bored and blasé with one bash after another?" Roger teased. It was his first hit show, too.

Jeanne shook her head. "No, but I'm sure we'll get more sleep when the novelty wears off."

"Well, that won't be until after the first of the year. Which reminds me. Mr. Scofield is planning a New Year's Eve cast party. He hasn't said where yet, but he did say there'll be plenty of champagne to celebrate. We're sold out through May—isn't that fabulous?"

"Yes, Roger," said Jeanne. "That's fabulous." Five more months of imagining I'm with Neal, she thought. A sudden pall appeared, though, as two words crossed her mind: *What then?*

"I'd better start my makeup, Roger." Then, with an affected, formal British accent, Jeanne said, "Do let me know what luminaries grace us with their presence in the house tonight?"

"Your wish is my command, madame," he said, bowing deeply. This, too, had become a ritual exchange. It lightened their pre-performance mood, which might otherwise have become nerve-wracking, considering the steady stream of box-office names that nightly invaded the Alvin Theater.

Next came Roger's tag line just before his exit. "Ah, madame, the trials of success . . ."

287

Jeanne's grin broke into a wide smile as Roger closed the door.

She had almost finished with her makeup and hair when Roger reappeared. This time his entrance was accompanied by a tentativeness he hadn't displayed since opening night. Half hour had been called, and although the stage manager's fifteen-minute warning was announced over the squawkbox, Roger generally stopped by in person to deliver the call and what he and Jeanne referred to as the celebrity list.

Then why should tonight have him quaking in his desert boots?

"Uh . . ." he began.

"Roger? What is it? You look as if you've seen a ghost."

"Well . . . I . . . um . . . don't know whether or not you'll want to hear who's out front," he said.

"Listen," she answered, "I'm immune. I mean, after Lady Bird Johnson, Tallulah Bankhead, and Joan Crawford on three different nights—*not* to mention the Hollywood vultures who would *kill* to play Alice—who on earth could matter so much that—"

"It's your sister. She's sitting third row center."

Suddenly Jeanne was at a loss for words. And banter wasn't going to help.

"Thanks, Roger," she said. "I . . ." But what could she add? Had Pia come out of curiosity? No, that wasn't like her. Pia was there for the same reason as all the other "vultures" who had come. She wanted the role of Alice. No word, no letter or call, not even to Mama. No attempt at contacting her sister. Ambition, not love, had brought Pia to the play, probably to New York.

Jeanne drew a long breath as she glanced at the

newspaper interview she'd read an hour before. Christmas shopping—for a *script!*

Jeanne didn't understand why the knowledge of Pia's presence in the house fueled her adrenaline, but if her previous performances as Alice had been "electrifying . . . gripping . . . stunning," as the combined adjectives of *The New York Times, The New York Herald Tribune,* and *Newsweek* had all proclaimed, then new superlatives would need to be coined for the evening on which Olympia Decameron saw *After Alice.*

Jeanne was in fact so emotionally charged that even during intermission she could barely focus on the real world of backstage life. Roger brought her chicken broth, which he did at the halfway mark every night, but he left the cup on her dressing table and didn't stay; Jeanne was seated on the little sofa in the corner and didn't seem to notice how or by whom the soup had been delivered.

Roger had the sense to keep her door clear of visitors. He wouldn't be able to fend them off after the final curtain, but at least no one was able to sneak past him while the performance was in progress.

While she was onstage, Jeanne wasn't conscious of Pia's presence. Even if she had been tempted to peer through the peephole in the curtain beforehand—which she didn't—once she had crossed the invisible threshold from the wings to the stage, Jeanne and Alice merged and became one. Anyone or anything that helped to infuse her role with life was permitted—encouraged—to surface; the smaller inessentials were left behind.

And still, as the love scene in Act Two began, Jeanne experienced a new sensation, one that excited yet terrified her: Just as she had "used" Pia at the

289

breakthrough dress rehearsal a month before, she was using her sister now. But tonight it was in a totally different way.

Now, as Andrew Thorne came toward her, Jeanne was aware of something more than an adrenaline rush. More than her unacted-upon feelings for Neal. In a flash, Pia's face darted through her mind and disappeared. In its place was a sense of *power*. Not power over Pia, or Neal, or anyone in particular. But power, nonetheless. With it came a tremendous, intense calm. Jeanne's heartbeat was no longer racing as it usually did with the heat of the approaching scene; her words and actions seemed to slow. She was conscious of being on two levels at once, as though she were acting out a part—which she *was* doing—while watching herself from the wings. And when her two "selves" melded, she was no longer Jeanne *becoming* Alice, as she had been before. She was Jeanne *portraying* Alice.

Her awareness did nothing to lessen the performance; rather, it *added* a deeper dimension, one that was larger than life. Only Jeanne understood. Those who had seen the play more than once—Lydia included—wouldn't have noticed. She doubted that even Neal would know.

Neal, she thought as Andrew Thorne embraced her. But these weren't Neal's kisses. Nor his touch.

Nor his love! a silent voice shouted. Oh, God! This *isn't* Neal! And *pretending* that it is will *never* be enough!

She was drenched from emotion at the final curtain. Her heart had resumed its faster rhythm, had doubled as though in compensation for its earlier, slower pace. Her eyes were blurred with tears as she took her final solo bow to a standing ovation. Usually the last act left her spent, drained of energy. Tonight it was the opposite. She likened the sensation to a highly revved-up motor.

She'd given the performance of her life. But what kind of Pandora's box had this new awareness opened?

By the time she had pushed past the well-wishers and congratulators and hangers-on and finally reached her dressing room, Jeanne was ready to scream. Suddenly she wasn't sure whether her performance had gone too far. Had Alice given too much? And if so, what was left for Jeanne?

As if in reply to her question, the door opened and Neal Genesco entered. He hadn't stopped by her dressing room—not without Lydia or someone in the company—since the afternoon of November 22.

Jeanne's throat went dry, but she managed to find enough voice to say, "Please, Neal. Come in . . ."

He closed the door behind him. For a moment there was an awkward silence between them. Then he said, "I . . . I wanted you to know how wonderful you were tonight."

She was standing three feet away from him, almost within reach. "Neal, I—"

She had removed several of her hairpins, and soft wisps of gold curled at the nape of her neck. Without thinking, Neal said, "You look wonderful, too . . ."

Whether she took the step forward or whether he did was unimportant. Suddenly they were in each other's arms, devouring each other with kisses, kisses that had been interrupted by a phone call only a few short weeks before.

"Neal, we *can't*—you *know* we can't!" Tears were running down her cheeks as she returned his caresses, her actions negating her own words.

"I love you," he said, his own eyes filled with tears.

"I've tried *not* to love you, but I can't help myself."

"You've got to! *We've* got to! For Lydia—and for us!"

Lydia's name seemed to shake them to their senses, but they were still in each other's arms.

"How do we manage, then?" he asked. "It won't just go away."

If she hadn't realized it before tonight's performance, Jeanne was painfully aware of the truth now.

"Then it's up to us to . . ." Her voice broke as she backed away from him.

"Up to us—to what? Lie to ourselves? We've been doing that, and it hasn't changed the way either of us feels—"

"But, Neal," she pleaded, "it mustn't be—*can't* be—any other way!" Looking up into his eyes, she asked, "You know I'm right, don't you?"

He didn't reply at first. Then finally, he answered, "You were right that night . . . and you are now. But you can't refuse me the joy of loving you."

"Please, Neal, that can only hurt . . . the three of us. We can't be more than . . . friends."

"Jeanne," he said quietly, "we already are."

"Neal . . . you've got to promise me—"

"Jeanne—"

"You've *got* to help me!" Tears were threatening again. "Neal . . . your strength will be my strength. Please!"

He was studying her as though seeing her for the first time. "You have enough strength for both of us. I saw that onstage tonight."

The love in his eyes was agonizing, and Jeanne couldn't reply.

Onstage. Tonight. That seemed so long ago. Finally through the blur she managed a smile. "Your . . . friendship . . . is very important to me, Neal. I don't ever want to lose that."

"You . . . never will," he whispered, coming toward her.

Jeanne wasn't certain she could maintain her own resolve if she permitted him to touch her. But she also knew the torture of denial; she'd been living with it.

Neal and Jeanne embraced, without kisses or caresses, with only tenderness and love.

They were in each other's arms when the door swung open.

"Well," exclaimed Pia, as a sly smile crossed her face. "If it isn't little sister and an old family friend . . . !"

Chapter Twenty

"Andy, I'm freezing!" Jeanne shouted.

"We're almost there!" Andrew Thorne yelled back over the gusting moan of the wind.

The New Year's Eve crowds had made finding a taxi impossible. The cast of *After Alice* had walked up Eighth Avenue from the Alvin Theater to Seventh Avenue and Central Park South. Tonight's arctic temperatures and snow flurries had transformed the usually pleasant seven-block stroll into an endurance contest.

Across the street and to their left, the park's naked trees struggled against the wind, which drowned out the jubilant cries of "Happy New Year!" from a few already inebriated passersby.

Jeanne pulled the collar of her mink coat tightly around her neck. She'd been so proud of her holiday purchase, bought with her own money saved from weekly earnings in the play. Then Pia had shown up . . . in sable.

Jeanne smiled to herself; it's ridiculous to even think about it—*or* about Pia. It's New Year's Eve. A night to enjoy. She was determined to have a good time and not let her sister interfere.

But Pia *had* interfered. Damn! thought Jeanne. *Why* did she have to walk into the dressing room at precisely *that* moment? It had plagued Jeanne for the past two weeks—both the significance of Neal's and her embrace—and the way it was sure to be distorted by her sister's warped imagination.

That night's embrace, Jeanne reflected. She and Neal had ended the possibility of something more; what Pia had seen was all there was—or was ever going to be.

The group had reached the shelter of the heated canopy over the entrance to the apartment building. The doorman tipped his hat and waved them cheerfully inside. They found their way through the vast marble lobby and rang for the elevator, which arrived silently a moment later.

Jeanne and her leading man and half a dozen others crowded in. Andrew said, "Penthouse, please."

"Oh, yessir, Mr. Thorne!" The elevator operator beamed happily. "Mr. Scofield's party is in full swing—sounds like they're having quite a celebration!"

Jeanne and Andrew smiled knowingly at each other. It was apparent that the building personnel were already having their own celebration.

The wood-paneled car lurched and began its ascent. Jeanne felt cozy and warm after braving the elements outside. It was good to be with friends and co-workers after a sold-out performance in a hit play. She glanced at the other members of the cast. Under various outergarments their party clothing ran the gamut from formal tuxes and glittering gowns to blue jeans and bulky knit sweaters. Jeanne had opted for practicality in the season's first cold snap. Her red wool jersey dress had its own matching mohair stole.

Some of the wardrobing was determined by taste, some by salary or status in the company. However,

Jeanne had noticed at other parties throughout the holidays that when everyone was together, differences faded away. Love of theater was the common bond, and that love transcended even the occasional disagreements that arose among so many personalities working in such close and constant proximity.

It's where I belong, Jeanne reflected, basking in a sense of well-being. Whatever the new year may bring, whatever the future holds in store, I'll always have this; home isn't so much a place as a feeling. *This* feeling.

"Penthouse! Happy New Year, folks!" announced the elevator operator, and the gleaming brass doors opened onto the vestibule of Herb Scofield's apartment.

A spate of polite applause greeted the cast's arrival. Their host called out, "Just throw your coats on the bed!"

The maid led them down a long marble corridor to the master bedroom.

A huge window, taking up much of one wall, offered a panoramic view of the city at night. Jeanne turned to find its lookalike image reflected in the antique mirror covering the wall opposite. Between the two skylines and over the enormous round bed hung a painting—amateurish, Jeanne saw at once—of Herb Scofield and his wife, Carol.

"Lousy, isn't it?"

Her producer stood smiling in the doorway. Now he came forward, kissed Jeanne on the cheek, and handed her a glass of champagne. "My cousin painted it. There's some better stuff in the living room."

She hoped he was right.

A large Christmas tree, covered with hundreds of sparkling ornaments, towered majestically over the guests and almost touched the ceiling. Twinkling lights sprinkled dots of color on the polished surface of the black lacquered baby grand piano alongside the tree. Strolling waiters proffered hors d'oeuvres and refills of champagne to accompany the sumptuous buffet set out on a seven-foot-long table.

Jeanne glanced up at the "better stuff" on the walls, as Herb said with pride, "It's Carol's taste. She knows art. Also knows a good investment when she sees it."

"Where is Carol tonight?" Jeanne asked.

The producer hesitated for a moment, then said, "She's . . . out on the Coast."

Jeanne knew the Scofields were partners in business as well as in marriage. It wasn't unusual for one of them to be in California while the other was in New York. Still, she'd felt his reluctance to answer. Jeanne hoped they weren't having marital problems; they seemed to be a devoted couple.

Aloud, she said, "Carol's missing a real bash. You've gone all out tonight."

He shrugged. "Carol arranged the whole thing before she left. She'll call later—at midnight, our time."

In her peripheral vision Jeanne could see Mathilde and Wes standing near the piano and chatting with another couple. Lydia . . . and Neal.

She swallowed hard and, as a waiter passed with a tray of champagne reinforcements, Jeanne exchanged her empty glass for a fresh one. The fortification, she decided, would do her good. Her host followed suit and downed the contents of his flute in two gulps.

"Excuse me, Herb," Jeanne began. "I haven't said hello to my mother, and—"

"Wait," he said, taking her arm. "Come into the study for a minute. There's . . . something you should know."

She followed him along another marble hallway. In the living room someone was beginning a medley of

Gershwin songs at the piano.

They entered the book-lined study and Herb closed the door. "Have a seat," he said, gesturing her to the black, tufted leather sofa.

"That's okay," Jeanne replied, remaining standing. He'd said a minute, and she was in a party mood for the first time in weeks.

"How'd the show go tonight?" Herb asked, setting down his empty champagne glass.

"Fine. Wonderfully, in fact—"

"You're terrific, Jeanne. I want you to know that."

"Thank you, but . . ."

"I'm going to have a *real* drink. Scotch?" He'd taken the Waterford decanter and two matching glasses from a marbletop table beside the black leather easy chair.

"I'll stay with champagne, Herb," said Jeanne, growing increasingly uneasy. "I hope I'm wrong . . . but you sound as if you're getting ready to fire me . . ."

He filled a glass with the amber liquid. His back was to her as slowly he said, "No, no. It's not *that* bad."

"But . . . it *is* . . . bad?"

Scofield took a sip of his scotch and faced Jeanne directly. "Carol called earlier with the news."

Jeanne tried to smile. "Herb, if Carol is in L.A., it means she's seeing movie people, so if you're trying to tell me that Hollywood isn't interested in Jeanne Lorraine for the film version of *Alice*, it won't come as a . . . surprise."

"Well," said her producer, "you're certainly realistic."

Belatedly she took his offer and sat down on the sofa. "I can't say I hadn't held out a *little* hope, Herb. But I knew it would be a long shot. Which studio bought it?"

He took another swallow of scotch. "None. An . . . independent company beat the other bids. New group called Zeus Productions. Ever heard of them?"

Jeanne shook her head. "Did they give any hints about casting?"

Herb Scofield's silence gave Jeanne her answer. She drank the rest of her champagne and, leaning back on the sofa, closed her eyes. "Zeus. A Greek god who lives on . . . Mount Olympus . . ."

"I'm afraid so," said Herb. "Carol signed the deal yesterday with someone named Berman. Barney Berman. Says he's a partner in the company."

"He's Pia's agent," Jeanne said listlessly.

"Honey, we didn't know Pia was behind this—I swear it! If we had—"

She laughed in spite of herself and opened her eyes. "Herb, don't. Even if you *had* known, you and Carol would be putty in my sister's hands."

"What do you mean . . . ?"

"Pia must want this role so much she can taste it. To be honest, she *is* perfect for the part. And she'd probably do anything to keep me from playing it. Believe me, Herb, if you'd said no, she'd only increase the offer till you had to give in. You'd be crazy not to. She'd spend every last dime she has . . . and Pia has . . . well, a lot of dimes."

Herb put down his glass. "I'm . . . sorry," he said.

Rising, Jeanne answered, "The only thing you should be sorry about is that you could have gotten *twice* what she's paying you for the rights—and you could have gotten it from *her*. It's business. I'm learning that, Herb." Walking to the door, she added, "I'm learning a lot."

More guests had arrived. Jeanne helped herself to another champagne and listened to the pianist, who had traded Gershwin for hot jazz. Laughter and chatter penetrated both the smoke and the music, and the air

299

was sweetened by the scent of expensive perfumes and exotic foods spread out on the buffet table.

Across the room, Neal caught Jeanne's eye; she acknowledged his tender smile with an almost imperceptible wave of her hand before she purposely turned away. It was difficult enough to shrug off Herb Scofield's news about Pia; Neal's presence certainly didn't help.

Maybe another champagne would. She wasn't planning to get drunk, but a little numbness might dull the heartache she was feeling.

At eleven fifty-five, the party guests gathered around the television set to watch the frenzy increase with the descent of the ball in Times Square.

Mathilde stood beside Wesley, her hand clasping his tightly. Her thoughts drifted to the past weeks. The holidays had been a family affair, marred only by Pia's absence. No, she reconsidered, by Pia's *estrangement*. We can be a family only when Pia is again part of us.

Mathilde had pretended to be unaffected by Pia's mid-December visit to New York, but it had hurt to know that her older daughter was in the city and hadn't called even once. It was no different when they were in California at the same time, but there it was easier to justify. In California, Pia was busy filming . . .

The countdown of the final seconds of 1963 had begun. Other couples in the room were standing hand in hand or arm in arm. Mathilde noticed Lydia stealing an early kiss from Neal. Herb Scofield was on the telephone to Carol in L.A.

L.A., thought Mathilde. What will Pia be doing at midnight in L.A., three hours from now? Will she be alone?

She glanced about Herb's living room. Everyone was

300

part of a couple, two by two, except for Jeanne, who stood slightly apart from the group. She was gazing half at the guests, half at the television set. Alone, too. Mathilde felt a sudden sadness. It doesn't seem right, she reflected. I wanted my daughters to be successful, but not without someone to share it with.

"Happy New Year!" everyone shouted as the ball dropped. Wes bent to kiss Mathilde, and as their lips met, she made a silent wish for 1964: Please . . . let my girls find . . . happiness.

Lydia would have preferred a longer embrace, but Neal pulled away and crossed the room to Mathilde. Meanwhile, Wes came to Lydia and they exchanged a quick, friendly kiss. Party horns and noisemakers blared as "Auld Lang Syne" was struck up at the piano. A few guests began to sing, then more joined the chorus. Lydia mimed the words, but her eyes were still on Neal, who seemed to be searching out someone. Then he found her and wove his way through the crush of people. Lydia watched Jeanne and Neal as their eyes met. She saw Neal lower his head to kiss Jeanne's mouth, and saw Jeanne avert her lips, offering instead the side of her cheek before moving away from him and going toward the master bedroom.

Thinking she was alone, Jeanne stood gazing at the cityscape through the vast expanse of window and let out a deep sigh.

But a voice said, "Happy New Year . . . ?" It was a question, not a wish.

Without turning, Jeanne replied, "I hope so."

Lydia eyed the champagne glass in Jeanne's hand. "Liquor's a depressant, contrary to popular opinion."

301

"Should we call Pia with the news?"

Lydia gave a short laugh and then asked, "What's wrong, honey?"

Jeanne related Herb's news about the film sale of *After Alice*. There was more, but the rest she couldn't share with Lydia.

"You know, Jeanne, I used to think you were . . . well, preoccupied . . . with your sister. Now I'm beginning to wonder if it's not the other way around."

Now Jeanne laughed. "She's got everything—why try to take anything away from me?"

"Pia couldn't ruin your mother's happiness," Lydia explained with a shrug, "but she can get at her . . . and Wesley . . . through you."

"But why?"

"Because she can. Because you're allowing it."

"I'm trying not to . . . but *this*—"

"Jeanne, you have to realize that Pia's . . . obsession . . . with you feeds off *your* obsession with *her*."

The words made sense, although Jeanne found it difficult to connect them with her feelings. The scene with Neal in the dressing room had replayed itself over and over in her mind.

Lydia interrupted her thoughts, then. "You may as well know . . . Pia called me."

"R-recently . . . ?" Jeanne stammered, trying to keep her hand from trembling.

But Lydia had seen it. "That's exactly what I mean. Look at what you're letting her do to you."

"I . . . I just never know what Pia's going to pull next." She brought the glass to her lips, but it was empty. "What . . . what did she . . . say?"

Lydia looked directly into Jeanne's eyes. "She told me she saw you and Neal . . ."

Jeanne leaned back against the wall. "Pia . . . saw . . . an embrace, and that's all. *That* wouldn't have even happened if *she* hadn't come to the play. Neal was only trying to calm me *down*—"

"All right," Lydia answered softly.

"It's a *lie*," Jeanne said, grabbing her friend by the shoulders. "There is *nothing* going on behind your back! Please, Lydia, you've got to believe me! I couldn't—I'd *never*—"

Lydia took Jeanne's hands in her own. "I know. Just as I know . . . that Neal is in love with you."

Jeanne turned her head away to hide the tears welling in her eyes. "Lydia, Neal and I . . . are *not* . . . lovers."

"I know that, too. But it's there. I'm not blind, honey. I saw it before either of you realized what was happening."

"Oh, Lydia!" Jeanne sobbed, letting her friend's arms come round her in a comforting embrace.

"You're very dear to me," said Lydia. "I hate to see you so unhappy."

Jeanne lifted her head from Lydia's shoulder. "But . . . I've caused *you* unhappiness—and I can't bear that!"

"Yes you can," Lydia said quietly. "We both can. We have to. Because, you see . . . I love him, too."

"I know it's not original," said a voice behind Jeanne, "but you look as though you've lost your best friend."

She'd been gazing blankly into the inky darkness of post-midnight Central Park. Her elbows still resting on the balcony ledge, Jeanne turned her head to see Andrew Thorne framed by the terrace doorway.

"Well . . . ?" he said.

"Well, what . . . ?"

"I looked for you at the stroke of twelve and couldn't

303

find you. I was afraid you'd fled from the ball." He was holding two glasses of champagne and handed her one, which she accepted and clinked against his in a toast.

"The carriage turned into a pumpkin," Jeanne quipped back, although she found no humor in either his line or hers.

"I understand," he said, placing his elbows alongside hers on the ledge. He straightened up a moment later, when he found that his height made the position comfortable for his co-star but awkward for him.

"You *don't* understand, Andy, but thanks for trying, anyway."

"At the theater, you said you were up for a party."

She shrugged. "At the theater, I was."

"So what caused the change of heart?" When she didn't reply, he added, "It's more than your sister's movie deal—"

"You know about it?" she asked, surprised.

"Herb told me a few minutes ago. That's one of the reasons I came looking for you."

Jeanne took a sip of champagne, expecting it to warm her; instead, it sent a chill through her, and she wrapped the mohair shawl more tightly around her shoulders. Then she reflected on Andrew's words.

One of the reasons? What's the other reason?"

"I just didn't think it was a good idea for my leading lady to be alone on New Year's Eve, that's all."

Jeanne looked up at him. She and Andrew Thorne worked so well together onstage, their timing and unspoken subtexts blending into a seemingly effortless duet, that *not* being able to immediately grasp his underlying meaning puzzled her.

Apparently it was one-sided, because he said, "Don't pretend to be perplexed. That won't help."

She turned her attention back to the view—the moonless, indigo skies, a few scattered cottony clouds,

304

and the black-green treetops scalloping the horizon. "Aren't you just a bit curious to know if Zeus Productions has decided on a male star to play Bernard?"

Andrew laughed. "I'm not worried. They won't pick me."

"You're a big name on Broadway—"

"Jeanne, first of all, they—your sister, that is—will want a *Hollywood* name. *Alice* isn't a musical. Not even a comedy. This story needs a star with the drawing power of a Paul Newman. Otherwise, it can win every prize in the book—even the Pulitzer—and it'll die at the box office."

"Andy, my sister may pay top dollar to buy the role of Alice for herself, but otherwise, she can be downright cheap. And she might feel threatened by a screen presence like Paul Newman's. I mean, he's handsome *and* he can act."

"Ah—and *I'm* just handsome? Thanks for the ego boost."

"I didn't mean that the way it sounded. I meant Newman would show her up—or quit when she started her tantrums."

"I thought you told me you haven't seen her in years."

"I haven't. But people don't change unless they see the need to change." She wasn't sure why, but her own remark put her off balance.

"Which takes us back to my other reason," Andy was saying.

"What *are* you talking about?" And why did it seem important to stay on the defensive?

"The reason I came out here to find you."

She was studying the champagne in her glass.

"The answer doesn't come in that kind of crystal," he said gently. "You can't hide your feelings from me, Jeanne."

"You only think you know me," she said, her face warming despite the damp cold of the air.

"Look, for the past couple of months we've had a . . . well, a rather intense relationship onstage. There's very little about Jeanne Lorraine that Andy Thorne doesn't know."

She turned away from the backdrop of the park and avoided his gaze by peering through the wide expanse of window facing the living room. The party was still going strong. The lights had been dimmed, except for those above the bar. Jeanne saw Herb Scofield pointing animatedly to one of the abstract paintings over the sofa, his guests' attention riveted to their host's words. Wes and Mathilde were seated under another painting and chatting with two people Jeanne hadn't met.

And then she caught sight of Lydia and Neal, off to one corner, alone. No, she amended. Not alone. They're together.

"As they should be," said Andy, breaking in on her thoughts.

"Wh-what . . . ?" Jeanne had forgotten for a moment that he was standing there beside her.

"Please don't think I'm being impertinent. It's just what I meant when I said I know you so well."

"But I . . ."

"Jeanne, you don't have to pretend. Not with me. I . . . well, I've known for quite a while."

"Known . . . what?" Oh, please, she begged silently, not you, too. Lydia's enough. I can't take more of it in one night.

His hand came to rest on hers. "The role of Alice is quite a stretch—and you're fabulous in it. You have a special kind of magic. And when we get to the love scene in Act Two, you're *so* good, you've convinced *me* that Alice is in love with Bernard. Which *we* know is acting, because *you're* not in love with Bernard. Thing is, you're not in love with Andy Thorne, either. And somehow I get the feeling you're not in love with that guy who used to stop by during rehearsals last fall." He paused to gauge her reaction.

She purposely displayed none. "Ted."

"Who?"

"The guy who used to stop by. Ted Sayers." –

"What happened?"

"He's on tour. Besides, I've realized that we're really better off as just friends."

"We've come full circle," he said, releasing her hand and turning back to face the park.

"I don't know what circle you mean," said Jeanne, also turning but looking down at the street twenty-some stories below.

Andy didn't explain. Instead, he lifted his champagne glass, clinked it against hers once more, and said, "Happy New Year. To friendships. They often outlast love."

Jeanne didn't realize that it was past two A.M. by the time she and Andy Thorne came inside. The party had thinned out, although more than a dozen guests remained. Herb Scofield rose unsteadily from a barstool to announce, "I'll make omelettes in one hour for anyone who's still here," while the champagne continued to flow.

Neal and Lydia left shortly afterward, Lydia hugging Jeanne warmly, Neal giving her a self-conscious kiss on the cheek. Andy Thorne stood beside Jeanne, his arm around her almost protectively, until the Genescos had disappeared into the vestibule.

Wes had gone to retrieve his and Mathilde's coats.

Jeanne saw the questioning expression in her mother's eyes, but before she could speak, Andy said, "Don't worry about your daughter, Mrs. Guest. She's my leading lady—I'll see her safely home."

They said good night at the elevator, then Jeanne and Andy strolled back onto the terrace for a final view of the park. Gazing uptown to her left, Jeanne said, "I didn't think of it before, but Mama and Wes's apartment is right up that way." It was too dark to pinpoint the location through the density of the trees.

"Maybe they're two of the little ants down there," said Andy, looking down over the street. But there were several sets of mink-coated and tuxedoed "ants," and it was impossible to distinguish one pair from another.

A couple was climbing into a hansom cab parked opposite the entrance to the Scofields' apartment building. "I'll bet *that's* Mama and Wes," said Jeanne. "They're incurable romantics. They'll probably ride around the park till the sun comes up and then go somewhere for breakfast."

"Not a bad idea," said Andy. "Certainly preferable to one of Herb's omelettes."

"That awful?" asked Jeanne with a grin.

"He's the only human being I've ever met who can make real eggs taste like the powdered yellow horror served up by the U.S. Army. Herb's cousin—the painter—taught him to cook."

Jeanne laughed at the thought of the portrait in the Scofield bedroom. "In that case, let's get out of here!"

The horse and driver had taken the hansom in and around the park for an hour—three of the cab's twenty-minute cycles, they were reminded each time one of the cycles was up.

The wind had calmed, and Jeanne felt cozy and warm snuggled beside Andy Thorne with the folds of her fur coat covering his knees as well as hers.

Finally, the driver pulled the cab over and reined his nag to a halt across the street from the Plaza Hotel. "Last stop, folks. Happy New Year, et cetera and so forth."

Andy reached into his pocket and withdrew his wallet as he had three times already, but the driver shook his head.

"It's after three A.M., mister. You've already been to your party. The bars close at four—I'll barely make last call by the time I say g'night to Queenie, here." He took a long, appreciative look at Jeanne, then turned to Andy. As though in a stage whisper, he said, "You two don't want to watch the sun come up from *outdoors*, do ya?"

After Andy paid the driver, he and Jeanne walked slowly, past the Grand Army Plaza fountain, past Bergdorf's, across Fifty-seventh Street, and south beyond the darkened storefronts along Fifth Avenue. The two didn't speak until they reached Rockefeller Center.

A few scattered couples lingered above the stillness of the deserted skating rink. Jeanne looked up at the towering Christmas tree opposite the RCA Building. Suddenly she was overwhelmed—by the tree's height, dwarfing everyone and everything beneath it; by the quiet that had settled over this small patch of city, while faint sounds of horns and noisemakers carried on the wind from Times Square and echoed through abandoned corridors created by the glass and steel and concrete towers about them.

"Hey, what's this?" asked Andy, his gloved hand brushing away a sudden tear on Jeanne's cheek.

"I . . . I don't know. I get silly on New Year's Eve."

She took a handkerchief from her pocket and dabbed at her eyes.

"That was last night," he said. "It's New Year's Day. Time for starting over. Resolutions to be made—or broken."

She tried to smile, but the sadness was still there.

"Jeanne," said Andy, sliding his arm through hers, "I know this is none of my business, but I'm going to say it anyway."

"Please, Andy, I wish you wouldn't . . ."

"Don't try to read my mind, Jeanne. The man you *think* you're in love with"—he put a finger to her lips to keep her from interrupting—"is not the love of your life. Oh, I'm not belittling what you feel for him—or the heartache you're having because it can't work out. But I repeat, he's not the love of your life. *Theater* is. No matter who you may love—or think to love—now or in the future, he'll always take second place. Theater comes first in your heart. And that's fine, as long as whoever he is can accept second place. Because it won't change, Jeanne. And, apropos of our talk on Herb's balcony, in this case there's no need to change."

"You seem to know me as well as you claim to," she said. But Jeanne wasn't on the defensive this time.

Andy nodded. "That's because we're so much alike. You and I live for the theater, Jeanne. Maybe it's selfish, but acting isn't just a 'job' you go to from nine to five every day. It's not something that works the minute you punch the time clock in the morning and stops the second you punch out at night. Even if I get married someday—and have kids—theater will always come first. It's in my blood. And it's in yours, too. I saw that from the first rehearsal, even when you were still fighting the role. I knew you'd get out of your own way and find the key—"

"How did you know?" she asked.

"Because you're a good actress. And you have what it takes to become a great one. You wouldn't accept less, would you?"

"No," she answered, surprised to find the sadness gone. Andy's words had struck the truth, and she was feeling newly alive. "Thank you, Andy. That sounds trite, but I really mean it."

Jeanne leaned up to kiss his cheek, but at that moment he turned and their lips met—accidentally at first, and then deliberately. She didn't pull away, even when his arms went around her and drew her closer. Their eyes seemed to reflect the difference between Bernard and Alice's onstage embrace and Andy and Jeanne's pre-dawn beginning of more than just a new year.

"Now," he said, lightly but with seriousness, "I happen to be a worse painter than Herb's cousin . . . but I make one hell of an omelette . . ."

"Is that a proposition?" she asked, half joking.

"It's whatever you want it to be," he replied.

Chapter Twenty-One

A soft late-spring rain was falling over Los Angeles and into Olympia Decameron's swimming pool. Brad Morrow lay stretched out on the seven-foot-long sofa. He turned a page of the book he was reading when, from across the room, he heard a loud snap.

"Owww!" he heard Pia cry.

She'd broken a fingernail. It might not be enough to ruin her day, but it was sufficient excuse to set her into the kind of fussy annoyance that generally made Brad wish he were somewhere—anywhere—else.

"Look!" she wailed, holding up the truncated nail.

"Poor baby," he said absently. "It'll grow back."

"I *know*. But it hurts."

"Come here. I'll kiss it and make it all better."

"No," she said, pouting. "You just want to lie there and read your dumb book."

Brad cast her a knowing glance. "And you just want attention, right?"

She nodded like a naughty, petulant child and flashed the famous, captivating smile that always made him forgive her. If only she could look like this all the time, he thought. Free of makeup and hairspray, Pia presented a fresh, healthy, wholesome picture. Well, almost wholesome, he noted silently. Brad, too, was glad to be rid of Hilda, but it couldn't be denied that the martinet had done her job: Pia had lost eight pounds, thanks to her reduced intake of liquor, and a moderate exercise program had helped to restore muscle tone. Her skin glowed. She was, in a word, gorgeous.

"What time is it?" she asked, glancing toward the bar.

"Not *that* time, yet. We'll wait till Barney gets here before we have a drink."

"Oh, Brad . . . !"

"Come on, Pia," he said, sitting up. "You got through three months of a difficult shooting schedule. Don't fall off the wagon now."

"I'm not *on* the wagon," she said haughtily. "I've cut down, but I haven't stopped drinking *completely.*"

"All right, all right," he answered wearily. He wasn't up to another evening of having to reassure Pia that she hadn't turned into a lush. "I just meant you're facing the start of another film soon. You ought to use this period to . . . preserve your strength."

Pia settled deeper into the coziness of the chair and curled her legs up beneath her. "I guess you've got a point. It's just that I get so . . . edgy. Oh, where *is* Barney, anyway!"

Brad rose from the sofa and came to kneel on the floor beside her chair. He ran a hand lightly over her leg.

"Calm down, baby. It won't be long now."

Pia stared at him curiously. "Why do you put up with me?"

"Damned if I know," he answered. "But it's almost worth it—when you're like this."

"Like what?"

"Approachable . . ."

Pia took his hand and removed it from her leg. "Is

313

that *all* you ever think about?"

He leaned against her chair, his back to her. "Pia, why do you always have to . . . misinterpret? Sometimes I feel that we're on the verge of . . . talking . . . and then you back off from any real communication."

"Darling," she cooed softly into his ear, "you want communication? See a shrink."

He looked up and she gave him a quick peck on the forehead. Brad knew better than to push the issue. The kiss was a truce, and harping on the subject would only start them fighting again.

Barney Berman walked into the living room and threw his raincoat over a white, silk-covered chair. Then he realized the coat was wet and removed it to the entrance foyer. Returning and placing a newspaper and his briefcase on the coffee table, he said, "Man, could I use a drink."

"Me too!" exclaimed Pia as Brad went to the bar.

"I've brought the revised screenplay," Barney said as he snapped open the locks of his leather case. "But the real discussion's gotta be about casting."

"*That* again," Pia said, folding her arms across her chest.

"Avoiding it isn't going to get you a leading man, sugar, and we're running outa time."

"I *still* think Paul Newman would be perfect," Pia insisted.

"So does everyone else. But you don't sign Newman on a month's notice. Or McQueen."

"Christ," Brad put in as he handed out drinks. "*I'm* even booked for the next six months."

"Well, I don't understand it," said Pia. "This is a *lead* in a big picture—opposite *me!* Who *wouldn't* want it?"

314

Barney kept his eyes on the briefcase while Brad turned to face the glass doors leading to the pool. Neither of them dared tell Pia the truth—that no male star equal to her stature needed or wanted to play opposite the temperamental Miss Decameron.

"The point is," Barney said finally, "who *does* want the part, Pia? Or needs it?"

"God, I'd almost *let* Andrew Thorne play it—if he was box office."

Barney laughed. "You really would, wouldn't you?"

"Sure. My sister's little boyfriend can act." She took a swig of her scotch and added, "Jeanne certainly dumped Neal Genesco quickly enough once the show sold out. She's getting as bad as . . . I *used* to be . . ."

"Well, skip the idea of Thorne," said Barney. "He's too young, the way the role has been rewritten. Besides, he'd never do it."

"No? Why not?" asked Pia.

"Because, doll, he's a *mensch.*" Barney finished his drink and held up the newspaper. "The word's out, though. We've gotta move fast."

"We're in the papers?" Pia hadn't read that day's edition; otherwise, she knew, she wouldn't have missed it. After almost eight years in films, she still thrilled to see her name and picture printed anywhere, whether as publicity or as scandalous gossip.

"Here," said Barney, tossing her the entertainment section. "Have a look. You girls are news again."

"Where?" Pia tore through the pages, taking out her impatience on the *L.A. Times.* She made a little "tsk" sound at not finding it immediately; she'd never yet been relegated to the back pages. She ignored an article on the New York World's Fair, turned past news about someplace called Vietnam, and at last saw her own face peering out at her. It was printed alongside an

315

excellent photograph of Jeanne.

"Fanning the Flames of a Famous Feud," read the banner.

"Jeanne Lorraine may be happy to have the Tony Award for her performance in Broadway's *After Alice*, but it wasn't enough to keep the play from closing last week, after a respectable six-month's run.

"With its closing, Jeanne's sister, film star Olympia Decameron, is contractually free to begin pre-production on the drama, which will star . . . who else?

"Some think it's dirty pool; others say that's show biz. But it will be a big and busy year for Miss D. In editing stages now is *Model Citizen*, a comedy about the fashion industry, due for release later in the summer. Insiders say that *After Alice* will start shooting next month and be rushed into theaters nationwide in time for Christmas—and Oscar eligibility.

"Meanwhile, younger sis Jeanne has been 'unavailable for comment.' Wesley Guest, stepfather to both girls and star on both coasts, isn't granting interviews, either."

Pia let the newspaper fall from her lap, while Barney and Brad waited for the explosion.

There was none. Instead, a smile began to form and grow bigger until it covered Pia's face. "Well, well . . . I don't know why I didn't think of it sooner . . ."

"What's that?" asked Brad.

"Just an idea. I've got to think it over, first. I'll call you tonight, Barney."

*　　*　　*

The rain had stopped by the time Pia walked Barney to his car. Brad switched on the pool lights and opened the sliding glass doors. A warm, humid breeze rippled through the blue water that lapped iridescently, invitingly. Brad walked out past the tiled patio and onto the wet grass, where the thin blades tickled his bare toes. At the edge of the pool he tested the water with his foot. From behind, he heard the tinkle of ice, and turned.

Pia stood in the doorway. Light from inside the house silhouetted her and served as a frame for the picture that was at once both demure and seductive. The thin fabric of her flowing white silk caftan swayed rhythmically against her body. She was holding another drink.

"That's your third," Brad said.

"No. I made this one for you."

She came toward him and handed him the glass. He took a sip and placed it on a lawn table. "Thanks."

"Think nothing of it."

"Barney's gone?"

Pia nodded. "He's ticked off with me."

"Why's that?"

"I told him I need some time to figure a few things out."

"Baby, you haven't got much time left."

"Don't *you* start, all right?" God, Pia thought, I sound just the way Mama used to. She turned away, but Brad grabbed hold of her wrist and pulled her back.

"What's this sudden secret of yours?"

"I said it's only . . . an idea," she said, freeing her hand from his grasp. "But it's . . . big. And I don't know if I can swing it."

Brad took a step toward her and began kissing her hair. "Want to go for a swim? The water's nice and warm . . ."

"N-no," she answered. "Brad . . ."

"Then let's lie down on the grass," he whispered, his tongue brushing her ear.

"The grass is . . . all wet," she whined.

"Exactly . . ."

His hands untied the tie closure at her neck, causing the filmy fabric to slide from her shoulders and breasts until the caftan lay in a silken heap at her ankles. Brad's tongue moved from one earlobe to the other, while his fingers traced the beautifully contoured outline of her body, moving downward, always downward. Pia felt the tension starting to ebb away.

Now he was kissing her temples, her eyelids, her nose, her lips.

But as his mouth met hers, she stiffened.

"What's the matter?" he asked.

She closed her eyes. "Don't kiss me. Don't stop . . . but don't kiss me."

"Whatever the lady wants," he murmured.

She dug her hands into his chest, heard the sound of his jeans unzipping, felt his hardness against her.

With her eyes closed, Pia's mind could summon any image of her choosing. She clutched the back of his head as her mental focus grew sharper and clearer. Brad sank to his knees before her, his tongue now working its way between her thighs.

For a split second, real life forced its way into Pia's mind. She wasn't wearing her diaphragm.

But the tug of his hand pulling her down on the wet grass obliterated the warning. He rolled on top of her and once more moved his mouth to hers. She squeezed her eyes tighter still and averted her lips.

"I get it," Brad said. "All right, lie there. We'll make believe that I'm your stepdaddy."

*　　　*　　　*

318

Pia heard the splash but didn't open her eyes. Her body was still tingling with pleasure. It had never been like this before. My God, she thought, he was amazing!

But when she opened her eyes and looked into the pool, it was Brad who was naked in the water.

She rose on trembling legs and picked up her damp caftan. Brad's drink was sitting on the table where he'd left it. The ice cubes had long since melted. She took it with her into the house.

Shivering as she ran her own hand across the front of her body, she dialed Barney's number. While the phone rang at the other end, she added more vodka and ice to the glass and took a few sips.

"Yeah?" Barney's voice barked into the receiver.

"It's me, Pia. I've made up my mind."

"It's about time. So what's this brainstorm of yours? And it'd better be good."

"Oh, it's good," she said. "And it's going to get even better . . ."

Wesley hung up and, leaning over, replaced the telephone to the night table beside the bed. Mathilde was in a sitting position, her back propped up against two pillows, her reading glasses on top of the copy of *Vogue* that rested among the folds of the quilted satin comforter.

She hadn't interrupted Wes's long-distance call from his agent in California, but she had immediately filled in Gary Sumner's half from listening to Wes's side of the conversation. If phone calls could be transmitted via television, the picture couldn't have been clearer: Gary was relaying the offer he'd received from Barney, which in turn meant the offer from Pia. Wes's jaw had tightened visibly, and that translated the whole story to Mathilde. It didn't require a clairvoyant *or* a business expert. All it takes, she mused, is knowing my daughter.

From the corner of her eye she caught Wes looking at her. She let *Vogue* slide to the floor and put her reading glasses on. When Wes's eyebrows rose quizzically, she said, "The better to see you with . . ."

"You think I ought to have said *yes?*" he asked.

"I think you ought to think it over," she answered.

"Darling," he said, turning on his side and observing the contradiction who was his wife. Tonight he perceived Mathilde as both a study in sensuality, in her glamorous black lace nightgown, and a down-to-earth pragmatist, with her hair still pinned into its tight, sophisticated French twist, her eyes framed by the horn-rimmed spectacles. They seemed to underscore an announcement: "All right, fun and games later. Now it's time for serious business."

He reached over and removed her glasses, which he placed beside the phone. He didn't mind talking over his career decisions with Mathilde—in fact, he relished sharing these aspects of his life with her. But without the glasses, she seemed a less formidable adversary. The word—*adversary*—brought a grin to his lips. She was anything *but* his opponent.

"Something funny in all this?" she asked.

He shook his head. "No. I was just thinking about the ironies involved. And about Pia's motivation."

"Darling, she's being practical, I'm sure that's all it is. The picture needs a strong leading man—"

"I'm too old to play the romantic lead. There are a dozen younger names besides the ones she's tried and can't afford—"

"But you'd be wonderful in the role. I thought so the first time we saw Andy play it at the dress rehearsal. Oh, not that he isn't good—"

"He's better than that. Why didn't she have Barney

call Andy's agent?"

"Because Andy isn't as big a name in Hollywood as you are. And besides, Jeanne said just the other day that he's signed to do another play. Neal offered him the London company of *Alice*, you know."

"I didn't know. You didn't tell me." Wes smiled to himself. His wife, who at one time knew nothing about show business, was now more informed than he was on a number of matters dealing with the entertainment world.

"Anything else you didn't tell me?"

"Such as?" She began unpinning her hair, and from habit, Wes moved closer to help.

"I was wondering if Pia had gotten wind of how badly you'd like to see the family reunited and if . . . well, if she'd decided to *use* that."

"I would have told you, Wes. You know I don't keep secrets from you." She never had, except for the incident of the cashmere stole, which seemed so long ago that it belonged to a previous lifetime. It was as though she had split, dividing herself into two parts: Before Wesley and Since Wesley. She easily preferred the Since part. But that excluded Pia, who remained the single source of unhappiness in her present life.

"I still think it's inadvisable," Wes said. "And I'm too old."

"How does Gary feel about it?" she asked.

"Well . . . he says Bernard can be played by anyone between the ages of thirty and fifty."

"You see? You'll bring a . . . maturity . . . to the role."

"Darling, this isn't MGM or Universal, or—"

"Of course not. They wouldn't do a film like this. It isn't 'commercial' enough. But that's the point. You've had commercial hits. You don't need to work for the next hundred years, if you choose not to." Mathilde paused to make certain he was listening and, seeing that he was, she continued.

"You've done more than fifty box-office smashes—"

"And a couple of bombs," he put in.

"Not enough to do any damage," she countered.

"You've really done your homework," he said, ruffling her hair and inadvertently sending hairpins all over the upper half of the bed.

"I believe in being prepared. Where do you think"— here she laughed ruefully—"*both* of my daughters got that . . . ?"

"All right, convince me . . . if you can . . ." Wes was surprised only by the fact that he was enjoying this. On the phone he'd felt a heavy weight across his chest.

"Wesley Guest, household name," she said to the air. "Known on both coasts for his strong stage and screen presence. Hasn't done a play in six months or a film all year. Basking in the late spring of suburbia. Don't you hate it?" This last she phrased as a news anchor might, warm but firm, like a female Walter Cronkite.

Wes began to laugh. "I don't hate it, because I'm with you."

"Well, that's grand," she said. "Major star falls to ruin for the love of a woman."

"Actually," he interjected more seriously, "I wouldn't want to play Bernard and have *that* cause my fall. The final print of the picture could make me look like . . . well, whatever the cutting room is *told* to make me look like."

"Darling, Pia isn't *directing* the picture!" Mathilde exclaimed. "Besides, she needs this to be a success even more than you do. It's her money and reputation at risk."

"Let's *not* discuss her reputation," said Wes. "That's another thing. She's totally unreliable. Darling, I know she's your daughter, but—"

322

Mathilde decided to use that as her ploy. It might be the truth. Where her girls were concerned, she could always find hope. "Wes . . . what if . . . if this is Pia's way of apologizing? She doesn't know how to come right out and say she's sorry. Maybe she's changed and wants a second chance. After all, Pia's twenty-two. She's no longer a child."

Wes remembered well the "child" who had disrupted his wedding to Mathilde. He also remembered Pia's acquisition of the screen rights to her sister's play less than six months before. "What about Jeanne?" he asked. "Won't she feel she's being betrayed by both of us?"

"She'll be happy for you, darling. And she told me herself she hadn't expected to play Alice in the movie."

"But if you're right . . . if Pia really wants a reconciliation, why didn't she ask Neal to direct the picture? Gary says she's signed Eric Archer—"

"Because Neal's going to direct the London company of *Alice*, which starts rehearsing during the movie's shooting schedule."

Mathilde didn't add her suspicions as to why Neal was accepting the offer. No one had to explain; her mother's eyes had taken in the scene at Herb Scofield's on New Year's Eve. Those same eyes had observed Neal and Jeanne, and later, Lydia. Without a word from any of the three principals in the drama, Mathilde had understood why Ted Sayers was no longer in her daughter's conversations at lunch and why the Genescos were packing for London. Andy Thorne was part of Jeanne's present; he probably kept her from being lonely. No harsh judgments from me on that count, thought Mathilde. I know what it means to be lonely.

She turned now to Wes, who was studying her intently.

"Did I miss a spot when I washed my face?" she

asked, still self-conscious whenever he stared at her, even after eight years of marriage.

"No," he said, taking her in his arms and kissing each brow. "I was just marveling over the woman I married. There's a lot more to you than meets the eye."

"When we met, you said you *liked* what met your eye . . ."

"Fishing again, Mrs. Guest?"

Mathilde nodded, touching his face. With her free hand, she swept the hairpins from the bed. At the same time, Wes turned off the overhead lamp.

"Mrs. Guest . . ." he said softly in the dark.

"Yes, Mr. Guest . . ." She snuggled closer as his hand began pulling the hem of her nightgown upward.

She shuddered with delight as the lace crept higher and higher.

"Shivering, Mrs. Guest?" he asked, beginning to massage her stomach.

A sigh escaped as his fingers reached her breasts. "Mmm," she murmured.

"So you think I should call Gary in the morning and say I'll do the film . . . ?" he asked lazily.

"Um-hmm," she answered.

"Warm enough . . . ?" he asked, his head moving beneath the comforter and his lips settling on her nipples.

"Um-hmm," she repeated.

"Then . . . why don't we slip you out of this pretty thing and get down to business . . . ?"

His fingers had parted her thighs as Mathilde uttered another "um-hmm."

Chapter Twenty-Two

The black stretch wig was pinching at Pia's temples. She tried to ease the elastic border, then readjusted her sunglasses to nestle more comfortably among the stiff, artificial curls that covered her ears. She felt perspiration breaking through the dark, heavy Pan Cake makeup on her face and neck.

The taxi shook with a loud thud as the trunk was slammed shut. Pia lit a cigarette as the driver climbed behind the wheel and started the motor.

"I don't like smoking in my cab, lady, *comprende?*"

Just what I need, thought Pia. "I'm paying for this ride. Drive."

"Lady, I don't like—"

"Here!" Pia shouted, her hands diving into her purse and pulling out a fifty-dollar bill. She threw it onto the front seat and leaned back. "That's over and above whatever the meter will read. Just let me smoke the goddamn cigarette!"

"Yeah, okay," he answered, rolling down his window.

The taxi sped off with a lurch, and Pia was overcome by another wave of nausea. Hang on, she told herself. You'll be all right once you get to the studio.

She turned her head just enough to see the airline terminal growing smaller and smaller. No cars seemed to be following behind. Good. She'd made it all the way to Mexico and back; three days, with no one the wiser.

Her major fear en route had been that fans or reporters might recognize her, but the wig, glasses, and makeup had apparently worked. She'd still have explaining to do, particularly to Brad. But she'd find a way to get around him.

The taxi hit a bump in the road, making Pia's stomach churn. Am I supposed to feel *this* lousy? she wondered. The doctor had assured her that everything had gone well. And he'd come highly recommended from two of Antaen's contract players who had formerly availed themselves of the same doctor's . . . services. Experienced and discreet, they'd said. And no coat hangers in dark alleyways.

That's for sure, she mused. *Better Homes and Gardens* could have photographed his suite of offices; the rooms had been paid for by stars and would-be-stars. All except for the room with the horrid antiseptic smells and the metal instrument trays, and . . .

. . . and it's better to put the whole . . . experience . . . in the past and think about now.

The problem was that Pia was feeling terrible. She was almost tempted to tell the driver to slow down, but that would make her even later than she was already for the first day of work on the picture. At least I'm going to show up, she thought. At least I'll *be* there.

She breathed deeply, inhaling hot, stale air from the freeway through the driver's window. Just my luck, with all the taxicabs at the airport, I had to get the only one without air-conditioning. But a studio limo would have been out of the question—too risky; and there hadn't been time to arrange for a private car.

Pia checked her wristwatch. It would be after ten

o'clock by the time she arrived for the read-through of the screenplay. Everyone would be furious with her. Time is money, Barney would insist.

Well, it's *my* money, she reasoned. A feeble rationale. And she'd already felt the animosity toward her. Stemming from envy, most likely, for being able to produce her own picture at the age of twenty-two. Even Wesley, although he had agreed to play the part, probably resented her. After all, he'd been a bigger star and had never financed a picture on his own.

So now I'll be late, she thought, and they'll accuse me of deliberately stalling so I can make an "entrance." Barney will be hopping mad. Not to mention Brad . . .

Brad. He'll be angry, but that can't be helped. He'll kill me if he ever finds out where I've been and what I've done.

But he won't know. *Nobody* will know. It's my secret, and I'm the one who has to live with it.

Nathan Schutz surveyed the room. Eight people were seated around an oblong oak table. The coffee urn in the corner had run dry. Half-eaten bagels lay beside pools of melting butter and cream cheese that was forming a yellowish crust.

Schutz checked his watch against the wall clock. Ten-fifteen, he fumed to himself; she should have been here an hour ago. He was livid for having accepted her offer; money wasn't everything, and he knew his client too well. That he'd gone against his better judgment in agreeing to act as press and studio liaison was already haunting him—and actual shooting hadn't even begun.

To counteract recent items in the gossip columns about Pia's backstabbing of her own sister, Schutz had choreographed a clever campaign that would publicize the Wesley-and-Pia-reunion for the filming of *After*

Alice. Jeanne's "brilliant stage career in New York" would be played up, therefore overshadowing the fact that Pia had bought the screen rights—and the role— out from under her sister's feet. Even Wes, mostly for Mathilde's sake, was cooperating.

And now, the newspaper photographers and reporters Schutz had so soothingly coaxed into showing up this morning had lost their patience and left. Pia herself had blown it.

Someone at the table speculated that perhaps she'd been delayed because of traffic. Someone else offered another possible reason. But Schutz was years past giving Pia the benefit of the doubt. From the expression on Barney Berman's face, the agent was thinking the same thing. Anyone present who knew Pia was probably thinking the same thing. Most of the people in the room, though, hadn't worked with their star before—which, Schutz reflected, is presumably why they've been hired. I'm the only one who's a glutton.

Wesley took the last sip of his tepid coffee and smiled wanly at Schutz. At least with the photographers and reporters gone, the publicist had stopped sweating so copiously.

No one had said anything or made any suggestions in minutes. The director, Eric Archer, was drawing doodles on a scratch pad. His assistant sat beside him staring into space. On Archer's left were three other actors, one an Oscar nominee, and Pia's personal secretary, Charlene Webb. She sat quietly next to the writer, Justin Ordway, who had finally ceased his muttering tirade against Pia only moments ago.

Wes wondered how long it would be before everyone got up and went home. He was suddenly seized by a

328

resurgence of anger. He'd signed the contract—and reluctantly at that—for Mathilde, and already he was feeling like a fool. If this morning was an indication of the "seriousness" with which Pia regarded the picture, no matter how great the role, he wanted out. And he had no one to blame but himself; his wife hadn't forced him into it.

He had closed his script and was rising from his chair when the door opened and Pia entered the room.

Whatever resentment had existed around the table dissipated the moment she appeared. *Ravaged* was the word best suited to describe her in Wes's mind; Nathan Schutz wondered if she had indeed suffered an accident. He was silently grateful that the press was gone, after all; at least she wouldn't be photographed in this condition.

Her customarily silken chestnut hair was dull and matted. Her darker-than-usual makeup was streaked, and failed to hide the sickly pallor beneath it. She wore a dark brown trenchcoat that seemed heavy enough to weigh her down.

She drew a deep breath and, with great effort, said, "I apologize to you all for my being so late." To Schutz she asked, weakly, "The photographers . . . ?"

He shook his head. "Gone."

"It's . . . just as well," she answered, running a shaky hand through her hair. Then she turned and, forcing a smile, said, "Hello, Wesley."

"Hello, Pia," he replied. He was no longer angry but concerned. She resembled a little lost child.

Her eyes filled with tears as her arms went out to him. An embarrassed silence spread through the room while the two embraced.

Pia's entire body was trembling, and she knew she

329

looked awful. But she didn't care. Wesley was here, with her, for her . . . and for no one else.

The coffee urn had been refilled and the room was now buzzing with lively chatter. Pia was seated next to her secretary, and when she opened her totebag to pull out her script, Charlene noticed a shiny black wig inside. She made no mention of it.

"Here are your messages," Charlene said, handing Pia several slips of paper.

Pia glanced quickly through them. Three from Brad, one from a reporter, one from her lawyer, and one that read "your mother." She crumpled them all and dropped them in the wastebasket behind her.

"Call Brad," she instructed Charlene. "Tell him I'm all right and I'll be home around four."

Returning to the table with their coffee cups, the various personnel reseated themselves. Eric Archer waited until Pia had lit a cigarette—nervously, he noticed—and then asked, "Well . . . shall we start reading?"

"Did she get my message?" asked Mathilde.

"I don't know. She hasn't called?" said Wes.

"No. They probably forgot to tell her. Did she ask about . . . us? Jeanne . . . or me?"

"No. There wasn't any time for that. She arrived very late."

"How is she, Wes? How does she look?"

"Frankly, like hell." He hadn't meant to phrase it so bluntly.

"What do you mean? I thought she'd curbed her . . . problem."

Wes put his arm around her. "She looks as if she's

330

been . . . ill. It may not be from drinking. It could be nerves. She was very tense. There's more to this role than meets the eye, and it's possible she's only realizing it now." He didn't mention Pia's physical weakness or the fact that the clothes beneath her coat had been drenched with perspiration.

"Poor Pia," said Mathilde. "And you. You're tense, too." She could feel the rigid muscles in his arm. "Here, put your head back and let me give you a massage."

Wes nodded, and Mathilde began working her fingers and palms into his neck and shoulders.

"Mmm, that's helping," he murmured.

"And you? How did Pia react to you?"

"She seemed glad enough to see me. She was gracious."

Thank God, thought Mathilde. Maybe there's a chance, after all.

But why hasn't Pia returned my calls? If not today's, why not those of the past three days?

It's going to take more time, Mathilde realized sadly. I'll just have to find the patience to wait.

The phone rang.

"Answer it, Brad, will you?" Pia mumbled from under the covers. She heard a second ring.

On the third, she turned over and reached out to Brad's pillow. Empty. He wasn't in bed. A momentary panic made her shiver, but then the persistent jangling cut through the fog and forced her awake. She answered the phone only to make it stop.

"Five o'clock, Miss Decameron. Your wake-up call. Time to get up."

"I *am* up," she said, dropping the receiver back onto its cradle. Then she willed herself into a sitting position and swung her feet onto the floor.

Her head throbbed and her stomach was still doing flipflops. There was a heaviness through her lower pelvic region that made her feel as though her insides were dropping out.

Pia splashed ice-cold water on her face. That helped. She pulled a robe around her and stumbled through the living room to the kitchen.

Brad, dressed in blue jeans and a sweatshirt, was seated at the table.

"There's coffee," he said.

"Thanks." She poured a cup and stood against the sink. "You never came to bed last night," she said after swallowing her first sip.

"Couldn't sleep. Want to talk now?"

Pia shook her head no. She'd sensed a fight brewing the night before, but she'd felt so terrible that she'd gone up to bed, exhausted, without an explanation of her three-day absence. She wasn't going to tell him the truth, and lacked the strength to invent a lie.

"I think you ought to see a doctor, Pia," he said.

"NO!" she burst out, slamming her cup down and splashing its contents across the countertop. "I've got a picture to make!"

"Pia . . . *you're* the producer. The boss. You can do whatever you want to."

"Don't you see? That's just what they're waiting for. I've got to prove to them that I can do it—prove to Wesley that I deserve this part!"

Brad didn't speak as he came behind her and placed his hands on her shoulders. His sudden touch startled her, and she moved away.

"What is it with you and Wesley?" he asked. "I thought you hated him."

"*What?*" she said, staring at him incredulously.

"You told me you did. Ever since their wedding."

"That's ridiculous!"

"Pia, you *told* me. They were your words."

"I *never* said that!" she insisted. "Besides, I was a kid. For Christ's sake, he's my father!"

"No," Brad corrected her slowly, "he's your *step-father*."

"Look," Pia answered, "the limo will be here in less than half an hour. I've got to get dressed."

He followed her through the living room and on up the stairs toward the bedroom. "Pia, I'm not *asking* you anymore. Tell me where you disappeared to for three solid days!"

She stopped outside the bathroom and leaned wearily against the door. "I wasn't sleeping with someone else. And I wasn't in an accident. That's *all* I'm going to say about it."

"Have it your way, Pia. But I'm not sure I can take much more of this."

"Oh, Brad," she said, "neither am I."

She took a pill to keep herself awake, but her mind refused to concentrate on the script in her lap. It was a short scene, not too demanding. Not even that many lines to memorize. But the limo seemed too hot, too stuffy, even with the air-conditioning set on high.

Pia touched her hand to her forehead. It was damp. One moment she felt feverish, the next in a cold sweat. She shuddered and tried to force herself back to the script.

She found it impossible.

She closed her eyes and tried letting the movement of the car and the whirring of the tires on the freeway lull her into some kind of calm. Instead, she felt enveloped by further confusion. Sounds seemed to rush at her from nowhere. A baby's mouth opened, let out a sudden, piercing cry, then was cut off just as quickly;

Wesley's face appeared and smiled at her, but immediately began to dissolve and reappear as another image. Another face . . . a familiar face. Also of a man. The smile now turned into a rounded O shape, open like the baby's mouth a moment before.

A gunshot went off.

Pia's eyes flew open.

"Sorry, Miss Decameron," called the driver from up front. "The exhaust backfired. I'll have it checked."

"Y-yes," she answered, gazing through the tinted window glass as the limo drove past the gate and stopped at the entrance to the soundstage.

Clarice, Pia's favorite makeup artist, was accustomed to compensating for what she termed her "boss-lady's nocturnal excesses." This morning's makeup session required more time than ever, but by Clarice's standards, the results were only acceptable. Poor kid must have really tied one on, she thought as Pia rose unsteadily from the high chair and headed for her dressing room.

Pia went into the bathroom and for a moment was gripped again by fear. She was still bleeding. Not profusely, and the nurse had said there might be spotting for a few days. But how much? And just how many days?

And how soon would these feelings end? Not the aching part; that was a monthly occurrence anyway, something she was used to.

Then what was it? Guilt? Where were those sudden maternal longings springing from? If she hadn't suffered a second's hesitation beforehand, why now, when it was over, done with, and too late?

*   *   *

Pia opened the dressing-room door and made her way to the set. Wesley was there already. The lights glared, and she could see her stand-in off to one side. Cameras and equipment crowded the areas that weren't filled with actors or technical personnel.

The atmosphere was claustrophobic. Pia wanted to run. She could think of only one thing, the single thing that was impossible. To turn back the clock, to undo what had been done. A different decision. A second chance.

"Ready, Pia?" asked Eric Archer.

"Yes," she answered.

Then she fainted.

Chapter Twenty-Three

Charlene Webb's neck was beginning to ache. For nearly forty-five minutes the receiver of the telephone had been wedged between her shoulder and cheek. At the end of one conversation, she'd automatically pushed the next blinking button, only to have another call come in on the line just freed. She was tempted to disconnect the trunk line altogether.

Brad sat in a corner of the living room watching the circus that Pia's house had turned into during the past week. He'd postponed his guest appearance on a TV-adventure series so he could stay close to Pia, fend off her visitors—intruders, as far as he was concerned—and allow her to rest.

But rest was proving impossible. A constant parade of men in three-piece suits tramped in and out, back and forth. Meanwhile, Charlene efficiently and diplomatically assured those lawyers, bankers, and studio officials who were *not* permitted an audience with Pia that "Miss Decameron will be back to work on the set as soon as she's feeling stronger."

Brad had tried to question Pia's personal physician, but Dr. Vincent's answers continued to be vague.

"It's not anything serious, Brad. Pia's suffered a mild

nervous collapse. She's under a great deal of pressure, you know." It was all the information he was willing to supply, and Pia was even more unapproachable on the subject.

At least her condition had improved over the past few days, despite the lack of privacy under her own roof. And it dispelled any rumors that might have accompanied a stay in a sanatorium.

Nonetheless, as another day went by without her presence before the cameras, the anxiety around her increased.

"No, Kathryn," Charlene was saying into the phone, "I don't think it's a good idea."

Brad jumped up from the sofa and leaned over Charlene's desk. "Is that Kathryn Paine?" he asked.

She nodded. "Kathryn, can you hold for a second?" She pushed a button and cradled the receiver. Then, rubbing her neck, she moaned, "Christ, I almost thought I'd need to have that apparatus surgically removed. What's up, Brad?"

"Kathryn Paine is one of Pia's few real friends. I think it'd be good for Pia if Kathryn comes over to see her."

"The doctor told me *no* visitors, Brad."

"I know—but his orders haven't kept *them* out!" He indicated the direction of the downstairs bedroom, where muffled voices had risen in anger. He and Charlene could both hear Pia as she tried to argue a point over the shouting.

Brad threw his arms up in disgust. "Goddammit! It's *friends* she needs, not . . . *that!*"

The door to Pia's room burst open and Nathan Schutz hurried out, yelling as he made his exit. "I can't get any straight answers from you with four other people trying to do the same thing, Pia!" He stormed into the living room and stopped when he saw Brad.

"Tell your girlfriend in there to call me when she's ready! And"—he turned to Charlene—"she is *still* expected to show up at the premiere of *Model* next week—plus the interviews and photo layouts. *Don't* cancel them!"

He went out and slammed the massive redwood door behind him.

Inside Pia's room, the shouting had not subsided. Brad grabbed the phone so fiercely that Charlene recoiled.

"Hello, Kathryn?" said Brad into the receiver. "Pia would love to see you—it'd do her a world of good. Why don't you come over in about an hour?"

When he hung up, Brad pushed, one by one, all of the blinking white button lights that were on HOLD. After he cut off the last caller, he took the phone off the hook. The ringing had stopped.

"Go home, Charlene," he said. "You can use the rest, too."

Before she could protest, Brad strode into the hall and headed for Pia's bedroom.

He found the doctor, with a syringe ready for injection, standing at the foot of the bed and trying to edge his way closer to his patient, who lay propped up against pillows and was staring ahead of her. Barney Berman was screaming at Eric Archer from across the bed.

"Just shoot *around* her!"

"I've *done* that, Bozo!" Archer yelled back. "I need her on the set!"

"Pia," one of the lawyers managed to put in, "every day you're out is costing you thousands—"

"And people have commitments in October!" added Archer. "They're not going to sit around waiting—and

338

that goes for me, especially! The picture has *got* to wrap by—"

"OUT!" Brad shouted over the din. "That means all of you!"

The room fell silent as everyone turned toward the bedroom door.

"I mean it!" cried Brad. "Out of this house—right now!"

Only the doctor spoke. "You're upsetting my patient."

Brad glanced at the hypodermic. "Upsetting your patient! Give me that!" He snatched the needle and broke it off the end of the syringe. "She doesn't need drugs, Doc. And she doesn't need *you*. Not any of you! What she needs is rest!"

"Brad, calm down," cautioned Barney. "We were only trying—"

"Out! I'm not kidding, Barney! If I call the cops, you and Schutz will have twice the work dealing with *that* kind of publicity!"

"All right, all right," Barney acquiesced.

"So what's *your* plan, Tarzan?" Eric asked sarcastically. "Just let Pia lie here and sleep it off—while the picture goes to hell?"

"My plan, Archer, is to have Pia see people who care about her—people she *likes*—or no one at all. Particularly *not* a swarm of business sharks with nothing on their minds but money!"

"*Her* money, Brad!" Barney yelled. "That's the point!"

"Excuse me," Dr. Vincent tried again, "but she really shouldn't have *any* visitors . . ."

"That includes medical men," said Brad. "You can get out of here, too!"

*　　　*　　　*

Ten minutes later, the house was empty, and Brad was sitting on the edge of the bed, his hand gently stroking Pia's fingers.

"Thanks for getting rid of them," she said.

"I want you to get well."

"I know . . . it's hard to believe."

"What is?"

"That you care that much about me."

"I just never say it 'cause you'd end up by using it," he said.

"Brad . . ."

"Get some rest. Kathryn's dropping by in a little while." He kissed her cheek and left the room.

Pia closed her eyes, grateful for the quiet. She was still feeling weak, but her earlier pain had lessened and she knew that in a few days everything would be back to normal. Dr. Vincent had said she'd traveled too soon after the . . . procedure. Fear of discovery had added to her physical distress. The two doctors—Vincent and the surgeon in Mexico—had warned that if disclosure of events should ever be made known, both men would be forced to claim ignorance of Pia's illegal . . . operation. Their licenses to practice, and Pia's career, were at stake. In more than one dream she had envisioned all three of them rotting in prison.

Gradually, though, her neurotic worries had subsided; no news had leaked to the press—nor, as far as she could tell, to Brad. Her physical discomfort had been real. But she'd suffered emotionally and mentally for nothing.

Still, Pia couldn't help thinking that her suffering was a form of retribution.

Well, she reasoned, as she had been trying to reason for the past two weeks, the point is that it's done. The next thing is to make myself strong again and get back to work on the picture.

On *After Alice*.
With Wesley.

"Mama," said Jeanne, settling into the backseat of Wes's Mercedes, "you needn't have come all the way to the airport. The studio offered to send a car, and I could easily have asked them to drop me off—"

"Nonsense," interrupted Mathilde. "My daughter and I have some catching up to do before she's whisked off by those moguls and publicity people. Why, I've hardly seen Wes at all since he's been shooting—" She stopped herself. It had required great effort to keep from mentioning *After Alice*, and she'd managed restraint during the interminable wait at Baggage Claim, only to blurt it out now.

But Jeanne smiled and squeezed her mother's hand. "Mama, let's get one thing straight. Any disappointment I may have suffered about not playing Alice in the movie has nothing to do with Pia. The subject isn't taboo—in fact, when Wes gets home tonight, I want to hear all about it."

"Well, darling, I'm glad—if you really mean that—but I must admit that Wes doesn't seem eager to discuss the film. I don't know if that's because he's exhausted by the end of the day, or if there's . . . dissension on the set . . ."

"You haven't watched any of the shooting?"

Mathilde shook her head. "I don't want to add to whatever tension there may be already. Frankly, I'm not sure it was a good idea for Wes to accept the role."

"I thought you were the one who convinced him to do it."

"I was. And just for the record, Mama doesn't always know best."

Tony, the chauffeur, had finished loading the trunk

341

with Jeanne's luggage. Mathilde dropped the subject as he opened the door on the driver's side and climbed behind the wheel.

Before he started the engine, Mathilde leaned forward and said, "Tony, let's drive through downtown Hollywood so my daughter can see how much everything has changed."

He nodded and glanced at Jeanne through the rearview mirror. "Been away long?" he asked.

"It seems like centuries," she replied.

Jeanne reflected on her mother's words as the car stopped for a traffic light up ahead. Everything *had* changed, so drastically that she felt as if she'd never been here before. Some of the buildings remained— Grauman's Chinese Theater; Frederick's of Hollywood, whose windows were crammed with the sleazy undergarments Jeanne recalled from the ads inside the covers of *Wonder Woman* comics. The polished stars with celebrities' names shone brightly in the afternoon sunlight, despite the blanket of smog. Jeanne smiled; she'd read in *Variety* that Pia's star had been added to those along the boulevard, but Andy had told her that it was possible to *buy* the status symbol; it would be in character for Pia to have purchased her sidewalk section of immortality.

Mathilde broke into her thoughts then. "Are you and Andy still . . . seeing each other?"

Jeanne laughed at her mother's choice of words. "Yes, Mama."

Mathilde glanced down at her lap. "I like him. He's a very nice young man. And a fine actor." She paused, waiting for Jeanne to add news of their engagement.

Instead, she heard, "Mama, please do me one favor. Don't try matchmaking."

342

"Darling, I wouldn't dream—"

"Yes, you would. So I'm nipping it in the bud. Andy and I have no wedding plans. We're close . . . very close, in fact—"

"Well then . . . ?"

"And theater comes first with both of us. That's why I'm out here and not in New York with him." She turned to Mathilde and said, "Look, I'm not living a wanton, wayward life, and Andy isn't leading me to ruin, so—"

"But you and he"—she glanced up toward Tony and then lowered her voice—"*are* . . . well, I guess the modern term is 'having a relationship,' isn't it?"

Jeanne smiled. "Yes, Mama, it is. And . . . we are. Let's leave it at that?"

"Darling," ventured Mathilde carefully, "you really mean it, don't you? That theater *is* why you don't want to marry Andy?"

"Mama, what exactly is going through your mind?" Jeanne felt sorry for Mathilde; one of the fringe benefits of being an actress was the ability, from habit, of analyzing others' words and moods. Her profession also helped Jeanne to hide any feelings she didn't want to reveal or share.

But Mathilde surprised her daughter. "Nothing, dear. As long as the reason isn't . . . someone else." She still was looking down at the creases in her skirt, and to cover the awkwardness of her prying, she began smoothing the soft wool fabric until Jeanne's hand stopped her.

"Mama . . . Andy hasn't asked me to marry him, for one thing."

Mathilde nodded mechanically. "And if he did . . . would you?"

"I told you, with both of us, theater comes ahead of everything."

"Yes, you told me. I just wondered if there might be something more . . . something you . . . *haven't* told me."

Without his name having been uttered by either woman in the car, Neal Genesco was suddenly there, seated in the backseat of the Mercedes with Mathilde and Jeanne as vividly as if he had flown all the way from London just for the occasion.

Jeanne, on impulse, threw her arms around her mother and said, "Mama, the only thing I haven't told you is how wonderful it is to see you." She was very convincing because her words were true.

Dinner was informal, served in the den due to the late hour of Wes's return from the studio. Jeanne noted that her stepfather looked tired, although his strong, handsome face had retained its matinee-idol look. If anything, the gray hair at his temples made him appear even more distinguished. It was easy to understand why female audiences adored him and why Mathilde had fallen in love with him.

With that thought came the unavoidable speculation: What, if anything, did Pia feel for Wes? Was she still harboring the girlish fantasies that had ruined her previous marriages? If so, how was it affecting the Alice-Bernard relationship on set? What would happen when they arrived at the seduction scene in the script— which would obviously be more graphic onscreen?

My God! mused Jeanne. Can Pia have cast Wes in order to find her way into his arms? Certainly she was capable of that—and more. She could go up on her her lines or find other ways to force retakes, to repeat the love scene over and over . . . all "for the good of the picture."

No, Pia wouldn't go *that* far, she reasoned. She wouldn't do that to Mama . . . would she?

Some of the dinner conversation touched on the picture, once Wes had seen that Jeanne wasn't bitter over not being cast—or by Wes's playing Andy Thorne's role. It enabled Wes to mention Andy; Jeanne knew Mathilde had probably put him up to it, but she knew also that her stepfather would exercise tact.

"I'm sorry he couldn't fly out here with you," Wes was saying now. "Once *Alice* wraps, the four of us could have flown to Palm Springs for a few days to celebrate your film debut."

"Andy's in rehearsal for a new play," said Jeanne. "Besides, this is just a 'cameo' role. Not exactly the stuff of Oscars. I'm really doing it because my agent feels I ought to learn to find my way around a movie set in something where the major responsibility falls on someone else's shoulders."

"Good advice," said Wes. "Wish I'd been that smart when I was doing my first picture. When do you start shooting?"

"In the morning. In fact, I ought to be getting to bed so I won't be groggy from jet lag tomorrow. All I need is to go tripping on cables and knocking cameras over. They'll ship me back East by noon!"

The three of them laughed. Then Wes rose from his chair, and Mathilde gave him her hand and let him pull her up from the sofa.

"It isn't the company," said Wes, trying to stifle a yawn. "I have an early call, too."

"That reminds me," said Jeanne. "Do you mind if I call New York? I just want to say good night to Andy."

"Oh, darling, of course! There's a phone in the guest

345

room, right beside your bed."

The delight in Mathilde's voice would have irritated Jeanne, except that she knew it stemmed from Mama's desire to see her happy. Yes, she mused, as first she kissed Wes, then her mother, on the cheek; as long as happiness means someone other than Neal.

Don't worry, Mama, thought Jeanne as she dialed the long-distance number; part of being a good actress is in knowing when to leave the scene.

"Jeanne!" Andy Thorne's voice came on the line.

"How'd you know who it was?" she asked.

"Because you're three hours earlier on your coast than I am on mine. Who else would be calling me at two in the morning?"

Jeanne glanced at her wristwatch. Eleven o'clock. She'd reset the time in the car on the way from the airport and hadn't looked at it until now.

"Andy, I'm sorry! I completely forgot—"

"That's okay. I was watching some junk on the tube to help me unwind. How was your trip? How's everything going out there?"

They exchanged news, chatted for a few minutes more, and then it was time to say good night.

Only after curling up on one side of the queen-size mattress did Jeanne realize she'd left room on the other half for Andy; it was his half of the bed in New York. It was also when she realized that, although her career mattered more than her heart, she missed him.

Jeanne Lorraine's first day on the set wasn't greeted with red carpets or fanfares of any kind. The studio limousine deposited her at the entrance to the soundstage before sunrise.

She pulled open the huge metal door by herself and experienced immediate and total disorientation. An assistant's assistant eventually came toward her, clipboard in hand. He checked off her name on a sign-in sheet and signaled—with a nod, not an offer to escort her—the direction of the makeup and dressing rooms.

"Oh, and if you need anything, Miss Lorraine, just ask Tina. She'll be by in a while." A moment later, the nameless young man was gone.

Thus abandoned, Jeanne followed the route he'd indicated and plopped down in one of the makeup room chairs. Someone had thought to provide a cardboard container of coffee. She lifted the lid and held the steaming cup under her nose, then took a sip; it tasted like mud, but at least it was hot.

The caffeine helped Jeanne to stay awake while a woman named Iris Pan-Caked her with highlight and shadow. Then Geoffrey, the hairdresser, sprayed and teased her long hair. Jeanne didn't feel very affable through any of this; jet lag had made its presence known, and reminding her that it was already nine A.M. in New York—normal rehearsal time—would have made no difference. Jeanne was in California, where it was hardly dawn.

She yawned as Geoffrey surveyed her from front, back, and sides. "Well," he said, grinning, "sorry to keep you awake, but we had to do *something* with you, didn't we?"

She tried to smile, although in the mirror's reflection it looked more like a smirk. *Why am I here?* she asked herself. What can this possibly do for my career? People must be crazy to do movies day in and day out—especially starting in the middle of the night!

As though in reply, Geoffrey said, "You'll get used to the routine after a few weeks."

Now Jeanne did manage a smile, and a short laugh escaped with it. "By then, I'll be going back to New

347

York. Besides, I don't think I could ever get used to this. How do you stay awake?"

Geoffrey winked. "Hysteria. Keeps me on my toes. Can I get you more coffee?"

"Thanks, that's the last thing I need," she said. "I'm sure I'll be fine by the time we start to shoot."

"Well, you have time for a little nap before they're ready for you."

It was an understatement. Jeanne could have slept for hours—at home—before they were ready to shoot her first scene. Not until midafternoon was she finally called to the set. Jeanne had spent more than half the day in her dressing room, completely made up and wardrobed. Tina or one of her assistants had stopped by hourly to say, "Just a little longer, Miss Lorraine."

There was no point in restudying her lines; there were so few in each of her half dozen scenes that she'd memorized them at the airport in New York while the jet was sitting on the runway awaiting takeoff.

Tomorrow, she decided, I'll bring along a book. A very *long* book.

At three o'clock, Jeanne rose from her canvas chair to shake hands with the film's director, Calvin Epstein. He was dressed in khakis, as though departing on safari. The only prop missing was a whip.

Epstein carried no script; Jeanne assumed he had each scene memorized and worked in the style of Hitchcock. But she soon began to wonder if Hitchcock would have placed his actors on marks as though he were a window-dresser and they were mannequins on display. Character motivation would obviously be dictated by camera angles already devised in his head but a mystery to everyone else.

That's great, thought Jeanne. I can handle motivation—but camera angles? Someone will have to point me toward the lens, or my motivation will play to the wall while my *backside* faces the camera!

Calvin Epstein, who had, except for his initial handclasp, ignored his "cameo" star from New York, now approached her. A tall, thin man with a beard stood alongside him.

"Miss Lorraine," said the director, "Joe here is my first assistant director. He'll walk you through the scene while I finish taking care of some minor details. It shouldn't be more than a minute."

Jeanne wondered which would take a minute—the minor details or the scene itself. She didn't ask, but smiled tenuously at Joe, who acknowledged her with a nod.

"I understand this is your first film," he said, coming closer.

"It's that easy to spot?"

"No. But your name has been in the papers. You know, 'New York stage star graces Hollywood with her presence,' et cetera."

"I'm hardly doing that," Jeanne remarked. "In fact, I'm hardly doing *anything*. I thought movies were like TV."

"They are," said Joe. "And both are like the Army. Hurry up, get ready, then sit around and wait."

"Oh. Well, I didn't mean *filmed* television. I've only done live TV. Soaps and interviews. The camera follows you. No technical knowledge required." She lowered her voice. "But what about *acting?* I mean . . . what on earth am I supposed to do when Calvin claps the chalkboard and calls, 'Action'?"

Joe laughed. "First of all, Miss Lorraine—"

"Please—call me Jeanne."

"Okay. In the first place, Jeanne, an assistant calls 'action.' Cal won't be doing much of anything. And

349

don't be intimidated by all the equipment you see around. Cal doesn't know much more than you do about any of this stuff."

"He doesn't . . . ? But he's the director—"

"Cal's got a cameraman and an editor. He decides what he wants for the overall, big picture. He may ask for a close-up, but God help us if he's the one who shoots it. Movies aren't what they were in Griffith's time. Nowadays, moviemaking is a team sport."

"You sound as though *you* should be the one who's directing," said Jeanne, beginning to relax.

"Well, you hang around movie sets long enough, you pick up information. I've been working in one studio or another since I was a kid. Started at Antaen Pictures as a gofer. Learned from the bottom up. Doesn't happen much anymore. Kids arrive with their briefcases and film-school degrees and think they know how to make movies." He drew himself up and cleared his throat. "The real way—the only way—to learn movies is by making movies."

"Joe," said Jeanne in a confidential whisper, "will you help me make this one so I don't wind up looking like a klutz?"

"You don't pretend to know it all. You're ahead of the game already. God, it's amazing—" He stopped himself abruptly.

"What's amazing?" she asked.

Joe had turned crimson and was nervously stroking his beard. When he spoke again, he didn't look Jeanne directly in her eyes. "I wasn't planning to mention it . . . in fact, I'd planned *not* to . . . but . . . I worked on your sister's first picture, too."

"You did?" She thought back to 1955 and Pia's screen debut with Wes. "Why weren't you going to mention it?"

350

Joe shrugged as the color of his face gradually returned to normal. "I guess because of the gossip stories in the papers. You know, all that stuff about . . . well, sibling rivalry . . . and your careers."

"Don't believe everything you read," said Jeanne. "But you still haven't explained. What did you mean about something amazing?"

He tried to avert his eyes, but he gave up. "It's just that . . . well, you're so *different* from Pia—you hardly seem like sisters at all."

"I'm not sure how to take that," Jeanne said, although she sensed it was a compliment. "After all, Pia knows her way around a movie set."

"There's more to life than a soundstage and a camera," said Joe. "There's knowing how to treat people." He hesitated, then added, "I shouldn't be saying any of this. She's your sister, and it's none of my business. Besides, you might think I'm bad-mouthing her because she didn't want to date me."

Dates. Suddenly Jeanne remembered. "You're *Joey,* aren't you! Joey . . . Crane?"

"Guilty. But we haven't said a word to each other in ages. Don't tell me she's ever mentioned my name—"

"Our mother did. Years ago. She liked you."

"Nice lady. I've never been able to understand how—" he stopped himself again.

"Neither has Mama, Joe," Jeanne finished for him. "Just call it an accident of birth."

Joe Crane became Jeanne's friend away from the studio and her ally on the set. By week's end she was comfortable enough in front of the camera to let herself relax; at the same time she was able to protract her performance to accommodate the more intimate scope

351

of the lens. She learned—and adopted Joe's phrase about on-the-job-training—that larger-than-life acting onstage would result in overacting onscreen.

Nonetheless, as she confided to Joe, she couldn't wait to return to New York. More and more she found herself missing the theater.

And missing Andy Thorne.

Mathilde was happy on all counts but one. She was glad that Jeanne's filming was progressing smoothly; that Joey Crane had moved up in the business and that he'd befriended her daughter; that *After Alice*, following innumerable delays, was heading into its home stretch. But she'd secretly hoped, despite all their various and hectic schedules, that somehow Pia and Jeanne would be reunited, just as Mathilde herself still hoped to recapture the closeness she'd once felt toward her older daughter.

Even if the closeness had been one-sided, it didn't matter to Mathilde. What mattered was that the girls—both girls—were her offspring. Hers and Hank's. She had no desire to rekindle the past; Mathilde loved Wes and cherished their family life together. Still, the phrase haunted her. *Family life together*. If that didn't include Pia and Jeanne, the picture remained incomplete.

When, shortly before the wrap of *After Alice*, she broached the subject of a reconciliation between her daughters, Jeanne's response was, "Mama, I spent my entire childhood trying to be her friend, but Pia always did something to sabotage it. She's done things I can never forget. She's hurt people with her lies. Just because we happen to be working in the same city doesn't mean we have to see each other. She was too busy in New York. Well, *I'm* too busy now. It's Pia's turn to make the first move."

Mathilde knew her older daughter well enough to realize that Pia would never make the first move. And now she knew that Jeanne wouldn't, either.

Well, she decided, after examining all the options. In that case, it's up to me.

Chapter Twenty-Four

"Look, Vince," Pia was saying into the telephone, "you're my doctor, not my shrink. So leave the advice out of it and just tell me, yes or no. Am I—"

"You're pregnant," he said. "And as your physician, Pia, I must warn you that to . . . terminate . . . another pregnancy so soon after the last one could seriously endanger your health. Furthermore—"

"Vince, nobody's talking about an abortion!" Her voice had risen almost to a shout, and she recoiled, surprised by her first use ever of the word. More softly she said, "I'm going to have this baby."

There was no response from the other end of the line, but Pia could hear a relieved exhale of breath. A moment later, Dr. Vincent said, "On a practical level . . . about the baby's father . . ."

"Oh for Christ's sake, it's Brad—who else would it be?"

The doctor again offered no reply.

Finally Pia said, "Vince, I want you to do me a favor. Don't say anything about this to Brad or to anyone else. I want to surprise him."

"Pia, if he's the father, he has a right to know—"

"I told you, he's the father. And I'll tell him. At the

wrap party. He's been making noises about getting married. I'll let him propose again and then say yes."

"I thought you were against remarriage," the doctor reminded her.

"I am. But I'm not about to bring a bastard into the world. I know enough of them whose parents *were* married. No, it's about time for Olympia Decameron to experience the joys of motherhood firsthand."

"Babies can't be discarded or sent away when the novelty wears off, Pia," said Dr. Vincent. "They're not the same as toys or pets . . . or lovers."

"I *really* appreciate your tact, Vince. But I'm aware of the responsibility."

"I'm glad to hear that, Pia. And I'm sure Brad will be a good father."

She smiled to herself. Whether she was carrying a boy or a girl, with her looks and Brad's, this baby would have the universe on a silver platter.

"Just remember, Vince—not a word to anyone till I announce it at the wrap party." She paused, then added, "I *can* trust you to keep the secret, can't I?"

"If I didn't know you better," he said, "I'd be insulted. Brad never found out about Mexico, did he?"

"No," said Pia. "And he never will."

Mathilde had noticed Wes's reticence all evening. He'd been unusually quiet that morning before leaving for the studio. Probably because it's the last day on the picture, she thought. Mathilde had learned during their years together that no matter how much money he made, the end of a film or stage commitment always brought with it a strange kind of anxiety, as though the next stop would be welfare or the unemployment line. Perhaps, she reasoned, it's a throwback from his early career; during the Depression the constant question hadn't been whether the show would run but if it would play long enough to fill the cupboard and pay the rent.

And so, when Wes returned from shooting his last scene in *After Alice* and was reluctant to discuss the final day's shoot, Mathilde shrugged it off as typical behavior because it fit a customary pattern.

She did wonder why he seemed equally reluctant to attend the wrap party, but she decided to leave the subject alone—at least until breakfast.

However, just before they went to bed, the matter came up. Mathilde, after rummaging through her walk-in closet, carried three different gowns into the room and laid them across the spread.

"Which one do you like best?" she asked. All three were made of silk chiffon and decorated with sequins or bugle beads. The decision was one of color.

Wes seemed distracted, so she said, "Darling, which one should I wear to the wrap party—mauve, peach, or blue?"

Now he looked over at her and seemed to notice the gowns for the first time. "What are those for?"

She didn't lose patience; he'd had a long day on the set. "For the wrap party at Pia's," she said.

She saw his jaw muscles tense slightly at the mention of Pia's name and hoped they hadn't suffered an altercation on the picture's very last day.

"We don't really have to go," he said.

"Not go . . . ! Wes—it's at her house—how could we *not* go . . . ?" Then she rephrased the question. "Why, Wes? Do you mean you don't *want* to go?"

He had removed his tie and said wearily, "Yes . . . I suppose that's what I mean."

"But darling . . . I don't understand! It'd be one thing if it were at a hotel or club. But it's at Pia's house—she'll expect us to be there—*everyone* will expect us—"

"We could drive up to Tahoe, instead. Or spend the weekend in Palm Springs. We haven't done that since Jeanne went back to New York—"

"Wes, something's the matter. And it involves Pia. Is she sick again? Is something the matter with her?"

He exhaled deeply, and Mathilde could see that his nerves were on edge. Just as she could see that harping about it would only make it worse.

Still, she had to ask. The more he avoided telling her, the more she needed to find out.

"Darling," he said at last, "there's definitely something the matter with Pia, and it isn't physical. I've tried—God knows I've tried all through this damned picture—but whatever it is, she ought to see a shrink, because I sure as hell can't figure her out."

"Wes—"

He interrupted. "And she doesn't care that you're her mother or that I'm—"

"Wes! Stop it, please! Unless you're going to explain everything, I don't want to hear another word about it!"

She had expected him to say all right, let's sit down and I'll tell you everything, from beginning to end.

It came as a surprise when instead he went into the bathroom and returned several moments later ready for bed.

"Wes . . . ?" said Mathilde in a small voice after he'd turned out the light.

She could hear the pause before he turned over and, very quietly, said, "We'll go to the party. For you. But don't say I didn't warn you about Pia."

She couldn't force him to say more. From the sound of his slow, steady breathing, Wes had either immediately fallen asleep, or he was doing one hell of a good job acting the part.

October's gaudy splendor was barely in evidence.
The freeway seemed oblivious to seasonal change, and
Mathilde's phone conversation with Jeanne the night
before had made her homesick for the house in
Connecticut. Jeanne had talked of leaves turning
orange and red, blown by crisp autumn breezes. Well,
thought Mathilde, a few more days and we'll be there,
too.

She smiled to herself. She missed the East Coast with
a nostalgia that descended each fall upon transplanted
converts; New Yorkers of her acquaintance took it all
in stride with a shrug. Instead, Mathilde was filled with
excitement.

Her jittery nerves were being caused also by the
anticipation of seeing Pia after such a long time. It was
a familiar feeling—hope, mingled with dread. Especially
after Wes's mood of the night before.

"We're almost there," said Wes. They had passed
perfectly manicured lawns of creeping-bent, which
carpeted the grounds of stars' estates along the
winding, palm-tree-lined roads climbing upward from
the canyon. Names and addresses were hidden from
view, but signs, warning trespassers of sophisticated
security surveillance, lined the paths at regular inter-
vals. Mathilde wondered how anyone who didn't live in
one of these houses could possibly find the right
turnoff.

She pulled down the windshield visor to check her
makeup in the mirror.

"You look wonderful," Wes reassured her.

"Thank you." She removed a stray eyelash from her
cheek and pushed the visor back in place. "Wes, I know
you really don't want to go—"

358

"I don't," he interrupted. "I don't want her to hurt you anymore."

She didn't pursue it. He still hadn't spoken about the previous day on the set, but at least he was willing to show up at the wrap party, though Mathilde knew it was in deference to her as much as to the rest of the cast and crew.

She saw the expression of concern on his face as they pulled into Pia's driveway.

"Darling," she said, "don't worry about me. I'm glad we're here."

He nodded. "I hope you'll feel that way later."

The door was opened by a young man dressed entirely in white. He took their coats and pointed them toward the bar, which was already crowded three-deep. A Beatles recording was just ending, immediately followed by the Supremes. A few couples were dancing.

Mathilde had seen at once that she was overdressed. The blue chiffon was far too fussy for the occasion, in view of the casual slacks and sweaters worn by the rest of those present.

"I thought you said *dressy*," she whispered to Wes, who was already perspiring in his linen dinner jacket.

"It's what Pia told me," he answered. "I should have known better." His arm slipped around her waist. "We don't have to stay."

"Yes we do. *I* do, anyway."

"Then so do I." When she glanced questioningly at him, Wes said, "Well, that's unless you've learned to drive while I've been working on the picture . . ."

Mathilde shook her head and glanced around the room. The house—as much as she'd seen of it so far—bespoke nothing of its owner or her taste. The furnishings fell into the category of easy elegance, the new standard of the Hollywood elite. The hand of a good interior decorator was obvious; the results exquisite but impersonal. Anyone might live here, thought Mathilde. Male or female, daughter or stranger.

And Pia was nowhere in sight.

Wes loosened his tie as they maneuvered their way across the room toward the bar. A woman called his name and both turned.

"Harriet," said Wes, introducing Mathilde to Harriet Hicks, "the best editor in town."

"Well, *one* of the best. Thanks. It's nice to meet you . . . finally," she said to Mathilde.

"Likewise. How's it going?"

Harriet ran a hand through her short gray hair. "I'm not glued to a movieola *yet*. We start tomorrow. It won't be an easy job."

"I suppose it never is," Mathilde said, accepting a vodka and tonic from Wesley.

"Well, we've got some matching prob—" Harriet stopped speaking in mid-sentence and flashed a nervous glance to Wes, then back to Mathilde.

"It's all right," he said. "Pia's . . . antics . . . aren't news at home."

"I *am* her mother, you know," said Mathilde.

"Yes, I do know. And Wes is being unfair. Pia's been . . . quite . . . disciplined. At least once the first two weeks were out of the way."

"Look, why don't you get to know each other?" said Wes. "I think I'm supposed to mingle."

The two women watched as he moved into the center of the room with his customary ease.

"You're lucky," said Harriet. "If he's as good to live with as he is to work with, hang on to him."

Mathilde laughed. "He is . . . and I will." She took a

360

sip of her drink. "Then I take it your matching problems don't involve Wes?"

"Not a one. People like Wes make my work easier. It's . . . well, it's Pia. She was too thin when we started shooting. It doesn't jibe with her appearance in the later footage. Somehow I'll have to get around it, and fast."

"Can't they reshoot?"

Harriet shook her head. "Money's tight. And they want this in the theaters before Christmas."

"But . . . you think it's a good picture, don't you?" No matter what differences had occurred between Wes and Pia during the filming, Mathilde knew the screenplay's possibilities.

"Yeah, I do. Ought to break even at the box office, and she'll probably have a crack at the Oscar. She's been on the wagon. Seems almost happy, too. You should be proud of Pia, Mathilde."

"Yes . . ." But where was she? "Have you seen her?"

Harriet glanced around and shrugged. "She was out by the pool with Nathan. He's the—"

"I know Mr. Schutz very well," said Mathilde with a smile. "Since before Wes and I were married."

"*Everybody* knows Mr. Schutz," Brad stage-whispered into Harriet's ear. He offered a crooked grin to Mathilde.

"Do you two know each other?" Harriet asked.

"No," Brad replied, extending his hand. "But we know *of* each other. I'm—"

"Already swacked," Harriet finished for him with a short laugh. "This is Brad Morrow."

"She's right on both counts," he said, hiccoughing. "Excuse me."

"Excuse *me,*" said Harriet, slipping between them. "My husband may be in the same shape, and *he's* driving!"

Brad seemed more sober when he and Mathilde were left alone. "So. At last. The mysterious queen mother. But I don't see your crown."

"It's in the car," she answered dryly, not certain whether to like or dislike him.

"You'll have to let me borrow it sometime," said Brad. "Consorts don't get to wear them, you know." He offered her a cigarette. Mathilde's hand reached out, then drew back.

"I've given up smoking," she said.

"Aha!" Brad laughed and lit up. "You almost took one, though. Nerves . . . ?"

"Do they show?"

"Just a little around the edges. If it's any comfort, she's nervous, too."

"Pia?"

"Of course Pia. She knows you're here. She may be playing hostess, but she's hiding."

"Well," said Mathilde, "I didn't expect this to be easy. For either of us."

"Pia's never easy. On anyone."

Mathilde found herself staring at him. "In that case, why do you . . ."

"Why do I stay?" He shrugged. "She's hardest of all on Pia. Always wants what she can't have." Brad leaned in close to her. "That's what you . . . and I . . . have to worry about. Good luck."

That they had just met hardly mattered; they understood each other. Whether it was because they were similar or whether Pia was their common bond, Mathilde couldn't say.

Brad started to walk away but, as an afterthought, turned back. "You know, you're not at all what I expected."

"Neither are you, Brad."

"I hope that was a compliment, 'cause I have a gut feeling that you're probably okay." He gave her the

362

thumbs-up sign and went off to dance with Charlene Webb.

The next half hour seemed unending. The longer each of them delayed the inevitable, the more apparent it became to the guests. Mathilde had seen Pia surrounded by people out on the patio near the swimming pool. At first sight of her daughter, Mathilde had to admit that her heart began to flutter.

Pia looked radiant. Her figure was fuller, her features and hair glowing with health. A star. The adolescent roundness of her face had grown into a womanliness that wasn't given justice when translated to the screen. Elizabeth Taylor was the only other woman Mathilde could think of whose in-person beauty far surpassed that of her image on film.

The only remnant of Pia's girlhood was, at each side of her brow, a carefully set spit curl.

Mathilde and Pia's eyes met only for an instant before Pia turned, giving her arm to Barney Berman as he led her toward the entrance to the kitchen. The exit didn't go unnoticed by Pia's immediate circle, and Mathilde looked away, searching desperately for someone or something on which to focus her attention. She had hoped things had changed for the better between them. Obviously they hadn't. And suddenly she knew that Pia had deliberately misled Wes—and thereby Mathilde—into thinking that formal attire was requested at the wrap party. A calculated humiliation which, although no one had made the slightest remark, had nonetheless cut deeply.

Mathilde felt tears threatening. She looked about for Wes but didn't see him anywhere.

Two women stood ahead of her, waiting for the guest

bathroom off the living room. They were soon joined by a third woman who seemed to know the other two. They smiled politely at Mathilde, who made a valiant effort at smiling back. Finally the bathroom door opened, and one of the women said, "We'll wait. Why don't you go ahead of us?"

Mathilde accepted, escaping into the safety of the small room. The tears she had kept bottled inside now burst forth, and she made no attempt to stop them. Damn the puffy eyelids, she thought. To hell with the makeup. Wes was right; we never should have come.

She ran the water faucet at full force to cover the sounds of her sobbing. She splashed cold water on her wrists, then to her forehead and cheeks. Little by little, she began to feel better. Maybe a touch-up of powder and mascara would disguise the pain. She turned off the water, dried her face, and reached into her purse for the silver filigree compact that Wes had given her for their anniversary.

She was working the tiny mascara brush over her lashes when she became aware of the voices coming from outside the closed bathroom door.

"She seems nice enough," said one. "You'd *never* take them for mother and daughter."

"I wonder if she knows. You should have seen Wes on the set—he looked angry enough to kill!"

"Can you blame him?" asked the first woman. "The bitch is his *daughter*—"

"*Step*daughter, hon. And you know the old saying . . ."

"What saying is that?"

"Oh, that vice is nice but incest is best . . ."

"*Now* who's being a bitch?"

"Yeah, but I was *there*. I mean, she practically raped him during the scene, and then, when Eric called 'cut,' she wouldn't stop! And that's in front of the whole crew—"

"Oh, come on—"

"Well," said the third woman, "you saw it. Christ, I wonder if her mother knows."

"She must—they haven't said a word to each other all evening."

"*That's* been going on for years," said the first woman. "She's been trying to fuck him since she was a kid!"

Mathilde was shaking so hard that she didn't see her mascara brush fall into the wastebasket. She willed the tears away and took three long, deep breaths, all the while staring, in shock and disbelief, at her reflection in the mirror.

"*. . . been going on for years . . .*" The words reverberated in her ears as she snapped her compact shut.

The brewing storm had gathered, choking her with rage. Mathilde didn't even notice the three red-faced women who fell silent with embarrassment as she flung open the bathroom door.

"*. . . since she was a kid!*" Well, Pia, she thought, it's been a long time in coming . . .

She pushed through the mob in the living room without excusing herself, without stopping for anyone until Wesley put his hand on her arm. "You seem upset. Anything wrong?"

Mathilde looked him directly in the eye. "The same thing that was wrong when you got home from the set last night."

"Darling, don't. Brad just told me that Pia isn't feeling well. This isn't the time—"

"It never *was,*" she said. "Let go of my arm, Wes." She spotted Pia, then, who was halfway up the staircase.

"I hope you know what you're doing," he said,

releasing his grip.

"I can't worry about that anymore, Wes." Mathilde brushed past him and rushed toward the stairs. As Pia reached the landing, she looked down and their eyes met.

Pia's face drained of its color as Mathilde quickened her step and raced up to the second floor.

Pia took one backward glance and, seeing her mother close behind, ran into the first room and slammed the door.

Mathilde swung it open before Pia was able to turn the lock.

"I want to talk with you," said Mathilde, closing the door and leaning against it for support.

Pia's earlier glow had vanished. Her face was pale white as she clutched at her stomach and sank down onto the edge of the bed.

"I'm . . . sick," she said with a groan.

"So am I," answered Mathilde tonelessly.

"Not now, Mama—can't you see I'm in pain?"

"Suddenly it's *Mama*. Why not Mathilde? *That's* what you've called me for *years,* isn't it?" Her voice was rising, and she was helpless to keep it down.

Pia fled to the bathroom and fell to her knees before the bowl. Mathilde moved closer only to keep the door open between them.

Pia tried to vomit, but nothing came up. Slowly she rose to her feet and, without looking at her mother, said, "You won't even allow me the dignity to be sick in private."

"Most people have forgotten more about dignity than you'll ever know, Pia. You're not sick, you're drunk!"

"I'm not! I haven't had a drink in weeks!"

"You're talking to *Mama,* Pia, *remember?* That's the word *you* just used! The *mama* who sat up with her child when she really *was* sick, Pia. The mama who wanted only the best for her daughters, Pia—while *you* laughed in her face."

"You don't know the half of it!" Pia screamed back, pushing past Mathilde and trying to reach the door.

"Don't you *dare* walk out on me! I have something to say to you, and you're going to listen!"

Pia wheeled around to face her. "You want to have this out, Mama? Then let's go! What've you got to say to me?"

"Simply this, Pia: Find a man of your *own!*" Pia started to interrupt, but Mathilde stopped her. "Don't open your mouth—I haven't finished, yet! When you were a child, I made *one* mistake, and we're *all* still paying for it! I neglected Jeanne and gave you all the love and attention—and you *used* it, you've *been* using it ever since! You've used *me,* Pia, but no more! You've stolen from your sister, tried to wreck my marriage, and you're ruining your own life in the process. You're a spoiled, manipulative, self-centered, egotistic *child* who destroys everything she touches! But I'm warning you, Pia"—she had to stop for breath—"*don't* touch *Wesley!* Do you understand me, Pia? *Leave him alone!*"

"He's my father!" she screamed.

"If you *believe* that, you're out of your mind! He's my *husband*—you've been trying to take *my husband* away from me from the beginning, Pia! I've had enough of you—and so has he!"

"Wesley loves me!" Pia shrieked. "He *has* to love me!"

"No, Pia!"

"*Yeeessss!*" she wailed feverishly, spitting the words into her mother's face. "It's *me!* It's *always* been me!"

Mathilde felt the dam burst. Her hand flew up and slapped Pia across the face. Once, twice. The third slap was so hard it made her palm tingle from the blow.

Pia collapsed in violent sobs and fell onto a footstool. Mathilde stood rock-still at the center of the room. Neither woman uttered a sound until Pia's hysterical spasms subsided and she regained control of her voice. Then, looking up at her mother, she said emotionlessly, "It's Papa. You never figured that out, did you?"

Mathilde chose her words very slowly, carefully, needing for them to sink in. "Pia, Wesley is *not* your—"

"No," Pia whispered hoarsely. "Not Wesley. *Papa.*"

Mathilde tried to swallow the sudden, dry lump in her throat. "H-Hank . . . ?"

Pia nodded listlessly.

"What . . . do you mean, Pia . . . ?"

With halting speech, Pia said, "All I ever wanted . . . was to . . . to have Papa back. I was . . . *his* little girl, first, before . . . Jeanne." Her throat was tightening. "B-but when . . . I saw . . ."

"Pia," said Mathilde softly, coming to kneel beside her, "I know you found him. I know it was . . . horrible. You were so young . . . We should have talked about this . . . years ago. It was a terrible accident, Pia—"

"I didn't say I *found* him, Mama. I said I *saw* him . . ."

"Pia . . . what . . . are you trying . . . to tell me?" And suddenly Mathilde was afraid to know.

Pia answered in an empty, lifeless voice, as terrifying as Mathilde's rage had been before. "I walked into the room . . . and Papa was holding . . . the gun . . ."

"He was cleaning his service revolver, Pia . . ."

"He was pointing the barrel, Mama . . ."

"Pia—"

"He saw me, Mama. He *looked* at me . . . and said . . . 'I love you, honey.'" She closed her eyes and began to gasp. "And then—he opened—his mouth—and—he

368

put the barrel inside—and—"

"NO!" Mathilde screamed, covering her ears. "It was an *accident!* It *had* to be an accident! *Pia—*"

Her own words raced through her brain. Words she had never allowed herself to speak, to think. And now they had penetrated the darkness. Twenty years after the nightmare. Twenty years too late.

Mathilde was barely capable of speech. "You've . . . lived with it . . . all this time . . . ?"

"Haven't you lived with it, too, Mama?" Pia asked weakly. "Can you honestly say that you never suspected the truth? Wasn't I your favorite because you were trying to make up for . . . what happened?"

"Pia . . . I . . ." Mathilde was struggling to make sense, but her thoughts were as jumbled as her words. Pia rose shakily, and Mathilde reached out to help her to her feet. "Why, Pia," she said finally, "in God's name, *why* . . . didn't you tell me . . . ?"

Pia looked up, her cheeks streaked with mascara-smudged tears. "Maybe I *am* crazy, Mama. I don't know. I felt that Papa was mine. That he . . . belonged to me." She shrugged. "I guess I wanted his . . . secret . . . to belong to me. But you're right, Mama. Wes . . . is . . . yours. He . . . he always has been . . . from the start."

She moved toward the door, and this time Mathilde made no attempt to stop her. But Pia, a hand on the knob, turned back for an instant. "You asked me why I never told you, Mama. I couldn't . . . I thought you wouldn't believe me. Besides . . . I . . . I always thought that if Papa had loved me enough—" Her voice choked off the rest of the sentence. Fighting new tears, Pia said, "Look at me, Mama, and tell me that whatever I am today has nothing to do with . . . Papa."

Then, on trembling legs, she opened the door and left

the room.

Mathilde remained standing at the center of the floor, her mind an empty void, her body immobile.

Seconds later, she heard a scream. Mathilde rushed out onto the second-floor landing to find several guests gathered around an inert form at the foot of the staircase.

Pia lay unconscious on the bottom steps. Brad and Dr. Vincent were shoving people aside and shouting orders.

"Give her room to breathe!" commanded the doctor. "And somebody call an ambulance!"

There was a blood-streaked gash on Pia's forehead. She was still wearing her left shoe, a black silk pump. Its right mate lay at the top of the stairs, where its dark color stood out against the stark white carpeting. It caught Mathilde's eye, but it wasn't until she picked it up that she realized its high spike heel was broken.

Chapter Twenty-Five

Except for the sparseness of the room's furnishings, the premises might have been mistaken for the bridal suite of a luxury Beverly Hills hotel instead of a private room in the hospital.

Flowers—in baskets, pots, and assorted, unmatched vases—were in evidence along every wall; nurses scurried along corridors in search of additional receptacles in which to arrange the latest delivery of floral get-well wishes.

Reporters and photographers were kept at bay by an army consisting of Nathan Schutz, Barney Berman, and Charlene Webb. Telegrams and messages flooded the switchboard, while boxes of candy arrived by the armload.

Outside the room pandemonium ruled; inside, Wesley stood gazing out the window, the post he had assumed since Pia had been returned from the recovery room following her emergency surgery. Brad paced quietly back and forth at the foot of the bed, while Mathilde, seated on a cold metal chair, waited numbly for her daughter to awaken.

Someone had given Mathilde a tranquilizer; she couldn't recall whether it was before or after she had

371

climbed into the front seat of the ambulance. So many random thoughts, truncated in midcompletion, collided simultaneously in her head and made Mathilde wonder if she, not Pia, had taken the fall.

But each time her mind replayed the scene of Pia at the bottom of the stairs, so too it repeated their confrontation. If Pia had lived with the horrible secret of Hank's suicide—there; she'd accepted it as fact—Mathilde realized that she, not Pia, must now live with the knowledge that their fight had triggered Pia's tumble down the stairs and caused her miscarriage.

Mathilde glanced inadvertently at Brad, who looked as emotionally dazed as she felt. She remembered their conversation earlier at the party and also recalled his reaction to the doctor's news. "What baby?" he'd asked, bewildered. I misjudged him, thought Mathilde. He's not another Rod Raynor. He really cares about her.

It made her want to reach out to him, to say something, but words failed her. Even Wes, whom she loved more deeply than she had known it was possible to love anyone, would never be able to erase the ugliness of what Hank had done and what Pia had witnessed.

A strange and unfamiliar fury gradually began to surface as Mathilde, her eyes closed, drew the memory of Hank into the forefront. All those years of mourning an accident—an accident that instead had been a deliberate, selfish, egocentric act, without a moment's contemplation as to the possible consequences! *"I love you, honey,"* he'd said to Pia. Words! Such easy words! Meaningless words to a child standing in the doorway and watching her father pull the trigger.

All those years, she repeated silently. I never stopped loving you. Even after I met Wes, there was part of me that went on loving you—the memory of you—*because*

I felt I'd failed you, Hank! I thought the drinking was to escape from pressures on the force . . . from responsibility . . . from the girls . . . and *me!* But I was wrong! You drank to escape from life! *We* didn't fail you, Hank—you failed *yourself*—and left *us* to pick up the pieces!

Mathilde's breathing, which had grown high and shallow, began to calm now as she allowed her mind to form the phrase she'd unconsciously buried for two decades: I know the truth, Hank, and that frees us both. My love for you is over, and I can cease to mourn.

Her anger and grief were gone; in their place was pity.

At that moment, a soft moaning sound came from the bed. Brad stopped pacing and Wes turned. Mathilde opened her eyes and leaned forward, as Pia, in a faraway, little-girl voice, whimpered, "Mama . . . ?"

Pia's face was almost as white as the pillowcase. Her hair, damp and matted, was the only sign of color on the bed. Her left hand was attached to the IV unit, her right hand clasped gently by Mathilde. Brad and Wes had understood that mother and daughter needed some time alone together; the two men had gone down the hall on the pretext of bringing back sandwiches. Whether minutes or hours had passed since then, Mathilde couldn't tell.

Initially neither woman spoke; Pia's throat was parched and sore, and Mathilde didn't know what to say. She poured some water and unwrapped one of the straws that the nurse had left on the night table. She held the glass while Pia sipped.

"I'm . . . sorry, Mama . . ." she whispered, almost inaudibly. "For everything . . ."

"Shh, we'll talk later. Take another sip."

The cool liquid brought relief as Pia swallowed.

"My throat . . . is scratchy . . ."

"That's from the tube that was inserted . . . during surgery," Mathilde explained.

"W-hat s-surgery . . . ?" Pia asked, trying without success to raise her head from the pillow.

"Because of your . . . fall . . . they had to . . . operate."

Suddenly Pia's face registered alarm. "Mama! T-the b-baby! What about—the—"

"Shh," said Mathilde, smoothing the hair at the sides of her temples the way she had when Pia was small. "The doctor said—they had no choice—"

Tears began to fill Pia's eyes as the realization sank in. Her throat became more constricted and all she could say was, "Why . . . ?"

"Pia, you took a terrible fall. There was nothing else they could do without endangering your life."

All Pia could make out in her foggy state was the unfunny irony: the clandestine abortion of one fetus—after no amount of bicycling, gymnastics, or hot soaks could shake it loose—followed by the legal, surgical demise of a much-wanted baby, a planned-for baby. Both pregnancies that she hoped to keep secret—one permanently, the other only until she had begun to show.

"D-does Brad know?"

Mathilde nodded. "He was surprised, of course, but your doctor explained that it was in the early stages and that you'd probably just wanted to be sure before you told him."

"W-was he angry . . . ?" Pia asked meekly.

"Angry? He cares too much about you to be angry."

"What about you, Mama?"

"What about me?"

Pia averted her eyes from her mother as she whispered, "Are you . . . angry with . . . me . . . ?"

Mathilde emitted a long, pent-up sigh. "I was, Pia. I was furious with you. Down deep I may have even hated you."

Pia turned back and reached for Mathilde's hand. "You said . . . *was,* Mama. W-what about . . . now?"

Mathilde's throat tightened. "You used to ask me that when you were a child, every time you did something that you knew was naughty. If I caught you in the act, you always looked up into my eyes and said, 'Are you angry with me, Mama?'"

"And you always . . . forgave me . . ." Tears were running down Pia's cheeks.

From habit as much as from memory, Mathilde squeezed Pia's hand.

With what little strength she had, Pia returned the pressure. "Mama . . . can you . . . forgive me . . . now . . . ?"

Mathilde's reply came through choking tears as Brad and Wes reentered the room. In a low, hoarse voice, she said, "I'll try, Pia. I can't promise you more than that, but . . . I'll try."

"She's asking too much, Mama," said Jeanne, pretending to study the menu. "Or perhaps you're the one who's asking too much."

"Darling," said Mathilde, "all I want is for you to give her a chance. I told you on the phone, I think your sister really wants to make amends."

"I hope for your sake—and Pia's—that you're right, Mama. But that doesn't mean I'm convinced."

The menu was covering Jeanne's face, and Mathilde reached across the table and politely tapped it. "Please don't use the menu as a prop to hide behind. You're talking to your mother."

Jeanne smiled, in spite of herself. "Yes, and I should have known that my mother didn't invite me to lunch just to discuss the fall foliage." The waitress arrived and took their order—and removed the menu-props from the table.

When they were alone again, Jeanne said, "Mama, in all seriousness, you have to understand something: Whatever Papa did . . . whatever Pia *saw* him do . . . still doesn't condone some of the things she's done to people—especially to those closest to her. You, more than anyone, must know that."

"Darling, I'm not condoning Pia's past behavior. I'm simply saying that Pia's trying to, well, you know the old saying about turning over a new leaf, and—"

"Yes, Mama, and there's another old saying: 'Actions speak louder than words.' If Pia is sincere, that's fine. But forgive me if I don't entirely trust one evening's catharsis and a miscarriage to have turned her completely around."

Their Mimosas arrived. Both Mathilde and Jeanne pretended to concentrate on stirring the ingredients of the drinks before sipping them—while each gazed downward into her glass.

At length Mathilde said, "She's seeing a psychiatrist, you know. And Brad's made a big difference. He isn't using Pia. He loves her."

"I'm glad, Mama. I'd like her to be happy. Just not at someone else's expense, that's all."

There was another awkward silence before Mathilde said, "She really wanted the baby."

"She'll be able to conceive again, won't she?"

"The doctor said there's no reason why she can't, in time, but . . ."

"But?"

Mathilde shrugged. "Nothing."

"Mama, there's more, or you wouldn't have brought

it up. And I have the feeling it has less to do with Pia than with you." Jeanne was looking into her mother's eyes with an intensity that Mathilde couldn't avoid.

"Your actress's imagination is working overtime," said Mathilde. "You're seeing things that aren't there."

"Or things that someone's trying to hide, Mama." She sat back against the tufted leather upholstery in the booth and observed Mathilde without speaking. At last, she said, "Mama . . . you're not blaming yourself . . . are you?"

"Not anymore. I did a lot of thinking at the hospital. I know I could have been a better wife to Hank. I'm sure I could have—"

"I'm not . . . talking about . . . Papa," Jeanne interrupted, halting as she measured her mother's reaction. As much as Pia had suffered in the past weeks, Mama had suffered, too. She needed no additional pain.

Looking down at her salad, Mathilde said slowly, "You mean about . . . the baby."

Jeanne nodded. "It wasn't your fault, Mama. Pia's fall *was* an accident—"

"Oh, darling, we'd just said horrible things to each other! Things that can't be taken back. And I slapped her."

"I'm sure it was a long time in coming," Jeanne said quietly.

"Funny you should say that."

"Is it? Why?"

Mathilde thought back to the conversation she'd overheard at Pia's party. "Those are the same words that flashed through my head before your sister and I had our . . . confrontation." She hesitated; the subject of Pia's aberrant behavior with Wes on the last shooting day of the film was the single detail Mathilde had omitted in her phone call to Jeanne from California.

Jeanne knew that something had been left out, but it didn't matter now. Instead, it was important for Mama to understand that she hadn't caused Pia's fall down the stairs.

"You said the heel of Pia's shoe was broken, didn't you?"

"I'd always thought those spikes were made of steel. It was just a cheap piece of plastic—and was cracked right through. It must have gotten caught in the piling of the carpet runner—"

"Then you see, don't you? It would have happened even if she'd been upstairs alone."

Mathilde took another sip of her drink, then absentmindedly began chewing on her swizzle stick. "I can't help thinking that if Pia hadn't been upset by our fight, she'd have been more careful about her footing."

"Mama, you *said* she was feeling sick. And you know why—"

"That's another thing!" Mathilde interrupted. "I accused her of being drunk—"

"Mama, you had no way of knowing she wasn't! *Stop* trying to take the blame. It won't bring back Pia's baby any more than it'll bring back Papa!" Jeanne had promised herself to maintain an even keel, for Mama's sake, and she was suddenly on the verge of losing it, right here in the restaurant.

But Mathilde surprised her. "You're right. I know you're right. I suppose I'm just expecting to change my thinking habits overnight, and it doesn't work that way."

Jeanne unwittingly echoed once more the words Mathilde had used so recently. "Don't make yourself any promises, Mama. All you can do is try."

Mathilde emitted a little, rueful laugh. "You know, darling," she said, taking Jeanne's hand, "I was wrong about you for so long. When you were a child, you went

378

off by yourself all the time, and . . . well, I was afraid you were weak . . . like . . . your father. But you're not. And"—her voice began to choke slightly—"I'm proud to know you. Not because you're an accomplished actress. Because you're my daughter. I admire your strength and . . ."

"Mama," said Jeanne, "I got that strength from *you*—don't you know that?" Jeanne laughed softly. "God, there were times I felt you couldn't stand me, and other times I was so jealous of the attention you gave Pia that I could have screamed. But I knew how difficult it was for you, raising two girls without anyone's help. And you tried so hard *not* to play favorites—"

"Your sister wouldn't agree with that."

"Then she'd be wrong, Mama."

"I wish you and she could talk that over. Among other things . . ."

Jeanne exhaled loudly, then picked up her glass and drained the last of the champagne at the bottom. When she didn't reply, Mathilde said, "You're determined to hold this grudge, aren't you, no matter what Pia does to win your forgiveness?"

"She hasn't done *any*thing yet, Mama. Not even a call."

"This has been very painful for her, Jeanne."

"I'm sure it has. But I've had pain, too, Mama— much of it caused by Pia. I'm sorry if I strike you as heartless. I'm just not going to let her *use* the truth about Papa to manipulate me."

Mathilde narrowed her eyes. "You can be damned stubborn when you want to be."

"Yes, Mama," agreed Jeanne. "It's another trait I inherited from you . . ."

* * *

Pia lay back against the cushion of the wicker chaise alongside the pool. The late afternoon sun had begun to fade, and Brad would soon be home from the studio.

A glass of iced tea sat within reach on the terra cotta tile. Although the air was cooler now than at midday, it was warm enough to cause droplets of condensation on the outside of the glass. Pia gazed absently at the widening ring of water on the tiling, turning it from a deep rosy coral to a darker shade of brown-red brick.

This had become her favorite time of day as well as her favorite spot in which to spend it. At first, these afternoon hours alone had frightened Pia, especially after her initial sessions with Dr. Kelly. But their exploration together into what Pia jokingly referred to as "her demon side" was becoming less horrifying as she began to understand the motivation for her past behavior.

Brad's presence helped, too. He had made no mention of the fact that Pia hadn't told him about her pregnancy, and if he'd heard about the love scene in *After Alice*—the scene that *wouldn't* appear onscreen —he'd either ignored or overlooked it. It was unclear to her whether Brad's patience was due to his own consultations with Dr. Kelly or if it was the result of Pia's determination to change. She still felt undeserving of anyone's devotion, but analysis had begun to chip away at that. Each hour with Dr. Kelly was followed by the agonizing examination of buried phantoms. But with every skeleton unmasked and cast aside, Pia discovered more about her own self-worth.

Except for those groggy moments in the hospital, though, she hadn't yet been able to face Wesley. Somehow it was different with Mathilde—possibly because they'd shared the loss of Papa, perhaps because at last they'd shared the truth. Whatever the reason, with Wes—and Jeanne—more time was needed. Time for them, and time for her.

Pia's thoughts again drifted to her sister. More than once, she'd considered calling Jeanne in New York. It hadn't proceeded beyond that point. How could she simply pick up the telephone and say she was sorry? Pia wasn't even certain why she'd treated Jeanne so wretchedly; had it been from an unconscious desire to destroy Jeanne's happiness in recompense for Papa's ruining hers? It held so little logic.

Although Pia and Dr. Kelly hadn't fully analyzed her relationship with Jeanne, Pia sensed that she and her sister had been driven apart at the moment their father had pulled the trigger. Resentment toward him—and toward Jeanne, who might have stopped the act—coupled with guilt at thinking that she, herself, was to blame, had filled Pia with hatred and a desire to shock, to lash out at those closest to her, as retribution for the horror she'd witnessed—and repressed—alone.

The layers were slowly falling away, but it was too soon for Pia and Jeanne. As the sun sank behind the trees and a soft breeze wafted out over the patio, Pia heaved a sigh and said aloud, "I can't blame you. If the situation were reversed, I'd never want to see you again."

She was unaware that Brad had arrived home and was now standing behind the chaise.

"What situation is that, lover?" he asked, coming around to sit on the edge of the cushion.

"I was just thinking. I didn't hear you drive up."

He leaned over to kiss her. "How are you feeling?"

"Better. Dr. Kelly's a slave driver—worse than any director I've ever worked with—"

"That means you two must be making progress—and that he doesn't let you get away with your old bag of tricks."

"I don't know what you're talking about . . ." But

381

she knew he was teasing. "I saw Vince today, too, by the way."

Brad bent over and picked up Pia's glass of iced tea, which was now completely diluted with melted ice cubes. Drinking it anyway, he said, "And . . . ?"

Pia sat up and gently pushed the glass away from his lips. He let it drop onto the grass that ran alongside the tiles.

"Vince said we can try again . . . whenever we want to . . ." She was smiling as her lips met his.

"And . . . do you want to . . . ?"

Pia couldn't believe how *much* she wanted to. "Brad," she whispered, "I don't know what's come over me, but . . ."

"Hmm . . . ?" He started kissing her hair, then her eyebrows, and again her mouth.

She pulled away from him then.

"Hey," he exclaimed, "you've never been a tease before—what's up?"

"*You* are," she said, reaching over and placing her hand on the erection that had become visible under his slacks.

"You really want to make a baby, don't you?"

"First things first," she answered. "I want us to make love. *Then* I want us to make a baby."

"You're sure about . . . both?"

"And in that order, please."

Brad stood and looked down. "Guess I'd better comply," he said, laughing at the bulge beneath the gray gabardine. In one movement, he scooped Pia up in his arms and carried her into the house. They got as far as the bearskin rug in the hall when Pia said, "Stop right here."

"What's the matter?"

"Nothing. I want to make love on the bearskin."

Brad gave her a careful look. "Is that a dignified

382

place to make a baby?"

"Not at all," she said. "That's exactly why I suggested it."

Whether it was the sensuous fur on the floor or the fact that they hadn't made love since the week before her fall downstairs two months ago, both Brad and Pia were aware of newfound tenderness that afternoon which neither had previously known with the other. The past, while daily being exorcised from Pia's mind, was firmly excluded from their embrace.

As for Pia, although she would never tell Brad, it was the first time since they'd met that she hadn't fantasized being with Wesley Guest. Or anyone else.

She was in Brad's arms, where she wanted to be.

Four weeks later Olympia Decameron Raynor Randall Price became Mrs. Brad Morrow. The marriage ceremony was performed by Judge Adler Willis at the local courthouse in a small town on the road to Lake Tahoe.

No reporters or photographers were present; the honeymooners' whereabouts remained unknown until the end of the week, when they sent telegrams to Barney Berman, Nathan Schutz, and Charlene Webb. A handwritten letter was mailed to Mathilde and Wesley. It was the first time Pia had ever addressed them as "Dearest Mama and Wes."

Upon their return to Hollywood in December, the couple held a press conference. Dr. Kelly stood by to lend support if needed, but Pia handled both the well-wishers and the scandal mongers with equal graciousness and aplomb. The smile on her face was as enigmatic as that of Leonardo's Mona Lisa, but Pia wasn't ready yet to reveal her secret.

Dr. Vincent, whose loyalty had been tested and

proven months before, knew of course that his patient was pregnant.

Only Brad and Pia knew, however, that the baby had been conceived one late autumn afternoon on a bearskin rug in the center hall.

What neither of them realized was the connecting link with that morning's therapy session, in which Pia had experienced a painful but revelatory breakthrough. She had at last been able to accept her own vulnerability, and in so doing, she had opened herself to love.

Part III

1968–1969

Chapter Twenty-Six

"Good night, Mr. Thorne," the chauffeur said. "And Miss Lorraine, once again, congratulations."

Jeanne thanked him as she gathered the skirts of her beaded gown and stepped from the limousine. She waited at the curb beneath the canopy while Andy tipped the driver.

The previous night's chill was waning with the oncoming dawn. Jeanne unfastened the closure of the collar of her sable jacket. She yawned and breathed in the air, which was perfumed with the scent of late-spring flowers and carried by a gentle, warm breeze.

The sleepy doorman offered his congratulations. As did the elevator operator.

Once inside the apartment, Andy and Jeanne made a beeline for the study and together they collapsed on the sofa. He asked, "How many times have you said thank you tonight?"

Laughing, she replied, "Probably a hundred. And I meant *most* of them."

On the wall over the fireplace hung the framed accumulation of honors that both actors had been awarded; on the mantel directly below stood what they called their brass collection.

"Well, now, there's Emmy, and Tony up there has a twin brother to keep him company. If you'd copped the Oscar last year, we'd have quadruplets." Andy was grinning, his arms crossed behind his neck.

"We can always borrow Pia's Oscar," Jeanne retorted without a smile. "It's Tony's cousin." She gestured to her first Tony, the prize she'd won for her stage performance in *After Alice*.

"Y'know, I'm very proud of you," he said, leaning over to kiss her.

"Thank you. And that makes it one hundred and one. As old as I feel."

"You must be tired. But you're not called for tomorrow morning, right?"

"Right, and thank God for it! Just the show tomorrow night. Ah, and then Wednesday the marathon resumes, with two weeks to go before I'm through shooting."

"Come on," he joked. "You love it. We both do."

"Oh, sure. I guess if there was only the picture, I'd love it more. But it's not like doing a play. And juggling both at the same time is just too draining—on me *and* on us."

"It could be worse," said Andy. "At least they're shooting the entire film in New York."

She nodded, chastised. "I know. Really I do."

"And don't forget about the Tony you won tonight—for the play you're doing *now,* while you're in the middle of a picture—"

"The play closes a week after the film wraps. Then what?"

"Find yourself another play."

"You make it sound as if it's easy to find a decent script—*not* to mention one with a strong role for a woman—*especially* a comedy."

"Comedy?" Andy repeated, genuinely surprised.

"It's what I need. I'm getting tired of playing hysterical and neurotic all the time. And audiences are getting tired of seeing me that way—think how depressing it must be for them!"

Andy laughed and she joined him.

"I'm *serious,* though. Audiences know what to expect from me in all this . . . turgid . . . drama. If *I'm* bored with it, just imagine how *they* feel!"

"Look," he offered, "after your play closes, why don't you take some time off?"

"That's fine, except you've got *your* show to do eight times a week. Time off alone wouldn't be any fun."

"I could take a few days' vacation, you know."

She turned to him, excited, and exclaimed, "Andy— *would* you?"

"Of course. We've been running for almost a year. My understudy can handle the role for a week."

"Only a week . . . ?" Her disappointment was evident and Jeanne couldn't conceal it from him.

"We can't push it, you know that."

She sighed. "Well, all right . . . I guess I should be grateful for that long. When . . . ?"

"As soon as I can swing it."

"You mean we'll actually see each other for more than two hours a night?"

His hand lifted her chin and he kissed her. "Six full evenings and two matinees' worth," he said.

She could hardly wait.

The telephone awakened her. Jeanne considered letting it ring; the answering service could pick it up. She snuggled down under the covers until only her face was warmed by the sun pouring through the windows. The bedroom was dark when she arose to work on the film. Sleeping in was luxury.

Then she noticed the hour. Almost eleven! Too late, even on a lazy day. She grabbed the receiver before the fourth ring.

"Good morning," her mother's voice greeted her cheerily. "Have you seen the papers?"

"I just opened my eyes."

"Well, darling, your photograph pushed the Democrats *and* the Republicans off the front page!"

Jeanne laughed. "You can't be reading the *Times*. Who got the headline?"

"An ax murderer in Queens," said Mathilde. "I'm so proud of you, darling. So is Wes."

"I missed him last night. How's he feeling?"

"Still has a cold. But he'll be fine by the time we leave."

Jeanne sat up. "Leave? Where are you going?"

"That's one of the reasons I called," said her mother. "We're planning a sort of holiday. Aspen. With Lydia and Neal."

"I can just imagine you on the slopes, Mama!"

"There's no snow there in June, so I'm told. They all want to go horseback riding. I'll stick to swimming." Mathilde hesitated, then added, "I . . . may even have some . . . company."

"Oh?" Jeanne had a fair idea of what was coming next.

"Yes . . . your sister . . . said she might join us."

"Good. You haven't seen each other for a while, have you?" Purposely she'd asked the question without inflection. "Will she be bringing the baby?"

Mathilde didn't bother to disguise her annoyance. "Of course. *And* Brad. Their marriage is working."

"I'm glad to hear it. Sorry, Mama."

"You should be. Jeanne . . . people *can* change."

"We've discussed that before, Mama. And I said I'm sorry."

"You . . . could see for yourself . . . if you'd join us. You've never even met little Alexandra, and—"

Mathilde was interrupted by Jeanne's laugh. Her mother knew the play's closing date and the shooting schedule for the film. "You never stop trying, do you, Mama?"

"No, Jeanne. And I never will—so you may as well get used to it."

Exhaling audibly, Jeanne said, "Mama, after four years, believe me, I'm used to it. And the answer is no."

"Your sister said she'd come only if *you* do . . ."

"Pia may have changed, Mama . . . but she still likes that kind of control, doesn't she?"

"I swear, there are times when you can be so . . . rigid, Jeanne." Mathilde paused, then added, "Not even . . . for me?"

"I always thought you were above emotional blackmail," said Jeanne. "But no, Mama. Not even for you."

Mathilde recognized the defeat and decided on a different tack. "What *will* you do when your play closes?"

Suddenly an idea struck Jeanne. "Well . . . since you're going to be away . . ."

"You'd like to borrow the house in Connecticut?"

"Oh, Mama, would you mind? A week in the country would be wonderful—for Andy and for me."

Mathilde agreed. It was the only subject that morning on which they did agree.

Jeanne thought about calling Andy immediately at his agent's office, but the hour was too late; they'd have left already for their early luncheon appointment with the French director. With luck, this evening Andy would have news of his starring role in the new film to

391

be shot in Paris. And Jeanne would have news of their forthcoming week in Connecticut. A good way to follow the Tony win of the night before.

Copies of the major dailies were piled outside the door to the apartment. Jeanne skimmed over them as she sipped her hot black coffee.

Apparently Mathilde had been reading the *Daily News*. Its front page was indeed divided between photographs of a brutal ax-murder victim—and the Tony Awards. And sure enough, items on the presidential campaigns were relegated to page two. In the *Times*, Jeanne's picture, and those of the other winners, appeared in the theater section—where she felt it belonged in the first place, no matter the paper.

But Jeanne's mind wasn't on the news or the awards. It was on her conversation with Mathilde. In all honesty, the possibility of her sister's presence in Aspen had served as a convenient excuse for saying no. Even if Jeanne had wanted to join them, she would have refused because Neal would be there.

She recalled the day thirteen years before, the day she and Mama and Pia had walked through the gates of Antaen Pictures. The day their world had changed. If the end of childhood could be pinpointed by a single moment, by an event, meeting Neal Genesco at Antaen most certainly was it. Then Wesley. And later . . . Lydia.

I do miss Lydia, Jeanne said to herself. But I'm not flying to Aspen to see . . . her.

Enough of this, she chided. Things are just as they should be. Neal and Lydia are together, and Andy and I are . . . content.

Connecticut *is* going to be wonderful, she decided. It *has* to be.

*   *   *

The night was hot and humid, and the stagelights hadn't made it easier.

Andy let himself into the apartment, enjoying the rush of air-conditioned cool that greeted him. He could hear voices from the television set in the bedroom. Jeanne was watching the late news, a pleasant reminder that she no longer had to be asleep at ten for a pre-dawn wakeup call.

He went to the bar and threw some ice cubes into a glass. "I'm home!" he yelled. "Want a drink?"

"No thanks!" she returned over the volume. "I'm just finishing up packing!"

"Be right there!" Andy picked up the day's mail from the table next to the telephone. Bills and junk. No surprises.

He carried his drink and a coaster into the bedroom, where Jeanne and organized chaos awaited him. Clothes lay everywhere, atop any and all available surfaces. Those items already packed had been folded neatly inside the small suitcases—his and hers—that were opened on the bed.

"My God, what happened in here?" Andy said, laughing as he began undressing for his shower. "We're only going away for a week—and at that, it's only an hour's drive . . ."

Jeanne was bent over a dresser drawer. She glanced up and pushed her very blond hair out of her eyes. For her movie role, she'd gone almost platinum.

"I know. But I thought I'd take advantage of packing and separate all our summer things and have the winter stuff dry cleaned while we're away. It looks worse than it is—and I'll have the place neat as a pin by the time I catch the train, you'll see."

She came over to kiss him. "How'd the show go tonight?"

"Okay. A little down, I think."

"Well, you can make up for it tomorrow and have a clear conscience about leaving. Did you watch the understudy rehearsal?"

Andy nodded. "Jim's fine. Excited. Bringing his mother up from Virginia to see him in it."

"Good. Oh, that reminds me. *Mine* called today from Aspen. She said the air is unbelievably clear." Jeanne smiled over the rest of her conversation with Mathilde. "Mama said the guest room in Westport is all ready for us. She underlined the singular."

"Really? No separate beds this time?" said Andy with a grin.

"Her words were, 'As long as I'm not there to see it, it's all right.' On second thought, mind if I have a sip of your vodka after all?"

He handed her the glass.

"Mmm, tastes good. Now, tomorrow I'll leave here around two. While you're doing your matinee, I'll run over to Bloomingdale's gourmet shop and pick up a few items, then I'll head straight downtown to Grand Central. Just remember to take *your* bag with you to the theater, 'cause I'll be carrying all kinds of goodies." She took another sip and returned the glass to him.

"Such as?"

"Well, champagne, caviar, smoked oysters, Brie . . ."

Andy put his arms around her waist and hugged her. "Sounds tempting," he whispered.

"Good. Then *you* won't be tempted to stop at Joe Allen's after the show."

"If I miss the train, I'll walk," he said, starting toward the bathroom door.

As he turned, his leg brushed against a stack of books, and the top one fell to the floor with a dull thud. He picked it up and straightened its colorful jacket cover. *Glass Slippers.*

"Everyone at the theater's reading this. Like it?"

"Love it. Lots of fun. It'd make a great picture. Probably why Larry gave it to me—I'm perfect for one of the leads."

"That's what smart agents are for. Anything in it for me?"

She laughed. "Actors! Unfortunately, no. The best roles in it are for women—and it's about time! Anyway, you've got Paris in October, Mr. Movie star . . ."

"Okay, okay," he conceded with a grin, his hands up in mock surrender. But his smile faded when he noticed what Jeanne was using as a bookmark. The edge of an envelope protruded from the pages, and Andy could see the London postmark to the right of the typewritten return address. It read: *Genesco.*

He said nothing, but Jeanne was watching as he replaced the book on the table.

"You may read it if you like," she offered. "It arrived yesterday."

"I thought . . . this . . . was out of your system," he said.

"That's not why I didn't tell you, Andy."

"If it isn't a secret, why didn't you mention it yesterday?"

"I . . . don't know," she answered slowly. "I guess I must have expected you to react . . . the way you're reacting. Andy, it's from *Lydia.*"

"Fine."

"Go ahead and read it."

"I said it's fine. Okay."

"Andy, please read it."

Without looking at her, he opened the gray vellum envelope and withdrew the matching sheet of engraved stationery.

"Dear Jeanne,

Just a note to say how sorry I am to learn that you aren't coming to Aspen. Unfortunately, flight connections at JFK won't even allow a quick drink or lunch—we'll barely have time to change planes.

Your mother has explained why you're not joining us (you'll read no lectures from me) and that as a result, Pia has decided not to come, either. I do wish you'd reconsider. Selfishly, because I'd love to see you, and it's been *so* long since you and I had a good heart-to-heart.

At any rate, we plan to be in New York toward the end of June, so we'll definitely get together then. I miss you very much. Neal sends his regards.

Love, Lydia."

Andy folded the letter and put it back in the envelope, then returned it to the place in Jeanne's book where he'd found it.

"All right?" Jeanne asked.

Andy nodded and went into the bathroom, closing the door behind him.

Jeanne glanced once more at the envelope in the book. The last line of Lydia's note had spoken volumes. She'd chosen the word *regards,* not *love.*

Mathilde pushed a button and the window lowered. A breeze caught her hair and tossed it about her head. Her first impulse was to raise the window and then wrap her hair in the scarf she'd tied around her neck. But she reconsidered. The hell with it, she decided happily. This is a vacation.

She was surprised at the effect the trip was already

396

having on Wes, after only one day. Beside her in the backseat, he was squinting against the sun's brightness that flickered through the trees. But the glare hadn't made him don his dark glasses; he seemed to be enjoying the warmth on his face. In a single day he had benefited from the pollution-free air and light; his skin tones were healthier than an army of makeup artists could have achieved, and his hair reflected golden sun-highlights.

"This feels . . . smells . . . so good!" Mathilde exclaimed to anyone who could hear her over the rush of the wind.

"Yes, but it's nothing like being on horseback," Wes answered. "I tell you, darling, we've *got* to get you riding. Until this morning I'd forgotten the joy of being up on a horse at a gallop. Enclosed by nothing—no motor under you, just a living, breathing animal."

From the front seat, Lydia turned around to face him. "Why, Wes—you mean that was really *you* on the horse in all those ten-cent westerns you used to do?"

Neal laughed as he turned the steering wheel to maneuver a difficult curve. "It was—I directed a few of them! Remember, Wes? They didn't want to pay extra for a stuntman?"

"I remember," said Wes. "It didn't matter, then, if the star broke his neck. They could have reshot all of my scenes in two days, anyway."

"Today's been full of surprises," Mathilde said. "I can hardly believe the two of you are here with us and not still asleep. Must have something to do with the climate."

"I may start fading early," answered Neal, "although I feel terrific. I must be getting used to jet lag. Of course, they do say you need less sleep as you get older."

Lydia didn't comment on his latter remark. Instead,

she took his free hand and squeezed it. He glanced across at her in response, but the car skidded and he quickly returned his attention to the road.

"Sorry," he called out, "these turns can be tricky."

"We're almost there," said Wes. "Tomorrow, we must *all* get on horses."

"You three have fun," replied Mathilde. "I'll sit by the pool and read my book."

"That *Slippers* book?" Neal asked. "How do you like it?"

"It's wonderful!" Lydia answered for Mathilde. "I read it in two nights. Couldn't put it down. By the way"—she nudged Neal's knee—"I don't know if it's been optioned yet, but whoever buys it is going to need a good director. You ought to start checking into it."

"I already have," he admitted. "And now, no business talk! We're on vacation!"

The car continued to wind through the mountain road. On paths to the left and right of them, people on horseback were laughing as they jaunted along.

"Look!" Lydia cried, waving to the riders as they passed by. "Oh, Mathilde—isn't it marvelous not to be bothering with makeup and hairspray and fancy clothes for a change?"

"Yes, it truly is." Mathilde was amazed by her own admission; years before, fussing with those very things had been part of a dream. Now that they belonged to her everyday life, she was happier to be riding along in denim jeans and a plaid western shirt. Just maybe, she thought, I *will* try getting on a horse tomorrow.

A few minutes later, Wes pointed out a turn, and Neal parked the car on a wide dirt shoulder.

Wes announced, "It's a short walk from here."

Neal carried the picnic hamper, while Wes led the

way toting the cooler chest.

"How did you know about this place?" Lydia asked, grabbing at a tree trunk to steady herself on the steep terrain.

"I came up here a long time ago with Clark and Carole—"

"Gable?" interrupted Mathilde. "And Lombard?"

He nodded and continued. "We wanted to do some camping. Of course, this wasn't rugged enough for them. 'Tourist camping' was what they called it." He laughed. "They were right. But it's perfect for a picnic. I just hope the spot is still here."

It was. And perfect for a picnic.

Two hours passed easily. Only once during conversation did the girls come up, and merely because Neal had mentioned Andrew Thorne as a possible lead in a film he might be directing. The subject was glossed over quickly and dropped when Neal realized the awkwardness of his remark.

The matter of the girls was the single flaw in the close friendship of the two couples. Pia's gradual metamorphosis had softened attitudes toward her. Nonetheless, she was seldom discussed, because the logical progression led to Jeanne. Lydia and Mathilde might talk about the girls in private but, by tacit agreement, not in front of Neal.

What remained of the roast chicken, the various cheeses and salads, and two chilled bottles of Muscadet, now lay strewn across the checkered tablecloth spread out before them. Mathilde poured coffee from a Thermos, and Neal accepted a second cup, although he had taken less than half a glass of wine. "I'll be the martyr and stay sober," he'd said, "unless someone else wants to drive back."

"Sorry," said Wes. "You should have offered before I sampled this." He drained his glass. "Excellent. We'll have to order a few bottles to have with dinner tonight." He noted the year on the label.

"Speaking of dinner . . ." Wes checked his wristwatch, then glanced up at the sky.

"Something wrong?" asked Lydia, chewing the last bit of chicken from a drumstick.

"It's awfully early to be getting so dark."

The others looked up. "Oh, I hope it isn't going to rain," said Mathilde.

"It's cloudy, but . . . I don't think it's a storm." Neal finished his coffee and watched as a flock of birds took wing, screaming as they flew off. From far away in the brush surrounding the picnickers' clearing, sounds of animals, stirring in a flurry of unseen activity and movement, began to overtake the tranquil scene.

"What is it?" asked Lydia.

A gray-black cloud passed over the treetops, and the day grew ominously darker.

"Smell that?" Neal said cautiously to Wes, who nodded and rose quickly to his feet.

"Pack up," he ordered. "We've got to get out of here."

"But Wes," said Mathilde, "we haven't—"

"Pack up! Now!"

He had never spoken to her in that tone of voice. The reason had to be that the group was in danger if they remained a moment too long.

Then, suddenly, the wind direction changed. Mathilde and Lydia smelled it, too. Their eyes met, mirroring each other's alarm as they recognized the acrid, stifling odor. The blackness gathering overhead was not due to storm clouds, or to fog. It was smoke.

Hastily they began throwing their plates and utensils and bottles into plastic and paper bags. The cooler and hamper, emptied of the food and wine, were light. Wes grabbed one, Neal the other, and the foursome hurried back down the dirt path through the trees that led to the road.

They knew the car had to be close, but by now it was barely discernible through the thickening plumes of smoke.

"Look!" Lydia cried suddenly, her voice filled with terror. Flames were already licking the upper branches of the trees.

"How could it happen so fast?" Neal yelled, choking as he inhaled the ever-blackening air.

"It's always like that!" Wes shouted back. "This time of year, fire can travel miles in minutes! There's the car—let's go!"

Wes and Mathilde climbed quickly into the backseat, while Lydia rushed around to the front passenger door and Neal slid hurriedly behind the wheel. They'd closed the windows before leaving the car, and now, slamming the doors immediately, they were able to keep too much smoke from entering.

"Drive!" Wes yelled, as Neal gunned the motor.

Riders on horseback were galloping through the brush and onto the relative safety of the main road. A lone, riderless horse, wild with frenzy, bucked up and down along the path and reared wherever burning leaves fell from overhanging branches.

Neal took the hairpin curves as skillfully as he could, but all around them the light was turning to darkness.

"Faster, Neal, faster!" cried Lydia. "The fire's behind us!"

"I can't see!" Neal yelled back. He'd switched on the headlights, but they simply cast brightness on more smoke—and on little of what lay beyond it.

In the rearview mirror Neal could see the lights of another automobile, careening back and forth across the road behind them.

Seemingly from nowhere, the riderless horse appeared once more—this time directly in front of the windshield!

"NO!" Lydia screamed.

Neal swerved, just missing the animal. But the sharp turn had sent the car flying off the road and down an embankment. It bounced over the rocky hills like a child's toy.

"Get down!" Wes cried out, grabbing Mathilde and pulling her to the floor.

Then, suddenly, the car came to a terrifying, earsplitting halt as it made impact. Shattered glass showered Mathilde and Wes, covering their shoulders and heads. The car horn began to blare in one long, continuous, unending alarm.

It was the last thing Mathilde heard.

Jeanne's tote bag weighed heavily on her right shoulder. Perhaps she had packed too much. Well, too late now, she thought, handing her Bloomingdale's charge card to the salesclerk. She was satisfied with the delicacies for tonight's late supper at the country house. In addition to the champagne, caviar, and Brie, she'd added grapes, Andy's favorite nutmeats— cashews and macadamias—olives, smoked oysters, and pâté. Jeanne had almost laughed at the clerk's question: "Will that be all?"

"Here's your card, Miss Lorraine," said the young girl with the carnation pinned to her lapel. "Have a nice weekend."

Jeanne slipped the card into her wallet and dropped it back in her bag, then checked her watch.

She was running late. It was already past five. Traffic would be coming *into* the city, and it was always impossible to find a taxi in this part of town at any hour. At least the commuter lines to Connecticut ran hourly on Saturday, too. She could catch the six o'clock train.

On the way out of the store, Jeanne saw a bank of pay telephones. It might be a good idea to call the apartment for any messages while I'm here, she thought. Better than looking for a phone that isn't out of order and a place to write on once I get to Grand Central.

She didn't have a dime, so she dropped a quarter into the slot and cursed under her breath at having to donate an extra fifteen cents to the phone company.

An operator answered after six rings, which annoyed Jeanne. Six rings meant that Andy wasn't home—and that the service wasn't intercepting calls on the fourth ring, as it had been instructed to do.

She was about to make a complaint, but the woman's voice was saying, "Your mother called, Miss Lorraine. She . . . sounded upset."

"Did she leave a number?" Jeanne's pen was clipped to the inside pocket of her tote bag. She used the back of a sales slip for paper.

"It's in Denver," said the operator. "The number is—"

"No, you mean Aspen."

"She definitely said Denver, Miss Lorraine. I wrote it down as she dictated it."

Jeanne scribbled the number, hung up, and dialed again. Perspiration broke out on her forehead, and she could feel her heart pounding loudly against her chest. At least I have plenty of quarters, she thought, dropping a series of them into the slot.

Her mother's voice, weak and hardly recognizable,

answered. As soon as Mathilde heard that it was Jeanne, she began crying. Between sobs, she choked out a disjointed story. "Accident . . . fire . . . all of us trapped . . ." At first, Jeanne tried piecing it together. Then she stopped. Mathilde was obviously under sedation and her words were coming out as gibberish.

At least Jeanne managed to pry from her the name of the hospital.

"I'm on my way, Mama. You get some sleep. I'll be there by the time you wake up, I promise!"

Her body was trembling when she replaced the receiver. A fire? Denver? What were they doing in Denver? And . . . how badly were they hurt? Hearing Mama's voice, Jeanne hadn't even asked about the others.

Stop, Jeanne commanded herself. Stop and think what to do next.

If Andy wasn't home, he must be at the theater. Then she remembered. He'd agreed to give an interview between the matinee and evening performance.

Depositing her last quarter, she dialed his dressing-room number. No answer. Then a busy signal on the backstage phone. The same at the box office. Jeanne hung up and pushed the coin-return button.

She heard a click, but the quarter didn't come back.

"Damn!" she muttered.

A man was staring at her. The other phones were still occupied and he probably thought she'd finished.

"I'm sorry," she said, "but this is an emergency. I have to make another call and the phone just swallowed my change."

With an impatient frown, the man reached into his pocket. Withdrawing a handful of coins, he said, "Aren't you Jeanne Lorraine?"

"Yes, I am. Please—"

"I've seen you onstage twice. And three of your movies—"

"Thank you, but—"

"When's your next—"

"Please," she all but shouted, "give me the dime!"

He did.

She dialed Information, then deposited the ten cents and called La Guardia Airport. The next flight to Denver was at six-fifty. She booked a single seat; Andy still had his last performance at eight-thirty tonight.

I can't just leave a message with the service; it would only confuse and upset him. Both of their agents' offices were closed on Saturday; impossible to reach Andy through them.

With luck—and if she could find a taxi—she could take a detour, stop at the theater to explain, and still make it to the airport in time for the six-fifty flight. She picked up her tote bag and packages and made her way to the heavy revolving doors leading onto Lexington Avenue.

Miraculously, a taxi pulled up to deposit a couple in front of the store. Another woman stepped off the curb and reached for the door handle as the couple exited the cab. But at that moment Jeanne pushed the woman aside and flung her tote bag onto the backseat.

"Bitch!" the woman shouted.

Jeanne grabbed the shopping bag full of delicacies she'd just bought. They'd be useless to her now.

"Here!" she said, shoving the bag into the woman's arms. "I'm sorry!"

Jeanne knew the cabbie was doing his best to speed her crosstown. But westbound traffic on Fifty-seventh Street was sluggish, even more than during a weekday rush hour. Jeanne sat forward on the edge of her seat, continuously bobbing her head up and down—from the window to her wrist and back up to the window. Her watch read five-thirty now.

405

"Driver!" she said, trying for patience and finding none, "you've *got* to find a faster route!"

"Every street goin' west is gonna be crowded, lady. The trouble's up ahead—y'see? Buncha hippies, that's the problem."

Jeanne craned her neck to the left and saw what he meant. A few cars ahead of them, a group of a hundred people or more—some not much younger than Jeanne herself—were walking in orderly, if noisy, formation down the street and blocking traffic in both directions. Their voices were raised in a chorus of "Where Have all the Flowers Gone?" The song was hardly audible over the blaring car horns and the curses shouted by crowds that had gathered along the sidewalk. Some of the marchers carried placards reading: OUT OF VIET-NAM and HELL NO! WE WON'T GO!

Jeanne couldn't blame them. Thank God Andy had already served his two years of active and four years of reserve duty before Vietnam.

Andy! she thought. At this rate, I'll never get to the theater and still make the flight. For the tenth time she checked her watch, then compared the time—five-forty—with the clock on the cabbie's dashboard. Spot-on.

"Listen," she said, leaning over the back of his seat, "can you do a U-turn here and head *east?*"

"Change your mind?"

"Yes. I have a plane to catch in an hour, and—"

"Which airport?"

"La Guardia."

"Good—it's closer than JFK. We'll make it . . . but hang on!"

Before she knew it, the cab took off and made a sharp, squealing left turn. Jeanne was thrown down against the seat on her right side, while the contents of her tote bag spilled out all over the floor.

But within minutes they were on the East Side Highway, headed uptown. She'd make the plane.

There would even be time to phone Andy from the airport before boarding the flight. She tried to think of anyone else she ought to call, anything else she ought to do.

Nothing.

That wasn't reassuring. It left her mind free to ponder what awaited her in Denver.

Not knowing was terrible.

Finding out, she feared, might be even worse.

Chapter Twenty-Seven

On the plane, Jeanne had downed two stiff scotches, but they hadn't dulled her brain enough to banish the dreaded thoughts colliding in her mind any more than the pilot's expertise had been able to avoid the air pockets that sent the cabin bouncing upward, then dropping suddenly; Jeanne's stomach had flipped upside-down with each leapfrog convulsion of the jet.

But the flight—and Jeanne's departure from New York—remained a haze, which had nothing to do with the scotch. Everything since Mathilde's phone call had assumed the aspect of fast-forward-speeding tape, while at the same time everything seemed, para-doxically, to be moving in slower-than-slow motion. During the taxi ride from Stapleton Airport to the hospital, Jeanne's nerves had reached such a state that a nearby car's backfire almost sent her flying from the seat.

She shut her eyes tightly at the thought. Mathilde's words had been fragmented by emotional upset, but her reference to the car crash and a fire had been sufficient; Jeanne's knee-jerk reaction from that moment had functioned at a purely practical level; just as she knew the apartment door was locked and the stove turned off, she knew also that focusing her mind on minutae would keep her from losing it altogether.

Mathilde was waiting in the visitors' lounge on the surgery floor of the hospital. Much of Jeanne's anxiety dissipated upon seeing that the only sign of injury to her mother was a bandaged right arm supported by a sling.

They embraced carefully, as though each feared the other might break. At first, Jeanne was solely aware of her own relief and of being with her mother. Then she glanced about and realized that the other people in the waiting room were strangers.

Mathilde said quietly, almost in a whisper, "It's not even broken . . . just a sprain . . ."

The phrasing sounded to Jeanne like an apology.

"Oh, darling, I'm so glad you're here!" cried Mathilde. "It was . . . terrible! I . . . I can't . . . let myself think . . . about it! One minute we were . . . and then—" Despite her attempts, she broke down in tears.

Again, Jeanne's arms gingerly encircled her. "Shh, Mama, it's all right. Everything's going to be all right."

She felt her mother's body stiffen and stepped back. When she saw the expression in Mathilde's eyes, Jeanne's earlier panic began to reappear. "Mama . . ." She was afraid to ask but *had* to know. "What . . . about . . . Wes?"

"He . . . wasn't badly hurt. A broken leg . . . the doctors have taken X rays to make sure there are no internal injuries, but—oh, God, Jeanne!" Mathilde covered her face with her left hand and blurted out the rest. "Jeanne . . . it's Lydia . . . she's . . . dead!"

Jeanne hadn't fainted, but when she opened her eyes,

she was seated on the vinyl sofa and a nurse was offering her a glass of ice-cold orange juice. "Drink it all at once," she advised. "It'll help."

Jeanne obeyed and gulped down the juice, ice chips and all. She shuddered from the cold shock, but the nurse was right. Maybe the antidote to one shock was another that followed immediately.

Whatever, it did the trick and Jeanne's head began to clear. She waited until the nurse had gone and then asked her mother, "What about . . . Neal?"

Mathilde shook her head sadly. "He . . . doesn't know, yet. He's still in intensive care." She sat down beside Jeanne. "Wes and I . . . were in the backseat . . . Neal was driving; the steering wheel probably kept him from . . . from going through the windshield . . ."

Apparently Lydia hadn't been so fortunate.

"Was she . . . did it happen . . . instantly?" Jeanne's throat tightened at the thought that Lydia might have suffered terribly. It pained her further to be speaking of her in the past tense.

But Mathilde had no reply. "We'll never know for certain. I . . . I'm afraid I took the cowardly way and" —she tried lightening her words—"there wasn't any orange juice. So I . . . fainted. When I came to, I was on a plane. Then I slept. The next thing I remember is waking up here."

Tears began to trickle down Mathilde's cheeks again, and Jeanne dug into her tote bag for a packet of Kleenex, which she handed to her mother.

"I didn't call your sister," Mathilde continued. "I know we're closer to L.A., but . . . I was worried that . . . well, she's so much stronger now, still . . . she's more . . . fragile . . . than you. And she was never as close to Lydia or Neal as—" She cut herself off abruptly and dabbed at her nose with the tissue.

Jeanne let out a long, drawn-out sigh. "Is Wes

permitted to have visitors?" She couldn't have faced Neal even if he was not in the intensive-care unit.

Rising from the sofa, Mathilde said, "He's asked me to bring you to see him as soon as you got here. I just thought it was better to talk with you alone first." With her left hand she clasped her daughter's fingers and entwined them with her own. "Oh, darling, you have no idea how much better I feel knowing that you're here. It's selfish of me, but I . . ."

Her voice broke once more, and Jeanne said, "You don't have to explain, Mama. I understand. Now . . . can I see Wes?"

As they walked down the corridor toward his room, Mathilde wondered what would happen when Jeanne was permitted to see Neal.

She didn't know that Jeanne was asking herself the same question.

On Monday morning, Wes was well enough to travel, so he and Mathilde made plans to fly back to California, where they would handle the arrangements for Lydia's funeral.

Neal's name had been removed from the critical list, also that morning; however, Jeanne hadn't yet been allowed to see him. Wes hobbled into the ICU on his crutches to say good-bye before the limousine arrived, but Mathilde was still too distraught about Lydia to put up the necessary front; Neal's doctors felt that any display of emotion might upset their patient further. As a result, neither Mathilde nor Jeanne had any details of Neal's reaction to the news of Lydia's death.

Jeanne had wanted to accompany her mother and Wes to the airport, but they wouldn't hear of it. So, Monday afternoon found her alone in the Guests' hotel suite, awaiting the hospital's call that would grant her permission to visit the only man she had ever really loved. At least, her only love before Andy.

She hadn't told Andy on the phone that Wes and Mathilde were flying home. It wasn't a deliberate omission, nor was it by accidental oversight. Too much had happened, and too many wounds had reopened. Jeanne needed time.

She'd slept fitfully since her arrival in Denver on Saturday and was taking a much-needed nap when the call came. Jeanne jumped from the sofa, startled by the jangling, incessant ringing of the telephone. The effect of the Librium was gone the moment she lifted the receiver.

"Mr. Genesco has been moved to a private room," said the impersonal, efficient-sounding voice at the other end of the line. "He's asked to see you."

"I'll be right over," said Jeanne, her stomach suddenly churning with opening-night butterflies.

Make yourself presentable, she thought. That'll help calm your nerves. A shampoo would have helped more; three days of low or zero humidity in the mile-high city had dried her hair and made it thoroughly unmanageable. She tried brushing it up into a French twist, but her trembling fingers were suddenly all thumbs. She opted for a bun at the nape of her neck. That was both easy and neat. But Jeanne recoiled the moment she saw her reflection in the mirror: it was Lydia's hairstyle. Quickly she pulled out the bobby pins and let her long blond waves fall loosely to her shoulders. Then she remembered. Neal had said he loved it that way.

"This isn't a *party* you're going to—so *what* in heaven's name are you doing?" she demanded of the mirror. But the face staring back at her offered no reply.

Finally, Jeanne parted her hair down the center and

tucked the sides behind her ears. She dabbed her chin and nose with powder, added a touch of pale lipstick, and rushed off to whatever might await her at the hospital with Neal Genesco.

He was asleep when she tiptoed quietly into his room. Voices carried from visitors in other rooms on the floor, but they blended into a white-noise blur, so Jeanne left the door open; the room was somehow less claustrophobic that way.

She lifted the folding chair from the corner and brought it alongside the bed. Then she rethought its position and returned the chair to its spot next to the window. After glancing around, she settled on a more comfortable-looking stuffed chair. It was closer to the door in case a nurse needed to be called. And farther away from Neal, she also realized.

How pale he was! The bottom half of his face was covered with beard stubble, which was growing in completely white. His hair, which had been salt-and-pepper gray when Jeanne had last seen him, was now closer in color to his beard. His left hand was stuck with the IV needle, and his right was bruised in several places; probably the intravenous apparatus had been moved from one hand to the other.

The blanket was drawn up under his chin, but Mathilde had told Jeanne that Neal had suffered several broken ribs in addition to other fractured bones. If he was able to sleep so peacefully, it had to be due to pain-killers or sedatives.

Jeanne smiled in spite of herself. She knew that her clinical appraisal was one way of intellectualizing the reality of the situation, of keeping all feelings at bay. She wasn't sure of what her reaction to Neal would be after nearly five years. Adding to her uncertainty was

Jeanne's own grief over Lydia's death. Their friendship had kept Neal and Jeanne apart, but the loss now only contributed to her confusion.

The irony of the situation struck her as she thought about timing; of prime importance in both the theater and in life.

The stillness in the room and the murmur of voices along the corridor had lulled Jeanne into a semi-dozing state. Her eyelids were closed, but apparently her senses were on alert, because the slightest stirring from the bed caused her to sit up immediately, ready, if need be, to ring for the nurse.

But when Neal finally awoke, he didn't call out for the nurse. In a hoarse, dreamlike whisper, he spoke Jeanne's name.

She rose from her chair and slowly approached the bed.

Jeanne couldn't take his hand; the left was the one with the IV. Her fingers gently rested on his arm, and the tactile touch sparked the tears that she had thus far been able to withhold. It required great effort to contain her emotion as she looked into his sorrow-filled eyes and said, "Neal." She could trust her voice to say no more than that.

"Wes . . . told me . . . you were here," he managed.

"Mama called. I . . ." But nothing could hide her sadness which, aligned with empathy, overwhelmed her. "Oh, Neal!" she said, letting the tears wash down her cheeks. "I'm *so* sorry . . . !"

"We . . . once spoke . . . about acts . . . of senselessness," he said. "That's . . . what this . . . was." His eyes were dry, but they held a hollow, vacant gaze, and Jeanne sensed that Neal was, in a way, beyond feeling. She was close to numbness herself.

She repeated the lines she'd heard in countless films, read in countless books. "Neal . . . don't talk . . . you mustn't tire yourself out . . ."

Jeanne wasn't sure whether she was grateful or annoyed when the nurse entered the room a moment later.

"I'm sorry, Miss Lorraine, but Mr. Genesco needs his rest. You'll have to say good-bye for now."

Jeanne bent to kiss Neal's forehead. "I'll come back to see you again tomorrow," she said, at last in control of her voice, thanks to the presence of an audience.

"Promise . . . ?" he whispered.

"Promise." It was as good an exit line as any, and she used it as one.

The following day, Tuesday, Neal was a little stronger, and Jeanne stayed a bit longer. They didn't say much to each other. This time she sat beside the bed; the nurse had moved the chair because "if you sit closer to Mr. Genesco, he won't have to project," she'd said. "We don't want him to strain his voice."

Jeanne purposely avoided telling Neal that Mathilde had telephoned the hotel after the funeral service. What good would it do to bring it up? she reasoned. If Neal wanted to talk about Lydia, she would comply, both for his sake and for the memory of her friend. But there was no need to add to his grief by initiating the conversation.

Jeanne couldn't get to sleep that night, so she turned on the television set, just to have the voices' company. The movie, a vintage film from the 1930s, was interrupted by too many commercials, and Jeanne found herself dozing.

415

She was shocked awake by the news bulletin. "The Democratic presidential candidate, Robert Kennedy, has been shot while leaving through the kitchen of the Ambassador Hotel in Los Angeles." A videotape replay of the horrifying act filled the screen.

Jeanne began to cry softly, as five years' emotions were catapulted onto center stage, eerily reevoking the past.

She didn't want to be alone, but where could she go at this hour? Who might she call? What time is it, anyway? she wondered, feeling a sudden need to concentrate on something logical, such as time.

By now the clock read 1:35 A.M. Jeanne stared blankly at the hour hand and minute hand dividing the face in half. Her own thoughts were split geographically. She couldn't phone Andy—it was past three in New York. Even in California it was after midnight, too late to phone Mathilde and Wes without alarming them—especially with what they'd just been through. No, she reasoned, drying her tears, I'll have to handle these feelings alone. She went to bed.

But she didn't sleep.

In the morning she found more than a dozen people in the ninth-floor hospital lounge awaiting the start of visiting hours. All eyes were glued to the TV replays of last night's assassination attempt.

Jeanne couldn't bear to watch it again. And again. Her thoughts went to room 903 . . . and to Neal.

Visiting hours wouldn't begin for ten more minutes, but the nurses' station was absorbed in managing the ninth floor while trying to catch occasional glimpses of the television set. Without actually sneaking by, Jeanne was able to make her way down the hall without being stopped by anyone.

416

Disconnected images floated randomly in her mind as she tiptoed down the tiled corridor: images of another Kennedy's small son, holding the American flag and saluting his father; images of Hank, Pia, and a long-ago afternoon in which the Decamerons' lives were irrevocably altered; images of Pia's daughter, the niece Jeanne had never met.

Little Alexandra must be the same age now, thought Jeanne, that Pia was when Papa—

She didn't finish the phrase. She was conscious of a melancholy aching for the closeness she and Pia might have shared if . . . events . . . had happened differently. That sadness surprised her; it hadn't surfaced in years.

But things were as they were, she reminded herself, and no matter what Mama tried to say or do, the fact remained that Pia had hurt others—others who had done nothing to her. Others who included Lydia Genesco.

Jeanne banished her ruminations as she knocked at the half-opened door of room 903 and heard Neal's voice say, "Come in. I've been waiting all morning for your visit."

There was a television set in his room, and despite Jeanne's protestations, Neal insisted that she turn it on. "Wearing blinders can't change things," he said. "They only shield our eyes from what we don't want to see."

She interpreted his words as reference to the shooting, but the tone of his voice had clearly said much more.

They watched the replays of the terrible moment in the hotel kitchen, interspersed with news updates of the senator's condition. Between them was a familiar silence, not unlike the silence they'd shared after John Kennedy's assassination a seeming lifetime ago.

Finally, Neal said, "I can't tell you how much your being here means to me, Jeanne."

She was seated alongside the bed, her head and body in profile to him, her eyes on the TV screen, although her thoughts were focused on the possible—or probable —intent behind his words.

"I . . . I promised Mama and Wes . . . that I'd stay until you were well enough to travel," she answered, still not turning to face him.

"And then . . . ?" The IV apparatus had once again been transferred to his right hand, so Neal's left hand was free. It came to rest on Jeanne's right arm.

She flinched as though reacting to a sudden chill, despite the heat in the room.

"I . . . I'll be flying back . . . to New York," she said.

"Jeanne . . ." His fingers exerted the slightest pressure on her arm, and she was grateful to be wearing a long-sleeved sweater so he couldn't see the goosebumps that had begun to appear.

"Jeanne," he began again. "I . . . want you to know something." When she started to interrupt, he squeezed her arm more tightly. "Please. I *have* to say this . . . you *must* let me finish."

"Neal, I—"

"I was faithful to Lydia, Jeanne, because of *your* strength. I cared for her deeply, and I'd give anything to bring her back." He lowered his voice. "But you've got to know that I've *never* stopped loving you. And Lydia knew. She even said to me, when we were in London, that if anything ever happened to her—"

"Neal, please!" Jeanne's heart was racing so violently that she felt close to suffocating.

"I realize . . . this isn't the . . . appropriate time . . ." he said in a halting voice.

Rising from the chair, she cut him off from adding

anything further. "You're right, Neal. This *isn't* the appropriate time."

When Jeanne reached the hotel, she headed for the desk to pick up messages and mail. But two busloads of tourists had just arrived, and everyone seemed to be checking in at once. Jeanne decided to forgo the wait in line; she could call down to check for messages later, when the clerk on duty was less harried.

She was the only person, however, taking the elevator to an upper floor. The other guests seemed to be evacuating their rooms in favor of the television set at the far end of the lobby. Jeanne understood their need to be in a group; her reaction earlier had been the same. Now, instead, all she wanted was to be alone.

But as she inserted the key into the lock, she noticed light coming from under the door. She hadn't left one on.

For a moment, Jeanne speculated that a thief might be trying to take advantage of the current news by breaking into rooms of guests thought to be downstairs. Then she shook her head and chided herself. "You've seen too many films," she said aloud, turning the key.

Two lamps were lit; one on the table in the living room of the suite, another over the round breakfast table in the dining area. The maid must have turned down the beds early this evening, she reasoned.

Jeanne wasn't ready for the surprise when she flicked on the lightswitch in the bedroom.

"Andy!" she exclaimed.

He'd fallen asleep, and her voice startled him awake.

"Hello, darling," he said, rising from the bed and coming to embrace her. "I came down with an attack of cabin fever, and since you're the best cure . . ."

She laughed softly. "I thought a burglar had gotten into the suite!"

"Didn't the desk clerk tell you? I distinctly told him that I—"

"I didn't stop at the desk. I was too tired, and besides, the lobby's so mobbed, you'd think the hotel is preparing to host a political convention!" The reminder made her step back from his arms. "You've . . . heard the news . . . ?"

He nodded. "At the airport. And on the radio all the way in during the taxi ride. Then again when I arrived here."

"Is there any change?" she asked. "I mean . . . is he . . . ?"

Andy shrugged. "That's why I turned off the TV. For lack of any hard news, they keep replaying the same scene, over and over. It starts to . . . cheapen . . . the tragedy."

Then Andy remembered. "What about . . . people closer to home?" he asked. "How's Wes? And Neal? And where's your mother?"

Jeanne kicked off her shoes and flopped down on the edge of the bed. She couldn't postpone telling him, now; first of all, he'd see right through any attempt to lie; moreover, Jeanne lacked the energy to relate anything but the facts.

So she looked up at him and said, "Wes is much better. He was released from the hospital two days ago." She noticed Andy's eyebrows rise as if to say, "Oh, really?" but she continued on. "He and Mama flew back . . . with Lydia . . ." Jeanne's voice trailed off at mention of her friend's name.

"You didn't tell me," he said. "When?" It wasn't asked in an accusing tone; nonetheless, Jeanne felt as though she were under interrogation.

She didn't answer immediately, so Andy said, "Did I

420

miss them? Don't tell me they were leaving the airport just as I arrived there—"

"No," she replied quietly. "They left . . . on Monday . . ."

"But darling, today's Wednesday—" He cut himself off. "I'm sorry. I forgot about Neal." Again, Jeanne felt as if her mind were being subjected to a microscopic examination that could read her innermost thoughts. She was certain, however, that the sensation was strictly from her point of view.

"How is Neal?" asked Andy.

"He's . . . coming along. His injuries were the most serious, so—"

"Darling, forgive me, but the most serious injuries were . . . Lydia's . . ."

Wearily Jeanne nodded. "I just meant . . ."

"It's okay. That was lousy of me." He'd been leaning against the dresser. Now he reached out to take her hand, and Jeanne let him pull her up from the bed.

"I don't know about you," he said, "but I could use a drink. We can call downstairs—"

"There's a fully stocked bar in the living room. Compliments of the management."

While Jeanne curled up on the sofa, Andy poured two scotches. "By the way," he said, concentrating on the ice cubes he was trying to free from the tray in the mini-freezer, "how is Neal handling the news about Lydia . . . ?"

"As well as can be expected, I suppose. He was behind the wheel, and I don't know if he's feeling . . . well, guilty, or responsible. I've purposely stayed off the subject. And he hasn't brought it up. In fact, neither of us has talked about it."

"What *have* you talked about?" Andy was measuring a generous jiggerful of scotch. When Jeanne offered no reply, he didn't insist. Instead, he said, "This hotel

421

certainly knows how to treat its guests—Chivas, no less!"

"I bought that," said Jeanne. "My first night here. I didn't want to get hooked on tranquilizers." Then she saw the amount of scotch Andy had poured. "Hey, I don't want to get hooked on *booze,* either—"

"Don't be worried. Andy Thorne will rescue the lady from temptation." He'd said it as a throwaway line; it was one of his acting tricks that came across so brilliantly onstage—not like a trick at all—and it could prove so frustrating when Jeanne wanted to interpret his meaning.

He crossed to the sofa and handed her a glass. Then he seated himself beside her and said, *"L'chaim."*

"I saw *Fiddler on the Roof,* too. That means 'to life.'" Jeanne was trying for a light, Noel Coward reading to match Andy's cheerfulness as she clinked her her glass against his and repeated, *"L'chaim."*

After several encores of *L'chaim,* Jeanne, from the combined effects of exhaustion and alcohol, was drunk. Not falling-down, passing-out drunk, but she couldn't have crossed a stage without fear of going over into the pit.

Andy wasn't in much better shape, although he wasn't yet slurring his words. "Must be the altitude," he kept insisting.

"Can't *possibly* be the scotch," said Jeanne, pronouncing her consonants with the utmost of care. "Y'know something? I can see how Pia turned into a—"

"Into a what?" asked Andy. "You'd better finish that sentence before *I* fill in the blank."

"Oh, never mind. Mama was right. Life's too short to carry grudges." Her *s*'s were growing sloppier by the minute, and she almost dropped her glass, but Andy grabbed it before it hit the floor.

"'S okay," Jeanne slurred. "The glass was empty . . ." She giggled. "B'sides, the carpeting's the same color as the scotch." A random thought appeared. "Pia should've stuck with vodka that night. It wouldn't have ruined Mama's stole." She bolted upright at the realization that she'd spoken the words aloud.

"What stole?" asked Andy. "And speaking of night, darling, I think we'd better tuck you in."

"Only if you'll come with me . . ." she said in a flirtatious voice, wagging her index finger in front of him.

"Booze is s'posed to make you sleepy, *not—*"

She planted a kiss on his lips. "Shh! I *am* sleepy. Just not *that* sleepy . . ." Jeanne's arms went around Andy's neck. "I've always wanted you to carry me off in your arms."

"Where to?" he asked, lifting her up off the sofa and pretending to groan from her weight.

"Aha! You may think I'm too drunk to give you d'rections. Well, you're wrong! It's thataway!"

He carried her into the bedroom, where they both fell onto the king-size mattress. Andy started to take off his shirt, but Jeanne's fingers were in the way.

"Let me do that," she said, fumbling with the first button.

"Darling, if I let *you* do it, it'll take all night."

"*That's* what I had in mind," she said.

She was making progress; the top two buttons were undone. And a second later, his fly. Andy was amused by her uninhibited behavior; he'd always been the one to initiate their lovemaking.

He watched, intrigued and increasingly aroused, as Jeanne's hands moved down to his belt buckle. She seemed to be having no difficulty with that, and suddenly he wondered if her amorous side was being fueled by the scotch or by a need to convince him that she wasn't still in love with Neal Genesco.

The question sobered Andy completely and brought with it a physical response.

"Sorry. I guess it's because it's been such a long day," he said, kicking off the pants Jeanne had just unzipped and shoving them to the foot of the bed.

But he hadn't expected her reaction. Jeanne pulled off her sweater and bra, tossing them to the floor. Then she slid out of her slacks and panties and sent them flying. Now she swung one leg over Andy and, straddling him, said, "You just lie back and relax, darling. I'll do all the work."

The inflection in Jeanne's voice and the sight of her bared breasts were sufficient to revive him. He drew her to his chest and began caressing her back. His penis had grown stiff and hard, and when Jeanne's hand reached down to fondle his erection, all thoughts of sleep had vanished.

She positioned herself directly over him. Then she spread her legs wide and, instead of easing herself down onto him, took him inside her with a single thrust, so sharply that it made him gasp. She was so wet from anticipation that if she had been under him, he would have slid out.

But Andy was deep inside her, and she was riding him faster and faster, taking him in with a ferocity that seemed intent on devouring him. As orgasm approached, she gripped his shoulders tightly and held on for life and love and for all she was worth. Together they could shut out the rest of the world—the world with its public and personal tragedies, its gunshots and car crashes. And Lydia—and *death!*

Only afterward, physically spent and emotionally drained, as Jeanne lay resting with her head against Andy's damp chest and listened to the steady rhythm of his heartbeat, did she reach the inevitable conclusion: that in shutting out the world, she was shutting out Neal Genesco.

That was also when she understood why she had wanted to get drunk, why she had needed to make love to Andy. To prove her feelings. But not to Andy.

To herself.

And now Jeanne wondered if she'd succeeded.

Chapter Twenty-Eight

The radio announcer's mournful drone, as he repeated the news of Robert Kennedy's death during the night, added to the dull ache at the back and sides of Jeanne's head.

Andy prepared the coffee. Then, after pouring a cupful and noticing Jeanne's trembling fingers, he asked, "Are you still planning to visit Neal today?"

She knew there was no choice, however confused she might feel. After all Neal had just gone through, his feelings had to be placed above her own.

Aloud she answered, "I told him I would . . . besides . . . he has . . . no one else . . ."

"Don't say I didn't warn you," he chided gently, refilling her cup almost to the top.

Jeanne glanced up before she realized that Andy wasn't in the habit of inserting hidden meanings between the lines; she was just touchy this morning.

She used her ebbing hangover as an excuse. "Fat chance I have of cheering him up today with the shape my head is in."

He'd seated himself beside her on the bench in the breakfast nook-dining alcove. "Tell you what. Why don't you relax, maybe have a long soak, take your

426

time getting dressed, and I'll drop in on Neal. You can meet me at the hospital later."

"But I promised him—"

"I'll explain. Neal will understand—he's a good director. And he knows what it feels like to tie one on. You remember some of those parties during the run of *After Alice*, don't you?"

It seemed to remind both of them of the long-ago New Year's Eve party at Herb Scofield's. "Listen, Jeanne," said Andy, "if . . . everything that's happened . . . I mean, if it stirs up the past . . ."

She touched his wrist reassuringly. "It won't. I'm not going to let it."

He was looking into her eyes. "There are some things we can't control, darling. Neal is alone . . . and vulnerable . . . his emotions have to be pretty raw right now." Andy caressed her cheek with the palm of his hand. "Vulnerability can be damned seductive . . ."

"That's what got you and me together in the first place, isn't it?" she asked, trying for lightness.

"Then you can see why it worries me, can't you?"

"Darling, Neal may think . . . well, he may not know his own mind just now. But there's no need to worry as long as *I* know mine."

The problem was that she didn't.

Andy knocked on the door to Neal's room. The nurse was in the process of disconnecting the intravenous equipment.

"Come in," she said.

Neal's face registered surprise at the sight of his visitor. "Andy! I never thought—"

"I got here last night. After your bedtime—and mine." He glanced at the bottle and the tubes the nurse had piled onto the top of a metal cart. "Seems that I arrived at an auspicious moment, didn't I?"

Neal grunted. "My hands will feel like pincushions for the rest of my life."

"But you'll be up and around in no time, thanks to those pins," said the nurse, wheeling the cart toward the door. To Andy she said, "Don't tire him out, though. He's not quite ready to qualify for the Olympics."

She was almost out in the hall when Neal called to her. "I've changed my mind about the TV. I'd like to have it back."

"I'll call down and arrange it, Mr. Genesco."

To Andy, by way of explanation, Neal said, "It's the news. I just couldn't stand it anymore. I told them to get the set out of my room. But"—he shrugged, resigned—"there's no running away from it, is there . . . ?"

It was clearly a rhetorical question, so Andy didn't reply; in truth he felt awkward and out of place. The "niceties" were out of the way, and suddenly Andy couldn't find the words that might comfort his friend.

"Where's Jeanne this morning?" asked Neal.

"We both had too much to drink last night, but I'm afraid she's a little worse for wear than I am."

"Is she all right?"

"She will be. And she'll be by later—in her words, 'when I'm more presentable.'"

Neal's eyes drifted into space. "Jeanne's always presentable." Then, turning toward Andy, he said, "She's been wonderful through . . . all this. Without her, I don't know how I . . . if I . . ." His voice trailed off.

Andy was still unsure of how to phrase his condolences. "Neal," he began, "I don't know how to . . . to bring up the subject." He threw up his hands. "I . . . I'm not very helpful in a situation like this. I . . ."

Neal shook his head in sympathy for Andy's discomfort. "It doesn't grow easier with practice, that I can tell you."

Andy didn't comment. He sensed that Neal wanted —or needed—to verbalize his feelings, but he didn't know if Neal would benefit by talking through his emotions, or if he would grieve all the more deeply for doing so.

And then Neal said, "You understand, Andy, that I loved Lydia. The two of us together . . . we . . . we made a good team. Even though it was my name up in lights, every success of mine was due largely to her advice, her vision, her . . ." He paused and reached over to the bedside table for a glass of water.

Andy again waited. He could see that Neal was filling the moment with "business," the way he might in a play.

"You must know, though," he continued between sips, "that it was never a . . . a passionate love . . . a deeply physical love . . . that kept us together. Lydia and I shared the love of two old friends who were accustomed to each other . . . of colleagues linked by a common interest. You can understand that. After all, you and Jeanne—"

Andy interrupted Neal by clearing his throat. He didn't want comparisons made between Lydia and Neal and Jeanne and himself. But a verbal protest would be out of place just now. He'd hold back, in deference to his friend. No need to reopen old wounds of five years past; Neal was suffering enough.

But it was Neal who persisted. "I'm sorry. It was presumptuous of me, wasn't it?"

"What was?"

"For me to assume . . . to talk of you and Jeanne. I mean . . . who am I to speculate about how . . . about the way the two of you feel about one another . . . ?"

But actor's intuition told Andy that Neal, whether consciously or not, *was* trying to speculate. He'd spoken with a rhetorical inflection; the meaning, nonetheless, was clear.

Andy opted for a line he'd used in a play that Neal had not directed.

"None of us can ever know exactly how another feels," he said. "We can make only an approximation." Onstage the line had worked and hadn't struck Andy as pompous. Here, instead, he felt like a cardboard cutout doing a second-rate stock production.

Apparently, though, it had held a ring of truth, because Neal nodded in agreement. "You're right," he said. "And I suppose that's the . . . most difficult part . . . for me to deal with."

"I'm not sure I understand."

Neal drew a deep breath. "Well, the accident . . . the stupidity of it . . . Lydia . . . such a senseless, terrible waste. But . . ."

"But . . . ?"

"Oh, God! How can I say it, Andy, without sounding like a callous, unfeeling bastard?"

"Just . . . *say* it, Neal. Whatever it is . . ."

For the first time since Andy had entered the room, his and Neal's eyes stayed fixed on each other, and suddenly, before Neal answered him, Andy knew what was coming.

Neal's voice was choking with emotion as he said, "Andy, I'm still . . . in love . . . with Jeanne."

Andy felt a souring sickness rising inside his stomach. A sense not of revulsion, or of sympathy for the man lying in the bed, but of a dizzying, churning fear.

Swallowing hard, he rose from the chair and moved toward the door.

He wouldn't speak his mind. He couldn't do that to

430

Neal. But at the same time, he wasn't about to lose Jeanne—no matter what his friend had gone through.

In a voice so low he could barely be heard, Andy said, "I tell you what, Neal. I'll come back later. With Jeanne. In the meantime . . . you get some rest . . ."

Their late-afternoon visit to Neal skirted personal issues. The television set had been returned to the room, and all three sat watching the videotaped replays of the events of the past twenty-four hours in the life and death of Bobby Kennedy.

Every now and then, when reference was made to the assassination of Bobby's brother John, Neal glanced up at Jeanne or she glanced up at him. Andy felt in those moments like a fifth wheel, but he said nothing. After all, the final outcome would be decided not by Neal or Andy, but by Jeanne.

Sunday night, Jeanne and Andy flew back to New York. Neal was improving daily, and Jeanne knew that if Andy went home and she remained in Denver, Neal might misinterpret her decision to stay. Her excuse was as legitimate as Andy's: his week's vacation would end on Monday and he'd be resuming his role in the play on Tuesday; Jeanne had spoken with her agent by telephone and he'd arranged a luncheon meeting, also on Tuesday. She didn't tell Neal that the appointment with the director was only tentative, pending her return to New York.

Andy slept on the flight east; Jeanne tried to doze, but every time she closed her eyes, she envisioned the lost expression in Neal's eyes as she'd kissed his cheek good-bye.

"I'll see you . . . both . . . in New York," he'd said.

431

She hadn't missed the hesitation before the word *both*. Neither, she was certain, had Andy.

The first few days were filled with activity; after a promising interview with her agent and the director on Tuesday afternoon, Jeanne sat through Andy's show that night; he'd been concerned about his energy level after a week's hiatus.

When they arrived home after the performance, Jeanne checked the answering service for messages.

There had been two, both long distance: one from Wes and Mathilde, the other from Neal.

Jeanne hoped Neal hadn't suffered a setback; the service said he'd phoned at eight-forty that evening. "It's earlier in California than in Denver," she said to Andy. "I'll return Neal's call first."

But with the two-hour time difference, it was still late enough for the hospital switchboard to say, "Sorry, miss, but patients can't receive calls after nine o'clock. You'll have to try again in the morning."

"Well, can you tell me if Mr. Genesco is all right? I mean, he *did* telephone me in New York."

The operator didn't seem to care where he'd called from. "I'm at the main board downstairs, miss, not on a patient floor. Those phones go off at nine."

Jeanne left a message and hung up. Then she tried her mother's number in California. No answer.

"I don't like it," she said aloud.

"They probably called before they went out for the evening, and they're not back yet," said Andy, reading her thoughts. "The two calls are *not* connected."

"How can you be sure?"

"I'm not. But worrying won't help, either. Your mother undoubtedly just wants to know that we arrived home safely."

432

"Why didn't she call yesterday? I told her we'd be flying back on Sunday."

"Because she and Wes have a life of their own, darling." He put his arms around her. "That does have its appeal . . ."

"What has?" she asked, nuzzling her cheek against his chest.

"The idea of a life together. You know, it's possible to have both."

"Both . . . ?"

Andy nodded. "Yes. Being together and having our careers."

"I thought we both agreed a long time ago that theater had to come first, ahead of everything."

His arms pressed her closer. "That was before I realized how much I love you."

Jeanne didn't reply, although she could feel the faster rhythm of his heartbeat racing in her ear.

"That's a cue, Miss Lorraine," Andy whispered softly.

"Is it?" she asked, looking up. "I'm not sure of my lines."

"Well, I'll rephrase mine. I think it's time you and I got married—maybe even start a theatrical dynasty of our own. What d'you say to that proposition?"

Jeanne's eyes widened in surprise. Andy had never before mentioned marriage—not in serious terms, anyway.

An image of Neal flashed through her mind. Stalling purposely, she said, "I . . . I'd say that sounds more like a proposal than a proposition."

"Well, dammit, it *is* a proposal—the first I've ever made!" A boyish grin broke out across his face, and he began to color.

It endeared him to her. But . . . marriage?

433

"Andy . . . this is . . . well, it's kind of . . . sudden, isn't it? I'll have to think about it. I'll need some time . . ."

"Darling, we've had four and a half years together—that seems like plenty of time to me . . ."

He didn't insist. Part of their success—both onstage and off—was in knowing when to emphasize a phrase and when to leave it alone. Andy knew that to press Jeanne for an answer now would only drive her away—and possibly into Neal's arms.

They returned Neal's call in the morning. He seemed buoyed by the sound of Jeanne's voice, subdued when she put Andy on the phone. But the doctors' prognosis was excellent; he was due for release in a week. "I'll be in New York before the Fourth of July," he promised.

Andy had been right; Mathilde had phoned just to hear that they were safely home. She sounded in better spirits, and it was the first time they had ever spoken long distance without Mama's mention of Pia. Maybe she was learning. They spoke of Wes's venture into directing, and then Mathilde added, mysteriously, "And I have a project or two of my own."

"What kind of project, Mama?" asked Jeanne. Her mother had redone the house from top to bottom just before the trip to Aspen, but could she be getting into interior decoration? Certainly it wasn't movies; Mama had given up that dream when she married Wes.

"It's a secret," Mathilde told her. "And if I spilled the beans, it wouldn't be a secret anymore, would it?"

Jeanne shrugged. No point in insisting. Mama could be as stubborn as her daughters when she wanted to. Whatever it was, she sounded younger than she had in years, so Godspeed to her, thought Jeanne.

"Have you heard from Neal?" asked Mathilde.

"This morning. He called last night while we were at the theater."

"Darling, it might be wise if you're at the theater tonight, too," advised Mathilde.

"I'm not sure I understand."

"And yet I think you do, dear. Just try to go easy on him, Jeanne."

"Mama what do you mean? How else would I behave with Neal, after what he's gone through?"

"Just remember your own words, dear. Look, I have to meet Wes at the studio. Give Andy a kiss—and call me if you have any news."

"I will, Mama. Love to Wes, too." And they hung up without Jeanne's having told Mathilde any news of Andy's proposal. Otherwise, she'd never have heard the end of it.

At a few minutes before nine that evening, Mathilde's wisdom became apparent. Neal telephoned. Instinctively, Jeanne knew why he had chosen that hour to call, both now and the night before: Andy was at the theater. That she had gone to see the play on Tuesday was something Neal couldn't have anticipated.

"Jeanne!" he said. "I'm so glad to find you at home!" His voice was sounding stronger with each day.

"I . . . I was just on my way out," she lied.

"Where are you going? Doesn't Andy have a performance tonight?"

"Yes. I'm . . . meeting a few friends for dinner." She realized it was past the dinner hour. "Actually, for a late supper." She told him of Mathilde's call, expecting him to say he'd also spoken with Mama and Wes.

He hadn't. That was when Jeanne decided that her mother's suggestion was a good one. Tomorrow night she'd be out when he called. And the night after

435

that. She didn't want to hurt Neal, but until she was certain of her own feelings, this was probably the best way to deal with the matter.

"I'll be back in New York in a fortnight," he said.

"That's wonderful news, Neal!"

That gave Jeanne exactly two weeks' time.

On Thursday evening, Jeanne really did go out. The stores were open late, and after buying a new pair of bell-bottom pants, she walked home from Bloomingdale's instead of taking a taxi. She checked her watch as she window-shopped along Madison Avenue. Fall fashions were already coming in, and miniskirts—even haute couture miniskirts—were creeping higher and higher. Maternity stores showed mannequins with short-short hemlines, too.

A baby boutique with nursery furnishings brought Andy's phrase to mind: *a dynasty of their own.* She smiled; did he actually think they were heirs to the Barrymores? I love children, she said to herself. It's motherhood I'm not so sure about . . .

She wasn't surprised, upon checking the service, to find another message from Neal. The surprise would have been if he hadn't called.

"What time did that come in?" she asked the operator.

"At eight fifty-five, Miss Lorraine."

There were no other calls.

On Friday night it rained, and Jeanne stayed home. She answered letters, then prepared a light dinner. Andy finished it off with coffee before leaving for the theater. Jeanne's meal was accompanied by a glass of wine, which she carried to the den to drink while watching Walter Cronkite and the CBS Evening News.

As Andy bent to kiss her, Jeanne's arms went around him and she said, "By the way, I've told the answering service to pick up any calls tonight, so if you try to phone from the theater—"

"I thought you were going to curl up with a book," he said, pulling on the sleeves of his trenchcoat.

"I am. I . . . I just don't feel very talkative this evening. So I figured it's about time the service started earning its money."

Andy nodded. They were alike in that area, too. "Okay, I'd better run, or I'll be late. See you round midnight."

It was as though someone had set a timer and trained a telescope on the windows of their apartment. At precisely eight fifty-five, the telephone rang. From habit, Jeanne put down her book and jumped up from the sofa. But then she stopped and waited. Three rings, followed by a click in the middle of the fourth. The operator at the answering service would tell Neal—by now Jeanne was certain the caller could be no one else—that Miss Lorraine had gone out for the evening. She felt guilty, while reasoning that in the long run this was the kindest way. Or safest. For whom, she wasn't sure.

At nine-forty, the phone rang again. And again Jeanne didn't answer. At least the service had heeded her reprimand; this call, too, was intercepted during the fourth ring.

And then, at ten-fifty, the door buzzer sounded. Jeanne had half dozed on the sofa and awoke with a start. It sounded once more.

She hesitated; usually the doorman announced visitors via the building's intercom. But it had been out of order for two days, and only now did Jeanne realize how much she relied on the system.

She hurried to the door and peered through the tiny peephole. Her heart leapt—and sank—at the sight on the other side.

She couldn't pretend to be out, even if she'd been tempted to do so; the doorman would have said already that she was home. Taking a long, deep breath, Jeanne opened the door and said, with forced poise, "Neal . . ."

He was drenched from the rain, and although his beard had been trimmed and his hair styled, the circles under his eyes betrayed his recent ordeal.

"C-come in," Jeanne beckoned, standing aside to let him enter the apartment.

She helped him out of his raincoat and took his umbrella, which she opened in the foyer to dry. The tasks gave her time to recover from the shock of seeing him standing here before her, let alone his presence in the city.

"When did you get out of the h-hospital?" she asked finally. "I th-thought you said next w-week . . ."

The need in his eyes filled her with profound sadness.

"I couldn't stand it anymore," he said. "I convinced the doctors that I'd heal much sooner outside that place than in it." They were still standing in the foyer, and except for the moment when Jeanne had removed his coat, they hadn't touched. She wondered if he'd sensed her awkwardness, too.

"I tried phoning you from the airport," he said. "When I got off the plane, and then again while I waited for a taxi. But I got your answering service both times."

She felt a sudden twinge, then said, "I just got in a

438

short while ago. I . . . I haven't checked yet for messages." She said it looking away from him. Like Andy, Neal could read her too well to miss a lie.

"I thought I'd stop here anyway, on the chance you might be back. Then if you weren't home, I'd go on to . . . the apartment."

The apartment, thought Jeanne. Third Avenue, where he and Lydia had lived together for so many years.

"Is that . . . a good idea?" she asked, preceding him into the living room. "I mean . . . for you to be there . . . alone?"

Very stiffly and cautiously Neal lowered himself onto a chair. He didn't answer her question; instead, glancing about the room, he said absently, "This is an attractive place. Warm . . . and inviting."

"We're c-comfortable here." She was anything *but* comfortable. "W-would you like a drink? Are you allowed—?"

Neal laughed softly, then winced at the pain it caused him. Holding his rib cage, he said, "I'm not allowed to do anything. The hospital would have turned me into a dependent child if I had let them. And yes, thank you, I'd very much like a drink. Scotch. With a touch of ice and water."

Jeanne busied herself at the bar and attacked the ice tray with vehemence, causing several cubes to fall to the floor. She picked them up and threw them into the small sink, then poured two drinks, adding the ice and water to Neal's, nothing to her own.

"I recall when your mother wouldn't permit you wine with lunch," he said, indicating her glass.

She handed him the other drink and said, "That was a very long time ago, wasn't it?"

"The Brown Derby, as I recall. When we first met."

"No, we met at the audition for Antaen Pictures,"

439

she corrected him gently. "I came down with hives and missed the screen test. Pia didn't, but Natalie Wood got the part." She laughed, remembering her sister's reaction.

"That's a good sign," said Neal, raising his glass to her.

"What is?"

"Laughter. It means old wounds are healing." He'd said it with more intent than that which applied to Pia. And Jeanne knew where he was probably heading.

"I . . . I wish you'd arrived earlier. I could have gotten house seats to Andy's play. He's wonderful in it."

"I'm sure he is," said Neal. "But I can't sit for two hours in one position. The plane trip was sheer torture."

"Perhaps you ought to have listened to your doctors and stayed a bit longer in the hospital."

"I couldn't," he said. "That would have been a worse torment. I had to see you and—"

"More scotch?" she asked, rising quickly to refill her own glass.

"We can't keep putting it off," he said. "I have a confession to make, Jeanne. I . . . purposely came here when I knew that Andrew would be at the theater."

Should I tell him I know that? she asked herself. And should I try again to stop him . . . or hear him out?

"Neal, I . . ." But the words weren't there.

"Jeanne, you told me at the hospital that the timing was wrong. And I couldn't argue then. But how long can I go on waiting for the moment to be right? And what exactly *is* the right moment? When the 'world' thinks it's right? You speak of timing—Jeanne, life doesn't stop, doesn't sit and wait until we're ready! We must seize the moment—we must *make* it right! I've come all the way from Denver to tell you that I love

440

you. Lydia *knew* I loved you—she'd be happy for us, Jeanne, because she loved us both. What greater way to keep her memory alive than for the two people she loved most to be together? Don't you understand, Jeanne? I'm asking you to marry me."

She was still standing at the bar. Her trembling hands clutched the glass so tightly that her knuckles went white. She was glad to be wearing slacks instead of a miniskirt, so that when her knees began to shake, their unsteadiness wouldn't be apparent to Neal.

But she hadn't finished her drink, and her physical reaction had nothing to do with the scotch. It was instead the sudden, unexpected culmination of years— years of wondering, of longing, of denying. And it was Lydia's oft-uttered phrase, borrowed from Stanislavski and drummed into Jeanne's psyche during hundreds of coaching sessions: *What do you want, and what are you willing to do to get it?*

It was the question she'd asked of every character she had ever played.

And it was the question she asked herself now.

She had skirted the answer since Lydia's death, partially from her own uncertainty, partially from a desire to avoid causing pain to those she loved.

Nonetheless, as Neal had said, life wouldn't sit and wait. Seize the moment. His words. Whatever she wanted—truly wanted—the outcome couldn't help but hurt one of them.

Jeanne felt a lump in her throat and tried to swallow it out of the way as she thought of Andy, of Lydia, and of the man, seated here now, who had endured so much anguish and sorrow.

I wish I could ease that suffering, she thought, rather than add to it. But . . . the moment had come.

With choking tears, Jeanne turned slowly to Neal, looking first away from him and then directly into his eyes.

"I can't . . . marry you, Neal," she said. "Please try to understand."

He shook his head as though to wave her words away. "Why, Jeanne? You must believe me when I say that Lydia—"

"It has nothing to do . . . with Lydia."

"Then . . . why . . . ?"

"Because," Jeanne answered as gently as she could, "I'm going to marry Andy."

Chapter Twenty-Nine

Pia was aware that heads turned and the room was
set abuzz as she made her entrance into the restaurant.
It pleased her that she could create such an effect on her
surroundings. She hadn't made a picture in almost a
year, so the reaction was particularly reassuring; it told
her she was still a star.

She spotted Mathilde in a booth near the window
and waved. The bright Hollywood sun was bathing her
mother's face in glaring, unbecoming light. Despite the
expert application of makeup and the smartness of her
watermelon-colored raw silk suit, Mathilde was showing the first visible signs of age, and Pia was quick to
notice.

She crossed the dining room to greet her mother with
a kiss, then instructed the hostess to draw the draperies
closed.

"Why did you do that?" Mathilde asked.

"Because I look awful in natural sunlight, Mama.
Lamps and candles are much more flattering when
you're past thirty."

"You're not thirty yet," Mathilde answered with a
laugh. "You're much too young to be concerned about
that sort of thing. *I'm* the one who should be—"

"You look marvelous," Pia interrupted. It wasn't a lie. She admired the poise her mother had acquired over the years. Her bearing was confident, but she hadn't sacrificed vulnerability. "I love your new suit," Pia continued, rummaging through her purse for cigarettes.

"Thanks," said Mathilde, removing a speck of the napkin's lint from the sleeve of her jacket. "I bought it in New York at a little boutique on Madison Avenue." Pia reached for a match, and Mathilde added, "You're still smoking."

"Yes, but not much—really, I've cut *way* down. I'll have one more later, over coffee, and that'll be it for the day."

The waitress's arrival ended that part of the conversation. "Would you ladies care for a drink?"

As it always did, the mention of alcohol in Pia's presence caused a fluttering sensation in Mathilde's stomach. "Nothing for me, thank you," she answered quickly.

But Pia said, "Nonsense, Mama." Then, to the waitress, "My mother will have Mimosa. I'll have a Virgin Mary. And please bring us some water."

Nothing more was said about it.

"How's my granddaughter?" Mathilde asked after her awkward pause.

"She has a little cold, so she's cranky. I think Consuela got more than she bargained for—housekeeper *and* nanny."

"You're lucky to have her. She's very good with children."

"Yes, she is. And you may find it hard to believe, but as it turns out, Mama, so am I—well, most of the time. I'll admit, though, I need some work on my patience. I'm not mad about motherhood, you know."

"Pia!"

"Don't be shocked. I love Alexandra so much that

444

sometimes it . . . it frightens me. I had no idea it could be such a strong . . . emotion. But I mean the *job* of being a mother—*that* gets to me every now and then. It's such a responsibility."

"Everyone feels that way. And most mothers *don't* have a Consuela. I didn't."

"And *you* had *two* of us!"

"Would you . . . ?" asked Mathilde.

Pia shrugged. "I'd love it, I think. But Dr. Vince tells me it's not medically advisable. Little Alixe was too much of a handful *getting* here!" Her face softened at the image of her daughter. "God, Mama, *she's* such a *good* child—how did you *ever* put up with *me?*"

"Well, you had . . . charm," answered her mother. Then, smiling, she added, "For a while."

Pia broke into a laugh. "I'm working on regaining that."

"With success, it seems to me," replied Mathilde.

"Well, thanks . . . I hope you're right." Pia opened her purse and withdrew an unsealed envelope, which she handed to her mother. "I wanted to ask your . . . opinion . . . of this before I send it."

The bright yellow envelope was addressed to Jeanne Lorraine-Thorne at hers and Andy's street number in New York. Inside, the card pictured a newborn baby girl, nestled in a cabbage patch. Mathilde nodded and opened it. The greeting bore a simple congratulatory rhyme and was signed, "Love from Pia, Brad, and Alexandra."

There was also a note, folded in half. Mathilde looked across the table at Pia, who said, "Go ahead and read it, Mama. Please." Mathilde opened the sheet of paper.

"Dear Jeanne and Andrew,
Mama tells me that little Julia is beautiful, healthy, and blond like her mother.

When the time is right I'm sure Alexandra would love to meet her new cousin.
Please . . . think it over.
Meanwhile, congratulations.
Love, Pia"

Mathilde replaced the note inside the card and returned both with the yellow envelope to Pia.

"Mama," said Pia, "you're getting weepy-eyed."

"I know." She sniffled and used her napkin as a handkerchief to pat the tears away. "Send it."

"It's all right, then? I mean, maybe the telegram I sent to the wedding was . . . too impersonal. I thought instead this might be—"

"It's fine. You're doing your best. Julia's almost a month old. Don't put it off any longer."

The waitress placed their drinks in front of them and took their lunch orders. But as soon as they were alone, the two women fell silent. Pia smiled as she realized that the Mimosa was not unlike a third presence at the table. She touched her mother's hand. "Mama, it's high time we had a little talk about this. *I'm* the alcoholic, not you."

"You're not anymore."

"I haven't had a drink in ages, but I'm *still* an alcoholic, Mama. That's *why* I can't have even a sip."

"All the more reason for those who love you to . . . refrain . . . from drinking in your company."

Pia shook her head and took a last deep drag of her cigarette before crushing it in the ashtray. "You're wrong. *I'm* responsible for my own sobriety. Not you or anyone else. So, Mama," she added gently, "don't take credit for keeping me dry. *I* do that."

"I wasn't trying to run down your willpower, Pia. You know that. I'm proud of you. I just don't like to—"

"To tempt me?" Pia laughed. "I start the day

446

tempted, Mama. I'm *always* thirsty. I get up in the morning and tell myself, 'I won't take a drink today. Maybe tomorrow.' Then tomorrow comes and I make the same promise. I'm sober for today. Eventually, the days add up."

Mathilde hesitated, then lifted her glass. Slowly she reached forward and clinked it against Pia's. "To . . . today, then," she toasted.

"Where to, ma'am?" the chauffeur asked.

Pia followed Mathilde into the backseat. "Let me think," she said. "I suppose you should take me home first, then drop my mother off at her appointment, Robert." To Mathilde, she asked, "You said it's on the way to the studio, didn't you?"

Mathilde nodded.

"Fine. You can pick up Mr. Morrow afterward, Robert."

"Very good, ma'am," he replied.

Pia giggled as the driver slammed the door and took his place behind the wheel. "He always says that," she whispered, imitating Robert and repeating, "Very good, ma'am."

Mathilde settled back against the soft velvet cushion. "You've loved limousines from infancy."

"Mmm. This is one of the nicest parts about getting what you want. Admit it, Mama—you love it, too."

Her mother smiled broadly. "All right, yes, I do. But isn't it easier for you to chauffeur yourself around?"

"Well, Brad usually takes his car to work. And I don't really drive much anymore, if I can help it."

"Brad's series—it's a success?"

Pia crossed her fingers. "It's been renewed for a third season."

447

"Good," Mathilde replied. "After that, they'll have enough episodes to go into syndication, even if it gets canceled—which, of course, we hope it'll *never* be."

Pia stared at her mother and marveled. "You really *have* learned the in's and out's of the business, haven't you?"

"Well, dear, I'm around it constantly, after all. Call it osmosis. Anyway, you can tell Brad that Wes and I stay home on Friday nights just so we won't miss the show."

"Out of enjoyment, or loyalty?"

"Both, really. Wes said it looks terribly strenuous on Brad, though."

"It is. There's so much action, and he tries not to use a double. Which doesn't please the stuntmen—or me."

Mathilde sighed contentedly. "I wish we were staying in town longer, but Wes will be through filming the guest appearance tomorrow, and we both have so much to do in New York. He was really hoping to join us for dinner last night, but . . . well, he's not the director on this picture."

Pia nodded. "I'm glad at least that Alixe got to meet him on the set yesterday." She was silently happy, too, that she and Wes had buried the past.

Mathilde was pleased as well. The only loose end, she thought, is Jeanne. If only she and Pia . . . Maybe the card would help. "You won't forget to send that note to your sister," she said.

"I'll take care of it right now." Pia pulled open the glass partition that separated them from the driver. "Robert, when you pass a post office or a mailbox, will you drop this off, please?"

She handed him the yellow envelope, which the chauffeur placed on top of a road map on the seat beside him. "Very good, ma'am," he replied.

Pia giggled again as she closed the glass. "Y'see?"

Mathilde nodded, then said, "I've meant to ask. Are

448

you interested in working again?"

"Oh, Mama, of course I am! But frankly, the scripts I've been reading are *lousy*. Especially the women's roles."

"Have you read *Glass Slippers*?"

"Who hasn't? And yes, I know I'm right for one of the two leads. But every actress in town wants either of those roles."

"You might produce it yourself," said Mathilde, almost adding, "You did once before," but stopping herself from saying it.

Pia was looking at her in an old, familiar way. "You know, Mama . . . I *had* thought of that."

"Then again," Mathilde went on, "it may be too late to make a bid. Surely someone else already has."

"Well," Pia answered with a smile, "there's no harm in asking, is there?"

Polly Meagan pushed the large baby carriage through the front door of the apartment and out into the hall.

Andy bent to kiss his tiny daughter. "Thank you, Polly," he said. "This won't take long. We should be through in about an hour."

"It's all right, Mr. Thorne. A bawlin' baby can be a nuisance when there's business t'be done," Polly replied with a chuckle. "B'sides, this here's the part o' my job that isn't work. It's a wonderful day t' be sittin' in the square with a beautiful baby—and t' be paid for it, t' boot."

"I envy you," said Andy. "It'll be a lot more pleasant than what we'll be doing. Now, have you enough money with you?"

She laughed again, her jowls jiggling. "Mr. Thorne, we're only goin' five blocks. I have Julia's bottle, diapers, plenty o' change if I need the phone, and a dollar or two for a hot dog and a Good Humor for m'self."

Andy rang for the elevator. "Don't you ever eat any of the marvelous things you cook for us?"

"How d'you think I got to be a size eighteen, sir?"

He tactfully avoided a reply. "Well, have a nice stroll—and would you check the mail on your way back?"

"Gladly, sir."

The elevator arrived and Andy watched as the operator and Polly argued over the best way to maneuver the carriage inside. "Try not t' wake her!" Polly hissed in a whisper, shaking her head and causing the head of gray curls to bounce. The doors closed as she waved good-bye to Andy.

She wheeled the pram along the marble floor of the main lobby and stopped in front of an enormous bank of mailboxes.

There was an armload today, and then some. Three magazines and at least a dozen envelopes of varying sizes, some of them thick enough to contain more of the plays her employers had been reading upstairs. Polly performed a juggling act, managing to close the mailbox and turn the key, then shoving most of the mountainous stack inside the canvas bag hanging from her left shoulder.

She considered leaving the mail to collect on the way back, but thought better of it and decided to take it along now; later, other tenants would be returning home from work and the mail room would be jammed.

Outside on the sidewalk, Polly turned the carriage left. It was a beautiful, clear spring day. A few blocks south was her destination, marked by the imposing arch at Washington Square.

She was waiting for the WALK light at the corner of Fifth Avenue and Ninth Street, when a teenager whizzed by on a bicycle, lightly grazing her backside as he sped past.

"Brats!" Polly cried. The pile of mail in her tote came tumbling out onto the pavement. Quickly she stooped to retrieve the letters before the wind could grab them.

But she was too late.

A single, bright yellow envelope escaped her reach. A sudden gust of spring breeze lifted and swept it out into the center of Fifth Avenue, where a taxi's front wheels bounced over a manhole cover. The yellow envelope stuck to the rear wheel and was carried off.

The light turned to WALK. Polly tucked the remainder of the mail into the carriage, under the wool blanket covering little Julia's feet, then she and the baby continued toward the park.

They'd finished eating, but a few matters still needed clarification. Jeanne offered to prepare coffee while Andy and Larry Martinson, her agent, continued their discussion in the living room.

Experience had taught Jeanne that, as a general rule, it was wise to be wary of agents. Larry had proven the exception. For five years, he had skillfully guided her career forward, not strictly for his ten percent, but because he was a theatrical rarity: an agent genuinely interested in his clients' professional longevity.

Andy's decision to seek new representation had prompted Jeanne to suggest today's informal lunch. Andy and Larry had known each other even before Jeanne had entered the business. They were almost friends. So both men were delighted with Larry's offer and Andy's acceptance to add his name to The

Martinson Agency roster. As for Jeanne, she couldn't have been more pleased.

"For that kind of money," Larry was saying as Jeanne served the coffee, "they should have thrown in half of a percent."

"It was a very low budget. It just seemed a lot to ask for." At the agent's attempt to interrupt, Andy added, "Larry, it was also the prestige of working with one of the best directors in the world."

"I know, I know," Larry said, pulling at his thin mustache. "He doesn't use that many Americans in his films. But believe me, over *here,* you work cheap and all you'll get is cheap work."

Jeanne sneaked a grin at Andy. Larry's habit of peppering his speech with phrases and clichés was part of what he considered his "style." She'd grown fond of it over the years.

"All right," Andy agreed. "Domestically, we'll go for whatever you say. Now, can you find a play that Jeanne and I can do together here in New York?"

"If it's out there. Nothing ventured, nothing gained. What's your availability, ladies and gentlemen?"

Andy looked across the sofa to Jeanne. "Well, let's see. This being May . . . we could aim for late fall, couldn't we?"

Jeanne was all in favor of that. "Once we open—assuming we're a hit, of course—I can have my days free to spend with Julia."

"Ah! That's another thing!" Larry exclaimed. "Jeanne, have you considered the potential publicity value of motherhood?"

She took a sip of coffee, then shook her head. "Larry, I know you can get us into the magazines with photo spreads of the 'happy family at home,' but I'd prefer that the baby not be . . . *used,* if you see what I mean."

"Absolutely. Just covering all the bases. Now, about your producing that picture—"

"What?" Andy interrupted.

"Don't get excited," Jeanne said with a grin. "I only asked Larry to check into the possibility of picking up the rights to *Glass Slippers*."

"But . . . produce it—yourself?" Andy couldn't believe his ears. "Jeanne, we haven't got that kind of money. We'd need a general partnership for financing, and—"

"It's not as if it hasn't been done *before,*" she interjected.

"Whoa!" Larry held up his hands. "You didn't let me finish! You waited too long, Jeanne. The rights are gone."

"They're what? How long ago were they sold?"

"Just last week. There were rumors circling about a movie deal even before the book was published, but that fell through. Too expensive, from what I heard. The rights were up for grabs again for months. And then along comes some private company with a lot of dough and blows everyone else out of the water."

Jeanne glanced over at Andy. "I've heard this song before."

"Jeanne," he said, "even if it *is* Pia, she *couldn't* have known that *you* were interested."

"Are you *sure?* Her name *and* mine have both been mentioned for those roles since the day the book hit the stores. Pia could guarantee keeping me out of the picture—literally—by controlling the project and starring herself."

"That's ridiculous," said Andy. "Larry, do you know who's bought it?"

The agent shrugged. "Some group calling themselves Three Muses Productions."

Rhetorically, Andy said, "That could be anyone,

couldn't it?" Then, to Larry, with a sidelong wink to Jeanne, he asked, "Look, to satisfy my lovely wife's paranoia, is there any way to find out just who the Three Muses are?"

"I doubt it," answered Larry. "We all know that the people in this business hold secrets like a sieve holds water. But when it's something they *want* to keep secret, you'd be amazed at how everyone becomes a clam."

"Well," said Jeanne, half to herself, "I think *I* might be able to find out."

The day was still sunny and bright when Jeanne and Larry emerged onto the street. Jeanne's hair was free and longer than usual; she hadn't had it trimmed since Julia's birth. She ran a hand through the tangled waves to keep the breeze from blowing hair into her eyes. While they waited for the doorman to hail Larry's taxi, he said, "I think Andy will be pleased with his decision."

"I agree," she replied, reaching out to grab Larry's hat before it flew off his head. "Here." She handed it to him.

"Thanks. You're quick."

"I can be. I didn't expect it to be so windy out."

"It's that little bit of winter that dies hard."

Coming from Larry, the remark surprised Jeanne. "Let me know what you find out about those Muses," she said as a cab pulled up alongside the curb.

"Likewise." But Jeanne . . . it doesn't really *matter*. I can still see about getting you a script. I'm sure they'll be interested—"

"Let me *know,*" she repeated with emphasis.

"Okay." He climbed into the backseat and closed the door.

Jeanne glanced down Fifth Avenue toward the square. It and the park looked inviting this afternoon. She and Andy might go for a stroll. Then she remembered that he needed to study his lines for a public service announcement he was shooting the next morning.

"Would you call upstairs and tell Mr. Thorne I've taken a walk to the park?" Jeanne said to the doorman. "I'll be back in half an hour."

He nodded.

Jeanne pulled her cardigan around her and started south. Maybe she'd even spot Polly and Julia.

She could see the housekeeper sitting on one of the benches surrounding the fountain. A mime in white-face was entertaining a small crowd gathered about him. His top hat lay upside down on the ground, and his silent performance was accompanied by the occasional clinking of coins tossed by his audience and landing inside the hat. Scattered applause and laughter greeted each new movement or trick.

Jeanne, too, had been caught up by his show when she came upon Polly and Julia. If only I had my camera along, she thought. The chubby woman was holding the baby over one shoulder and obviously trying to induce an after-bottle burp. But Polly's gaze was fixed on the mime, her eyes alive with amusement at his antics.

"I'll take her," said Jeanne, holding out her arms.

"Oh, Mrs. Thorne! How nice t' see ya!" Polly made room for her on the bench and handed over the baby.

"Enjoying the show?" asked Jeanne.

"I am, that. Can all of you theater folk do what he's doin'?"

"Well, it's an art that some of us study—for body

control and communication. But not many of us are as good as *he* is."

"Why's he doin' it here?" Polly asked. "I mean . . . he's practically beggin', isn't he?"

Jeanne watched the mime for a moment and considered Polly's question. Whether entertaining in a public square for loose pennies, or performing in theatrical splendor for thousands of dollars, they shared one basic, common ground.

"He does it because he has to, Polly," she answered at last.

"I thought you'd say 'twas for the love of it."

"Oh, that, too. There are many kinds of love, I suppose." Jeanne caressed Julia's tiny face as she rocked the baby in her arms.

"Ah, you're right, there. But him"—Polly gestured toward the mime again—"what kind o' livin' can he make, doin' that just for love?"

"Probably not much," said Jeanne. "But that's not only what he *does*. It's who he *is*."

"Sounds t' me like a sickness o' some kind," said Polly. "Or slavery, maybe."

Jeanne's eyes were on the mime. "Maybe he'll get lucky. Maybe someday he won't need it anymore."

"An' then what?"

"He'll be free. No more conditions."

Polly wrinkled her nose. "But what's he left with?"

"The love," said Jeanne.

The sun broke through a passing cloud. Jeanne looked down at the baby nestled in her arms. Julia's hair shone golden in the afternoon light. Once more Jeanne began rocking her to and fro, while singing in a whisper the Beatles song that had inspired her daughter's name.

*   *   *

Andy was on the phone when they arrived home. "Hold on a sec. She just walked in."

Polly handed the mail to Andy, thinking she ought to mention the envelope that had flown away. She hadn't thought of it in the park. Mrs. Thorne had shown something of her personal side, and it had seemed special. Polly loved little Julia, and had grown fond of the baby's parents, too. She was eager to better understand people of the theater, their thoughts were so . . . different . . . from her own.

The baby awakened just then, and Polly went quickly to lift her from the carriage. Time to change her diaper, she noted.

She and Julia were already in the nursery when Jeanne said into the phone, "No, Mama, I never received it . . . of *course* I'd remember it, and not because it was yellow, either . . . Well, she probably changed her mind about sending it . . . if she ever really intended to at all . . ."

But Polly was busy with safety pins and Julia's tiny hands and feet, which she had to gently keep pushing out of her way. It required Polly's complete concentration. Besides, she wasn't in the habit of eavesdropping.

Perhaps it was the meeting with Larry, or her long-distance call from Mathilde, that had tired Jeanne. Whatever, she decided on a nap before dinner.

But sleep eluded her. Words and phrases repeated and replayed through her mind. Her mother had said that she'd personally investigated the purchase of the film rights to *Glass Slippers*. "I'm *positive* that Pia doesn't own it," she'd insisted.

Of course, reasoned Jeanne. That's what Mama *wants* to believe. On the other hand, if it's true, I might have a chance to play one of the roles—even if I can't

457

produce it myself. All right, let Larry handle that end. So relax.

She closed her eyes, but another thought kept her awake: What if Pia *had* sent a note? Or is Mama still trying to bring us together? I *can't* do it just to please Mama. Not after everything Pia's done.

A small, silent voice seemed to ask why. Was it pride? Childish stubbornness?

Mama had called Jeanne rigid. And Lydia . . . dear Lydia had once referred to her as *obstinate*. Could they have been right?

The half hour in the park had added to her growing restlessness. Polly's observation had struck a nerve. Jeanne had always perceived her profession as a calling. Andy, too. Their relationship—indeed, their marriage—was based on it. The world they'd carved out for themselves was forged of their devotion to their art, the practice of their craft.

For the first time it posed a question. What had Polly said—a sickness? Slavery? Acting had given them much. But acting *demanded* so much—demanded complete devotion, above and beyond all else.

Conditions.

And, Jeanne thought slowly, pulling herself into a sitting position on the bed, I'm not willing to make that sacrifice anymore. There . . . that's *it!* My career is important to me, but it doesn't mean *everything* . . . Andy and Julia mean *more!*

Although the sun was setting and the room had turned cool, Jeanne was enveloped by a sudden, wonderful feeling of warmth and light. And love. Tears welled up in her eyes, and initially they puzzled her.

Gradually, however, she began to realize that these were tears of joy. Of freedom and release. And they were tears shed over a loss . . . over a kind of abandonment. Whether it was Jeanne abandoning a

458

former love, or the former love abandoning her, she had no way of knowing.

She understood, however—and for the first time—that nothing, whether theater, career, or fame, meant so much to her as the tiny child sleeping in the nursery, and the husband who would soon be home.

She lay back and softly wept into the pillow.

I wouldn't change things even if I could, she thought. I have Andy. And Julia.

Chapter Thirty

The following week was uneventful at first. Jeanne relished the time she was able to spend with the baby. Andy attributed this new calm and relaxation to Jeanne's relationship with their daughter. In addition to her cheerful personality and Gerber-baby face, Julia was, even at the age of only five weeks, good-natured and affectionate, especially with her mother.

But Jeanne knew the change in her was due to more than motherhood. She now looked at her career as an enhancement to her life, not as a primary goal. She also suspected that her new objectivity would make her the better actress for it.

On Thursday, Larry Martinson called. "I've got a script," he said. "I read it last night. It's dynamite."

"Great," said Jeanne. "Can you send it over by messenger?"

"Yes, but . . . there's something I'd like to talk over with you personally. Can you make it uptown to my office sometime today?"

"Well, I suppose so. Polly's due here at any minute, but Andy's already left for—"

"It's okay," he interrupted. "Andy can judge for himself later. How's elevenish?"

She glanced at the clock. "I'm not even dressed yet."

"It's nothing formal—just you and me. No fashion show necessary."

Jeanne laughed. "In that case, eleven's fine." She hung up and was tucking a gray silk blouse into the dropped waist of gray flannel bell-bottoms when Polly arrived, panting and out of breath.

"Sorry t' be so late, Mrs. Thorne, but the traffic this morning is just—"

"It's okay. Look, I'm in a rush. I'll explain later. Julia's formula is ready, and I've bathed her, and—" Jeanne, too, was out of breath. Kissing the baby, she said to Polly, "I'll be back by one, in case Mr. Thorne calls." Then she dashed out the door.

The morning rush hour was long since over, but finding a taxi was still a problem. She chatted with the doorman and drank in the fresh air of another glorious spring day while she waited.

Once inside the cab, Jeanne speculated on the urgency of Larry's words. She trusted his taste, even if in the past year it had leaned toward fluff. He was right, lightweight comedy *was* a better commercial risk—and *she* had been the one to insist on a change of pace. But right now, she hoped the "dynamite" script was quality writing, especially since the last time she and Andy had starred together in a play was in *After Alice*, and that *had* been dynamite.

My God! she reflected, that was six years ago! How different we all were then—and how things have changed! Jeanne's thoughts for a moment went to Neal and to her confused feelings over him only the year before. She'd heard that he was in Europe now, directing a film. Then Lydia came to mind, as she so often did. Jeanne missed her.

But doing a play again with Andy would be such fun! And Julia will see her parents onstage! Silly, she chided

461

herself, Julia's a baby! Still, Polly can hold her on her lap for now, and then later, when she's old enough . . .

With a sudden burst of joy, Jeanne realized that her "spark" was back. For all her recent self-discovery, the love for her profession hadn't diminished.

She alighted from the cab at Sixth Avenue and walked the half block west on Fifty-seventh Street to the building where The Martinson Agency was headquartered. The brisk breezes blew her hair wildly about, but it was a good, alive feeling, and Jeanne didn't brush it out of the way.

After a few minutes' wait in the spacious reception area, an assistant ushered her into Larry's office.

As always, he was on the phone when Jeanne entered. He gave her a perfunctory wave and, without rising from his desk chair, gestured her to a seat. Behind him, the picture window afforded the viewer a magnificent panorama of the city's theatrical district. It served as an appropriate backdrop to an agent of Larry's stature.

He was still on the phone when the receptionist came in with a coffee tray. Larry nodded his thanks, while pulling so vehemently at his mustache that Jeanne thought he might actually tear it off. He mimed an apology to his guest, then said, "That's right!" into the mouthpiece. His ear glued to the receiver, he picked up a script lying on the desk in front of him and handed it across a stack of papers to Jeanne. Apparently, at that moment his caller put him on hold, because Larry said, "Take a look while I get rid of this guy."

The binding was green leatherette. The title, printed in gold letters on the cover, was a surprise.

Jeanne glanced up at her agent, but he was scribbling something on a notepad. She opened the script.

462

Tucked inside was a letter addressed to Larry Martinson. The name Three Muses Productions was engraved at the top of the stationery.

"Dear Mr. Martinson:

Enclosed herein is a copy of the screenplay entitled *Glass Slippers*. We stand firm in our conviction that your client, Jeanne Lorraine, is the ideal actress to portray the pivotal role of Helen in the forthcoming filmed version of the best-selling novel.

We are currently in negotiation with several other artists. The director is yet to be decided. We expect to complete principal casting by early next month, with principal photography scheduled to begin this July and continuing through late October.

As you may know, the project is being independently produced and financed. To this end, we plan to be in New York during the coming week, at which time, in the event that Miss Lorraine is both available and interested in the project, and pending our mutually acceptable fee for her participation in the film, we would like to set up a meeting to discuss contractual terms.

Please consider this to be a formal offer, and let us hear from you at your earliest convenience.

Sincerely,

Three Muses Productions, Inc."

Jeanne was stunned. Flabbergasted, she looked up at Larry, who was finally off the phone.

"The play's taking a little longer," he said with a sly grin.

"Larry! You did it!" She jumped up from her chair and leaned over the desk to kiss him on the forehead.

463

"All I did was make *one* call. The following day, *that* was delivered, by hand."

"And you didn't say anything!" she exclaimed.

"I wanted to read it first. It's good, Jeanne. And they're right. You'll be great. But—"

"There's a but?"

"Only one. We don't accept till after you've read it through."

She nodded. "And Andy."

"Right. Between the two of you, you might come up with a few ideas to make it better."

"Better?" she repeated.

"Jeanne," he said slowly, "we wouldn't want to let them think you don't expect approval of any changes . . ."

She laughed. Larry was a good agent, and examining every option was one of the qualities of a good agent. "All right," she agreed, "I'll read the script today, show it to Andy tonight, and I'll call you tomorrow."

Most afternoons, after Polly had taken Julia out for a ride in the carriage, Jeanne played with the baby. Or sometimes, while Julia napped, Jeanne sat beside the bassinet and watched the rhythmic breathing of her sleeping daughter.

But on this particular afternoon, she let the housekeeper tend to Julia. Jeanne instead spent the rest of the day curled up on the sofa in the den, the script opened on her lap.

She was delighted to find that the story faithfully followed the plot of the novel, although the writer had, of necessity, pared it down to the most salient points. What emerged was a powerful screenplay that could be, in the hands of the right director, an important film—with two memorable roles for its leading ladies.

464

She couldn't help wondering who would play the other part.

It seemed safe enough to assume that it wouldn't be Pia; her thwarted effort to secure the property for herself must have canceled her out of the running.

It *better* have, thought Jeanne. I'd *never* do the film with her.

She laughed wryly. Pia wouldn't do the film with *Jeanne,* either. The fact that she was being offered one of the roles meant that Pia *hadn't* been offered the other. No producers in Hollywood would pit Olympia Decameron and Jeanne Lorraine together on the same movie set.

Or would they . . . ? It would ensure a box-office smash, but what producer—even in such a cutthroat business—would stoop so low?

"They *all* would," Larry said when she telephoned her agent a moment after the thought occurred. "But they didn't. I checked. Three Muses assures me that Olympia Decameron is definitely *not* playing the other role. What's more, she's not even under consideration. They're talking Dunaway or Fonda. Bancroft, if they decide to go older."

Jeanne remembered *The Miracle Worker* and the Oscar that Pia had lost to its star. "My sister'll *love* that," she said.

By the time Andy had read the script, it was agreed. Jeanne didn't wait until the next morning to call Larry. She telephoned him that night.

"Tell Three Muses the answer is yes," she said. "And Larry, get what you can, but don't price me out of the picture. I *want* this role."

*   *   *

Even Jeanne was impressed at the speed with which the contract agreements were handled. "The Three Muses people want to be free to discuss the script on an exclusively creative plane," Larry told Jeanne. "It's a great idea. Leave the business end to the business people."

"And art to art?" Jeanne countered. Larry had expected to haggle—"I'm ready for anything," he'd said—but it hadn't been necessary. Jeanne would be paid the highest salary she'd ever made, would have full approval of wardrobe and script changes, and a chauffeured limousine to and from the set. She would share equal billing with her co-star. The name of Jeanne Lorraine would read left to right and second, top to bottom.

She'd smiled at the age-old studio ploy at satisfying stars' egos, but the producers' willingness to meet almost every demand was gratifying; it assured her that they very much wanted her in this picture.

Jeanne had taken extra care with her appearance today. Three Muses had signed a star, and she was dressed for the part. The ensemble was elegant and understated, a mocha silk shantung suit, accented by an eggshell-colored crepe de chine blouse and matching scarf. For the occasion, she'd even swept her hair into a French twist, and over it she wore a cut-straw pillbox hat.

Jeanne exuded confidence as she stepped from the taxi at the corner of Seventh Avenue and Fifty-second Street. Memories converged as she glanced west toward the Alvin Theater, where she and Andy had starred in *After Alice*. Next to it, although she couldn't see that far, was Jilly's; she recalled the last time she'd been there: on the night of the President's assassination. With Neal. She remembered the Chinese restaurant across the street where they had stared at, not eaten, their dinner.

In front of her the Americana Hotel had taken its position as part of New York's skyline. It seemed only yesterday that the enormous hostelry had been no more than a vast hole in the ground.

Jeanne walked east, past the deli on the corner and beyond Joe's Pier 52, until she reached the building where the Three Muses' production office was located. She recognized the entrance immediately. Often she and Lydia had come here to browse through plays at the Drama Book Shop, upstairs.

This visit took her only to the third floor. The elevator deposited her in a nondescript waiting area painted in muted tones of slate-gray and blue. Behind a desk, a receptionist was busy pushing buttons on a Call Director bank of phones. The moment Jeanne appeared, the girl put all the calls on hold and looked up with an awed expression of admiration.

She's *got* to be an actress, or else she's studying to be one, Jeanne mused, even before noticing the published acting edition of *After Alice*.

"I . . . saw you in it . . . when I first came to New York," the receptionist explained, blushing. "I'm working on it for my acting class."

"Which scene?"

"The . . . love scene in Act Two."

Jeanne smiled warmly. "It took me three weeks to get it right. But I had a lot of help."

"Oh," said the girl, "my scene partner is really quite good."

"So was mine," Jeanne replied with a wink.

The room was empty. Jeanne had seen dozens like it before. A large rectangular table stood at its center. Small vases of flowers had been placed on occasional tables at the two ends of the corduroy sofa. A sideboard held the expected coffeepot and Danish pastries. There was one surprise: a bottle of Veuve Cliquot chilling in an ice bucket.

Jeanne filled half of a plastic cup with coffee and was considering adding a drop of milk when she heard the door buzz and then open.

"Am I late?" asked the voice behind her.

"No, I'm early," Jeanne answered, turning to face the new arrival.

It was Pia.

They stood as though rooted, staring at each other and unable to speak for a full thirty seconds.

Pia had obviously decided on a star's wardrobe, too, her taste, though, running to the more flamboyant. She wore Chinese red, from the small silk hat with red-and-black jet-bead trim to the matching red-and-black Chanel sling-back pumps. The famous spit curls were gone, and her lustrous dark hair was brushed softly into a flip that touched the shoulders of her red linen jacket. She was magnificent.

Although Jeanne had seen her sister's movies, she understood now the frequent comment that film didn't do justice to Olympia Decameron's face. In the years that they'd been apart, Pia had grown more beautiful. But for the first time, this did not undermine Jeanne's own sense of identity. They were facing each other not as sisters, but as women. Stars.

Equals.

It was Pia who at last broke the silence. "You're . . . looking well. Motherhood becomes you."

"Likewise," Jeanne replied, putting down the coffee cup. She paused, then said, "I suppose it was naïve of me not to know."

"Know what?" Pia asked as she pulled off her three-quarter-length black gloves.

"That you were behind . . . this."

"Oh, Jeanne," said Pia, "I'm not. I'm as surprised to see you as you are to see me. I'm here because I've agreed to do a role in a film. If that's why you're here, too, well . . . the joke's on us, I suppose."

"Pia, do you expect me to believe that Three Muses *isn't* your company?"

"Yes, I do, because it isn't." She thought for a moment. *"Why* would I do *that,* anyway?"

Jeanne shrugged. "I don't know. One last effort to—"

"To patch things up between us?" Pia walked to the coffeepot and poured herself a cup. "The baby's card was my last attempt, Jeanne. I've tried. But not anymore."

"The card you *told* Mama you sent."

"The card I *did* send. If you didn't receive it, blame the post office." She took a sip of coffee. "I should have stopped after you didn't respond to the wedding telegram—which you *did* receive, I assume?"

"Yes," Jeanne admitted. "I thought Mama sent it and signed your name."

Pia gave a short laugh. "I wouldn't put it past her. But no, I sent the telegram. You're so . . . suspicious, Jeanne."

"Goddammit!" Jeanne suddenly felt the pent-up emotions of decades rising inside her. She tried to control herself as she continued. "I am *tired* of having *everyone* say that to me, Pia! I am *weary* of being called obstinate, rigid, and now . . . suspicious! I've reacted normally to defend myself against a . . . a predator!"

Pia emitted a long sigh. She had anticipated the inevitability of this or of an eventual confrontation. Now there was no running away. So be it, she thought silently, taking a seat on the sofa.

"All right, Jeanne. Go ahead. Get it out. I'm predatory. What else?"

Her sister was taken aback. "My God!" Jeanne exclaimed, beginning to pace the room. "Even *now* I don't trust you! For years you've been able to . . . to take people's words and . . . twist them . . . to serve you! I'm afraid to speak my mind to you, for fear that you'll find a way to *use* it—against me!"

"Jeanne," said Pia almost calmly, "I have everything in the world. There's nothing of yours I want."

"Why the sudden change?" asked Jeanne. "Are we all supposed to believe in some miracle that's turned you into a saint?"

"Look," said Pia, leaning toward her, "I was . . . a mess. That's not an excuse—it's a reason. There's a lot I . . . regret . . . and I've tried to make . . . amends. But I can't control how you'll—"

"Oh, stop it, Pia! You can't just sweep aside the things you've done! You tried to drive Mama and Wes apart so you could have Wes for yourself! You *stole* a role out from under me, and almost destroyed Lydia and Neal's marriage with your . . . lies! You *did* damage my friendship with Lydia—and now you try *this* stunt, and expect me—"

"I expect *nothing* from you!" Pia shouted back, rising from the sofa. "I am not responsible for this . . . *stunt!* And since we're finally having it out, tell me— what makes you think *you're* that important?"

"What?" Jeanne asked.

"All I'm hearing is what *I* did to *you! You* were never the objective—you were *in the way* of the objective!"

"What objective?"

"Importance! *Being* somebody! Love!"

"You *always* had that! And you had the looks! *And* the voice! Things *I* had to learn!"

"You didn't have to fool everyone into thinking you

470

had *talent!*"

"I *worked* for it! I studied! I deserve it!"

"So do I!" Pia yelled, tears welling in her eyes.

"And you've gotten it, haven't you?" cried Jeanne. "We've *all* got your footprints on our backs to prove it!"

"That's a despicable lie!"

"That's a line from your latest movie, isn't it, Pia? God, you can't even be honest with me *now!*"

"I can! I am!"

"No, Pia, I haven't heard *why,* yet. You're right— you *were* a mess. Well, we've *all* been *that,* once or twice over the years, and *we* didn't do what you've done!"

"I told you! I wanted—"

"Love—*Wesley's* love!"

"No!" Pia screamed, sinking slowly onto the sofa once again and burying her face in her hands.

Jeanne stopped pacing and looked at her sister. She thought back to Mathilde's phone call from California after Pia's miscarriage. To the revelation about their father's suicide. Was it possible—could such an act have controlled her sister's behavior for so many years? Jeanne tried to envision Pia at age three, standing in the doorway and watching as Hank Decameron ended his life. Deliberately. *"I love you, honey."* The words Mama said he had used. For what purpose—to exonerate his actions in the mind of a child?

What if I'd been the one in the doorway?

Jeanne hadn't considered this before, any more than she had considered that Pia might have changed. Until this moment, Mama's disclosure had answered questions only about Papa. Jeanne had never examined it from her sister's point of view.

Taking a seat on the sofa, she turned toward Pia, who still hadn't looked up, and said quietly, "You were the firstborn. You were always Papa's favorite."

"Till you came," Pia said between sobs. She raised her head and said in a choked voice, "You wanted to know the reason. Well, it's taken a lot of work to sort it all out, Jeanne. But I . . . I blamed you. For such a long time."

"Blamed me? Why?"

Involuntarily, Pia shivered. "It was more than sibling rivalry. When you were born, everybody said you looked just like him . . . and he paid so much attention to you. Then . . . after he was gone, I guess—no, I *know,* now—I must have really hated him for it. Not just for *leaving*—but for the *way* he left! He'd needed help—but back then, who was there to analyze such things? I only realized a few years ago how much *I* needed help—how I'd been blotting it all out by taking it out on you—and by trying to replace Papa with . . . with Wes . . ."

Glancing tentatively at Jeanne, she said, "He's . . . been able to forgive me . . ."

Jeanne felt her throat tightening as her sister's words sank in. I *have* been obstinate, she thought. Selfish, too. And, when we were younger, yes, I *was* jealous. Maybe Mama's right. If she and Wes can forgive Pia . . . maybe . . . I can, too.

Jeanne reached out then and gently pressed Pia's arm.

"I'm sorry, Jeanne," Pia whispered, her voice almost breaking. "For everything."

Her eyes misting, Jeanne answered, "I'm sorry, too, Pia."

The sisters' arms went around each other and they embraced for the first time in fifteen years.

Then the door buzzed and they both looked up.

*   *   *

Mathilde stood at the threshold.

Her face displayed no expression as her eyes went from Jeanne to Pia and she pushed the door closed with her elbow.

"I've taken to eavesdropping," she said.

"*Mama . . . ?*" said Jeanne, rising from the sofa.

"*You're* Three Muses . . . ?" asked Pia, incredulous.

Mathilde nodded. "Only one of them. I'm hoping that you girls are the other two."

Jeanne was still recovering from the shock of seeing their mother standing in front of them. "It isn't . . . possible," she said.

"I don't see why not," answered Mathilde.

"But . . . *why,* Mama?"

Matter-of-factly, their mother replied, "I'm a producer. I wanted the perfect cast for my film."

Jeanne was thinking back over all the subterfuge—the offer through Larry, the terms of the contract. "You know, Mama," she said with a glance toward Pia, "my agent was assured that . . . Olympia Decameron was *not* going to be in this movie."

"Then your agent was lied to," replied Mathilde.

Pia, looking at Jeanne, said, "Isn't that called a breach of contract?"

"Only if you have it in writing—and you'd still have to prove an intent to defraud . . ."

"It's a *verbal agreement,* Mama," said Jeanne.

"She's right, you know," added Pia.

Mathilde walked to the sideboard and leaned against it. "Well, if I may quote Mr. Goldwyn, 'a verbal agreement isn't worth the paper it's printed on.'"

"You're . . . *serious* about all this, aren't you, Mama?" Pia asked, still astonished.

"Absolutely. And I'm convinced that the script could win us an Oscar."

Neither Jeanne nor Pia could argue that.

After a pause, Jeanne said, "You really think it would . . . work?"

"With the three of us together, I can't imagine how it couldn't," said Mathilde.

Silence followed, until at last, their mother, standing next to the coffee urn and the ice bucket, asked, "Well . . . do I open the champagne . . . ?"

Jeanne turned slowly toward her sister. "What do you say, Pia?"

Pia didn't reply immediately, but it wasn't from indecision. She stuffed her handkerchief into her purse, then moved to her mother's side. "I say that . . . the three of us will make one hell of a picture!" She lifted the bottle from the bucket. "The two of you can kill this—I'll have the coffee."

Jeanne reached for the bottle. "Mama," she said, "you're a great manipulator, but how did you manage to pull it off?"

With a gradually increasing smile, Mathilde replied, "I've studied with masters."

Jeanne popped the cork and filled two plastic cups with champagne. Mathilde accepted hers and sat down at the head of the table, while Jeanne and Pia took chairs on either side.

Raising her cup, Mathilde said, half to herself, "I've done it." Then she amended the statement. "No . . . the *three* of us have done it."

Epilogue

The three women were seated on cushioned wrought-iron chairs around the matching table on the tiled patio of the Morrows' palatial new ranch-style house. Sounds of giggling could be heard inside as the children played with their dolls on the living-room floor. Wes and Andy were doing laps in the swimming pool, and Brad was climbing the ladder to the diving board.

Mathilde took a sip of her iced tea and shook her head, as though in conversation with herself. Then, aloud, she laughed.

"What's so funny, Mama?" asked Jeanne, reaching for a handful of salted cashews from the bowl on the table.

Still wearing a broad grin, Mathilde said, "We are. I was just thinking. All the talk these days about women's liberation, and will you look at the six of us? The men have spent half the afternoon in the water, having a grand time and behaving like little boys"—she stopped until the splashing noise of Brad's dive subsided—"while the three of us sit off to the side by ourselves, with our ears on alert in case the phone rings

475

or one of the children falls down. Things haven't changed so much since you girls were little, after all."

"Mama," said Pia from behind her dark glasses, "don't tell me it was anything like this when we were kids. Jeanne and I were there, remember?" But she'd spoken in an almost wistful manner.

"We've come a long way," said Jeanne, thinking back to her childhood and Pia's. "I'm not referring to women in general," she added so there would be no misinterpretation. "It's probably too soon for that. I mean that the three of *us* have come far."

They were looking out over the lush, manicured gardens beyond the pool. The house had been designed according to Pia's and Brad's specifications, and although Mathilde might have chosen a somewhat more traditional interior rather than the black ebony furnishings against a white backdrop throughout, she had kept her suggestions to a minimum. They'd wanted a "showplace," and they'd built exactly that.

"You're right, dear," said Mathilde, "we have come a long way."

Wes climbed out of the pool then, and began toweling himself dry, after which he stretched out on one of the cabana chairs.

Jeanne glanced from him to Pia. She couldn't help wondering, every now and then, if her sister was completely free of the past.

But the answer became clear as Brad waved to Pia from the diving board. The expression on Pia's face, as she removed her dark glasses and waved back at him, was a vision of loving affection. And, Jeanne noted, her sister wasn't "acting"; in fact, Pia was unaware of the scrutiny.

Jeanne's eyes moved toward her own husband as Andy dried off, then changed his mind and headed for the diving board once more. She was glad they'd agreed to this week with the family. The word *family* reminded eanne that the six of them hadn't spent any time ogether since last year's Academy Awards—and *Glass lippers*' Oscar for Best Picture. She smiled, recalling Mama's philosophical shrug when Jeanne's and Pia's nominations for Best Actress had canceled each other out: "If one of you had won and the other had lost, it night have undone all of what you girls call my . . . manipulations. So why don't we celebrate the film's success—and the family's—with a vacation?"

Just now, Mathilde seemed to be reading her mind. It's really all I've ever wanted, you know. To have my amily around me in my dotage."

Pia burst into laughter. "Mama, for God's sake— you always told me *I* was the melodramatic one! Dotage—you talk as though you're ancient!"

"Well, forty-eight *is* halfway there, dear."

"You don't look it, Mama," said Pia. "And you could cover those gray hairs if you were really worried about it."

"Not a chance," said Mathilde. "The gray gives me more credibility when I'm talking deficit financing with the money people. Gray means I'm serious—and above' vanity."

"Do you wear glasses to your board meetings, too, Mama?" Jeanne teased. "For credibility, that is?"

"I never go anywhere without them, dear." Then, in a confidential voice, she said, "If I did, I'd never be able to read the fine print in a contract!"

The three of them laughed together.

It was cut short by a shout from inside the house. "Give that back to me—it's mine!" Alixe yelled.

Julia's whimpers broke into a full-scaled cry. "Nooooo! *I* want it!"

"Ouch!" wailed Alixe. "What do you think you're doing!"

"Uh-oh," said Jeanne, jumping up from her chair. Pia and their mother rose as well.

"Those are crocodile tears," said Mathilde. "Can't you tell the difference, after so much practice?" She shook her head with amusement and started toward the door. "This is a job for Grandma."

But they wouldn't hear of it, so a moment later Mathilde, Pia, and Jeanne were on their way inside the house.

The sounds hadn't come from the living room. The children's dolls had been abandoned, and other playthings had left a trail leading up the three stairs and down the hall to Alixe's room.

It was Mathilde's favorite room in the house. It had been papered on all four walls. The wall against which Alixe's dotted-Swiss-canopied four-poster bed stood was a light apple-green. Whimsical ballerinas danced across the room in pastel tutus of pink, yellow, and blue. The remaining three walls were of palest yellow with all-but-imperceptible flecks of gold shot through the color, giving it an iridescent, textured appearance.

It's just the way I would have decorated Jeanne and Pia's room if Hank and I had been able to afford it, thought Mathilde. Funny, I can think of him now without any feelings of anger or remorse. I wasn't sure that would ever be possible.

The sight that met Mathilde, Jeanne, and Pia when they arrived at Alixe's room required the self-control of all three women.

On sections of each of the three yellow-papered walls, Alixe and little Julia had been—and still were—hard at work. So deeply were they immersed in their "art" that even now, with Grandma and their mothers standing in the doorway, they failed to look up.

Alixe was using red crayon to complete her drawing of a house, a swimming pool, and a family of stick

478

gures holding hands across the wall.

Julia, not to be outdone, had scrawled unintelligible
lue lines up and down and across the masterpiece.
pparently the yelling had been over territorial
oundaries of each's respective "canvas."

Jeanne touched Pia's arm as her sister opened her
1outh to speak.

But Mathilde was ahead of them. "Children!" she
xclaimed.

Both of the little Rembrandts whirled about in
urprise.

Julia was holding two crayons and a green pencil.
lixe's "paints" were in the Crayola box on the floor
eside her.

In the flash of an instant, the two-year-old toddler
hrust the incriminating "evidence" into her six-year-
ld cousin's hand. Then she blinked her double-thick
ashes in a wide expression of innocence, and beamed a
hirley Temple smile at the three women who stood
taring at both girls in disbelief.

Alixe lowered her head guiltily toward the crayons
nd pencil she held in her fist. Her face, a miniature of
ia's, was a study in wonder.

Jeanne was unnerved by the display of her small
aughter's behavior. Pia didn't know whether she was
1ore shocked by her niece's action or by the mess on
he walls. Still, when the two sisters' eyes met, it was
ifficult to refrain from smiling.

But under her breath, Mathilde whispered to them,
If either of you dares to laugh, you'll be ruining them
oth for life."

The crayons and pencils were confiscated. Pia said,
Alixe and I are going to have a little talk. We'll be out
n a moment," and she closed the bedroom door.

Jeanne, still bewildered, scooped Julia up in her
rms and headed down the hall. Mathilde followed

behind, watching as her little granddaughter giggle
and exclaimed merrily, "Mommy! Mommy!"

"I swear, she's never done *anything* like this before!
exclaimed Jeanne.

Mathilde shrugged. "I'm sure she hasn't. But tha
won't keep her from doing it again. Some children ar
born with a strong sense of will, you know."

Then, squeezing her daughter's wrist as they entere
the living room, she added, "Mine certainly were."